C000242722

JAN TURK PETRIE

TIME
TO CHOOSE

ALSO BY JAN TURK PETRIE

Until the Ice Cracks – Vol 1 of The Eldísvík Trilogy

No God for a Warrior – Vol 2 of The Eldísvík Trilogy

Within Each Other's Shadow – Vol 3 of The Eldísvík Trilogy

Too Many Heroes

Towards the Vanishing Point

The Truth in a Lie

Running Behind Time – (Cotswold time-slip series Book 1)

Still Life with a Vengeance

Play For Time – (Cotswold time-slip series Book 2)

Turn Back Time – (Cotswold time-slip series Book 3)

'Time to Choose' is the 4th volume in Jan Petrie's highly rated Cotswold time-slip series.

The story begins with vol 1 – *'Running Behind Time'* . The author strongly recommends you read the series in order.

Contents

"Yesterday is but today's memory and tomorrow is today's dream." – Kahlil Gibran

"For the present is the point at which time touches eternity." – C.S. Lewis

TIME
TO CHOOSE

Chapter One

Cheltenham, Gloucestershire.

April 2036

Tom

The front door slams, a violent blow that shakes the house out of its previous air of calm. Could have been tugged by the wind, though Tom doubts it. Footsteps on the hard floor of the kitchen below him. A heavy burden is dropped onto the countertop. Hinges groan as the fridge door opens and then closes. He thinks he hears the swoosh of a canned drink being opened, but possibly the latter is only in his imagination.

The sound-effects cease, but only for the second that precedes a shout of, 'I'm back!'

As if he might not have noticed. 'Up here,' he says reluctant to raise his voice to her level. No need to elaborate – he's always in his study at this time of day. He's been so deep in thought he failed to register it's gone four. Outside the window the branches of the magnolia tree scrape at the glass. Encouraged by the spring sunshine, those creamy-white buds are about to burst open. He looks through the tree to the street beyond where a parking attendant is about to issue a ticket to the poor sod who's left their Kia out there longer than the permitted time.

Vega thumps up the wooden treads of the staircase. Coke can in hand, she's framed in the open doorway of his study. Most of her golden-brown hair has fallen out of this morning's neat ponytail. Her untucked school shirt has an orange stain down the front that will probably be hard to get out. Her new school jumper is precariously clinging to her waist. Below her regulation plaid skirt, Vega's thin legs end in the enormous pair of thick-soled black boots she insists on wearing everywhere. Little wonder his mum has taken to calling her Minnie Mouse.

'Hi, sweetheart,' he says, his eyes flicking down to one of the photos on his desk – Vega as an angelic looking toddler, all chubby limbs and blonde curls haloing her head.

'Yeah,' she says, reading his mind. 'Kids grow up, Dad. Get over it.' After taking a sip of her drink she pulls a face. 'Why d'you keep buying this organic decaffeinated shit?'

'Because it's a lot better for you than the alternatives.'

'Except it tastes nothing like the real thing.' After a final swig, she crushes the can and launches it across the room. It lands with a clatter in the wastepaper basket – an impressive shot Vega takes for granted.

She comes to perch on the edge of his desk and begins recounting a complicated argument between two of her friends. It's a convoluted tale of 'Rani said' and 'Yana said'. While his daughter is talking, for a moment Tom recognises her mother in her face, especially those blue eyes. The next second her expression changes and the resemblance all but disappears.

At the mention of Ollie, he tunes back in. Tom holds up his hand to stop her mid flow. 'Hang on a minute – are you telling me your brother now has a girlfriend?'

'If you'd been listening, you would have noticed I was careful to separate the word *girl* from the word *friend*.'

'I see. So, he simply has a new friend who happens to be a girl.'

'Pretty much. At least as far as I can tell. These days he's way better at shielding his thoughts from me.'

'So, what's her name this girl? Is she someone in his class?'

She shrugs. 'No idea yet. At least seeing the two of them walking past shut Rani and Yana up for a bit. None of my mates recognised her; we guessed she must be new to the school. She's got fairish hair and sort of olive skin. I'd say she's, you know, normal looking. In fact, she's pretty – from what I saw of her.'

Vega tugs at the scrunchie holding back the rest of her hair and then slips the band over her wrist to make a multicoloured bracelet. The resulting big hairstyle looks like something more appropriate to the 1980s than the mid 2030s. She smooths it down a little though its volume remains. 'As usual, Dad, you've missed the salient point. Ollie having a new friend is a big deal by itself. When they walked past us, the girl was actually laughing at something he'd just said.'

'Why's that so remarkable?'

'Come off it. You know as well as I do it was probably some

feeble joke like the one he came out with last night.'

Tom takes a moment to think back. 'Oh, you mean the one about the subatomic duck that goes quark-quark.' Tom chuckles. 'I happened to find that rather amusing.'

'Did you really, Dad?' She gives him a long look he can't escape from – one that suggests he's as socially inept as his son. To avoid her further scrutiny, he turns his attention back to the screen in front of him.

'What is it this time?' She huffs in that dismissive manner she adopts when it comes to his work. 'Maybe you ought to project some sign from the roof like the bat-signal so anyone wanting the services of *Tom Brookes Cosmic Private Eye* will know exactly where to come.'

As she leans over his shoulder, Tom wishes he'd shut down the screen – not that he can hide anything from her. 'Listen,' he says, 'at the end of the day, my recovery work not only helps people who are distraught over a loss, it also pays the bills. I'd call that a win-win.'

'Except your latest case is an actual missing human being.' She points to the man on the screen. 'I recognise him. It's that bloke David Bainbridge who went missing after a night out. It was on the news a while back.'

'His name's actually David *Baynton*. And yes, in spite of all the surveillance cams, he somehow disappeared from Central London without a trace.'

Her face grows serious. 'You know the Guardians aren't going to be happy if you break their precious rules again.'

'I haven't even decided whether I'll take this case.'

She tousles his hair. 'Oh, I think you have.'

'Well, in any event, I'll be careful not to go beyond what we've agreed.'

'Hmm.' She stands up. 'No offence, but this man's family really must be desperate if they've asked *you* to help track him down.'

'You know, saying "no offence" before you offend someone doesn't neutralise the insult. If anything, it amplifies it.'

'I just meant this is way more serious than your usual assignments. Hopping back in time to locate a stray dog, or somebody's lost engagement ring, is one thing – this is different. Anything could have happened to this Baynton bloke. If you're planning to trail him, what's to stop the same thing happening to you?' She narrows her eyes at him. 'You'll need to stay well out of it. Like Grandad always says, you mustn't intervene whatever happens.'

'I don't need reminding of that.'

'Well, if you're aiming to be inconspicuous, I wouldn't turn up in that hat you're so fond of.'

'Are you dissing my vintage fedora?'

'No, but it's not exactly the perfect disguise for a private eye, is it?' She tousles his hair again before planting a kiss on top of his head. 'I hope they're paying you plenty for the risk you're about to take,' is her parting shot before she leaves the room. At least she doesn't slam the door this time.

It's not long before the beat of her music comes thumping through the wall. Not the usual indie stuff, but the insistent piano and drum intro to Nina Simone's Sinnerman. He remembers Beth, then heavily pregnant, dancing and singing along to the same track only a week or so before Ollie was born.

Chapter Two

Ollie

It's another hot afternoon and Ollie is dawdling along in the vague direction of home. As usual, loads of other kids stream past him like he's invisible. Above his head, seagulls are wheeling and squabbling. A long way from the sea, their sheer numbers suggest they've moved further inland to escape a coming storm.

The ice-lolly he's eating is doing little to cool him down. Before the last part of it drops onto the pavement, or down his school shirt, he manages to catch it in his mouth then drops the sticky stick into a nearby bin.

His school enforces a strict ban on the use of personal electronic devices in class, which means there's lots of catch-up conversation going on around him – all of them one-way. There's only a few weeks left of regular school before his final exams. Then what? He looks up into the sky hoping for divine inspiration.

Ollie is studying the cumulonimbus formation on the horizon when Cerys Roberts materialises alongside him.

Presuming this to be unintentional, he keeps walking, his attention glued to the clouds.

Perhaps he had been happier B.C. – Before Cerys. Like some ethereal being, her sudden appearance mid-term has changed everything. It wasn't only her perfect tan which made everyone around her seem paler by comparison. In the maths class they share, she's head down and working most of the time. Occasionally, he's heard her groan with confusion or frustration. It's odd that she arrived so close to the final year exams. Unlike all his other classmates, he can't tell what she's thinking.

Yesterday, after catching up with the other girls in the corridor, he'd overheard her explain that her dad had previously been seconded to Australia for six months and the family had gone with him. 'Alice Springs is a bit different to Cheltenham,' she'd assured Minnie Blackman.

'Yeah, I bet it is.' Minnie casually threaded her arm through Cerys's in the way girls do. 'So how come you moved here, then?'

'Oh, cos of my dad's work,' she said with a shrug and in that way Ollie's come to recognise. Lots of the kids' parents work at GCHQ – the government's intelligence gathering centre in Cheltenham. Ollie joins the dots having read about Pine Gap – the Australian surveillance base near Alice Springs.

In this town, it's never a good idea to ask about what people's parents do.

Ollie's aware of stuff like that. He knows too that as the sole fifteen-year-old in a year group of eighteen-year-olds, his natural place is on the periphery. And yet, the first time Cerys's deep brown eyes looked up into his, he'd felt her gravitational pull. Since then, he's been constantly alert to her presence, averting his gaze whenever he's in danger of letting it stray in her direction. Out of his league doesn't even come close.

'Hi, Oliver.' Cerys is a little out of breath because, he's shocked to realise, she's walked fast to catch up with him and is now falling into step by his side. He knows what she is about to ask him. 'Everybody reckons you're a bit of a maths genius,' she begins, taking an obtuse angle. 'Well, along with being brilliant at lots of other stuff – or so they say.'

Concentrating on his shoes, he feels himself blush. 'I wouldn't, I mean I don't think that's entirely accurate.'

'Modest as well eh? So anyway, the thing is, Oliver, I was wondering if maybe you might be willing to help me with my maths revision. Just 'till I can catch up. I thought, you know, we might possibly meet up before school if you can spare the time?' Her accent is mobile – lots of influences that are hard to pin down.

Before he has a chance to answer, she adds, 'I'd make it worth your while.' Cerys holds up her hand to block the implication. 'Wait.' It's *her* turn to be embarrassed. 'That sounded a bit pervy, didn't It? I just meant that I'd be happy to buy you a coffee and that. Or maybe spring for a burger and fries, or whatever, to compensate you for your time.'

She comes to a halt in front of him in a way that forces him to stop too. They step to one side, out of the pressing mainstream. 'The truth is, Oliver, I'm really struggling to get up to speed. Take tonight's homework – it's meant to be revision but, for a start, I have no frigging idea whether some number is a surd or not.'

'That's easy,' he tells her, then regrets his flippancy. 'If you work out a square root and find it can't be simplified as a number that makes much sense, that means it's a surd.' Seeing her unconvinced expression, he tries another approach. 'Take a simple example like the square root of 2. If you work it out, it's actually 1.4142135 and so on.' He can't help but laugh. 'That's a pretty irrational, nonsensical sort of number, right – so it's a surd. Whereas the square root of 4 is 2 – so it's not a surd.'

'Yeah, I see,' she says, 'I suppose that makes sense.' Her tone is still uncertain.

Before he can stop himself, Ollie adds, 'Al-Khwarizmi – the Persian dude (Christ, he's never uttered the word dude in his life before) who, um, is often referred to as the father of algebra, he called irrational numbers *inaudible*. Later on, Fibonacci, you know the bloke (slightly better than dude at least) who's famous for his sequence, used the word surd, which was actually a simplification of the Latin word *sudus* meaning deaf or mute – hence we have the mathematical term surd.'

'Wow,' she's staring at him. 'You really do know a lot of stuff.'

For once, this isn't a criticism. 'Possibly too much.' He grins, his eyes focused on the top of her head but straying no lower. On a bit of a roll, he says, 'An easier way to remember might be that *surd* sounds like *absurd* which, after all, means something quite similar to irrational – although granted they're not exactly the same. And obviously it doesn't mean inaudible.' He takes a breath. 'I should probably have stopped talking some time ago,' he mutters, his cheeks on fire.

She bursts out laughing, then catches his arm before he

can walk away. 'Don't get the wrong idea, I was laughing *with* you, not *at* you.' She shakes his elbow. 'I promise. I think you might be the most interesting person I've met in ages, Oliver Brookes.' She means it too.

'Everyone calls me Ollie,' he tells her.

'I didn't like to presume – not until I got to know you better.'

Up ahead his sister and her mates are sitting along a wall, legs swinging as they argue about something. He groans under his breath. As they draw level, out of the corner of his eye, he sees Vega and the rest staring open-mouthed at the two of them. Introductions are out of the question. Instead, Ollie turns away from their stares while struggling to think of something to say to distract Cerys. On a weird impulse he asks, 'Why's it never cold in the corner of a room?'

There's a long awkward moment before she responds with, 'I don't know, Ollie, why's it never cold in the corner of a room?'

Wishing a sinkhole would open under his feet, he has no choice but to utter the punchline. 'Because it's always ninety degrees.'

Giggling, she releases his arm to run for her bus. Once on board, she calls through an open window, 'I'll be in the library at eight o'clock tomorrow morning.' With no chance to reply, Ollie's left staring at the back end of the departing vehicle.

After that he loses track of time while he stares at the pavement pondering this development. It's a date then. Well, sort of. More of an appointment than an assignation.

Vega and her mates have scattered. His imagination racing in all sorts of unlikely directions, he waits for the green light before crossing the road. On the other side, he finds himself staring into Cullimore's window, for once not checking out any of the books on display. Catching his own reflection in the glass, he takes out a tissue and wipes at the lolly stain from around his mouth, wishing he'd done so earlier. If only he had the sort of square jaw and shoulders many of his classmates have developed.

He rakes his unruly hair behind his ears then studies his profile. Perhaps a haircut would make his features seem more distinctive. Whichever way Ollie turns his head, his cheek-bones aren't what anyone would describe as chiselled. The line of hair above his upper lip barely shows. In fact, he looks sort of unformed with nothing much to distinguish him from any other lanky school student. If he ran into the shop and grabbed an armful of books right now, apart from his dark hair, the customers would probably struggle to come up with a detailed description of the culprit. Although, obviously, Mr Cullimore wouldn't have a problem identifying him.

An elderly woman is now staring back at Ollie through the glass, her eyes narrowed with suspicion. Aware that people of her age often see the young as a threat, he smiles in order to demonstrate his harmless nature before moving away.

When he kicks at a loose stone, he misses.

At the beginning of the year he didn't think much about his appearance. Moving up from Year 11 to the upper sixth, he'd welcomed the lack of restrictions on what he's allowed to wear to school. White shirt, black supermarket trousers and jumper, mid-range trainers – he's done his best to blend in. And it helps that he's tall for his age. In the Easter holidays, his gran persuaded him to ditch his specs for contact lenses, though half the time he couldn't be bothered to put the bloody things in. Until the last few weeks, that is. Now he never leaves home without them.

To meet Cerys tomorrow morning he'll need to get up earlier. She's taken it for granted he'll be there. Girls like her must be aware of the power they exert over mere mortals. Although, strictly speaking, he's not your average run-of-the-mill human.

Ollie turns into his home street. He shouldn't have hung back because his sister is home before him. In fact, he's aware that she's already told their dad about seeing him with Cerys – not that she's found out her name yet.

Under his breath, Ollie practices saying it out loud with that flat-tongued stress she puts on the first syllable, '*KEH-riss.*' An appropriately exotic-sounding name. 'KEH-riss,' he repeats – louder this time and with more accompanying spittle. Hopeless. If he attempts to pronounce it correctly, she'll assume he's taking the piss.

Chapter Three

Vega

In the sanctuary of her bedroom, Vega unlaces her boots and kicks them off one at a time, relishing the satisfactory thud as one, and then the other, hit the floor. Reduced to her proper height, she wiggles her toes to cool them down. Listening to Nina Simone, she gets lost in the raw power of her extraordinary voice.

Once the song's finished, she opts for silence. She lies down on her bed, not to shut her eyes and have a nap (if only) but to exhale as she stares up at the ceiling ready to view her socials. Though she complains about it to her outraged friends, Vega's secretly pleased her dad restricts her browsing time to two hours max after school.

She savours a further moment of tranquillity before it begins. Like the hungry caterpillar, socials are never satisfied no matter how much they get fed. Filters help to eliminate the worst of it, but that still leaves plenty to plough through. Thanks to the Porn Laws, at least dick pics and all that sort of crap are a thing of the past.

Vega stares up at the projection while a seemingly infinite series of faces vie for her attention. When it's someone she knows, she checks out the way their imperfections have been erased often to the point where they're hard to recognise. She's careful to big-tick Jennifer's new trainers and then Yana's latest hairstyle, which, in real life, doesn't suit her one bit. Here and there she's entertained by a clever mash-up or gif, or somebody's pet doing something ridiculous or cute. (Or ridiculously cute.) Mostly, she's bored out of her skull.

. To make a show of participating, Vega posts a few things. She has an eye for weird angles and edits that help make her feed appear quirky and enigmatic – stuff that can be misinterpreted as meaningful.

Comments run back and forth amongst the people in her year group and beyond in what passes for bants, though it's impossible to miss the critical edge to much of it. Like she does every day, Vega plays along. She's good at that – at fooling the eye. And, after all, acting is in her blood.

Dad calls up the stairs wanting to know what she fancies for supper. She ignores him because she needs to concentrate – any tiny slip could be disastrous. She marshals her responses, scatters comments and symbols, which she's confident will be taken at face value. Too little versus too much is always a tricky balance.

Her gran's unbelievably naïve about how all this stuff works. She keeps telling her and Ollie they should express and defend their own opinions. In her day people said what they really thought and, apparently, that was seen as a good thing. Shows how much she understands about today's world where the smallest of missteps on the socials tightrope will feed you to the ravenous creatures below.

Today the school corridors buzzed with talk of Leonard Scott's big gaffe. Okay, what he posted was stupid, and possibly offensive to some, but, in her unspoken opinion it didn't warrant him being ghosted by everyone. Spotty and nervous, Leonard's online existence, at the age of thirteen, has effectively been erased. It's just possible that, if he sucks up to the right people and keeps his head down, he'll eventually be re-friended by a few. That's as much as he can hope for now.

Pitying the poor idiot, Vega is tempted to go back in time and intervene before Leonard thought of saying what he did. (She doubts he thought it through.) She's never spoken to him in person, so it's hard to think how she could accurately locate his bedroom – assuming that to be the scene of his "crime". In any case, if she were to materialise next to his bed, he'd scream the place down and her cover would be blown. If she goes to his home, he'll get the wrong idea. The thought of being subjected to the boy's awkward advances makes Vega shudder.

The smell of cooking is drifting up the stairs. Something tomato-and-herby. Most likely pasta, though it could be pizza. Vega signs off early, mustering her selfie-honed smile along-side an Italian flag and the word *Yum!* She doesn't elaborate. No one seriously gives a crap about what anyone else is about to eat, but she's done her bit, been seen to play the game.

Life must have been way easier in the past – before socials were a thing. Her dad was lucky to grow up in the nineties and noughties. Although, by the time he'd reached Ollie's age, they already had iPhones, Facebook, YouTube, and Twitter. To be entirely free of it, you would have to go further back – back to her mother's era.

The aroma becomes more enticing as she descends the stairs. Not looking up from chopping herbs, her dad says, 'Vega, could you drain the pasta?' He doesn't bother to add a *please* or a *would you mind*.

Hands on her hips, she stands her ground. 'Why's it always me and not Ollie that has to help? Talk about gender stereo-typing.'

Dad scoffs. 'That's utter nonsense and you know it.'

Glancing up from his screen, Ollie has a smug expression on his face. 'And I chopped a load of veg while you were piss-ing about upstairs.'

'Hmm.' Forced to concede, she unhooks the colander and drains the tagliatelle over the sink. Her friends' parents hardly ever cook anything from scratch, but her dad's a bloody dinosaur. He insists they sit around the table and share a meal every evening.

The three of them have healthy appetites, so conversation at the table is kept to a minimum. Afterwards, leaning back with a too-full stomach, it would be tempting to relax, though that's precisely when she could be caught off guard. It's easy enough to avoid her dad's scrutiny or fob him off with a straightforward denial, her brother is a whole other ball game.

Ollie is studying her face in that annoying way he does when he's on to something. She pushes her chair back eager to avoid further scrutiny though a silent dialogue has already begun. Infuriatingly, he can crystallise her thoughts before they're fully formed.

Don't go there, he silently instructs her. *Vega, I mean it. Don't even think about it.*

Who put you in charge of the Thought Police? I can think about whatever I bloody well like because what I choose to do, or not do, is none of your sodding business.

His expression softens. *I know it's tempting. Believe me, I've thought about it many times. And I know it's only natural to be curious, but it won't help. In fact, it'll just make everything a whole lot worse.*

She stands up so quickly her dad's forced to catch the chair before it falls. 'Whoa,' he says, 'where's the fire?'

'Ask Ollie,' she tells him. 'He's the one with the hots for this new girl in his year. Her name's Cerys by the way and she's eighteen. She's using him, though, like a mug, he's far too besotted to realise.'

'Bitch!' Ollie calls after her.

Dad's on him right away for that. 'Whatever the provocation, I won't have you using such a disrespectful word to your sister.'

'Sucker!' she yells back. One foot on the bottom step, she pauses, 'You know, for the elimination of doubt, you should get that tattooed across your forehead.'

'At least I'm not deluding myself about...' He stops short of betraying her.

'I do so enjoy these frank exchanges of views.' Dad looks from her to Ollie. 'As usual, I have no idea what this argument is about, and maybe it's better that way. All the same, I expect the two of you to disagree in a civilised fashion.'

'Yeah well, Ollie is such a sodding pushover.'

'And you're a dreamer. A fantasist who needs to wake up and smell the espresso.'

'How original – I don't think. Anyway, I'd rather be a dreamer than a sap.'

'You're deluded.'

'And you're a patsy.'

'Patsy!' Ollie sneers. 'Have you been watching those old Godfather movies or something?'

'Enough you two!' Dad shouts. He shakes his head, does that annoying thing with his hands that's meant to make them calm down. Then he tries distraction. 'By the way, did you know the term patsy is a corruption of pazzo, which is the Italian word for fool.'

'Yeah, well Ollie's that too,' she mutters climbing the stairs.

Dad scoffs. 'And they say the art of conversation is dying.'

Chapter Four

Tom

Something about the kids' latest spat continues to niggle away at him. Both of them have now retreated to their rooms. Whatever they're up to in there, at least they're doing it quietly. As an only child, he needs to remind himself it's natural for siblings to squabble. Teenagers more so.

Unable to settle his mind, as with any problem he's confronted by, Tom tries to break things down into their separate elements. First off, it seems Ollie has a crush on a girl. And an older one at that. Hardly an earthshattering revelation for a fifteen-year-old boy. Vega is convinced he's about to be taken for a ride and yet, given his advantages over others, Ollie's unlikely to be all that gullible. And pretty much every adolescent experiences unrequited love. Lust more often. However painful, it's more or less a rite of passage.

He remembers the way Sandra Lewis had sniggered after he declared his feelings for her. Forced into a volte-face, he'd pretended it was a joke, a wind-up she'd just fallen for. Looking back, he doubts she was taken in. If Ollie is about to make a similar fool of himself, so be it. He can only hope this Cerys girl will let him down lightly.

Though he's certainly not telepathic like his children, Tom's learnt to trust his instincts, and right now he has a strong inkling that Vega is the one he should be more concerned about. Is she going to do something rash she'll later regret?

On the plus side, she's super bright and in many ways far more worldly-wise than her brother. Given her abilities, she's unlikely to face physical danger. And even if she were to, she'd be able to extricate herself without lifting a finger. And yet… However much he tries to reason it away, something Tom can't quite define continues to bother him.

From various things they've let slip, it seems Vega and Ollie have learnt to shield some, but not all, of their thoughts from each other. He's never sure – doesn't really want to know – to what degree they can see right through him.

Should he ask his dad to get to the bottom of whatever it is? These days his dad – the man he still calls Matt – looks like a regular grandfather with his iron-grey hair and wire-rimmed, reading specs. He likes to give the impression he's lost most of his power since his "retirement" from what he calls the "Organisation". (He seldom utters the word Guardians out loud.) A fat chance. Like some cosmic hound dog, Matt can still sniff out anything and everything. Whenever he's with his dad – which is less often these days – Tom's all too aware the man can see right through him. In response, he tries to keep his mind as blank as possible. Too often he then struggles not to think of something deeply inappropriate, if not downright pornographic. Matt must think he's some kind of degenerate.

Tom rubs a hand across his face. Even if Matt could discern whatever it is Vega's up to, he's not sure he would tell him. Probably just as well. The fact remains that if she's in any danger, his dad won't wait to be asked before he intervenes. Yes, there's no doubt the old man would be on her case like a shot.

Plus, though the two of them bicker a lot, Ollie has always looked out for his little sister. Whether she welcomes it or not, he'll step in before Vega gets involved in anything foolhardy or dangerous.

So, all bases are covered – he can stop worrying about the kids and try to relax.

Except he can't afford to relax because he needs to focus on the rather pressing matter of his dwindling savings. He's never had much of a gameplan, but maybe he needs to develop one. In the world according to Warren Buffet, diversification should be unnecessary if you know what you're doing – after all, Henry Ford didn't need to diversify. For those less driven, it seems a lot safer not to pour all your eggs into one omelette.

The figures in front of him show he's currently shelling out way more than the amount coming in. He needs to address that gap without falling back on betting. (A misnomer to call it *betting* when he can discover the result of any wager he makes in advance.) How lucky can one man get without arousing suspicion? Not least from HMRC.

Over the last few years, and almost by accident, he's developed two very different but bona fide income streams. His series of "lost kingdom" sculptures – the mini villages grouped around a central castle he constructs in his garage – have proved very popular – especially with the obscenely wealthy "Cotswold set". Designed as a whimsical feature to float on the surface of a lake or pond, he'd made the first one for a charity auction. Since then, he's taken on a series of commissions from people with big enough gardens, or grounds, to indulge in such fantasy objects. The only downside is the amount of time each one takes to customise.

He's had little opportunity to work on his latest commission due to his booming recovery business. They were still living in Bristol when he started *Tom's Track & Trace* as a bit of an experiment. It then morphed into the *Brookes Detection Consultancy*. His kids may take the piss, but demand for his services has grown to the point where he can pick and choose assignments. His accountant keeps advising him to raise his day rate and make sure his expenses are fully covered.

It may be getting late, but there's something else he ought to think about. It's been three days since that tearful call from Mrs Baynton about her missing son. Taken by surprise, he'd pointed out as gently as he could, that it wasn't his usual line of work. Her obvious distress had stopped him turning her down flat. He heard her out, noticing her slight Edinburgh accent, the desperation she couldn't conceal.

He listens to the recording again. Towards the end she says, 'The police are no further forward than they were at the beginning.' (Audible sobs) 'Frankly, Mr Brookes, I'm at my wit's end. I can't sleep, can't begin to find any peace of mind with all these questions buzzing around in my head.' After a long pause, 'For better or worse, I need to know what happened to my boy.'

It's not hard to imagine the pain and uncertainty consuming her. Sniffing back tears, she says, 'My great friend Julia, Julia Tanner, can't stop singing your praises. She swears you can work miracles.'

'I always try to do my best,' is his flat, non-committal reply. Turning off the recording, he remembers Julia Tanner and the Samoyed puppy abducted from her back garden in broad daylight. By hopping back a few days, he'd been able to follow the culprits to an outbuilding on a rundown farm. Instead of going in there all guns blazing, he tipped off the local police who subsequently recovered Mrs Tanner's puppy along with several more. He was cock-a-hoop when the gang were denied bail. Reunited with Snowflake, Julia had been in tears.

Figuring it couldn't do any harm, he's been looking into David Baynton's disappearance. It's more than two months since the last confirmed sighting of him walking rather unsteadily along the riverside close to Tower Bridge. A young city trader, he'd spent the evening celebrating the sizable bonus he was about to get. With so much still to live for, Mrs Baynton's only child had then disappeared without trace.

Tom would rather not think about what it must be like not knowing where your child is or whether they're safe. If he were to take the case, it would involve going back more than just a few days. Which means he'd need to factor in time to get over his initial nausea and disorientation.

He's studied the known route David took after leaving the pub alone. Tom's familiar with that area of Shad Thames, he's even identified an out of the way spot where no one would be likely to witness his sudden appearance. If he gets there

23

well ahead of time, he'll have recovered before David walks past and he'd be able to follow him. He would need to keep his distance, or he'll be picked up on the cams as a potential witness. Or even a suspect.

Tom's managed to rule out any superposition issues – on that same night he was at home approximately 120 miles away. He remembers going to bed early that evening with a bad cold.

He hasn't really thought about his fee. With a missing pet, or a lost item of jewellery, it's easier. His accountant has been urging him to ask for a percentage of an item's insurance value. How can anyone begin to value the life of a twenty-four-year-old with his whole future ahead of him?

As Vega took pains to remind him, he can't ignore the strict terms of his agreement with Ford. Interfering in a dog's destiny is highly unlikely to change the course of history; human beings are a different matter altogether.

It's late. He yawns as he turns off the screen, then sits on in the semi darkness. In her public statement, the inspector in charge of Baynton's case had speculated that, given his drunken state, David could have lost his footing and fallen into the river. The tide had been strong and swift at the time, so his body could have been washed out to sea. The only clue is David's distinctive paisley scarf, which had washed up on the foreshore at low tide.

There remains the possibility he was attacked. When pressed, the DCI in charge had admitted they were unable to rule out foul play. He rubs his eyelids. If he witnesses David stumbling and about to topple into the river, or if someone is lying in wait for him, will he have the self-control to stand back and let it happen?

Tom gets to his feet and heads for bed. He's as ready as he'll ever be for his meeting with Mrs Baynton in the morning. Once he hears what she has to say, it ought to be easier to make up his mind.

Chapter Five

Vega slams the front door as she leaves. After muttering about the detrimental effect on the hinges, Tom attempts to gather his thoughts in the peace that now descends. Mrs Baynton isn't due for half an hour, which gives him time to clear up a bit and grab a shower.

For once Tom has no idea what this potential client looks like. In the only image available online, she'd had her head down, her face averted from the photographers. The woman doesn't do socials; has no profile he can find on any of the platforms.

The smell of burnt toast lingers as he shovels blackened crusts into the compost bin. Based on her accent alone, he tries to picture Sarah Baynton, conjuring up a rather stiff individual dressed head to toe in some sort of tweed. Or tartan given that she's Scottish. Ludicrous stereotypes aside, he's discovered that she's a forty-seven-year-old divorcee and that her missing son's twin sister, Elspeth, died at the age of six from a rare form of cancer. Tom can only imagine how devastating that must have been for the whole family. The couple were divorced fifteen months later, and the following year David Baynton Senior remarried. He'd gone on to father four more children. Someone claiming to be a close friend of his had felt the need to inform the media that the father was "understandably devastated by the accidental death of his eldest son". Assuming this is an accurate quote, unlike his ex-wife, David's dad appears to have accepted the New Met's conclusions.

He surveys the kitchen pleased to have imposed a bit more order. The shriek of a siren is getting closer. Peering out into the street, for a split second he glimpses flashing blue lights, then the pitch drops as the ambulance passes on by. Relieved it's someone else's emergency, he heads for the bathroom hoping there's some hot water left.

Tom turns off the shower. Did he imagine that buzzing? There it goes again. Damn it – the bloody woman's early. Hair dripping and with a towel around his waist, he turns off the visuals before answering. 'Is that Mr Brookes?' she demands.

'Mrs Baynton, I assume.' More irritated than he has a right to be, he doesn't buzz her in but leaves her on the doorstep. 'Hold on,' he says. 'I'll be there in a minute.'

He hastily pulls on yesterday's clothes before running down stairs in his socks. Opening the door, his first thought is that she looks younger than he'd imagined. Her mid-brown hair is cut into a shiny, shoulder-length bob. He notices some grey regrowth along her central parting. Minimal makeup – a touch of mascara and not much else.

After clocking his shoeless state, her blue eyes dart around the hallway seeking clues as to what sort of person she might be dealing with. There's an awkward moment before they shake hands. Hers is cool to the touch.

He shows her into the cramped little room off the hall he reserves for interviews with clients. Inside, he's kept things to a minimum. There's nothing on the pale grey walls except his ABI and SIA certification. The only furniture is a table and three rather upright wooden chairs. He ushers her inside. 'Take a seat, please, Mrs Baynton.'

'Call me Sarah, please.' She remains standing while examining his professional qualifications.

'Then I'm Tom.' He smiles, thinks of telling her how he's sorry for her loss, but that seems inappropriate under the circumstances. Instead, he says, 'These last few months must have been very hard on you.'

'They've certainly taken their toll,' she says, taking off her jacket to reveal the pearl grey blouse underneath. No sign of tweed or tartan. Her perfume has a citrus edge. An attractive woman under different circumstances. After looking around for somewhere to hang her jacket, she gives up and drapes it over the back of a chair before she sits down. Her slim legs end in a pair of understated shoes – his mum would call them court shoes. Beth used to say you can learn a lot about a character from their shoe choice. (Right now, his "not rocket science" socks must be giving out a strange message.)

Seating himself opposite her, with the table to one side, Tom clears his throat. 'Thank you for coming. I prefer to hold the first meeting with my clients face to face. Before we begin, I should point out that everything we say in here is being recorded.'

'I see.' Sarah looks around trying to spot the technology involved.

Confident she won't be able to, he ploughs on. 'These recordings are purely for my own use as reference material. I assure you that anything you say, anything at all you choose to tell me, will remain strictly confidential. At this point, should either of us decide not to proceed, all record of this meeting will be deleted.'

She seems unnerved by this. He says, 'If that's a problem…'

'No, no, it's fine.' She looks directly at him before glancing away. 'It's just, well, I'm rather a private person, Tom.' Her smile is almost girlish. 'My son's always telling me; he, um, keeps joking that I should sign up for the twenty-first century.'

He smiles back. 'Client confidentiality is essential in my line of work. I promise our conversation this morning will go no further than this room.' Instead of leaving it there, he adds, 'Although theoretically, if a client were, for example, to tell me that he, she or they were about to commit a serious criminal act, I would be obliged to reveal this information to the police.'

'Then it's lucky I have no criminal inclinations.'

'Glad to hear it.' Tom clears his throat again. 'I'll be perfectly honest with you, Sarah, this is the first time anyone's asked for my help with a missing person case.'

She winces at the word case. 'I'm aware of that,' she says. 'Julia told me you specialise in missing pets and lost jewellery.'

'Exactly.'

'But she also said you managed to find Snowflake when the police had got nowhere. She thinks you must have some sort of sixth sense.'

'Yes well, unfortunately, I don't possess any psychic powers…' He can't circumvent what he needs to say next. 'Forgive me if

I come straight to the point, Sarah. The police are convinced your son must have leant over the barrier – possibly to vomit or maybe stare down into the river – and accidentally fell in. Once he was in the water, it's likely he would have been caught in the tide and swept downstream.'

She shakes her head several times. 'The issue I have, Tom, is that right from the outset the police adopted this seen-it-all-before attitude. Instead of keeping an open mind, they were reluctant to consider any other explanation for my son's disappearance.'

'So, you don't accept that scenario could have been what happened?'

'I don't accept it's the *only* explanation. David was an exceptional swimmer, Tom. He once swam the length of Loch Lomond and that's nearly twenty-two miles.' A look of pride crosses her face. 'He did the whole thing in under eleven hours. So whilst I realise he'd had a few drinks that night, *if* he fell into the river, wouldn't the shock of hitting the water have sobered him up?'

'As I'm sure you've been made aware, the Thames has some very strong tides and eddies. Even the ablest of swimmers would have trouble contending with that sort of force.'

'I take your point.' She leans forward. 'I'm sure you will have done your homework, Tom. So, I assume you know that my daughter, David's twin sister, she died when they were six.'

Deciding to stay silent, Tom simply nods.

'His father and I… We separated less than a year after we lost Elspeth. She was only a wee girl… Then it was just the two of us. Naturally, David saw his dad in the holidays, though he was often preoccupied with his other children. From being a family of four, David and me – we were on our own. I like to think we were close. We may not have seen as much of each other since he moved to London…'

Sarah takes a moment, then, with closed eyes, she goes on. 'The thing is – and I know this may sound fanciful to you – but I would know if he… I can still feel him here.' She presses a hand to her chest then moves it over to her heart. 'If David was dead, believe me I'd know.' Her hand may be shaking but her conviction is absolute. 'A parent's instinct is easily dismissed, but I truly believe in such things.'

Not wishing to offer false hope, he chooses his next words with care. 'Instinct can be a powerful thing.' He waits until she meets his eye. 'As an investigator, my job first and foremost is to examine all available facts. I start with an open mind. Then I try to piece together the sequence of events leading up to any disappearance or loss. Once I have that information, I try to imagine – to go back in time, as it were, to the last known sighting and then take it from there. I do my best, but I can never guarantee the outcome a client would like.'

'From what I've heard, your track record is extraordinary.'

'That's very flattering, Sarah, but I wouldn't like you to get the impression I'm infallible. I should also remind you that the Met police are very experienced when it comes to this type of investigation. And I'm sorry to say that, despite what your instinct tells you, it's entirely possible your son may have drowned.'

After staring at the floor for a few moments, she meets his gaze again. 'I just need to be sure. Ever since Elspeth… I've been haunted by doubts. If I'd noticed the signs earlier, if we'd seen a doctor before we did, could she have been saved?'

He hesitates before he reaches out to squeeze her hand. Between sobs she says, 'And now, with her brother… And that other investigator – oh, he was pretty keen to take my money, that one. Not that he found out a damned thing. And you see, the point is, I need to believe that I've done everything I possibly can.'

Tom swallows. 'Okay then.' He lets go of her hand. 'Why don't we start at the beginning. Before we get to the events of that night, I'll need to know more about David. I've read all the statements from his employers and his friends, but to piece together everything that led up to his disappearance that night, I may have to delve into your son's personal life. Are you okay with that, Sarah?'

'If it will help.' She looks at him in earnest. 'I want you to do whatever is necessary.'

'And just so we're completely clear,' he tells her, 'I need another couple of days to weigh everything up. If I believe there's a chance, if I do decide to take this case on, it'll be on a no-result-no-fee basis. I won't ask for any payment unless I'm able to find out exactly what's happened to your son.'

Chapter Six

Vega

She drums her fingers on the desk in the rhythm of galloping horses. When Joel Edwards shoots her a frown, Vega stops. Today is as boring as the day before and the one before that, their lessons on rinse and repeat.

What would happen if she actually stood up and let out the scream that's inside her head? She's read about some scientific experiment in Virginia where they'd stuck people in a bare room by themselves for ten minutes with nothing to occupy them. Instead of chilling, most of them quickly became anxious. When they varied the experiment by introducing some electronic equipment, with no other options to *do* something, many of the subjects chose to give themselves mild electric shocks to help pass the time. One person had shocked themselves almost 200 times.

She knows the teachers are equally bored with trying to ensure their students ingest whatever random bits of knowledge the curriculum dictates thirteen-year-olds ought to know. The world might come to an end should anyone deviate from the course.

Vega inspects her nails, nibbles the jagged edge she's spotted on her middle finger, then holds it up to judge the result. (Not at all in a gesture of defiance.) She uses it to tap the *submit work* icon before slumping back in her chair.

They're in the last period of Double English; she's completed the assignment and now can only wait for the buzzer that will release them to break time. The classroom is really stuffy, the air loaded with other people's sweat. They're up on the third floor, so only a tiny section of the windows is able to be opened in case a student – or a member of staff – should feel suicidal. Looking around no one meets her eye because they're busy working on the task of comparing two poems.

At the front of the room Ms Kelly is reading. She's laid her book flat on the desk so no one can spot it's a novel which isn't allowed on the English syllabus due to its disturbing "adult" content. Right now, Ms Kelly is so *disturbed* she's re-reading the page that's raised her pulse and made her cheeks flush with borrowed excitement.

This term's topic is Power and Conflict. Before she sat down, and despite the fact that the full guidelines are on the screen in front of them, Ms Kelly had felt the need to add value to this educational experience by scrawling her own instructions on the interactive screen.

They read:

A) **"Unpack" the words and phrases being used.** (She pictures a line of poets like tourists just arrived, dragging their inspiration around behind them in little wheely cases.)

B) **Compare & contrast two poems of your choice.** Their choice has been limited to four poems unlikely to trigger anyone's anxiety. No mud, or blood, or corpses are allowed – they've taken the guts out of war poetry.

C) **Think about each poem's POV. Do you agree? Construct YOUR argument including relevant quotes.** This is just a box to be ticked. No one gives a crap about your opinion, they only want to know you know what the poet's going on about.

When Vega gives a loud sigh, Ms Kelly's head shoots up. Disappointed to find herself still single at 44, Lianne Kelly had, on her friend's advice, actually paid for the injections that now prevent her from frowning. Or looking half human. Instead, the woman's general expression hardens into a stare – a silent reminder that, if Vega wants to remain in this school, she *must not disrupt the education of others*.

Though it doesn't show on her face, the teacher's disappointed when Vega smiles back. After a while, and though not entirely convinced, Ms Kelly looks down at her book. All those negative thoughts have killed her buzz.

Vega's attention drifts towards the line of windows. The sun is shining and there's still some blossom on the trees beyond the two-metres-high perimeter fence topped with ugly metal spikes that's there to protect the students from whatever threat might be lurking in the orderly streets of Cheltenham Spa. It also stops the students escaping. Vega grins, safe in the knowledge that no barrier would ever be able to prevent her leaving if she chose to.

Her friend Yana is sitting directly in front of her. Vega can tell she's struggling with question A). The unpacking's not going well. Her long fair hair was recently shorn and shaped into what's known as an "ultra-radical bob". (Which sounds like some dodgy activist.) A quick visual survey tells her that about half of the girls in the room now have the same unflattering style. While Vega likes to be aware of fashion trends, she has no intention of following this one.

In the locker room earlier, Yana and Rani had made up after yesterday's row. (Neither of them admitting to the underlying jealousy that sparked it.) They'd bumped fists in a gesture of reconciliation, but then chosen to sit on opposite sides of the classroom.

When it comes to Power and Conflict, they should study the behaviour of teenage girls. During Vega's first year at the school, it really got to her. Without a mum to turn to for advice, she'd asked her dad – though she doubted he knew a lot about blending in. 'Stay out of their squabbles,' he told her. 'Be like Switzerland – neutral.' Then he actually laughed like it wasn't serious being the class pariah.

For obvious reasons, she hadn't asked Ollie for help, but he felt the need to pitch in anyway, not by suggesting something potentially useful, but by questioning the neutrality of Switzerland during World War Two.

Rolling her eyes, Vega had gone off to her room to call Gran. 'Keep your chin up, dear,' were her sage words. Along with, 'It'll pass – these things always do. Be nice to everyone. A smile gets you a long way in this world.'

She'd tried to follow their suggestions; her face muscles stiff from smiling, she took care to stay out of their petty squabbles and still ended up a Billy no-mates.

At the start of year nine, Vega changed tactics. Studying the pecking order, she noticed the girls having the least shit time were "the cool gang". (Though they'd never used the word cool.) A group of alpha predators who always listen to the same music, big-up or diss the same films etcetera, etcetera, ad nauseum. Despite coming from diverse backgrounds, they shared a specific "cool-speak" vocab. She noticed how they all wore their regulation blouses with the first and last two buttons undone, with the front bit but not the back tucked into their waistbands.

All she needed to do was figure out how to infiltrate the gang. If she simply aped them, they would sniff her out as fake. Better to approach from an unexpected angle.

And so, Vega raised the stakes. She made sure the key players overheard snatches of the music she was listening to. (Obscure indie bands tipped for wider success.) Though they sometimes pinched her feet, she wore her highest, blackest boots. She sprayed her naturally fair hair a variety of lurid colours. Her tights didn't just have minor holes; they would have fallen apart if it wasn't for dozens of blobs of nail varnish.

When a passing member of staff criticised her scruffy appearance, unfazed, Vega snapped back with, 'My dad's a single parent, sir. I'm afraid he doesn't earn very much.'

Muttering something sympathetic, the teacher had backed off. Witnessing her "secret" smile as she walked away, the gang were impressed. In the space of a few weeks, Vega made the transition to socially acceptable and then, unbelievably, to popular. Looking back, she is almost embarrassed by their collective gullibility; how easy it was to fool them all.

Ollie noticed – of course he would. Shaking his head, with one of his serious faces on, he asked, 'Are you genuinely any happier as a result?'

'Hell yes!' she told him straight. Without her having to say a thing, he knew her friends weren't exactly her soulmates. How could they be since she belongs to a family of frigging freaks?

Across the room Rani looks up between paragraphs. Vega makes a point of catching her eye, grins to confirm their continued alliance in spite of any contrary signals.

Ollie has found his own way of coping. For Vega, her friends are the first line of defence. Like that old sixties song, she's in with the in-crowd, and that's where she intends to stay. Individually, they can often be petty and annoying, but collectively they make up her Praetorian Guard.

Chapter Seven

Tom

Deep in thought, Tom returns to what his kids refer to as his Interrogation Room. Once he activates the screen, a new image of Sarah Baynton appears on the wall. 'Go to topic *personal life*,' Tom demands. The system finds and then replays the part where he'd mentioned delving into David's personal life. Watching it back, he's struck by her physical response – that flicker of alarm in her eyes, the cough intended to disguise the unease in her voice. Yes, Tom suspects there is something she doesn't want him to find out about her son.

Is digging into David's background strictly necessary? After all, he hadn't asked the neighbours whether Snowflake seemed happy with her new owners. Or visited the Samoyed bitch who'd given birth to her. In his usual line of work, there's little point in bothering with any of that when he simply has to arrive unseen just before the disappearance of the animal or object and then follow the trail. His clients tend to be remarkably incurious about his methods, caring very little once what they've lost has been recovered. In principle, following a soon-to-be-missing person ought to be no different.

Tom asks for a slower re-run, watching for the precise moment when Sarah's expression had altered. Or slipped. There it is again – the tell.

Intrigued, he scratches at the growing stubble on his chin. If he decides to take this case, he'll need to uncover new evidence to explain *how* he knows what happened that night. There's also the emotional aspect to consider. If David Baynton drowned and he can prove it, what impact will that have on Sarah? And not just her – there's the rest of the man's family and friends to consider. How would he feel if, God forbid, it was one of his kids? Although obviously, he's in a unique position. All the same, if he was an ordinary, worried father, would he prefer to know they were dead, or would it be better to hold onto a sliver of hope that one day they could still walk through the door?

He can't decide.

Given the complications, bearing all of that in mind, the smart thing, in fact the *only* sensible and sensitive thing to do is to decline this case. He slaps the table. Yep, easily the best decision all round.

About to erase the interview, Tom hesitates. He draws his hand back. No rush, no need for such a drastic step just yet.

He utters the necessary words to call up the part where Sarah talked about her mother's instinct; her belief that, despite the Met's conclusion, her son is still alive. Watching it again he finds himself moved to the point of tears.

The interview plays on until the screen goes blank. Tom stares into nothing, unable to unsee or unrecognise the pain in her eyes. Though they might seem outwardly okay, he knows how loss can shatter a person. For those left behind the broken fragments never go back together in the same way they were before.

He draws a hand down his face and holds it over his mouth. Why not do a bit of preliminary digging? Maybe he could have a chat with a few of David's friends and colleagues. He can weigh up any new information before deciding to pass on it or not. Sarah Baynton isn't his client right now, so there's no obligation on his part.

According to the reports, David's colleague, Simon Yardley, was the last known person to see him before he disappeared.

After a call, Yardley readily agrees to meet him in the same pub they'd been drinking in that night. Tom rubs his hands together at the prospect of getting some answers at last.

His kids might be old enough to manage on their own after school, but Tom's not comfortable leaving them alone all evening. (The what-ifs just multiply.) Fortunately, Athena assures him she's more than happy to pop round later. The kids get on well with her, which is handy as she only lives a few doors down. They'll love it if she knocks up some of her famous gemista or a batch of their favourite tomatokeftedes. And with luck there'll be some tasty leftovers in the fridge when he gets back.

His destination is a brisk ten-minute walk from London Bridge tube station. It's a miserable, unseasonal evening, the sky prematurely dark and loaded with the threat of rain. In front of him the famous Tower Bridge comes into view, lit up as befits such an icon of engineering ingenuity. Tom takes a moment to consider how it's been spanning the ever-restless water of the Thames since 1894.

On a previous visit, he'd climbed down some side-steps to Dead Man's Hole – a sort of alcove built into the bridge next to the waterline. It served as a mortuary back when anonymous bodies were frequently fished out of the river using boathooks. The water-logged corpses were propped up against the alcove's tiled walls in the hope that someone searching for a lost person would be able to identify them. Apparently, most of the dead still ended up in unmarked graves.

Close to Tower Bridge on its eastern side, the Dean Swift pub is tucked away amongst the converted warehouse blocks and cobbled streets of Shad Thames. Tonight its lights shine out into the quiet streets like a homing beacon.

Tom steps into a crush that's generating a stifling amount of body heat and noise. Everywhere, raucous conversations are punctuated by laughter. Named after Anglo-Irish satirist and cleric Jonathan Swift, the interior still has its wooden floors and long mahogany countertop. The large blackboard behind the bar lists a dizzying choice of craft beers and gins. As he makes his way through, a deafening cheer goes up from the crowd gathered around a giant screen. Other punters surround a series of high tables – the sort you can only stand at.

Peering over the tops of heads, he spots the man he's come to interview though he has trouble squeezing past all those expensively dressed young guns to get to him. Glass of beer in hand, Simon Yardley meets him halfway. Considerably more dishevelled than his image on the company's website, Yardley's free hand rakes his brown hair into slightly better order. 'You must be Mr Brookes,' he says with a slight slur.

'Call me Tom.' Smiling, he offers the man his hand and it receives an enthusiastic, though rather clammy, shake. 'Thank you for seeing me.'

'Anything to help.' A lanky man in a creased suit staggers past them, knocking Yardley's arm and spilling beer down the front of his jacket. The culprit's 'Sorry mate,' is accepted with a raised hand. 'No worries,' Yardley says, studying the resulting dark stain with an air of resignation.

'So, Simon,' Tom begins, 'as I explained, I'm investigating David Baynton's disappearance on behalf of his mother.' Yardley nods. 'I understand you worked with David. Would you describe him as a friend?'

'Well, we were good enough mates. Though, if I'm honest, I can't say I knew that much about the bloke. We saw each other mostly at work. He kept his cards close, did Dave.' Certain vowel sounds suggest Yardley grew up in the north, though living in the south has modified his accent.

'What about his personal life?' Tom asks, 'D'you know if he was seeing anyone at the time of his disappearance?'

'Sorry, what was that again?'

'I was wondering if David ever mentioned a girlfriend. Or maybe a boyfriend?'

Distracted by the match, Yardley shrugs. 'No, not to me he didn't. But then, like I said, we mostly talked about work and stuff. Well – that and football. He's an Arsenal fan…'

Tom misses the last part of the sentence. He leans into Yardley's ear. 'I don't want to spoil your evening, Simon, but could we possibly go somewhere quieter for a quick chat? I noticed a café just across the street.'

'Yeah, it is a bit lively in here.' Yardley swallows the rest of his pint, gives a loud burp and then, swaying a little, says, 'Lead on, MacDuff.'

The café is almost deserted, the baristas busy getting ready for the following morning's rush. Over a double espresso, Yardley's manner sobers into self-importance. Wagging a sage finger in Tom's face, he says, 'It seems to me we're faced with a number of possible explanations for Dave's disappearance.' Though his use of the first-person plural irritates, Tom tries not to let it distract him. After looking around to exclude any possible eavesdroppers, Yardley judges it safe to continue. 'First off...' He holds down his left index finger. 'We accept the police's theory that he accidentally falls into the river and gets swept away. Or...'

Tom raises a hand to interrupt him. 'There are substantial barriers all the way along the side of the Thames. David was on a wide, tarmac path so it's difficult to imagine how he could have slipped and fallen in.'

'Yeah, but then we have to remember he'd had a skinful – all of us had. Maybe he's pratting about and decides to walk along the top of the wall. Or he thinks it'd be a laugh to climb over the railings.'

'Does that type of reckless behaviour seem in character?'

'Well, no, not especially,' Yardley says. 'Which brings us to our next potential scenario.' He taps his middle finger. 'Some bastard – or possibly bastards plural – attacks him. Think about it – he's wearing a big-ticket suit, flashing a decent watch... A vintage Rolex Submariner as a matter of fact. Dave told me it was a birthday present, though he didn't say who from.' Simon leans forward, the stench of beer on his breath. 'That watch of his catches somebody's eye. Dead giveaway to a mugger. He tries to fight 'em off but he loses his balance and...' Yardley's hand nose-dives onto the tabletop. 'The poor sod topples over the barrier into the water.'

'That's certainly a possibility.' Leaving a moment, Tom clears his throat. 'Did David seem depressed at all?'

Yardley snorts. 'What, you think he jumped?'

'It's another possible explanation to consider.'

'I seriously doubt it. We'd had a great night. The man was in high spirits when he left.' Yardley shakes his head with vigour, hair flopping into his eyes. He sweeps it back. 'Lucky bugger had just had the first instalment of a *pretty sizable* bonus. No way would he have topped himself.' He tosses his head back as he rakes at his errant hair. 'Take it from someone who knows, we can dismiss that possibility outright.' He finishes his coffee and then pulls a pained face. 'Which brings us to our last possibility.'

'Which is?'

Grinning, Yardley taps a third finger. 'That our Dave is actually alive and well, but, for reasons of his own, he's lying low.' He raises a defensive hand. 'Before you say anything, remember there's no proof he hasn't gone to ground. Why he should choose to, well...' He throws up both hands. 'Who can tell, eh?'

'You're right, Simon, that's another possibility.' Thinking of Snowflake, Tom says, 'Or he's being held somewhere against his will.'

'Bit unlikely.' Yardley knits his brow. 'This is London mate, not bloody Bolivia. Besides, if he'd been kidnapped, there'd have been a ransom demand ages ago. Hasn't happened, has it?' His dark eyes narrow on Tom. 'Unless, of course, you know otherwise.'

Chapter Eight

Ollie

Third period and their teacher this morning, Mr Snell, is taking the class in place of Mr Khan, who's off sick. The science block has that ingrained chlorine-and-burnt-metal smell. Ollie's sweating; it's really stuffy in spite of the through-draught from the open windows and door.

In the first five minutes, Snell feels the need to mention that he'd studied at Oxford. He's in his twenties and his clothes, hairstyle and much of his language conform to current trends, so he imagines this affords him a greater bond with his students than, for example, Miss Harrison, the Head of Physics. Snell has a habit of sweeping back his fringe with a dramatic flourish, refers to everyone as *chaps* and *chapettes* and likes to inappropriately quote from the lyrics of The Tin Wasps and vintage Taylor Swift. In summary, Mr Snell is, by general consensus, a total bell-end.

Today promises to be more boring than usual because they're revising. The set task relates to Newton's second law of motion. Yawn. No one is paying attention as Snell-end scrawls the usual force-mass-acceleration formula on the interactive screen at the front.

A balled-up piece of paper sails over Ollie's head and lands on the floor in front. Before Snell notices, Paul Gregg stamps on it. He scrapes his foot back, picks it up and surreptitiously spreads the paper out on the bench before turning round to raise a thumb at Aaron Jenkins. Everyone's perked up because passing a boring note about football practice represents a small triumph in the perpetual student v teacher struggle.

After a further mind-numbing ten minutes of explanation, several dumb-arse questions about how Newton's law relates to vehicle design appear on their screens.

When somebody lets out a loud fart, a ripple of laughter runs around the room. Look of disgust on her face, Sukie Jones alternates between pointing an accusing finger at Paul Gregg – who hasn't looked up – and wafting her hand in front of her face. Next thing, everyone around her is doing the same. 'Settle down now, chaps,' Snell tells the class.

Ollie works on the assignment though he's distracted by thoughts of Cerys. Earlier, their first one-to-one in the library seemed to go okay. He thinks. Except he'd found it difficult to explain the maths while trying not to stare at her mouth (a total giveaway). He'd then fixated on the line of freckles leading down into her collar.

As they'd packed up their stuff, Cerys assured him he'd been a big help. 'We'll have to grab a coffee sometime, Oll,' she'd said shouldering her schoolbag. No specified time. Pathetically grateful, he'd tried to match her nonchalance, tried not to mind having his name reduced to one syllable – which has got to be a sign she feels comfortable with him. Although, it might also suggest he's been relegated to the dreaded friend-zone. Hard to tell because he can't read most of her thoughts. Ollie puts that down to the affect she has on him. Sod it, he's not used to all this uncertainty.

His sigh is loud enough to attract Sukie's attention. Ollie gives her a twitch of a smile before turning his eyes back to the screen. Grandad would tell him to stop *mooning* over Cerys. Being from another century, the old man's pep talks tend to include archaic phrases such as *brace up* and *knuckle down*. Sometimes he wishes he had an ordinary grandad instead of one that, like some cosmic mole, can pop up anywhere, anytime he chooses. Right now, he could be hovering somewhere over his shoulder. Thoughts of his grandad materialising there in the science lab send a shudder through Ollie. After a backward glance to reassure himself, he focuses on finishing the set task.

Snell-end breaks off from the Nintendo game he's been playing (not very well) to stroll around the room, peering down at everyone's screens to check their responses. 'Read the question more carefully,' appears to be his standard advice. Coming to a stop behind Aaron, Snell raises his voice to the class. 'Remember you need to show *all* your calculations, chaps and chapettes. Explain *exactly* how you've reached your conclusions.'

After several more aimless circuits, Snell's orange and blue trainers come to a halt beside Ollie. In a sneering tone, he says, 'You appear to be looking at entirely the wrong screen, Mr Brookes.'

'Oh, I've already completed the set tasks and submitted my work, sir.' He switches pages to show him the relevant screen with its orange FULLY COMPLETED banner. Before Snell-end can respond, Ollie turns back to the article he'd been reading.

'Well, then I very much doubt you've fully grasped the complexities involved,' Snell declares. 'Might I suggest that, instead of attempting to fly before you can walk, you choose the reassess option and take another look at the questions.'

Red in the face, Ollie says, 'I think you'll find my answers are correct, and my examples and conclusions detailed enough for *anyone* to follow, sir.' He stops short of adding *even you*.

'Ollie's the class genius, sir,' Ryan Elliot pipes up. 'Mr Khan always lets him do his own thing once he's finished.'

'Does he indeed,' Snell-end says, letting his down-with-the-kids persona slip. 'Well, in *my* classes, all students are expected to stick to the curriculum. Even a supposed *genius*. (He makes the word an insult.) 'Once you've completed the initial assignment, you should move on to the supplementary questions. At this stage it's all about re-enforcement. Drilling things into here.' Snell taps his own temple. (If it was allowed, he'd love to rap that finger against the back of Ollie's head.) Like it's some crap slogan, Snell announces, 'Repetition is the key to knowledge retention.' Then, pleased with his own wit, 'I can't say that often enough. Seriously chaps, you need to drum this stuff into (he mimics Poirot's accent) *the little grey cells*.'

There's a scraping of stool legs. Ollie stands up along with everyone else because Miss Harrison is lingering in the open doorway. Despite the hot weather, she's wearing her regular burgundy jacket and skirt combo. Advancing into the room, she pats the air in front of her as a silent signal they should all sit down and get on with their work.

Those sharp eyes of hers dart around the class missing nothing. 'Everything alright, Mr Snell?'

'Perfectly fine, thank you Miss Harrison. I was, in fact, just in the process of explaining to Mr Brookes here that, in this school, there can be no special treatment for *any* student. No exceptions to the general rule.'

'I see.' Under her usual emollient tone, there's a hint of steel. 'And yet young Oliver is just that – exceptional.' Her stout heels drum the hard floor as she strides over to join them. Ollie scents wallflowers – a fleeting reminder of his granny's garden. Miss Harrison pauses before she speaks. 'We must always take care to *differentiate*, Mr Snell. To make appropriate adjustments in order to cater for the full range of our students' differing abilities.' Snell-end gets the full laser-stare. 'As I'm sure you agree, we would be remiss, as educators, if we failed to recognise a gifted student.'

Her beneficent smile attempts to soften the admonishment. She glances down at Ollie's screen. 'Ah, I see you're currently wrestling with the theory of LQG, Oliver.'

He clears his throat. 'Yes, miss.'

Taking in Snell, her attention widens to the rest of the class. 'For the uninitiated, the acronym LQG stands for Loop Quantum Gravity. Those of you who continue to study physics beyond this school, will no doubt come across the theory. In essence, it's a quantum theory which, instead of treating gravity simply as a force, employs Einstein's geometric formulations.

The theory postulates that space and time are, in fact, made up of finite loops woven into an extremely fine fabric known as *spin networks*.' She chuckles. 'To my mind it sounds like our creator may have gone in for a bit of cosmic knitting.'

A polite laugh runs around the room. Miss Harrison beams at them. 'Anyway class, my apologies for having distracted you from the task in hand, and possibly boggled a few minds in the process.' Leaving no doubt, she adds, 'Carry on with your reading, Oliver.'

Upright as a general inspecting her troops, she strides towards the exit. 'Please continue where you left off, everyone.'

Clearing his throat, Mr Snell goes to respond and then thinks better of it. Instead, he follows Miss Harrison to the front and, after checking she's some way along the corridor, and in spite of the heat, he shuts the door.

Snell does his best to appear calm though Ollie knows that he's seething. He sits down. Too riled-up to concentrate on Nintendo, he stares down at the chemical staining on the surface in front of him, conjuring up images of retribution like it's a Rorschach test.

For the remainder of the lesson, the man barely looks up. When he does, he's careful to ignore Ollie.

First out of the door as soon as the buzzer sounds, Snell-end stomps off along the corridor. Head down, he's busy fantasising about the various ways he might even the score.

Chapter Nine

Tom

Tom's meeting with Yardley has thrown up more questions than answers. Before taking this further, or not, he needs to get the measure of the missing man and where better to start than his home. He makes the call posing as a would-be tenant. In her boarding-school accent, the agent he is put through to assures him the apartment is still vacant, and by the end of the month they expect it to be available to rent for a 'very reasonable' eyewatering sum. They arrange to meet in the building's lobby.

Just before the appointed time, Tom steps into the glass fronted atrium of the high-rise – an edifice designed to reflect the corporate world rather than offering a retreat from it. In contrast to the street outside, the inside of the building is cool and hushed like it's holding its breath. Marble flooring gives way to thick carpet as he approaches the hardwood reception desk. Tom produces his alternative ID for the concierge and waits for their system to verify his right of entry.

The lobby's interior walls are punctuated by massive

colour-block paintings devoid of any emotion. He notices there's a separate lift for the gym and swimming pool in the basement.

'Ms Fitzwilliam is expected shortly,' the elderly concierge informs him before he turns away to deal with a pot-bellied man demanding information about a missing package. To placate him, the concierge morphs into obsequious mode.

After ten minutes, Tom begins to pace, prompting the younger concierge to come across and strongly suggest he, 'Might like to take a seat while you're waiting.' His impatience must be spoiling the vibe. Tom acquiesces. Fortunately, he's built in a margin for error. The clockface projected onto the floor reassures him there's still ample time.

Ms Fitzwilliam arrives a full twenty minutes late, gushing her apologies together with a story that undermines the blurb about the apartment's convenient transport links. Dark blonde hair, cream blouse, tailored black trousers; she finally remembers to introduce herself as Katrina. No last name.

Her spice-edged perfume fills the lift as she escorts him up to the eighth floor. Spiked heels ringing on the hard floors, she walks him through the apartment's hallway straight out onto a sizable faux-wood deck. As she talks, the soundscape of the city is a constant intrusion. Making the most of this major selling point, Katrina's bracelets jangle when she wafts an arm to encompass the 'fab city view'. She invites him to appreciate the skyscrapers she identifies by name as if introducing him to the impressive social set he could potentially find himself mixing with. The next part of her pitch is lost when a pneumatic drill starts up in the street below.

Giving up on her spiel, Katrina leads him back inside. Tom eyes up the sparse collection of personal items knocking around the apartment. Noticing, she says, 'The previous chap left in rather a hurry we understand. His belongings are due to be removed in the next day or so.' She doesn't say by whom and betrays no hint of what might have befallen the missing tenant.

Katrina's movements are staccato; she's anxious, flustered about something. Following a heavy sigh, she comes clean. 'I'm most dreadfully sorry, Mr White, but as you know I'm running rather later than I'd expected and I have a couple arriving to view one of the penthouse apartments they're interested in acquiring. In fact, they're actually due here in about four minutes.' She checks the slim gold watch on her wrist. 'If I show you the lie of the land here, so to speak, would you mind awfully if I leave you to carry on looking around by yourself for a little while?'

Tom tries not to show how pleased he is at this stroke of luck. 'Of course. Don't worry about me. I know what it's like – been there, got the thong.' (Wrong audience – she looks more alarmed than amused.) He clears his throat. 'No problem, it'll give me a chance to imagine what it might be like living here.'

Katrina seems torn – probably weighing his trustworthiness. 'It's absolutely fine, honestly,' he tells her. 'I've studied the floorplan and the layout seems pretty straightforward.' He bats away any remaining concern. 'I can manage to work out what's what. In fact, I expect you'd like to spend a few minutes checking the penthouse over before your viewers arrive. Brew up some coffee and that sort of thing.'

'Well, if you're absolutely sure you don't mind. The penthouse is on for eight figures, so I would like to make quite sure everything passes muster up there.' A frown creases her otherwise smooth forehead. 'I would hate you to get the impression this flat is any less important to us…'

'Perish the thought.' Tom gives her his most reassuring smile.

No doubt envisioning the hefty commission at stake, she says, 'Right then; well enjoy that view. And explore. In fact, my colleague did mention that there's some sort of underfloor wine cellar to look out for. I'll be back soonest. And, of course, I can answer any questions you might have then.'

On her way out, she stops. 'If, for whatever reason, you have to leave before I get back, would you mind signing out with the concierge. Fire and security regulations…'

'Don't worry,' he says, following her to the outer door. 'Honestly, take all the time you need Katrina. I'm in no hurry to leave.'

Once she's gone, Tom goes to work like some scene-of-crime officer. He strides along the apartment's wide hallway into the second bedroom/study. The room is empty. A dark patch on one wall marks the spot where something must once have hung. Faint indentations on the floor suggest the ghost of a desk. Nothing else remains.

Disappointed, he moves on to the impressively large master bedroom suite. Its sheer curtains are pulled back to give a dazzling view of all the glass-sided buildings surrounding this one. Waking up in here, a person might feel on-show; exposed.

Staying away from the windows, Tom slips on transparent

nitril gloves before beginning his search in the ensuite shower room. (A pro investigator never compromises the scene.) In the old days, people stashed things in the toilet cistern, but that was before such fittings were hidden inside the walls. No sign of any loose panels. Fancy toiletries are lined up in the shower. Perfectly folded matching towels descend in size order. David's electric toothbrush still sits on its dedicated shelf. Tom opens the mirrored wall cabinets to find the usual over-the-counter medication arranged according to the relevant ailment. Has someone curated this stuff, or did David Baynton really live like this?

The walk-in closet holds a short row of freshly laundered shirts and two seemingly identical grey-blue suits. Nothing in any of the pockets. On the rack below a lone pair of black shoes show no sign of any wear.

Tom goes through to the bedroom. Its king-sized bed has been made up in the standard hotel style before being artfully dressed by a blue tartan throw and stacked cushions in a variety of toning tweeds.

No paintings or decorative objects on any of the walls. A hardback copy of The Blind Assassin sits next to the lamp and coaster on the nearest bedside table like a prop. No bookmark inside, no corners turned down or passages highlighted. The spine is broken in quite a few places suggesting it may have been read and re-read. He fans the pages, holds it upside down but nothing falls out, all the same he's careful to put it back precisely where it was.

Moving on, he searches the drawers underneath. One contains paracetamol, a box of fabric cufflinks and an opened pack of condoms with one missing. In the middle drawer several pairs of designer underpants are neatly folded. Nothing's hidden in-between. The bottom drawer holds half a dozen paired-up socks. Thinking of his own over-stuffed bedside drawers, he wonders how often Baynton stayed here.

Tom walks around the bed to examine the other bedside table and finds it empty. Had David reserved the space for some potential new partner, or has it already been cleaned out? He slips one hand between the mattress and the sprung base and, stretching to his fullest, works his way around feeling for anything that might have been missed.

Coming up empty handed, he tries the living room next. The layout is open plan though carefully zoned. On the back wall there's a kitchen area equipped with every gadget an enthusiastic cook might need. No sign of wear and tear; none of it appears to have been used much. The fridge is pristine inside and must surely have been emptied out and thoroughly cleaned.

There's not a single smudge or fingerprint on the glass-topped dining table. The set of grey leather and metal chairs around it are all neatly tucked in. Again, there's no artwork on any of the walls. Maybe looking out over the vast capital was more than enough for David to take in.

In the lounge area, Tom steps onto a deep-pile, denim blue rug. Arranged to face the view, there are two very large white sofas. The same shade of blue is echoed in what his mum would call scatter cushions. There's a central glass and brass coffee table with a stack of travel books on the shelf below its empty surface. Given enough time, he plans to examine these.

A pair of Eames-style black leather chairs with matching footstools sit on either side of the vast entertainment screen. Tom sits down in the nearest, puts his feet up and stares out at the view. He's perfectly placed to see into a nearby apartment block. Like stacked up reptile terrariums, the occupants of these high-rise homes must be happy to live in full view of countless others.

Making himself comfortable for a moment, he shuts his eyes to the vast amount of light pouring in through all that floor-to-ceiling glass. He has a strong sense that he's entered a stage-set; that the real David Baynton had acquired these accoutrements as an outward illustration of his financial success, but he'd been putting on an act, adopting a glamourous lifestyle no more real to him than it feels to Tom.

Time is ticking. Getting to his feet, he focuses next on the long, narrow side table it would be easy to overlook. A towering pair of stone table lamps are the only objects on its polished wooden surface. Below this sit two shallow drawers. Searching the first, he finds tablemats along with an unused scented candle. The other drawer holds odds and ends: a metal tape measure, a torch, a set of screwdrivers, some unidentifiable bits and bobs and, underneath all that, an old remote control with two unmarked buttons. Like the torch, it could be some sort of back-up in case all his voice-activated electronic gadgetry were to fail. Or maybe it operates the fabled wine cellar he'd almost forgotten about. Tom presses the top button, and like an inappropriate erection, it sets off a slow growing bulge beneath the rug. He turns back the edge of the rug a metre or so to reveal an open pop-up wine rack just large enough for the dozen or so prostrate bottles it contains. Various labels confirm they're vintage wines from well known, high-end vineyards. The pub trade has taught him a bit about wine and, as far as he can tell, none of them are especially rare or valuable enough to warrant being hidden like this.

One bottle – a 2007 Medoc – is lying more awkwardly in its cradle than the rest. He lifts it out with care. Underneath it, where the neck had lain, is the sort of plug-in flash drive he hasn't seen in years.

The outer door gives a tell-tale groan. 'Hello?' Her spikey heels ring out along the hallway, marching his way. 'Mr White, are you there?'

He slips the flash drive into his trouser pocket before replacing the bottle. 'In here. I was just checking out the wine cellar you mentioned.' He strips off his gloves and stuffs them into a pocket hoping the bulge won't look suspicious.

After checking the room for anything amiss, Katrina exhales, no doubt pleased he hasn't made off with anything. 'So I see,' she says, towering over him. 'Whilst this is a lovely flat, I have to admit that particular feature is a bit of a disappointment. I'd describe it more as an underfloor hidey-hole than a wine cellar.'

Tom gets to his feet. 'Yeah, I'd play it down if I were you. Reserve it for a second visit, which, I'm afraid, I don't think I'll be making.' He presses the lower button on the remote and the bottles soundlessly descend. Once in place, he doubts anyone would spot the join. He flips the edge of the rug back into place.

'You know, I think I'd like something a bit more... How can

I put this?' He gives a vague wave to illustrate his uncertainty. 'A bit more *me*, if that makes any sense?'

'Absolutely. I think we all get that indefinable, je-ne-sais-quoi tingle when somewhere feels right for us.'

'So anyway, how'd it go with the penthouse?' he asks. 'Did they like it?'

'Matter of fact, they loved it.' Katrina smiles. 'I'm cautiously optimistic.'

'Then I'm pleased your afternoon hasn't been wasted.'

She ushers him towards the door. 'Viewings are never a waste of time, Mr White. As we always say, identifying what doesn't suit a person is an important step in any property search.'

'I couldn't have put it better,' he tells her.

Chapter Ten

Back in the lobby, they sign out. Promising to keep in touch, Katrina strides off on those spiky heels, already on another call. Tom lingers by the front desk. 'Turns out I actually knew Mr Baynton,' he tells the grey-faced concierge. 'David Baynton?' He hikes a thumb towards the lift, but the man doesn't respond. 'He was the previous tenant of the flat I was looking around just now?'

Stonewalled.

'Anyway, turns out I knew him, you know, from a while back. What are the odds? Small world, eh?'

Finally, the man opens his mouth. 'If you say so, sir.' Faced with his indifference, Tom gives up.

The man's sandy-haired assistant is holding the front doors open for a couple manoeuvring two very large suitcases. 'Allow me, madam,' Sandy-hair says, relieving the woman of her burden. Tom stands aside while he helps them into a waiting cab. There's a sleight-of-hand exchange. Sandy's quick to squirrel away the tip he's just received for doing what he's paid to do.

Sharing the pavement, the two of them watch the cab pull

away. Tom opens the proceedings with a friendly smile. 'Like I was just telling your colleague at the desk, it turns out I knew Mr Baynton – the previous tenant in the flat I was just looking round. Quite a coincidence in a city of ten million people.'

'Happens more often than you might think.' Sandy gives a backwards nod. 'You've heard he's missin', right?'

'Yeah, I couldn't believe it when his name came up on my newsfeed,' Tom says. 'I hadn't seen Dave in a while, but all the same...'

'He kept his cards closer than most.' After checking his boss isn't watching, Sandy looks down at his empty palm and then back up at him. A not-too-subtle hint.

Taking the bait, Tom hands over the only option he finds in his wallet – a twenty. This had better be worth it.

'I make it a rule not to gossip about residents, but then again, Mr Baynton's no longer one of our tenants.' A conspirator's smile. 'After he went missin', this policewoman – police *officer* I suppose I should say – she came here askin' questions. I told her straight up he wasn't the chatty sort. Plus, he was away quite a bit. On business, I presume. None of us knew much about the man.'

Tom raises an eyebrow. 'And yet...'

Sandy rubs the side of his nose like someone playing a snitch in a bad film. He takes a step closer. 'This bloke I happen to know – a good mate – he works for this plumbing maintenance outfit that specialises in high-rise residential buildings.'

'Sounds quite niche.'

'Yeah well, it's the complexity of it all see – can be a

plumber's nightmare. Anyway, a few months back, Mr Baynton happens to walk past me while I was out here chattin' to my mate and, like always, I greet him by name. This was well before the man went missin'. My mate had just finished a job up on the ninth. Anyway, after he sees Baynton, he swears blind that – unless it was his identical twin – he's the same bloke who owns this big fancy apartment in one of them new blocks down Greenwich way.'

'Dave wasn't a twin,' Tom says. 'Maybe the Greenwich apartment belonged to his lover. Or possibly a good friend.'

'All I can tell you is my mate got sent there to fix a leak in the kitchen up in one of the penthouse apartments. Big swanky place like you might expect. Took him the best part of a day to sort it out and Baynton – or his double – was there alone the whole time. The place hadn't long been finished so everythin' was still under guarantee – which means the developer has to carry the can. Baynton wasn't pickin' up the tab, but he needed to sign off the work as the owner. Which he did.' Sandy nudges him. 'My mate was pretty certain he wasn't goin' by the same name.'

'I suppose he could have bought the place to let.'

'What, a posh gaff like that?' Sandy whistles his scepticism then shrugs. 'Maybe. Or p'raps he'd won the lottery.'

'So did you pass on this information to the police?'

Sandy scoffs. 'You got to be jokin' me.' After a swift glance over his shoulder to check on the other concierge, he says, 'The bloke's gone missin' presumed dead, right? If he was livin' in two separate apartments in the same city and usin' two different names…' He shakes his head. 'Whatever he might've been mixed up in before he died… Well, put it this way, I'd sooner stay well out of it. Besides, nothin' I can tell them is gonna bring the poor bugger back.' Tom manages to dodge the next nudge. Remembering his duties, Sandy re-positions himself ready to open the door. 'You didn't hear this from me, alright? Want my advice, you'll stay well clear of whatever, or whoever, caused him to drown himself.'

'One last thing,' Tom says, 'Did your plumbing friend happen to mention which building this penthouse apartment was in?'

'Not that I remember.' A middle-aged woman is heading towards them. Without turning his head, Sandy says, 'There's loads of new apartment blocks down that way.'

'Could you give me your friend's contact details?'

'No chance.' Sandy looks him in the eye. 'Listen mate, I weren't born yesterday. Why you've come here to snoop around his old flat – well, that's your business. I definitely don't wanna know.' He raises a hand to block Tom's denial.

'Afternoon, Mrs Deacon.' Sandy's nod is halfway to a bow.

'Good afternoon, Lenny.' She fails to make eye contact with either of them.

After she's safely out of the way, Tom changes tack. 'I'll level with you, Lenny. I actually came here on behalf of Dave's mum. When I heard about him drowning, I went to see her to offer my condolences. As you might imagine, the poor woman's been through hell. And she's desperate for answers. Who wouldn't be in her situation? So I promised her that, when I was next up in town, I'd try to find out more about Dave's disappearance.' He opens both hands like he's hiding nothing.

Lenny's expression softens. 'Can't tell you any more than I have.'

'Yes, well thanks anyway,' Tom says. 'I guess it's a start...'

'And an *end* – if you've got any sense.' Before he walks away, Lenny delays him with a hand on his arm, 'For what it's worth, my mate keeps being called back to the same buildin' to sort out the mess these cowboy plumbers made of it all. Seems there's this sculpture outside the entrance he was really taken with. Apparently, when you first walk towards it, you think it's just these random shapes and colours hangin' off a load of metal rods. But then, as you get closer, the whole thing alters and slowly comes together to make up this massive bird with its giant wings spread out.' Lenny spreads his own arms to demonstrate.

'The parallax effect,' Tom tells him without thinking.

'If you say so, mate.' He gives Tom a curious look. 'Thing that really blew my mate's mind was that the bottom bits are all made out of raw copper, so, if you're standin' at the right angle when the sun hits it, this giant gull, or whatever it's meant to be, looks like it's on fire.' He laughs. 'Maybe the bloke that made it had had his chips swooped on too many times.'

'Wow, that sounds extraordinary,' Tom tells him. 'Listen, you've been a great help.' He pats the man's arm. 'Thanks.'

Sandy gives him a long look. 'Mind how you go.'

On his walk to the tube station, Tom gets the jitters. Feeling spooked, he pretends to study a restaurant's menu so he can check the window's wider reflection. People continue to pass by without showing him any interest. As far as he's able to tell, no one is lurking on the periphery.

Tom walks on shaking his head, dismissing the idea as nonsense – a product of his overwrought imagination. How could anyone know about the flash drive in his pocket?

As for the concierge's suspicions, it's quite possible that anonymous plumber mistook Baynton for some wealthy lookalike. The phoenix sculpture he mentioned sounds distinctive enough to easily track down.

He's always loved the story of that mythical bird rising from the flames. In some versions, it ascends from the burnt remains of its dead predecessors. Other versions have the same bird dying in the flames before being reborn. If Baynton passed it on a regular basis, might it have inspired him to "die" before reinventing himself?

Tom checks the time before picking up his pace. He glances back several times expecting to catch sight of someone on his tail. No one appears to be following him, no one accosts him on the tube or in the tunnel leading up to the maelstrom of Paddington Station. All the same, as he waits for his train, Tom experiences a prickling sensation across his scalp – a feeling he's learnt to trust. Someone amongst the throng of fellow travellers is watching him.

Chapter Eleven

Ollie

Ollie off-loads the weight of his swim-kit and school bag onto the pavement. The sports centre is on the outskirts of town and Dad's late picking them up. Hair still wet from the pool, his eyes are sore and he's beginning to shiver a little. Above them the sky looks ominous – a shit day about to get shitter. A few heavy raindrops land the first blows.

Fresh from tennis practice, Vega is prancing about, swiping at incoming imaginary balls with her covered racket. 'We could start walking.' She stretches for the next fictional shot. 'Beats hanging around here until our beloved father deigns to show up.'

'He'll be here soon,' Ollie tells her, though of course she knows that already. 'It's not his fault the train was running late.'

'Two trips to London in one week is a bit excessive.' She mimes an overhead smash. 'I doubt it's gone unnoticed. He ought to have turned that Baynton woman down point-blank. Would have if he wasn't such a soft touch.'

'Yeah well, let's not guilt-trip him when he arrives.'

'Why not? Why shouldn't we get priority over some missing bloke he's never even met?' Ollie doesn't respond. After a backhand swipe, she says, 'You know there's a much easier way for us to get home.' She stops bouncing on her feet to give him one of her all-knowing glares. 'I'm just saying. There's absolutely nobody about. All we'd need to do is dodge behind those bushes over there, and voila!'

Ollie shakes his head, which predictably sets her off on one. 'Pray tell me, oh saintly brother of mine, aren't you *occasionally* tempted to break their sodding rules? I mean, it's not like Dad always sticks to them.'

'Except he drives an ordinary EV. And this morning he caught a regular train up to London like everybody else. In any case, the answer to your question is emphatically no. I'm not planning to risk it. And you shouldn't either.'

She chops the side of the racket against her open palm several times. 'What is the point of being able to do all sorts of amazing things if we're never allowed to actually do them? Shouldn't we be practising – honing our skills?'

'When we're older–'

'D'you think there's some sort of legal age we need to reach before it's okay – like with drinking alcohol or having sex?' She goes for a winning forehand down the line. 'When we were tiny we didn't play by the rules. Remember?'

'Yeah, well that was before we fully understood about unforeseen consequences.'

'How do they know that stuff anyway?' When he doesn't answer, she says, 'Do the Guardians have some sort of council or committee that decrees what we can and can't do?'

Ollie shrugs his *search me*.

'Aren't you even curious?' She's serious now. 'When I first realised just how different we are, I sort of felt… I don't know, ashamed I suppose. Guilty even. I was ordinary looking on the outside, but really some kind of hideous abomination – a freakish excuse for a human being.'

He nods. She knows there are times when he's felt the same way.

Staring at the pavement, Vega is lost to her memories. 'I started to wonder, you know to *postulate* – don't you just love that word?'

'Not especially.'

She raises her head to look him in the eye. 'It's possible *we* are the normal ones and someday in the far future *they* will be the oddities.' She pats his shoulder in a gesture of solidarity. 'Don't pretend you haven't had the same thought. We've both been down that particular rabbit hole.' She clears her throat. 'Both of us are in disguise trying to pass as normal.'

'Very profound.' He can only make light of something he can't deny.

'Have you ever wondered if maybe we were born this way for a reason? This might sound pretentious, but what if it's for some sort of higher purpose?'

The idea silences him for a moment. 'Since when have you been religious?' he says, to disarm her, to discredit such a grandiose notion.

'Not what I was getting at, and you know it. I'm just saying that, if you follow the logic, even when we were tiny embryos in our mother's womb, you and me were destined to be different.'

'You and *I*,' he corrects her. A wind-up she ignores. He says, 'Since you mention Mum…'

'We have an inalienable right to be as we are,' she declares. 'Inalienable rights can't be taken or given away.'

'I know what the word means.'

'Then you have to agree we have a God-given right to find out exactly what we're capable of.' She swings her racket close to his head making the air whoosh inside his ears.

'I think you should leave God out of this.' He doesn't want a debate. Not here, not now. He says, 'Grandad's explained to us loads of times why we shouldn't do that stuff. Like he says, if you knowingly step into a minefield, you can't pretend to be surprised if things explode in your face.' He grabs the head of her swinging racket mid-stroke. 'We can't ignore unintended consequences – the potential for collateral damage. To quote Voltaire: "With great power comes great responsibility".'

'Wasn't that what Uncle Ben told Peter Parker in Spider-man?'

'I think you'll find Voltaire said it first.'

She frees her racket to swipe at a passing blowfly. 'If I can't mention God, you're not allowed to bring some long-dead French dude into it.'

'Except, what Voltaire said happens to be highly relevant.'

'Whatever.' She looks away. 'Always the same bloody song, with the same monotonous lyrics I'm sick of hearing.' The racket becomes a guitar. Tunelessly, she sings, 'Don't go there, don't go anywhere…'

When he covers his ears, she laughs. 'I don't imagine they'll let us do what we like once we're eighteen. Or even twenty something. The age of majority – the whole concept is stupid. And totally arbitrary.' She's in his face now. 'Seriously – why should we stick to their rules? Why not experiment a bit?' Wordlessly she adds, *Live a little.*

'Because we mustn't risk it, alright,' which sounds lame even to him. Without speaking he tells her. *We've been through this. You know about the possible dangers – the chain of events you could inadvertently set in motion. Mess about with fate – or whatever you want to call it – and you risk screwing things up on a cosmic level.*

Then perhaps someone should remind our father of that.

The threatened rain starts to spot the ground. Peripheral movement draws his attention to Paul Gregg and Aaron Jenkins who are heading their way. Ollie groans. Joined at the hip, those two like to stay behind after swimming to "pump iron" in the gym.

Vega says, 'It's like never being able to flex your muscles properly.' She scoffs. 'Talking of which, here come Dogberry and Verges.'

'Shakespeare – isn't he another long-dead dude with no relevance for today?'

Her racket becomes a swashbuckler's sword. 'Touché – I don't think.'

The two boys saunter up to them. Aaron says, 'Alright Oll? Vega?' not to be friendly, but because the prat is eyeing up his sister, hoping to engage her interest in the six-pack his wide-open shirt is intended to showcase. Subtle or what?

Undeterred by the age difference, or the disdainful expression on Vega's face, Aaron glances up at the tarmac-coloured sky. 'Want a lift? Looks like it's about to piss down.' He rearranges his shoulders to seem unconcerned either way, then nods in the direction of the car park. 'My new motor's over there. Two-seater, so there's only room for one more.'

Paul widens his legs. 'His *new* car's older than my brother.'

'You tryin' to throw shade, man?' Turning to his friend, Arron deploys his signature loud laugh, his teeth impressively even and white. 'Mazda MX5's a classic, innit. 130 top speed. 2 litre engine – the one with all the torque.'

'Yeah, like you,' Paul quips.

Don't laugh at that. Don't even smile, Ollie tells her. *Engage in any way and they'll never bugger off.*

'Wheel-to-wheel that baby Fiat of yours would be coughing on my fumes.'

'Seeing's we're flexing, man, mine can seat four, minimum.'

'Two's company, innit?' Smirking, Aaron lifts one eyebrow at Vega. 'More than that's a crowd.'

Vega gives him her die-now stare. 'As entertaining as this conversation has been, gentlemen, GTG – our lift's here.' She waves her racket at Dad before turning on Aaron and Paul. 'Adieu: I must away. Exit, pursued by a stare.'

Watching her stride off towards the car, Paul mutters, 'What's she on about?' Suspicion narrows his eyes. 'Your sis stoned or somethin', Oll?'

'No, she's just high on life,' Ollie tells him. As if.

'Be seeing you then,' Aaron shouts after her.

Vega's already bagged the front seat leaving him to dump his gear in the boot then scoot into the back. 'Sorry you had to wait,' Dad tells them. 'At least I arrived before the heavens open.' He peers up at the sky, then over at the two boys watching them. 'Friends of yours? Do they need a lift?'

'What, those two clowns?' Vega scoffs. 'Ollie's not that desperate.'

'They've got their own wheels,' Ollie tells him.

'Okay then.' Dad pulls away just as the rain arrives all at once, bouncing off every hard surface.

'How'd it go in London?' Ollie asks raising his voice.

'Not that interesting.' Peering through the frantic wipers, Dad says, 'I'm surprised you need to ask.'

'We don't,' Vega tells him. 'Oll's only being polite.'

'Don't call me Oll.'

She turns around. 'What's it matter, bruv? What's in a name?'

'You wouldn't say that if they started calling you Veg. Or Vague.'

'Wouldn't the shortened version be Vegg?' Dad suggests. He stops for the lights. 'I don't think Tom can be made shorter.'

'You could be T,' she says. 'Known by a single initial like a spy.'

'And you do do a lot of snooping around, Dad,' he adds.

Vega laughs. 'Lose the T and you'd be Om – like the chant. Ommm...'

'Though that would actually take longer to say than Tom,' Dad points out.

'So anyway, changing the subject.' The rain hammering on the roof forces Ollie to shout. 'How was the glorious capital?'

After steering around a massive puddle, Dad says, 'Oh, you know, probably just a waste of time.'

'Really?' Vega says. 'What about that mysterious flash-drive you found?'

'That's classic sneaker-net,' Ollie tells him. 'That Baynton bloke must have been worried–'

'Damn it!' Dad thumps the steering wheel. 'Can't a man have any secrets in this family?'

They all know the answer to that question is better left unsaid. 'I could look out that old laptop of mine with the USB port,' Ollie suggests. 'If you like, I'll fire it up when we get back so we can see exactly what he was hiding.'

'Let me make myself clear, I do not require your assistance.' In his your-father-has-spoken voice, Dad adds, 'and *we* plural are not going to be looking at whatever's on that thing. *I* will be viewing it alone. Got that?'

'Yeah, okay. I suppose it would be inappropriate for your kids to get involved in your investigation,' Ollie says. 'Unprofessional and all that.'

'Quite.' Dad is pleased to have made his point, choosing not to acknowledge the obvious flaw in his apparent victory.

Chapter Twelve

Tom

The phoenix sculpture is a dead giveaway. Sitting at his desk, all it takes is a couple of clicks and he's looking at an image of it against the recently completed Grenewych Heights building. Aside from having such a stunning artwork right outside, the edifice is pretty much indistinguishable from its neighbouring glass and steel tower blocks. If, prior to his disappearance, Baynton was leading some sort of double life, there's a chance he's not dead after all but holed up in his secret apartment.

According to recorded property sales, both penthouses were purchased around eighteen months ago. The new data disclosure regulations prevent him from discovering at what price or the name of either purchaser.

Against his working theory, when Baynton was first reported missing, the man's face was all over the media. Wouldn't a neighbour, or the agent who sold him the apartment, have come forward to identify him? Heaping speculation on speculation, he wonders if Baynton might have taken steps to avoid being recognised.

Tom shakes his head. He should drop this case like a hot brick.

Decision made, he can't help but wonder how Baynton might have pulled it off. For a start, he could have purchased the apartment under a false name or simply bought it through an intermediary. Simple to arrange for deliveries of anything he needs to be left outside his door. If he gets stir crazy looking out from his tower like some modern-day Rapunzel, maybe he disguises his appearance when he goes out. He could get Clark Kent style glasses. Shave his head or grow his hair and/or a beard. Dye his hair even. Or any combination of the above.

Why would he go to all that trouble? What was, or is, he playing at?

Before his disappearance, Baynton had felt secure enough to let that plumber see him. Which suggests that, at that time, he wasn't too worried. Or he might have simply trusted to the anonymity of the city.

Pointless conjecture. Tom stares up at his favourite photograph of Beth with her arms round the kids when they were both tiny. What would she say if she was here? He knows the answer. Yep, whichever way he views the conundrum, red flags are popping up all over the shop.

And yet his eyes keep returning to the little flash-drive lying there in front of him. In spite of its bad juju, the one thing he knows for certain is that Baynton took pains to hide whatever it contains. Such a trifling object, cheap and outmoded, but the mystery it might throw light on nags away at his resolve – a veritable Pandora's box he might well regret opening.

(Poor old Pandora, along with Eve in the Garden of Eden, their stories pin the blame for everything bad in the world on an over-curious woman.)

Hmm. Tom drums his fingers. Gone the way of microdots and optical disks, tech manufacturers tend to assume no one uses flash-drives anymore. The *how* of finding out what's on it is easily solved by a versatile bit of kit designed to get around such incompatibility issues. Tom retrieves the Tex-Connex from the bottom drawer, locates the right-sized dock and slots the stick into it.

The little gadget lights up as it scans the contents. A flashing green light verifies the absence of detectable malware. Augmenting its state-of-the-art firewall, his system has a "view only" mode with zero danger of any undetected nasties transferring or corrupting anything. Bottom line, should he choose to do so, he's all set to find out what Baynton was hiding.

How long did it take Pandora to break? Tom stares at the flashing green light for a couple of minutes at most before he capitulates.

He presses a key, and his screen is populated by data arranged in grid form. The widest left-hand column consists of rows of random letters, while the four corresponding columns each contain a series of numbers.

David was a city trader; could this information relate to his job? Market predictions? Insider trading? – if that's even a possibility in the mid 2030s.

Tom takes a closer look at the first cell in row one and its seemingly random series of letters. No spaces to suggest words. No recognisable combos. Could be a foreign language or more likely some sort of code.

Various online sites offer to encrypt your sensitive information using quantum-resistant algorithms. However, since these sites are considered by many to be highly dubious phishing exercises, if he was Baynton he wouldn't want to take that risk. Instead, he might resort to more old-school encryption.

Tom remembers how Uncle Matt – as he'd known him back then – would write clues to hidden goodies in various codes or ciphers his younger self needed to solve. Often it was a Caesar cipher using date numerals to shift each individual letter on by a specific number. He recalls one Easter when the clue "moon landing" had given him the UK-style date of 20061969, which he then used to decode the location of an enormous chocolate egg. Without that clue – the key – decoding the directions would have been impossible.

Concentrating on the first few rows, Tom tries all the obvious substitution ciphers including the numbers in the adjacent columns. Nothing translates into anything meaningful.

What if David had jumbled the substitute letters in a pattern of his own devising? To test this idea, Tom compares the standard letter frequency distribution in the English language – the most popular being e t o i n and so on – with the frequency of the letters used. There's no discernible correspondence. He tries the same thing with several other European languages and comes up blank.

Thinking back to the man's apartment, he's struck once again by the oddness of that lone hardback book on the bedside table. The Blind Assassin. During the 2020 lockdown,

Tom had read an old copy of his mother's and been impressed by its Russian doll structure of a novel, within a novel, within a novel. A multi-dimensional story first published more than thirty-five years ago strikes him now as rather unlikely reading material for a young trader.

If Baynton used a Vigenère cipher, he would need a source of unlikely key words or phrases. He could have chosen something memorable to himself alone but, for added security and possibly inspired by the many spy stories in which books provide cribs, he might have wanted to vary the key with each entry.

To test his theory he'd need to know the exact edition of that book. Even then, he'd still have to figure out which pages and paragraphs contain the key or, more likely, keys.

The puzzle he's staring at holds him in thrall. If he could just get his hands on David's copy of the book…

Suppose he calls Katrina, the agent, and claims to have accidentally left a book on the man's bedside table – the large volume she won't have seen him carrying in the first place.

No chance – she'd see straight through that bullshit.

He could try blagging his way past that grumpy concierge with the same story, though his odds of success are just as long. If he goes back there and somehow manages to persuade the concierge to let him into the apartment, by the time he gets up there Baynton's possessions could already have been removed.

There's a far easier alternative. It's late – well past midnight. At this hour the other residents are most likely asleep or pre-occupied. A quick in and out – the briefest of forays – and the book will be his. He knows its precise location, so that's not an issue. Once he's got his hands on it, he'll be able to try the obvious stuff like the opening or closing phrase of each chapter. Give it a few hours, and whichever way it goes, he'll pop the book back where it belongs before anyone's aware it was ever missing.

The first obstacle in his path is the state-of-the-art security system highlighted in the particulars. Also, with so much ambient light coming in through all that glass, he could be picked up by a random cam, or spotted by any number of residents in the surrounding apartment blocks.

Due to privacy regulations, it's now illegal to install cams in bedrooms or private bathrooms. In high-rise apartments, security engineers must assume no intruder is going to scale the outside of the building. Most likely they concentrate on the obvious entry points. If he can pull off a precise leap, he'll simply need to extend a hand and the prize will be his.

Perhaps, as an added precaution, he should wear a bathrobe so any casual onlookers will assume he's just a regular bloke relaxing at home.

He strips to his underpants before putting on his dressing gown. (The coffee stain on the front reminds him it could do with a wash.) Thinking of Bruce Willis crunching broken glass under his bare feet in the Nakatomi Plaza building, he slips on a pair of soft trainers just in case.

Tom takes a few deep breaths before he shuts his eyes and conjures up a vivid image of Baynton's bedroom and the exact spot he wants to arrive at.

A moment later he's plunged into profound darkness.

Chapter Thirteen

Vega

She wakes sweating and terrified. As her heartrate slows, Vega reaches under her pillow to cancel the alarm. The specifics of her dream are already lost though something of it lingers formless in her mind. She shrugs it off, tells herself there's no such thing as a bad omen.

A quarter to two and the house is as quiet as Vega hoped it would be. Moonlight is bathing the room in silvery tones. A hare moon apparently – a symbol of feminine power and said to be auspicious. She'll take that.

Vega slips out of bed. Taking care with every footstep, she creeps across the landing to crack open the door of Ollie's room just enough to be certain he's sound asleep, and unlikely to intervene. Reassured by his steady breathing, she retreats to safer ground.

After soundlessly shutting her own door, she risks turning on a lamp.

The Kylie t-shirt is hidden beneath the others in her drawer. (The singer's name picked out in pink shiny letters on a white background.) Vega pulls it on over the type of push-up bra she would normally disapprove of. Her jeans look fine after she turns up the bottoms a few centimetres like they'd worn them in an old Bros video she watched. A snake-head belt draws the waistband closer. At the back of her wardrobe, she finds the pink, leather trainers she hasn't worn in ages. They still fit, her feet settling into the soles' ready-formed indentations.

Her hair's next. She's practiced scooping up a section from the middle crown. Comb in hand, she gathers a sizable hank together and holds it in place with a sparkly scrunchie. It makes her hair seem more voluminous.

She seldom wears makeup, but if she hopes to get away with this, it's essential. Following the instruction from an online tutorial, she applies a foundation base then brushes on different shades to create contours, finishing with blusher along her cheekbones. In the mirror her face is already unrecognisable – a doll-like, blank canvas awaiting definition. Vega inhales to steady her hand before sweeping black eyeliner as close to her lashes as she can. Some baby blue shadow across her lids and then mascara to finish – lashings of it. She goes easy on the lipstick – just a hint of extra red to her mouth.

Is it too much? Vega studies her reflection, turns her head this way and that to get used to this newly created version of herself. Next, she shrugs on the genuine 80s bomber jacket she'd found in a charity shop. The turquoise leather creaks whenever she moves; its lining still holds the cloying scent of someone else's perfume. In the same shop she discovered the dozen bracelets she now divides between her wrists.

Vega picks up the little box containing the St Christopher

necklace her mother gave her all those years ago. When she opens the box, the little golden disk glows up at her like a welcome. She takes it out, fastens the chain around her neck and then hides it beneath her t-shirt.

On impulse, she grabs her multi-coloured, gran-knitted scarf for its familiarity – a style she's certain has never been in, or out, of fashion. She flicks the trailing end over one shoulder to give a jaunty air to her ensemble – a hint of the don't-give-a-fuck confidence she needs to project.

She tucks her phoney ID into an unremarkable shoulder bag. Its zipped pocket is big enough to hold her mascara and eye shadow in case her look needs a touch up. She adds a purse that's stuffed with authentic banknotes snaffled from the wad her dad has squirrelled away in his top drawer. It feels weird not to be carrying any tech – to be setting out on a journey with no way to communicate her whereabouts or what she's doing.

Vega gives her reflection a confident grin. Fake it till you make it, as they say. She could pass for sixteen. Eighteen might be pushing it.

Time to put theory into practice and quell any lingering doubts. With luck, all her research is about to pay off. A final moment to clear her head and then, ready or not, here she comes. She shuts her eyes. Whatever happens next is going to happen.

The underpass is darker than she'd imagined. Colder too. Vega allows her eyes to adjust. No witnesses visible in either direction – an excellent start.

Without warning, she's poleaxed by nausea which rises in successive waves giving her just enough time to lean forward and miss her trainers. As she voms, Vega finds herself staring into the eyes of a balaclava-clad disembodied head with the letters IRA scrawled underneath. FUCK THATCHER. someone has sprayed in blue along the bottom of the wall. Between retches, she tries to concentrate on the full stop at the end of the word Thatcher. Why didn't they add a vertical line to make it an exclamation mark?

When there's nothing more to bring up, she straightens her back. Her eyes are drawn to the rustling she can hear amongst the piled-up cardboard and newspapers in the corner. Vega leaps back when an enormous rat emerges, its whiskers twitching. More scrabbling and then a couple of its ratty mates follow its lead. Disgusted, she watches the trio scurry towards what she's just regurgitated. Gross. Vega heaves. If she hadn't already emptied her stomach…

Lightheaded, she stumbles out into a side street, her breath clouding the cold air. Time to pull herself together, act like she belongs. The street name on the corner confirms she's precisely where she'd planned to be. Okay, she might feel a bit shit, but the worst of the nausea has now passed. She's desperate to rinse out her mouth and repair any damage to her makeup. Given the occasion, she wants to look her best.

The Prince of Wales pub is further along the street in the right direction. Vega pushes open its heavy door and steps in to too much noise and light along with the stomach-churning stench of cigarettes and spilt beer. Everyone inside is loud and animated. (No phones to check.) Snippets of their conversations crowd her head, the cigarette smoke casting a blue haze her eyes are already smarting from. Following signs for the toilets, she makes her way through a fug of body heat to the end of the room and then down a wide staircase littered with cigarette butts.

The queue for the ladies stretches out into the corridor. She only wants to use a basin, but there's no way she can squeeze past all those women. Cursing under her breath, Vega joins the end of a line that doesn't appear to be moving. She clears her throat, finds the courage to speak up. 'Excuse me...' All heads turn her way. 'Can anyone tell me the time, please?'

Wrists are consulted. 'I make it ten to eight,' a petite red-head tells her.

'It's ten-past by mine,' a mousy-haired woman says.

'Yeah, well I put mine right by the radio before I came out.' Taking a drag of her cigarette, Red has the decency to blow the smoke off to one side. 'Ten-to is definitely right.' Other heads nod in agreement.

'Thanks a lot,' Vega says. They appear to want more. 'It's just, um, a bit later than I thought.' Inside, a toilet flushes. 'I only want to use the basin.'

'Then in you go, sweetheart.' Stepping back to make room, an older woman beckons her forward. 'Breathe in, ladies. No need to look so forlorn, darlin'. If he's worth his salt, he'll wait a few more minutes.'

Though she worries the water might not be sterile, Vega takes several large gulps from under the running tap. She swills more water around her mouth before surreptitiously spitting it out. Her makeup isn't as ruined as she'd feared. Though some mascara has migrated down her cheeks, she manages to rub it off with a damp paper towel. Better. A few more running repairs and she's good to go.

'Thanks for letting me through,' she tells them as she squeezes past the waiting queue.

'Good luck, sweetheart,' someone calls from behind.

Vega heads for the exit, pushing her way through people reluctant to move. Outside, the cold air hits her afresh. She breathes in the comforting smell of her old scarf, trembling possibly more from trepidation than anything else. Her destination is now a mere five-minute walk away.

Tucked between two closed-up shops, she might have missed the entrance altogether but for the flashing neon sign above its narrow doorway. 'Ticket?' the man on the door demands squaring his shoulders. Moody jazz drifts down the stairs behind him. His open palm is impatient to be filled. Tall and impressively muscled, he has the distracted air of someone who'd rather be someplace else.

'I'll need to buy one,' she says, 'if it's not sold out.'

'Four-fifty.' He gives her a sideways grin. 'And believe me there's plenty of room up there.'

She extracts a ten-pound note from her bag and hands it over. The man's eyes narrow as he raises it to the light – giving more attention to its authenticity than hers. Vega holds her breath hoping they both pass scrutiny.

After a satisfied grunt he hands her a cloakroom-style ticket, then extracts some coins from the leather bag slung round his waist and counts the change into her hand. 'Performance starts in ten minutes,' is his only nod to professionalism.

Tatty posters of past productions festoon the walls of the narrow stairway. Above the sultry jazz, she can hear the audience chatting. On the landing a blackboard A-frame has chalked up information about an upcoming show.

She gets her first glimpse of the performance space through the curtained doorway ahead – an area bigger than she'd feared. Rows of upright chairs are arranged along three sides of a raised stage where a single spotlight is trained down on the dishevelled sheets of an iron-framed bed. The available seats are half-empty or, from a different perspective, half-full.

A poster is sellotaped to the open door. Poised on the threshold, Vega stops to study it. The play's title– Cat on a Hot Tin Roof – is printed in curly letters along the top. The striking image below shows a beautiful, dark-haired woman embracing a man from behind. He's fully-dressed while she's only wearing a silky petticoat with spaghetti straps – the type women wore under their frocks in the 1950s. The man is clean-cut and handsome despite his greased-back hair. His face is turned away from the woman, his eyes off someplace else. The man's body language suggests he's in the act of rejecting her sexual advances.

Below the main image, there are heads-shots of the cast and the various characters they're playing. The second person along is the beautiful, rejected woman playing the part of Maggie Pollitt. Her real name is printed under her smiling portrait: Elizabeth Trevino.

Vega walks through the curtained doorway on unsteady legs. She selects a seat that's well back from the stage. A few people glance her way, though no one comes over to challenge her right to be there. She sits back with a heavy sigh, stares down at her sweaty palms. So far, everything's gone to plan, but is she really ready for what comes next?

Too late. The house lights drop. This is it. Alone and anonymous in the shadows, Vega holds her breath as she waits for her mother to walk out onto the stage.

Chapter Fourteen

Ollie

He drags himself from a feverish dream. Hot and sweating, Ollie's instantly on his guard. Something's wrong. Very wrong. It's 3:20 in the morning and, unless he's very much mistaken, he's alone in the house. And not just the house, but in this precise temporal reality.

He climbs out of bed and goes to check his dad's room before his sister's. As he expected, Dad's bed hasn't been slept in. Vega's clearly has been, though her bed is now empty. Fuck! Ollie kicks at the pile of junk on her floor. How come he's the only person in his sodding family capable of sticking to the rules? And now, inevitably, they're both in way over their heads.

Before Grandad gets scent of this (which would have been instantaneous a few years ago) he needs to put things right. He can't split himself in half, so who gets priority?

Ollie hurries back to his room to change into jeans and a plain sweatshirt. Pulling on his cheapest trainers, the dread he'd felt on waking begins to crystallise into something altogether more graphic. He tells himself to stay calm, to rise above the adrenaline flooding his body, demanding to know if it's fight or flight.

He grabs his grey jacket and then runs downstairs to seize the handle of the largest, ugliest knife in the block. The edge of the blade glints in the moonlight. Without some kind of sheath, how can he even carry the thing safely? He stops, remembering the teary-eyed, bereaved dad who had visited their school and begged the students never to carry a knife. A weapon can be the catalyst that causes an altercation to spiral out of control. Duly castigated, Ollie slides the knife back into the slot where it belongs.

Shame they don't have a pet Alsatian or Doberman to unnerve a would-be assailant. With nothing else to hand, he hopes the element of surprise will prevail over brute force. (He makes a mental note to acquire some pepper spray, or possibly a taser on his return.)

Ollie puts on his jacket, zips it up and pulls the hood over his head. Armed with just his wits, he tries to steady himself for what's to come.

When his sight clears, he sees her up ahead. It's late and she's walking alone down a poorly-lit street – a slight figure despite her oversized coat. The shops on either side are shuttered, their interiors dark. Hasn't she learnt anything from all those movie openers?

He's feeling no ill effects from the time-switch, which is good because she's setting a fast pace and he's some way behind. He's shivering due to the breath-capturing cold of the night air. She's not alone; exactly as he'd feared, a tall, powerfully built figure in a black leather jacket is following her, biding his time, matching her step for step. Head down and hunkered into his raised collar, the man could be following a scent trail not a person. His long, loping legs will cover the ground a lot quicker than hers when he chooses to make his move.

Unaware of either of them, her footsteps continue to ring out in a brisk rhythm on the cobbles. Up ahead, Ollie can make out the brighter lights of a busy main road she could sprint towards, but instead of choosing to do anything as logical and self-preserving as that, she turns into a narrower, darker side street for fuck's sake. Where's she planning to head next – an abandoned tunnel or some derelict building with crumbling steps leading down to a dead-end cellar?

The man picks up his pace, makes the same turn to keep her in his sight. Ollie's thankful for the silent soles of his trainers as he jogs to narrow the gap. Rounding the corner, he can just make out the pair of them. The distance between them has narrowed.

She's preoccupied, thinking about tonight, how things had gone better than expected, the future possibilities that could be about to open up. She can sense she's not alone on the street but makes nothing of it. Doesn't look over her shoulder, doesn't respond but simply carries on walking, absorbed in her dreams.

He needs to intervene before anything irreversible occurs. One thing's for sure – physically, he's no match for this man. At this precise time, the man trailing her has done nothing wrong – this isn't Minority Report. (Not that either of these two will have seen the film yet.) If he's going to stop him, it has to be now.

Ollie pushes back his hood to show them his face. 'Hey there! Can either of you help me?' he calls out, his voice wavering more than he would have wished. Both heads snap round in response. He's got their attention at least. To make up for the weakness of his words, he takes a couple of steps towards the man. With Leatherjacket distracted, this would be a good time for her to size up the situation and make a run for it. But, of course, she does no such thing.

'I'm a bit lost,' Ollie says, projecting his voice. 'I was just, you know, wondering if either of you could, um, possibly direct me to the nearest tube station? I suppose *any* tube station will do.' Babbling is doing little to disguise his nerves. 'I assume they'll have one of those big maps at the entrance, so, you know, I'll be able to work out where I need to go next. It's great how they have those different colours for the different lines.' Where the hell is he going with this?

Leatherjacket looks to his right, then his left and then over Ollie's head before taking a couple of steps towards him. He stops, legs splayed as he assesses the situation. Under a heavy brow, his eyes are hidden in shadow. He clears his throat as if about to say something but doesn't.

'They're pretty iconic, those tube maps,' Ollie says, swallowing down the defeat in his voice. 'Did you know that that particular schematic representation was invented by a man called Harry Beck and, um, at the time it was totally ground-breaking. London Transport first introduced it way back in 1933, which was what – fifty-two years ago?'

'You've made a mistake, sonny.' The man rearranges his formidable shoulders. 'Early 1933, would make it fifty-six years ago. If it was later in the year, it would be fifty-five.'

Ollie pretends to count on his fingers. 'You're absolutely right. I stand corrected,' he says. 'I've never been very good with numbers.'

A bystander until now, she speaks up at last. 'Southwark station is just round the corner. I'm heading that way so I can point you in the right direction if you like.'

Hearing her familiar voice almost chokes him. He manages to say, 'That would be, um, really great thanks.' He scoots past the man to stand in between the two of them; a feeble barrier but a barrier all the same. 'I lost track of time,' Ollie says, 'and it's now way past my curfew hour. My parents will be worried sick. Overprotective doesn't even come close. In fact, they've probably already been onto the police. My dad will be scouring the streets right now.'

He hears the sound of an approaching car engine – deep and throaty. A diesel. Leatherjacket shields his eyes as the headlights of a taxi swing into the end of the street. 'My dad's actually a cabbie, so that could be him.' Ollie waves both hands overhead in a not-waving-but-drowning style as if flagging down the driver.

When he turns around, Leatherjacket is striding away.

The cab comes to a stop some thirty or so metres from them, its engine idling as it disgorges a couple of passengers. Unsteady on their feet, two men are searching their pockets for the fare.

When she smiles across at him, Ollie is overwhelmed. It's

a struggle to speak, to say what he needs to. 'That man – the one who was here just now…' He nods in the direction Leatherjacket headed off in. 'He was following you. I don't wish to alarm you, but his intentions weren't exactly honourable.'

'You couldn't possibly know that.' She narrows her eyes and then shakes her head. 'He probably just happened to be heading in the same direction.'

'Listen to me!' Ollie swallows down his rising emotions. He needs to sound calmer. 'Take my word for it – he was thinking of attacking you.' She remains unconvinced. 'Flagging down a cab would be a hell of a lot safer,' he says. 'In fact, why don't you hop into this one right now?'

'Hold on a second. You're what, fourteen – fifteen tops? And you're wondering around late at night alone and lost, and you're giving *me* safety advice.' She scoffs. 'Besides, I'm not made of money.'

She comes closer, the taxi's headlights illuminating her face. He can see just how young and beautiful she is. Despite her dark hair, she's so very like Vega. 'I'm what they euphemistically call a *struggling actress*,' she tells him, putting air quotes around the last two words. 'I can't afford to go catching cabs home after every performance. I was supposed to get a lift back tonight, would have done if I hadn't got waylaid by an over-eager young fan.'

'I know.' He clears his throat. 'Or at least I can imagine how that sort of thing might happen.' He can't leave it there; her there. 'I strongly suggest that, after what nearly happened here tonight, you think about prioritising your personal safety.'

She stares at him open-mouthed and then bursts out

laughing. 'I don't wish to be rude but you're a funny little chap.' She wrinkles her nose like she always did. 'And oddly familiar. Are you an actor because I feel sure I know you from somewhere?'

He's too choked up to answer.

'Seeing's you're the one who's lost and out in the big city all alone way past his bedtime – why don't you take that cab?'

'Oh, that was all utter nonsense – something I made up to get that man off your back. I'm not lost. In fact, I know exactly where I am.' The two drunks have now managed to stump up the fare between them and the cab is about to pull away.

'Is that right?' She regards him with her head on one side. 'So, d'you want to share this taxi ride with me?'

'No thanks.' This is no time for self-indulgence. 'I actually live in that house just there.' He points to the next but one. 'I couldn't sleep and just happened to see you and him out of my window.' Ollie takes his house key out of his pocket as proof. 'He could still be lurking about.'

She pulls a face. 'Seriously? I mean–'

'I'm deadly serious. Please believe me. I haven't got any money with me otherwise I'd give you the damned cab fare myself. You were in grave danger just then – who knows what might have happened if I hadn't popped up and put him off.' He stares right into those so-familiar eyes. 'Trust me, please.'

She glances over her shoulder. 'Okay, now you've really freaked me out.' She shivers then holds up her hand. 'I get the message.' She delves into her shoulder bag, then opens her purse. 'I'll take this cab as long as it's not going to cost more than a fiver.'

'It won't.' The cabbie has just put his light on. Ollie beckons him towards them and, tyres crunching, the driver responds.

When it pulls up alongside them, she leans in to ask, 'How much to Shepherd's Bush – the top end of the Goldhawk Road?' She waves a paper note in his face.

'Seeing's how I'm nearly at the end of my shift...' The cabbie wipes a hand over his mouth. 'I reckon that ought to do it.'

She turns to Ollie. 'Well goodnight then my young, would-be knight in shining armour.'

He slams the door shut on her like this has been some casual encounter. 'Stay safe.' Choked up, he watches the taxi make a tricky U-turn. Ollie gives her one last wave, which she may or may not have seen, as the cab heads off, carrying her out of his life all over again.

Rooted to the spot, he can't get his head around what just happened. He wants to laugh out loud and cry at the same time. Watching her disappear into the night would be unbearable if it wasn't tempered by relief that he'd rescued her from impending harm. Motionless, though far from unmoved, he stands alone in the dark, the cold air seeping into his body along with a sadness that would overwhelm him if he let it.

Chapter Fifteen

Ollie finds her where he knew she would be a few streets away in the Prince of Wales pub. Almost unrecognisable as his sister, she's just downed her second whisky – paid for by a man with floppy hair and an oversized denim jacket pulled up at the sleeves.

'I don't believe it,' Vega says breaking away from the group she appears to already be part of, 'What the hell are you doing here?'

It's hot and crowded in the pub; and noisy as hell with everyone struggling to be heard above the piped eighties music. Sensing trouble best avoided, Vega's drinking companions have now stepped away, closing the gap she'd just occupied. 'My mind is just... you know, blown,' she says, her hands miming an explosion.

Ollie scoffs. 'And so, naturally, you felt the occasion called for a spot of underage drinking.' *And batting your eyelids at some random older man so he'll buy you the alcohol.*

'It wasn't like that. Patrick was only being kind. He noticed I was really shaken up. You wouldn't understand.'

'No, I get it – of course I do. It's only natural to want to make the most of the evening and, you know, break a few more rules while you're about it.'

'For fuck's sake drop the sarcasm. I was literally shaking all over – in aftershock.' *I mean to meet and actually speak to our dead mother. It doesn't get much weirder, right?*

Smudged mascara is making her look hollow-eyed. She says, 'I was dead nervous at first, but we actually had, you know, a proper conversation about acting and stuff.' Unsteady on her feet, she keeps waving her hands to illustrate. 'I know you just talked to her too. It's weird to think she's here in this same city, right now. Don't you find that's, like, totally *extra*. Yet, you know, at the same time it feels so natural, so right. Like it was meant to be all along.'

She doesn't wait for his response – doesn't stop to consider what he might be feeling having been dragged into this. She says, 'I can't believe I was talking to her, that she was right there – as close as you are now.'

A nearby group are joining in with the chorus of "Tainted Love". It's too much. Talk about overload… And now a few people are checking him out, noticing he looks underage – more so than this ludicrously made-up version of his younger sister.

While Soft Cell are selling it to the crowd, he says, 'Yeah well, thanks to you, my brain's now equally deep fried.' His voice might be raised, but he needs to keep his emotions under control. 'Come on,' he says. 'Let's get out of here.'

'Hold on a second.' She pulls back. 'What's the rush? I really like this era. Look at them all singing and laughing – totally in the moment.'

He knows what she means but this is hardly the time for a philosophical debate on the alienating effects of 21st century technology. 'We're going.' He grabs her elbow to steer her away. *Neither of us belongs in this place or time and you know it.*

'Lighten up, Oll.' She shrugs him off. 'You're such a fun-sponge.'

'Yeah well that must be why whatever you call me bounces right off again.'

The two of them are a discordant note – people have moved further away, the collective shunning couldn't be clearer, even to Vega. Which may be why she acquiesces and allows him to lead her outside and around the corner to a quiet spot where no one will witness what's about to happen.

He had expected some contrition on her part, but of course she goes for the full counterattack. Now they're alone a toxic word-salad pours from her lips. Emboldened by alcohol, she refuses to accept her actions could have put their mum in danger. 'So, this bloke hadn't actually attacked her or anything when you showed up?'

'No, he hadn't, not when I got there, but he was following her with what I knew was *intent*. He was weighing up *when*, not *if*.'

'Yeah, but thinking's not the same's doing, is it?' Slurring her words now, she presses a finger to his breastbone. 'We all have fantasies. And some people's are, like, really gross. But he might not have done what he was thinking about doing. 'S'like in that old movie… Can't remember the name of it now.'

'Let's not get into that whole pre-cog debate.' He lays a hand over his heart. 'I *know* for sure he was about to attack her, okay?'

'Oliver Brookes – the inheritor of the all-seeing eye.'

Given the unreasonable mood she's in, further discussion is pointless. 'Sod this.' After checking the street is empty, he grabs her arm to ensure they make the leap together.

On the upstairs landing, he steadies her before she falls, though she soon pushes him away. 'Whoa. You might have fucking warned me before you did that.' And then, 'Anyway, you can't stop me. I can go straight back there whenever I want to. You're not the boss of me.'

'And I'll just come and get you again if you try it. Plus, you seem to have forgotten tonight's a school night.'

'Tonight's a school night,' she singsongs back at him. Eyeball to eyeball, she blinks first. 'Yeah well, I was actually about to leave anyway before you showed up. But only because I'm knackered.'

Muttering something about paracetamol, she stomps off towards the bathroom and slams the door – her signature move these days. He hears the bolt shoot across. His sister is safely back home and that will have to do for now.

Chapter Sixteen

Tom

He's in Baynton's bedroom as planned. Though the room is unlit, with the curtains drawn back the lights of the city are bright enough to be certain he's on the right side of the bed and in the precise spot he'd been aiming for. He raises a clenched fist. Yes! The movement causes a red light on a security monitor to wink back at him. A bad move. As far as he can tell, no alarm's been triggered – unless of course it's the silent type. Under his breath he curses his own stupidity. Time to cut his losses, grab what he's come for and go.

Except, one glance at the bedside table tells him the book is no longer where it was. Damn it – he's too late; in the intervening time David's personal effects must have been cleared.

Tom's stomach is beginning to churn, his mouth watering the way it does before he throws up. With an effort he swallows it down. Like one of those spot-the-difference puzzles, he registers the various discrepancies in the room since his earlier visit. The covers and the cushions on the bed are in disarray suggesting someone's been lying on it. A white shirt is draped over the back of a chair which also wasn't in the room before. His head feels light and yet, recovering his other senses, he's aware of music playing – something instrumental though not classical. Guitars and drum. If it's coming from an adjacent flat, the building's soundproofing must be crap. And the place has a different smell; instead of air-freshener and cleaning products, there's a warmer, earthier aroma which, after a couple more sniffs, he narrows down to cumin, possibly harissa. Someone is, or recently has been, cooking or eating North African or Middle Eastern food.

He must be in the wrong flat. Before he can take stock of this new situation, the music swells as a door opens, those duelling guitars follow the trajectory of someone who's whistling along and is undeniably heading his way.

Shit a brick! He only has time to dive behind the doubtful cover of the sheer curtains before all the overhead lights are triggered. A rabbit caught in headlights, he dare not move. When the person stops whistling, he holds his breath.

He can sense they sense something is different about the room – that a new element has been introduced. Instead of striding over and throwing back the bunched-up curtain to expose him, they begin to hum along to what he now recognises is Polyphia's *Playing God*. Through the gauzy material he can see the person is tall and broad shouldered. The deep notes they're now whistling suggests it's most likely a man. Whoever this person is, he turns on his heels and heads off into the walkin closet – assuming the layout doesn't vary much between apartments. During the mellow finale to the track, he hears a sound which suggests empty hangers knocking together. Tom fights the urge to scratch the annoying itch from the curtain resting against his nose. More irritating, the bloke in the closet is tone deaf and in the process of murdering a decent track.

Under brighter lights he recognises the throw on the bed is in the same blue tartan, the cushions an identical tweed combo. This must be Baynton's apartment – at least he'd got that bit right.

Intrigued, he maintains his sentry-stiff pose while trying to piece together a scenario that incorporates another man gaining entry to Baynton's empty flat and discarding his shirt before or after lying down on the bed. The same man then orders and eats a spicy meal while filling the apartment with his own niche music played at an indiscreet volume while he packs up the missing tenant's stuff. Unlikely doesn't come close.

The music morphs into another Polyphia number. He recognises *Ego Death*. The intro's eerie tones gather pace and intensity, those three guitarists vying for supremacy like the soundtrack to a movie that's about to end in a shoot-out.

Again, he swallows down what is threatening to come up. High time he got out of here. Though Tom is loath to accept failure, he has no wish to confront whoever this is. When he shuts his eyes to summon up the necessary concentration, the music auto-mutes because the man is now talking. Either he's in the habit of soliloquising or he's on a call. Who's he talking to? What's he saying? He must be moving around because some words are clear and others incomprehensible. His "Excuse me?" just then was definitely not an apology but a demand for clarification.

Emerging from the closet, the man comes to a halt less than four metres from him while he buttons-up a blue shirt. 'We agreed...' Whatever the reply, he butts in with, 'Wait. Now hold on just a second. I seem to remember you were entirely happy with the terms we agreed. Now you seem to be singing from a whole other playlist.'

He looks up at the ceiling and shakes his head, his face momentarily spot-lit. Even through several layers of material there can be no doubting the man's identity – living and breathing, it's David Baynton.

Tom starts when Baynton yells, 'No! There's no fucking way that will happen.' Clutching his forehead like he's experiencing a migraine, he walks over to the floor-to-ceiling windows. Absorbed in his argument, he stares out on the restless capital. 'This has got to be a joke.' Baynton certainly isn't laughing.

From this new angle, if he were to glance to his right, he couldn't miss seeing Tom. Luckily, he turns left, spinning on his heels in what is nearly a dancefloor move. 'Wait, now just hold on a minute. Are you trying to threaten me?' He thumps the wall with his fist. (He must have really felt that.) 'Yeah well, that's what it sounded like.' Giving no time for a reply, 'I thought we'd agreed.'

There's a swagger to Baynton's walk as he heads towards the bathroom. 'Yeah, well I'm not in the habit of renegotiating.' Another about-turn and now he seems to be peering straight at Tom. 'Good. Then we understand one another. I'll be in touch,' signals he's done talking. No pleasantries or goodbye.

The guitars resume their tense contest. Rubbing at his chin, Baynton's attention seems to have shifted to the person-shaped anomaly he's detected behind his drapes. Shit! Tom could step out with his hands raised, though providing any plausible explanation for his presence in the man's apartment would be a challenge. Time to go. He's trying to will himself out of there when Baynton changes direction and strides off into his closet. Tom's breathing through his relief, when he comes striding back towards him, this time carrying something which looks suspiciously like a baseball bat. Caught like a rat in a sack, he's rooted to the spot.

There's a loud and insistent buzz. Baynton's head snaps towards the sound. The buzzer goes again – longer and more demanding this time. Weapon still in hand, his would-be assailant strides out into the hallway to investigate.

Tom can't believe this stroke of luck. He tries to muster the focus he needs to escape. When that fails, he dives under the bed, pulling the covers down to the floor so that he's hidden from view from the front angle if not the back.

'Good evening, Mr Baynton. I apologise for disturbing you.' The amplified voice belongs to the older concierge. (Why is the man still on duty at this hour?) 'A package has just been dropped off for you.'

'Okay, thanks. I'll pick it up tomorrow.'

'The courier insisted it was extremely urgent. He assured me you'd be highly relieved to have whatever it is back in your possession. In fact, he wouldn't leave until I promised to inform you immediately.'

'Could you bring it up?'

'I can't leave the desk unmanned, sir.'

'I see. Okay, then I'll come down and collect it right away.'

He watches the man's polished shoes re-enter the bedroom, hears the swish of the hooks dragged along the curtain pole followed by a brief snort. Is Baynton amused by his own baseless paranoia, or gleeful at the prospect of a cat and mouse chase? Either way, before he decides to check beneath the bed, Tom shuts his eyes and concentrates hard on getting the hell out of there.

Chapter Seventeen

Ollie

His head is oddly light, his brain half-scrambled. There's been no time to reflect on what's happened. Thinking on, or possibly *with* his feet, Ollie heads off to Dad's study where, sitting right there on his desk in front of him, he sees the flash drive – an insignificant tiny timebomb.

Inspired, Ollie snatches it up. Should he add some bulk, or ballast to give it more weight – the physical presence it deserves. He runs downstairs to rummage in the re-cycle bin where he discovers a discarded small box that smells okay. It'll do the job. Some parcel tape to seal it and, hey presto.

His hood pulled up, his face averted, Ollie lingers at what he hopes is a safe distance from which to observe the concierge's desk through the glass wall. Like a tableau, the atrium is lit up against the wintery gloom of the city. He's reminded of those Hopper paintings where solitary people sit in picture windows being observed from the darkness outside. The concierge could be a lone figure on a stage where some action is about to occur or might already have happened.

Dressed in his thin hoodie and jeans, Ollie stands out from the passing pedestrians hunched inside heavy coats and wraparound scarves. In the space of a few warmer months, he's forgotten how the cold night air can seep through your clothing and chill you to the core. He's shivering so hard he has to set his jaw to stop his teeth knocking together.

The cold is a welcome distraction since he has no spare bandwidth to process everything that's just happened. As usual, Vega had gone off like some unguided missile, forcing him to masquerade as a stranger in order to talk to his own mother. Seeing her again only a matter of minutes ago, looking just the same as she did when she was his mummy... And so young, with the rest of her life ahead of her and no memory of the bereaved family she'd left behind.

Movement breaks his train of thought. A large black SUV – commonly known as a Wank-Panzer – glides past him, splashing through the puddle he's glad he's standing well back from. Operatic music is leaking from inside it. The SUV slows and then comes to a stop opposite the apartment building. It's impossible to see the occupants through the blacked-out windows.

At the same time, and after a side glance, he notices the elevator doors have opened. A youngish man steps out. He recognises Baynton from the photographs on his father's screen. He's dressed smartly, fashionably even, as if he's planning to head out to some upmarket club rather than go to bed. He strides across the space with his arms loose at his side, a walk that exudes an enviable air of confidence, a ready-for-anything kind of vibe.

Baynton heads straight to the desk where, after a brief exchange with the concierge, the package is handed over. Having received it, he takes a moment to weigh the box in his hand, no doubt wondering if it might be empty given how light it is. Some instinct makes his head flick around to check that this isn't an elaborate decoy, a ploy to draw him into the open. Can he sense he's being watched? Ollie shrinks back into the shadow of the shuttered shopfront, checks his phone like he's hanging around to meet someone.

The Wank-Panzer – an obscure Chinese import – moves off. Left standing out in the cold night air Ollie's relief turns to anger. He's furious with Vega for her recklessness and his dad for his sheer ineptitude at screwing up his entry time and arriving a month before Baynton will go missing. Dad wouldn't have been in this position in the first place if he hadn't been too stubborn to accept that decoding the stuff on that bloody memory stick was beyond him. Perhaps this will teach him not to go blundering into things he only half understands.

Ollie leaves it a bit longer before he checks the atrium again. His suspicion clearly aroused, Baynton is holding the package Ollie's just delivered away from his body like some UXB he'll hand straight back to the concierge. An unexpected delivery at this hour would make anyone wary. Baynton turns it over no doubt looking for a tell-tale label or some sign of its contents. When that fails, he sniffs it. Despite its clumsy wrapping, it must have passed the test, or his curiosity wins out, because he tucks the box under one arm. Instead of opening it there and then, Baynton gives the concierge a friendly wave and heads back to the lift. Once the doors have closed on him, Ollie relaxes, glad that the damned thing is out of the way and back in the hands of its rightful owner.

Mission completed, he retraces his route around the corner and along the street to the same deep doorway he'd arrived in only a matter of minutes ago. No one else is sheltering inside. He surveys the murky streets unable to detect anything except the weather that's ostensibly different. Nothing stands out. Again, Ollie checks for possible onlookers and, satisfied, he disappears.

Chapter Eighteen

Ollie is relieved to be back in the comforting familiarity of his bedroom. Though he's normally unaffected by time-leaps, tonight's quick turnarounds have left him disorientated and exhausted.

The room's residual warmth begins to thaw the chill in his body. There's a stale, unpleasant smell to his clothes – the residual stench from that smoky pub.

He should be delighted that his intervention gave Dad the opportunity to escape. And, in the process, there's the added bonus that he's closed the loop with that flash drive. Why then does a sour note remain – a lingering sense of some misstep he hasn't yet identified?

Steady snoring is coming from his father's room. Although he hasn't been back long, Dad's already out for the count. After tonight's close-shave, and with nothing else to go on, unless he's an irredeemable moron, Dad will give up on the Baynton investigation and go back to locating people's stray pooches. (Dogs don't wield baseball bats for starters.)

Without needing to check, he knows Vega hasn't gone back to that pub like she'd threatened to. Instead, she's fast asleep in her room.

Ollie would feel better if his head would stop lurching like he's just stepped off one of those roundabouts in the park. Not a bad night's work to have thwarted their mother's would-be attacker *and* prevented his father from getting a beating.

He rubs a hand over his eyes and waits for the room to settle into its usual solid state. Both his interventions were pretty ingenious. Can things be *pretty* ingenious – he doubts such an accolade can be modified. As for Baynton, he's now, or rather *was* a few months back, in possession of the flash drive Dad found after snooping around his empty apartment. Baynton will, sooner or later, have stashed it away in his underfloor "wine cellar" where, it will, or was, found by Dad who takes it home and fails to decode it before it inexplicably disappears from his desk.

Circle closed. End of.

Ollie's sense of victory is short lived since it's immediately and catastrophically superseded by doubt, followed by a sinking pit of dismay at his own fucking idiocy. By giving that flash drive back to Baynton, did he open up a paradoxical can of worms?

What if he was the means by which Baynton received a duplicate of his own memory stick? Superposition theory might allow the two objects to exist at the same time, but if the information on the original was only known to Baynton, as soon as he viewed the content of the second one, he might have concluded that someone else knew the secret information it contained. Fucking hell – what if he's caused a serious temporal displacement?

If that isn't bad enough, there's an alternative, equally

worrying scenario. What if the memory stick originally belonged to someone else – some Mr Big Vicious Bastard. And what if, in the time between receiving it via him and his unexplained disappearance, Baynton had managed to decode the information on it? Could that new knowledge have made him act in a way that put him in danger? Have his own actions tonight played a crucial role in the events that led to Baynton's disappearance? Or even his death?

Angered by his own lack of forethought, Ollie turns his indignation on the person who provoked him to go there in the first place. If he's the one who's just screwed up big time, it's down to Dad's impetuousness.

Fury grips him with an intensity that spreads through his veins, tempting him to go and shake Dad awake and have it out with him. Maybe he should have let him take that beating after all.

The logical part of Ollie's brain knows the anger he's experiencing is due to an excess of stress hormones, a crude biological knee-jerk he needs to rise above. To stave off the emotions threatening to overcome him, he takes a series of deep breaths. After a dozen or so, he begins to calm down. Okay, he might be guilty of acting injudiciously, but it's possible the outcome won't have been as bad as he first feared. Perhaps it'll all work out in the end – come out in the wash, as Gran would put it.

Overtaken by mental and physical exhaustion, Ollie ventures a few steps towards the bed. Though he's less dizzy now, his thoughts refuse to form an orderly queue. Maybe everything will make better sense in the morning.

He undresses and lies down to wait for the sleep he needs.

In a few hours, he'll have to get up and get ready for school. After adjusting the covers, he tries to settle himself, but as soon as he closes his eyes, the what ifs come at him out of the darkness thick and fast. To escape them, he tries to envisage something more pleasant. Whatever Vega says, tonight he averted one disaster, even if he might have ballsed-up his other intervention. He acted in order to keep his family safe, and he's achieved that. He wasn't the one who went rogue. It shouldn't be down to him to sort out their screw-ups.

Could it be time to bring in the big bazooka in the shape of his grandad? His dad and sister have demonstrated they can't be trusted to act responsibly, so dobbing them in would be justified. It was their ill-considered behaviour that forced his hand tonight.

Would telling Grandad make him a snitch? At school, dobbing someone in is the ultimate transgression. Well, not as bad as stuff like bigoted or personal abuse. Or grabbing someone's genitalia without their consent. Though not so far below in the hierarchy of potential sins.

Ollie yawns and turns over. Trying to think of something more positive, his mind strays to Cerys and the perfect teeth she reveals whenever she smiles. The way she runs a finger along her bottom lip when she's trying to figure something out…

As he relaxes, he loses control and Cerys's features grow distorted, transforming her into a gnarled version of Grandad. A gruesome image that jolts him awake.

Is his subconscious telling him he should talk things through with the old man? But what if Grandad snitches

115

and tells "The Organisation"? The last thing anyone wants, or needs, is a visit from Ford or one of his equally terrifying cronies.

Does Grandad's loyalty to the Guardians outweigh his loyalty to his family?

Good question. On balance, Ollie's not sure he wants to know the answer.

Chapter Nineteen

Vega

Friday morning and they've all overslept. Vega's head feels heavy and yet as fragile as an egg that could crack any minute. She swerves to avoid colliding with Dad on the landing and, of course, Ollie is hogging the bathroom again. She bangs on the door to get him to hurry while she waits cross-legged. When he emerges, they exchange bleary-eyed grunts like passing gorillas. By unvoiced agreement, everyone's energy is reserved for the herculean task of getting their shit together.

Downstairs in the kitchen, pale faces averted, the three of them look like they'd been out partying all night. Unless Dad gives them a lift to school, they'll be late. Fortunately, he can't refuse since he has to drive more or less past it to get to his appointment with the dodgy accountant he pays to finesse (or falsify) his tax returns.

She downs a glass of water. With no time for breakfast, Ollie grabs a banana to eat in the car while she snatches something in a big red and yellow packet.

Vega sits alone in the back, their schoolbags piled on the

seat next to her. Turns out the red and yellow packet contains a load of worm-like, luminous-orange nurdles about as tasty as packing material. Hard to believe Dad would have purchased something at once so unhealthy and so bland. Whatever – she munches them by the handful hoping the calorie hit will kick in along with the additives' hyper.

Ollie is texting Cerys to apologise for standing her up. (Not a date, more of an opportunity for the girl to pick his brains.) When he's done, he sighs to gain their attention. 'We need to talk.' He leans towards her, his breath smelling of masticated banana. 'As a family,' he adds. 'Around the table in a civilised fashion.' The civilised fashion bit is something Dad's fond of saying and so a tactic to get him onboard.

'Well, I for one am done talking,' she tells him. And then silently, *you'd better not be planning to snitch on me.* She opens the window to let in fresher air. (Also, in case she throws up.)

In the rearview mirror Dad is frowning. 'What's all this about, Ollie?' He wears the puzzled expression of a man who has so far failed to join the dots.

When he slams on the brakes, Vega's thrown forward, the seatbelt digging into her chest. Dad swears at the scruffy, grey dog trotting across the road with a nothing-to-see-here expression on its face. Several metres behind and like some useless urban angler, a flustered middle-aged woman is failing to reel the animal in.

Dog and owner have reached the opposite pavement when Dad lowers the window. The woman pre-empts things with a mea culpa, it's-a-fair-cop hand gesture. 'Awfully sorry,' she squawks above the rush-hour din, 'I'm afraid Archie can be a trifle impetuous at times.'

'Dogs are by nature impetuous, madam,' Dad shouts back in his snottiest voice. Behind them someone leans on a horn which elicits a two-fingered response from him. Pulling away, he shouts at the woman, 'You need to keep that dog on a shorter lead.'

Ollie says, 'Which brings us to the subject of last night.' Smug faced, he morphs into lecture mode. 'And the fact that the two of you decided to go AWOL.'

'Excuse me.' Vega leans forward. 'Don't you mean the *three* of us? It's not like you were fast asleep in bed the whole night.'

'Don't I wish,' Ollie spits back.

'Hold on a second,' Dad says, distracted. When the light turns green, he's straight off the mark. 'What is it I don't know?' Neither of them answers. 'And what makes you think I was AWOL?' The man is fooling precisely no one.

Ollie's cheeks burn with self-righteous indignation. 'For fuck's sake!'

'Watch your language, young man,' Dad tells him.

'Ha! You can talk,' Ollie snaps back.

Dad indicates left. 'You were the one who said we should discuss whatever this is about in a *civilised* fashion. Civilised hardly includes the use of expletives.'

Vega guffaws. 'What about you back there then, Dad? What was it you called that woman? I seem to remember it began with a B.'

'Only because I was severely provoked. You saw the way that wayward dog of hers nearly caused an accident.'

'Bigger picture,' Ollie says, 'at worst, that would have been a trifling incident; a fender bender.' They've pulled into the sideroad that leads to the school. 'Dad stop!' he shouts.

No response. Instead of dropping them off, Dad drives right up to the gates before braking. 'Vehicles aren't meant to enter the red box,' Ollie reminds him. 'It's there for everyone's safety.'

'Yeah well, it's too late now, I'm in it.' Dad is visibly rattled at the prospect of the post-mortem to come. 'You two can either pile out here – in which case you might just make it to registration in time. Or you can wait for me to turn the car around and then drop you at the end of the road we've just driven down so you can walk all the way back here.' He throws up his hands. 'Your choice.'

She's already out of the car. 'Thanks Dad.' She slams the door and legs it through the gates. With her destination in sight, and her school bag bashing her thigh, she breaks into a full-on run. Doesn't look back to see what her brother's decided to do. There's no need.

The first two periods are a nightmare. She feels better after downing a bottle of Coke Max and half a scrounged fruit and nut bar at breaktime. Fingers crossed her elevated blood sugar and caffeine levels won't nosedive until lunch.

Period three is a doddle because it's history. To chime in with their English Lit syllabus, they're studying Conflicts of the Twentieth Century – a whistle-stop tour of the major screw-ups and deranged ideas that dealt the deathblows to European colonialism.

This morning their personal screens inform them the topic is: The Role of Serbian Nationalism in World War One. Mrs Kingsley has handwritten and doubly-underlined the same heading on the big interactive screen at the front. Below that she's written:

Nationalism

Positives – shared identity, sense of allegiance, promotes pride etc.

Negatives – xenophobia, potentially divisive, can sow the seeds of conflict.

Focus – why and how did the assassination of Archduke Ferdinand "light the powder keg"?

Marking her last assignment, Mrs Kingsley had written in the comments box: "*Try to keep things simple at this stage*, Vega". In person, the teacher had warned her about "*getting ahead of yourself*", as if some annoying duplicate of Vega is always skipping in front to enter the room before she arrives.

Around her everyone is heads down working. Catching Mrs Kingsley's shrewd glance, she nibbles her thumbnail in a pensive manner as if she's marshalling her thoughts re the assignment and not revisiting the life-changing experience of last night.

She fingers the medallion hidden beneath her school shirt. Just a toddler when their mum disappeared, until yesterday the memories Vega had of her were derived from that strange visit and a mix of poor-quality stills and faded vid footage in which she's always smiling. Hard to imagine her mum's true character by piecing together fragments from family stories. Ollie might be angry with her, but he has no right to be. Why should she have to settle for a few vague impressions of the woman who'd given birth to her when she has the ability to discover so much more?

All the same, nothing prepared her for the shock of seeing Elizabeth on stage – a living and breathing incarnation. And the performance she'd given – wow! Vega wasn't the only one held spellbound. The audience clapped wildly at the end, demanding a crazy number of curtain calls. (The actors didn't know there was a Time Out journo in the house about to write a glowing review of the play in which he would single her mother out for high praise.)

Mustering her courage, Vega had been super nervous waiting to ambush her mother on the pavement outside like some drama-loving groupie. 'I just wanted to say that was a great performance,' she told her. 'You're such an amazingly talented actor.'

'Actress,' Elizabeth corrected her, smiling at the strength of the compliment that had taken her by surprise. 'You're very kind.' A stock phrase – a played-down response to an overenthusiastic fan waylaying her when all she wanted was to head off home. They'd discussed the play and her role as the rejected woman. Animated, her mother gave off a palpable energy, charismatic on and off stage. As they chatted, Vega recognised herself in the shape and colour of those eyes and then in her whole face. Aside from her mum's hair being much darker, she could have been looking at her mirror-image all grown-up and independent.

'You're the picture of your mother,' Gran's told her often enough. Until last night, she'd assumed it was an exaggeration – something people say to make you feel better about losing a parent.

Her mum had been within touching distance, and yet,

paradoxically, she'd seemed almost as far away and unreachable as she's always been. Vega recalls her distinctive smell. She'd wanted to lean in to sniff her, but that would have been super weird. It was hard to believe she was chatting to her own flesh and blood, though Elizabeth Travino is not, and can never be again, Beth Brookes. If it wasn't for all the makeup she'd plastered on, the resemblance between them might have been more obvious to her mum. Uncanny, she might have said. With her memory of those missing years erased, at twenty-five, her mother couldn't and wouldn't ever be able to guess she was talking to her own thirteen-year-old daughter. Or to anticipate she was about to meet her interfering fifteen-year-old son.

In the car this morning, Ollie sounded like he was planning on staging an intervention. He's keen for them to talk things through, have everything out in the open like some school counsellor trying to get you to agree on a code of conduct going forward. He hasn't decided whether to snitch on her to Dad. (A terrible idea on so many levels.)

Like the worrywart he is, her brother long ago declared any visits to their mum were strictly off-limits. 'Nothing will be gained from it if you do,' he'd repeated many times over the years. 'Consider the damaging psychological impact of such a meeting,' had been another one of his cautions. She'd thought about it alright, convinced herself she was pre-adjusted to the idea – that it wouldn't faze her as much as her brother had predicted. If you went to a counsellor for advice on how to get your head around meeting up with your long-dead mother, they'd section you in a heartbeat.

Ollie must have known the temptation would be too great in the end. It's too late now because it's happened – it's a fait accompli. He might wish she hadn't gone there and done that, but she did, and she has. Or had. And it's pointless to revisit choices once they've been made.

Thinking back over the conversation she had with her dead mum is sending Vega's brain into spirals. Last night she dared to go there and now there's no going back. It doesn't surprise her one bit that Ollie chose to exaggerate that whole sinister-bloke-following-their-mother story to put her off any inclination she might have to repeat the act.

Maybe that possibility shouldn't be ruled out.

Chapter Twenty

Tom

Rain clouds are gathering as Tom steps outside his accountant's office. 'Bring it on,' he says, looking up. After their summation of his current financial situation, nothing the elements can throw at him can dampen his mood any further. With Ollie about to head off to university, or some other form of training, his accountant had more than hinted that he needs to get his act together.

A day that started badly appears to be set on a downhill course. He woke up heavy-headed. After dressing in a hurry, he only had time to gulp down an instant coffee before they were all out the door. On their way to the school the atmosphere in the car was odd – strained even. Preoccupied with the task of driving, he paid only half a mind to what Ollie was saying. He should have listened. Whatever's going on with the kids could be serious. Once they're back from school he means to get to the bottom of it. Meanwhile, he heads home in desperate need of proper coffee and something to eat.

Nibbling at a piece of toast, through the window he sees the storm appears to have passed on by. Above the din of grinding beans, he hears the outside buzzer. An amplified voice says, 'Hello?'

What now? Tom turns off the coffee machine – which tends to play up when interrupted mid-sequence – and checks the intercom screen. His visitor appears to be a woman. Though she has her back to the lens, she has the mid-brown hair and slim figure of Sarah Baynton.

Shit. What's he going to say to her? He'd assumed finding out what happened to her son would simply involve a hop back to the night he disappeared and then tailing the man at a safe distance. His accidental encounter with Baynton last night confirmed it was a whole other ballgame – one he'd be a fool to take any part in. The way he'd wielded that baseball bat suggested something beyond self-defence. Baynton may have been living a double life before he disappeared. All the evidence suggests the man had been swimming in some murky waters up to his neck in the sort of poisonous blue algae they warn dog owners about.

It still niggles him that he hasn't been able to decode the information on the memory stick Baynton had taken pains to hide. All the same, he's determined to turn down the assignment. Knowing what he now knows, only a complete idiot would let themselves get dragged into the same cesspool. In fact, he probably ought to advise Sarah to cut her losses, accept the official verdict on her son's disappearance and move on. Obviously, he won't put it in those exact words.

Tom waits for her to turn around. When she doesn't, he

prompts her with, 'Hello?' Is she checking to see if anyone's watching? When she spins round to face the cam, he's surprised to find it isn't Sarah Baynton but a complete stranger – possibly someone with the wrong address.

Before he can suggest this, she says, 'Hello' again, leaning into the lens in a way that distorts her face like a fairground mirror. 'Have I got the right address? Are you Mr Brookes?' The edges of her deep brown eyes wrinkle with a set-hard smile. When she pulls back a little he can see she's attractive and smartly dressed. She could be selling something expensive he won't be buying.

Resisting the urge to lie, he says, 'I'm Mr Baynton – sorry, slip of the tongue there. I meant to say Brookes. I'm Mr Brookes.'

Her pink-lipstick grin drops. 'You don't sound too sure?'

'You rang my buzzer. Which means *I* don't have to prove my I.D. This isn't an especially good time so maybe you can tell me what it is you want.'

'I was, um, wondering if I might have a quick word, if you're not too busy, that is.'

'About what exactly?'

'Forgive me, I should have introduced myself. I'm Gwen Roberts – Cerys's mother? I understand your son Oliver's been helping my daughter with her maths homework.'

'Oh. Right. Yes. Sorry for being rather abrupt just then.' He tries levity. 'Ollie's not been charging her for his tutoring services, has he?'

'Not as far as I'm aware.' She's frowning. 'If you can possibly spare a moment, Mr Brookes.' In a not-too-much-to-ask tone, she adds, 'If we might have a quick chat – preferably face to face.'

She's a parent at his kids' school so he ought to hear her out. 'Give me a second and I'll be right with you.'

In the flesh Gwen is undeniably easy on the eye. 'Come in,' he says, aware that the kitchen is a mess, and he must look like an unmade bed while she's all poise and confidence. She walks past their discarded shoes, doesn't take her own off though those heels look like they might leave rings behind.

He considers showing her into the living room but that seems too formal at this hour. So, the kitchen it is. 'We left in a bit of a rush this morning.' After scratching his head, Tom catches a glimpse of himself in the microwave and tries to rake his hair into better order. 'I haven't had a chance to clear up yet.'

The woman's eyes dart to all the wrong places. Her straight face delivers a damning verdict on his housekeeping. 'I was just making some coffee before I got started on this lot,' he says. 'Can I offer you a mug? Although actually, it better be a cup since all the mugs appear to be dirty. I usually turn the dishwasher on before we leave in the morning…'

'Smells good. I'd love a cup; that's if it's not too much trouble.'

'Not at all.' The table is a disaster zone. He moves a pile of Vega's crap off one of the stools at the breakfast bar, dusting off stray crumbs with his hand. 'Please – take a seat.'

She checks the surface before she perches. Understandable given her business suit is pale blue and looks expensively tailored.

For once the coffee machine forgives the interruption. Its din relieves them of the need to speak for a minute or so. During the hiatus, Tom clears a space on the work surface then wipes it down with a dishcloth. (Although that too could do with a good wash.)

Once the noise has subsided, she says, 'I'm sorry – I would have phoned first, but I don't have your number. Someone mentioned you lived down here, opposite the park entrance. Anyway, I happened to be passing and I thought I might as well strike while the iron is hot, so to speak.'

'Sounds like I'm in for a roasting.'

'That was just a metaphor…'

He chuckles to put her out of her discomfort. 'It's fine. Only joking.' His attempt to bat the air in a dismissive manner narrowly misses her face and she flinches. 'So sorry,' he says, 'I wasn't trying to… My coordination's a bit ropey this morning.'

'Heavy night last night?' She has the grace to blush after that question. 'Sorry, that is, was, none of my business. Please forget I said that.'

'It's okay. It's a fair assumption.' He shakes his head. 'But no. I was stone cold sober. It was an eventful night. Disturbing on many levels. I didn't get a lot of sleep in the end.' Way too much detail. 'Anyway…' Tom opens the fridge. 'Milk? Sugar?' One sniff confirms the milk's on the turn.

'Black, no sugar, thanks.'

He fills the last unchipped cup, finds a mismatched saucer, and puts it down in front of her. 'We did have some chocolate biscuits, but I think the kids must have finished them off.'

She pats her stomach. 'I would have refused in any case.'

'You're slim enough to handle a few extra calories.' It's his turn to blush. 'Did I actually say that out loud just then? Creepy or what?'

She snorts. 'It was rather a *bum* note.' Her dark eyes are alive with amusement.

Tom fills the last cup standing – with its hairline fracture he ought to have thrown it out before now. An accident waiting to happen, he hopes it'll hold itself together this one last time. He gulps a greedy swig of coffee. The second slug hits the spot – so much so he can't stifle a groan of satisfaction that sounds positively orgasmic. 'I really, and I do mean *really*, needed that.'

'Then judging by the sound of it, I'm glad I'm having what you're having.' She holds up her cup in salute. Manicured nails, barely-there pink varnish. After a sip, she gives her verdict, 'Not bad.'

'Damned by faint praise as usual.'

'I have high standards when it comes to coffee,' she says. 'I once tried kopi luwak, I'll have you know.'

He whistles. 'Wow – the most expensive coffee in the world. Made from beans shat from the arses of captive civets, I believe?'

'Yep, the very same.'

'And…'

She shrugs. 'It wasn't bad.' For a moment they grin at each other, then her face falls into seriousness. 'Joking aside, I called round because I'm worried about Cerys.'

'Oh?'

'When your son didn't meet her in the library this morning,

she called me in a complete panic asking if she could take the day off school because she hadn't finished her maths assignment. I don't know what arrangement the two of them have made, but I told her straight she'd have to hand in her work, sink or swim on her own merits. Your boy really shouldn't be doing her homework for her.'

'Hold on a minute.' Tom raises a hand in protest. 'I haven't spoken to Ollie about this *yet*, but I do know one thing for certain – he would never complete another student's assignment. Obviously, you don't know my son, but let me assure you that cheating like that is simply not in his DNA.'

She looks sceptical. 'I'm sure we've all been tempted to bend the rules on occasions. Especially if it means getting into the good books of someone we happen to find attractive.'

'Uh-uh. No way. I'm not suggesting Ollie isn't smitten by your daughter, I'm just telling you the boy is an absolute stickler for doing what's right. I'm not sure where he gets that from…'

'Then why would Cerys be in such a panic when he didn't show up before class?'

A fair question. While he tries to think, she sips her coffee. He says, 'The thing is, Ollie's a bright boy, and I mean super-crazy bright. Again, I'm not sure where he gets that from…' She doesn't react to the bait. 'And he's also highly principled. I'm more than happy to have a word with him about this, but my guess is he's been tutoring her and nothing more sinister than that.'

'There's a fine line between tutoring and taking over. Maybe the two of them have unintentionally strayed across that line.'

Hand to his chest, Tom grins. '*I* may have trespassed across a good many boundaries in my time…' Now he's back to sounding pervy. He clears his throat. 'But Ollie is guided by firmly held principles – the boy never strays from the path of righteousness.'

'Really?' Gwen is giving him a look that might be interpreted as flirtatious. She says, 'I've always thought things would be a lot duller if no one ever deviated from the straight and narrow.'

'My son is the first to pull me up on my own misdemeanours. In fact, sometimes he acts like he's the parent around here and I'm the rebellious offspring.'

'Tell me about it. Cerys is certainly not averse to correcting me if she thinks I've said or done anything the least bit out of order.'

'So, Gwen – can I call you that?'

'Of course.'

'And I'm Tom, by the way.'

She nods in acknowledgement, her shoulders relaxing. That shared-secret smile makes a reappearance.

'I think we're both singing from the same lyrics sheet on this one,' he says. 'Naturally, I'll speak to Ollie, but I very much doubt he's doing anything other than explaining a few mathematical principles to your daughter.' He chuckles. 'You know how that sort of stuff can turn a girl's head…'

Her laugh is loud and possibly just a little bit too much. 'I need to talk this through with Cerys,' she says. 'I don't want my daughter relying on someone else to do her thinking for her.' She stands up. Raising her drained cup, she delivers her verdict, 'Not bad at all.'

She takes a couple of steps toward the door. 'I'd better run.' She doesn't say where to. 'Thanks for the coffee, and for hearing me out.'

'It was a pleasure to meet you, Gwen. Let me know if there's anything more I can do to help.'

She pauses in the doorway. Her perfume has the heady smell of blossom carried on a salt-laced breeze. (Did he really just imagine such a thing?) 'Can I suggest we keep the lines of communication open between us,' she says.

'Delighted to,' he tells her.

Chapter Twenty-One

Ollie

The rhythm of his day is all wrong. Dad drops Vega off while, sticking to his principles, he walks the whole way back to the gates. The school grounds are empty because everyone is inside. Since joining the sixth form he's never been more than a minute or so late to registration.

'Is everything alright, Oliver?' Mrs Fulmer asks as he walks in. He'd have preferred it if she'd told him off, but instead, with a look of sympathetic indulgence, she adds, 'It's not like you to be late.'

'Maybe he's human after all,' Aaron Jenkins quips, setting off echoing laughter at his expense.

'You gonna give him a detention, miss?' Leon Bailey demands from the back.

'I'm sure there are extenuating circumstances,' she says, prompting him with her eyes and then a slight nod to come up with a viable excuse to justify her assumption.

'We overslept,' is his honest answer.

This is greeted by jeers of disbelief from the usual suspects.

'They can only get 4G in their house, miss,' Paul Gregg calls out.

'Ollie still uses one of them wind-up alarm clocks, miss,' Hal Robbins shouts.

Paul G comes back with, 'Yeah but, to be fair, that's only since his cockerel died.' Mrs Fulmer is still struggling to quieten them down when the buzzer for first lesson sounds.

Ollie hates being the butt of their inane jokes. Trooping off with the others to his first lesson, he decides the only way to survive the next few hours is to ignore them and concentrate on the work. Everything else needs to be boxed up and put away inside a part of his brain labelled: DO NOT FUCKING OPEN.

The strategy works until just before first break when a vision of his mother puts in an unexpected appearance. Even after he shuts his eyes, she lingers on beneath his eyelids before dissolving into red-tinged darkness.

Turns out it's a good learning day after all. He'd thought the crippling loss and awful longing he'd experienced as a three-year-old abandoned by his mother had faded away to nothing. How stupid of him not to realise that, like a virus waiting to reinfect you when you're most vulnerable, those feelings had been lying dormant, on the lookout for the right moment to re-emerge and overwhelm him all over again.

Sitting on his own in French, he is no longer a confident linguist in a busy schoolroom, but an infant standing in a country lane enveloped by freezing air laced with the terrifying smell of escaping petrol while he watches in mesmerised disbelief the plume of hot steam rising from their twisted and broken car. Their rusty but trusty old Fiat had reforged itself into a death-trap. Once sprung, it had every intention of hanging on to its victim. In that frozen moment, he and Vega hadn't understood that their attempt to turn back time would only mean a temporary stay of execution. They were tiny children, no match for the forces determined to drag their mummy back to where she belonged – a place that wasn't, and never could be, with them.

Call it her fate, or an anomaly righted, he'd learnt to accept the outcome until last night when she'd emerged from the dark streets transmogrified – no longer a faded memory but a living person with no idea who the hell he was.

In ordinary, normal families, the dead stay dead.

Of all people, Vega should have understood what is likely to happen if you go up against the natural order of things. He'd warned her so many times, was sick of saying, *don't go there.* Parroting Gran with, *out of sight is out of mind.* The collective wisdom of ages distilled into seven words of one sodding syllable. But, no, quelle fucking surprise, Vega ignored him. Last night she was all, *I was only planning to watch her from the audience,* like there was a fat chance she'd stick to it. Once isn't likely to be enough. Why can't she show some self-restraint? Keeping his head well down, he wipes his cheeks with the heel of his hand.

Ollie dumps his school bag on the hall floor, relieved to have its weight off his shoulders, more relieved that the school week is over. He rubs his shoulder muscle where the strap's been, but it does nothing to lessen the ache. He takes off his shoes

– house rules – and stares down at his socks. His feet really stink. Assessing his reflection in the hall mirror, he sniffs back angry tears. Nothing pleases him about the tall, awkward boy staring back at him.

Ollie squares his shoulders because that's exactly what he needs to do. Reason and logic can face down apparitions. He can force his mother back where she belongs inside the DO NOT FUCKING OPEN compartment of his brain.

He concentrates on the vinegar whiff from his socks, the sun-warmed wood under his feet. In this reality, he's late back from school with loads of homework to do. That's enough to worry about.

He's leaving damp patches along the floor. (The house rule could do with an update.) Walking into the kitchen he sees Dad and Vega are sitting opposite each other at the table – less than half a metre apart but immersed in their separate concerns. Dad has cleaned up and something that smells pretty good is in the oven. Maybe he ought to tell him more often that he's doing an okay job as their sole parent.

'Hi, Ollie.' Dad musters a welcome-home-son smile he's quick to drop. His thoughts are unreadable though Ollie can detect a subtle change in him since the morning. Yes, something has shifted.

Vega deigns to acknowledge his arrival with her usual offhand greeting of, 'Hiya.' Though she's trying to act nonchalant, she's out of sync with herself; her thoughts flitting between too many things. She's avoiding his eye, hoping to hide the fact that she's also trying to get her head around meeting a woman she has so little memory of. His unspoken, *I told you so* is the hollowest of victories.

She looks up. *Are you going to rat on me, or what?*

Depends. My silence comes at a price.

I'm not planning a repeat performance, if that's what you think.

He mimes the Scream emoji.

What's that supposed to mean?

You know.

Oh, for fuck's sake...

Ollie turns away from her attitude. He clears his throat. 'Something smells good.'

'Lasagne,' Dad says. 'Should be ready in about ten minutes.' He frowns. 'Has either of you seen the flash drive that was on my desk?'

They shake their heads in unison.

'I've looked everywhere but it seems to have gone walkabout.'

Ollie steers him away. 'So, you met Cerys's mum this morning.'

Dad shrugs. 'Gwen – yeah, she popped round to have a quick word about–'

'You were right – what you told her about me not doing Cerys's homework. And, just so you know, I'm not taking any money for helping her.'

Vega sniggers. 'He's just doing it for love, aren't you, Oll?'

Ollie ignores her. 'Fair enough,' Dad says. 'There are worse motives.'

'Look, she's new to the school and the exams are looming,' he says. 'She asked me for help because she's really struggling to catch up with the rest of the class. I'm only pointing her in the right direction so she can work things out herself.'

Vega says, 'How very noble of you.'

'Yeah well, unlike *some people* I would never do anything stupid I might live to regret.'

'Never doubted that for a minute,' Dad says. Which is the truth, as it happens. 'Anyway, seeing's now is as good a time as any and we're all here, what was it you were so keen for us to discuss, Ollie?'

'There's a lot maybe we need to get straight between us,' he says. 'Though I'm really not sure I can be arsed to go into all of it right this minute.'

'Suits me,' Vega turns her face away so Dad can't see how relieved she is.

'Okay.' Dad shrugs. 'Then we'll save it for another time.' Absentmindedly, he goes back to thinking about how to make more money. Then back to picturing Cerys's mum. More precisely, the way she'd smiled at him as she was leaving. The Roberts family do a good line in smiles.

When Ollie opens the fridge, he finds they're out of cold drinks – out of almost everything. Looking at Dad, he says, 'You might want to order some food.' Getting no response, he goes over to the sink and slurps water from under the tap. 'Think I'll take a quick shower before we eat.' On his way out of the room, he says, 'You know Gwen Roberts has a husband, right?'

Dad tries to appear unconcerned. 'Your point is?'

'Just suggesting that's maybe something you should, you know, factor into the equation.'

Chapter Twenty-Two

Vega

She's still half asleep when she hears and then recognises the raised voices coming from downstairs. Shit! Her grandparents are far too fond of springing unannounced visits on them. (Dad calls them spot inspections.) When it's just the three of them, Saturday mornings are a time for lingering in bed followed by lazy, half-dressed brunches. Though she's always delighted to see Gran, it's tempting to hide under the covers from their grandfather. Fortunately, his eye-of-Sauron gaze is a lot less penetrating than it used to be. He'll be far more suspicious if she doesn't put in an appearance.

Out of bed, she's careful to remove her St Christopher pendant before pulling on jogging pants and an outsized t-shirt. A trick she's learnt to help shield her thoughts, is to imagine an impenetrable force-field around her head. A bit literal but it seems to work. She goes for a pee and then, at the top of the staircase, takes a deep breath. 'Shield wall,' she mutters to herself as she walks down the stairs and into the kitchen where they're standing around chatting.

'Vega sweetheart, there you are.' Gran greets her with a tight hug, swaying her backwards and forwards as she envelopes her in the roses-and-warm-body smell that's unique to her. If only she'd come alone. When they draw apart, Gran continues to hold her by the shoulders, appraising her for any differences.

'So, what's your verdict then?' Vega grins. 'Don't tell me, let me guess. You think I've grown a bit, but I'm too pale and probably need to eat more greens or red meat.'

'Since you can read my mind, you'll know I was thinking no such thing but simply how lovely you are. No ifs or buts. And how grown up you're getting.' She doesn't add, *And more like Beth every day.*

Gran refuses to dress like an old lady. Today, in her knee-length shorts, blue floral shirt and white trainers, she looks young for her age though, up close, it's a different story. Her tanned skin is way more wrinkly now. Her stylish haircut helps to disguise the fact that her hair is a lot sparser than it was.

Ollie's discussing with Grandad the latest refinement of the chemical process used to make aviation fuel from bacteria. Gran's not listening – shocker. Instead, she's thinking about how much she misses Beth at times like this. As she sits down, Gran surreptitiously leans on the table for support. And afterwards her bony hands look jittery. Dad hasn't noticed because he's busy clearing away the remnants of last night's meal.

Gran is the only "normal" member of their family – apart from it being quite tricky to calculate her age. Though her passport states she was born in 1959, it was actually 1923 – which would make her 112 and a contender for Britain's

141

oldest woman. Of course, in their family nothing is ever that simple. Lana fell for Matt during the Second World War after he'd heroically rescued her from her London digs which had just been flattened in an air raid. Not long after they hooked up, she discovered she was pregnant with Dad, (Talk about irresponsible!) which forced Matt to come clean about his unusual abilities. He persuaded Lana to go with him to the safe, though terminally boring, Cotswold village of Stoatsfield under Ridge in the early 1990s. If you allow for that forty-eight-year time-hop bit in the middle, Lana's cumulative biological age is only 64. Not all that old and yet there's a new weariness about her, a distance in her eyes that suggests time is catching up.

'And how's my favourite granddaughter?' (Grandad's usual, well-worn joke.) His hug is as tight as Gran's. Intended to demonstrate his affection, today it puts her in mind of a crocodile's death roll. After letting her go, his opening gambit is, 'So, what have you been up to recently, young lady?'

'Oh, you know, just the usual this and that. Boring school stuff mostly.' She shrugs, acts like she has nothing to hide by reaching past him to tear off a piece from the croissants they've brought with them.

'Plate,' Dad says to demonstrate his parental authority. He nods towards the croissant pile in the centre of the table. 'Why don't the rest of you take a seat while I nip out for some fresh milk?'

'We're running low on lots of other stuff,' Ollie says. Her brother's bed-head hair makes him look like a cartoon version of himself. 'In fact, why don't I come with you, Dad?' A blatant tactic. 'To help you carry stuff and that.'

'Why don't I go instead?' she says. 'It won't take me a second to get dressed.'

'There's no need.' Dad gives them his stern-eyed stare. 'I'm guessing Mum and Matt would like you both to stay here and chat. I'm sure they'd love to hear how you're getting on at school.'

'Given their outstanding abilities, I think we can assume there are no concerns in that department,' Grandad says, with an edge they all feel. He pulls his cream-coloured trousers up at the knee to preserve their creases before he sits down at the head of the table. (In Dad's place.) Leaning forward, he interlaces his fingers like he's waiting for the rest of them to come to order. Over his right shoulder, his Panama hat rests on the countertop like a witch's familiar.

'I'll be back shortly,' Dad says, making good his escape.

Vega sits down in her usual place which means she's right next to Grandad. Ollie chooses the other end by Gran. He grabs a plate followed by a huge chocolate croissant. 'So, your garden must be looking lovely right now,' he says knowing it will set Gran off, which it does.

While she's describing the various wildflowers that have sprung up in their uncut grass, Vega's attention strays to the photos on the wall behind. She studies the framed shot taken on their trip to Brighton. The pier's wavy-striped helter-skelter is directly behind them. She must have been around eight at the time – so only five years ago. All of them, even Grandad, had had a go on various rides. After their beach picnic, both their grandparents swam in the sea though the freezing water chased the rest of them out. Their heads became dots further out from the shore than all the other bathers before the two of them turned around and headed back to the beach. It's hard to believe these are the same two people.

'Lana is making a virtue out of a necessity,' Grandad says. 'Truth be told, all that mowing had got a bit much.' He spreads his age-spotted hands wide. 'Mortality has a way of catching up with us all in the end.' He says it deadpan, like he's reading from a fortune cracker and it's no biggie.

Gran tut-tuts him. 'We're not dead yet, Matt. I prefer to think of these as our golden years.'

He tuts her right back. 'Golden years – ha! Sounds like something from one of those awful brochures they keep sending us. "Enjoy your golden years at The Sheltering Arms Care Home." They might as well say, "Welcome to the Twilight Zone for old codgers".'

'Well, this is a cheerful conversation,' Gran says. She winks like this is just the usual bants between them and Vega shouldn't take it seriously. It's an effort to smile back. Their grandparents have been a constant in their lives since Mum left. Naïvely, Vega imagined losing her mother as a baby would be the end of her bad luck. Rani was really upset when her gran died of a heart attack a few weeks ago. She'd sympathised while sort of assuming that, because her own grandparents are different to everybody else's, they'll be around for years to come. But maybe they won't.

Grandad leans forward, his eyes narrowing. 'Everything alright, Vega?' he asks like he can tell it's not.

'Fine,' she says. 'I'm doing well at school. And I've been picked for the under 14s tennis squad. We're playing some posh London school next week.'

'Well done you,' Gran says. 'I was very fond of tennis when I was younger.'

Grandad doesn't respond. He hasn't even blinked. She concentrates on maintaining that forcefield then decides more deflection is needed. Sometimes sacrifices have to be made. 'Guess what,' she says. 'Ollie's in love with an older girl who's in his class.'

'You absolute–' When Ollie tries to stand up, Gran's hand restrains him.

'Her name's Cerys and she's really pretty and way out of his league.'

Red in the face, Ollie shakes his head. 'Vega's talking crap as usual because she's trying to divert attention away from what's she's been up to.'

'Oll pretends he's only *tutoring her...* ' She puts air quotes around the words. 'She's crap at maths and the exams are coming up, so Cerys goes and bats her eyelashes at him, and, like a sucker, he agreed to coach her. F.Y.I. Oll, she's still got the hots for this boy in her old school even though he's ghosted her. Oh, and Dad *really likes* Cerys's mother, Gwen, though she's married–'

'That's enough!' Gran's anger is directed at her alone. 'I'm shocked, and I have to admit, disappointed in you, Vega.' A hard blow. 'Lord knows a private life is a difficult thing to maintain in this family. All the same, the nature of Oliver's relationship with this girl is a matter for him and her alone. As for the poor girl's own feelings or motives – that is definitely not something any of us are entitled to hear about or speculate over. I believe you owe your brother an apology.'

Usually her ally, Vega can't remember the last time Gran spoke to her like this. The shame of her disapproval makes her eyes water. Gran isn't finished. 'And as for that tittle-tattle about Tom – that's also none of your business, young lady. There's no place for the Orwellian Thought Police in this family.'

'It's not my fault. When you know, you know,' Vega offers in her defence. 'I can't unknow all the stuff in people's heads. And I didn't ask to be born like this.'

'Granted,' Gran says. 'But the very least you can do is keep that type of personal information to yourself.'

Chastened by such harsh criticism, she says, 'Sorry, Oll,' meaning it for once. Her brother's stare doesn't waver. She hopes he's not about to throw her under the bus in turn. 'You're right, Gran,' she adds. 'We're all entitled to a private life.' She glares first at Ollie and then her grandfather. 'Don't you agree, Grandad?'

Chapter Twenty-Three

Tom

It's weirdly quiet when Tom walks back into the kitchen; except for his mum's slight nod, no one acknowledges his return. They're all still sitting at the table in an atmosphere that could be cut not so much with a knife, more like a chainsaw. The croissants have barely been touched. 'Okay,' he says, 'What did I miss?' A question that's met with silence. Abandoning the refinement of a jug, he plonks the milk carton on the table. 'Anybody care to enlighten me?'

His mum clears her throat. 'We've been discussing personal privacy. Clearing the air a little, I hope.'

Tom frowns. 'Really? Only it feels more like a thunderstorm brewing.'

Matt says, 'Reiterating the conversation that occurred in your absence would, I suggest, prove rather counterproductive. I think we'd probably all agree on that much at least. Suffice to say, everyone has had an opportunity to express their opinions. Since no one disagrees, can I suggest we turn our attention to the more pleasurable topic of breakfast.' To illustrate his point, he reaches for a plate, then stares down at its empty surface as if conjuring up a spell that would magically fill it.

'Okay, then.' Tom unpacks the rest of the shopping. 'Moving on, you now have a choice of bacon, sausages, eggs, mushrooms, oh and tomatoes. So, who's up for the full English brekkie?'

Ollie and Matt raise their hands.

'Think I'll just have a croissant,' Mum says. 'Perhaps with some coffee.'

Vega pulls a pained expression. 'I'd rather have a boiled egg – which I'm happy to do myself, by the way. I'm going to grab a quick shower first.' Pausing in the process of standing up, she adds, 'Assuming I'm granted permission to leave the table.'

His mum covers Vega's hand with her own. 'I'm sorry if what I said seemed a little harsh. Just doing my best to set you on the right path while I still can.'

'And I'm sorry if I fail to live up to your high expectations.' Before anyone can argue, Vega flounces out of the room and stomps up the stairs. Counting to three, Tom waits for the door slam, is disconcerted when it doesn't come. He can't decide if that's a good or a bad sign.

'Why don't I give you a hand cooking breakfast,' Mum says, getting to her feet with some effort.

'Stay where you are,' Matt says. 'I can help Tom.'

'Let's leave them to it while I show you the garden,' Ollie says. 'You should see the tadpoles in our pond, Gran. There are loads of them at the moment.' He crooks his arm, and she threads hers through like it's an affectionate gesture rather than her worrying need for support. 'Did you know the skinnier ones with golden flecks are frog tadpoles?' Ollie tells her. 'The fatter all-black ones are toad tadpoles.'

'We always called them toad-poles,' Mum says.

Tom gets the impression he's been set-up in some way for this one-on-one time with his dad. Matt waits for them to leave the room before he picks up the egg box. 'I've recently discovered something interesting,' he says.

'Enlighten me.'

'The secret to achieving perfect scrambled eggs is to add an unhealthy amount of butter and…' Matt points a knowing finger. 'Above all, to take your time about it.'

'Then I'm happy to delegate the egg cookery to you while I try not to burn the rest.'

They work side by side in a companionable silence that's unlikely to last. After he cracks another egg into the bowl, Matt pauses. 'So, I gather you've branched out from locating stray pets to tracking down missing humans.'

'Ah – so now we get to the nub.' Tom turns the grill to max before handing Matt a whisk. 'You've been misinformed. Whatever you've heard, the simple fact is a lonely, bereaved mother came here to ask if I would try to find out what happened to her missing son. I heard the poor woman out and then told her that I'd need to think about it. Which is exactly what I've been doing.'

Matt cracks another shell on the side of the bowl. Poised to smash the next, he says, 'Who could fail to be touched by a grieving mother's plight?' in that annoyingly smug tone of his. 'And, of course, you felt the need to investigate in order to make an assessment.'

'I did. Seems to me that's what any normal human being would do in the circumstances.'

'Although this assessment of yours involved going beyond your normal modus operandi.'

Tom submits the sausages to the fierce heat of the grill. 'Before you say anything else, you should know that I'm planning to turn Mrs Baynton down.'

'*Planning to.*' Matt is piling up the empty shells on the worktop instead of throwing them in the bin. 'I see.'

'What does "I see" mean?' The sausages are already beginning to spit; time to turn the temperature down a couple of notches.

'I'm merely observing that, despite your resolution to refuse the assignment, you haven't yet made the crucial call to tell her of your decision.' Matt stops beating eggs and does that thing with his eyes – like he's X-raying your soul – before reaching for the pepper grinder as if nothing of consequence is occurring. 'If you want my advice–'

'I don't.' Tom holds up a hand to stop him right there. 'I can assure you I'm quite capable of figuring things out for myself.' He spears the raw rashers with his fork and lays them down one at a time next to the sausages.

'I must warn you against any further involvement.' Matt waves the whisk around like a weapon. 'You discovered that before he disappeared David Baynton had been leading a rather complex life.'

Tom nods. (No point in trying to hide anything from old eagle-eyes.)

'Then you must realise that any further involvement in the

matter would be very ill advised. I have no wish to exaggerate, but suffice to say, if you don't let this go, you may well regret it.'

'Is that so, Dad? You know, if I didn't know better, I'd say that sounded more like some sort of threat than concerned fatherly advice.'

Matt tips the beaten eggs into the pan. 'Can't a man give his son a well-meant warning without it being seen as a threat?'

'Tell me, Dad, is this so-called *"well-meant warning"* coming from you or are you acting as a messenger for others?'

'Those concerned for your safety have your best interests at heart.'

'Does that include my son?'

'The boy can hardly have failed to be aware of your activities. Indeed, he was obliged to intervene to keep you from coming face-to-face with a very angry David Baynton.'

'Now you've lost me.'

'Ollie was the so-called courier who delivered that mysterious package. His arrival interrupted Baynton before he could discover you lurking in his apartment.'

'Shit a brick.' Tom covers his mouth with his hand. 'So that package delivery – that was Ollie?'

'It was indeed. The boy saved your bacon as it were.' Matt nods towards the cooker. 'Talking of which, I believe I can smell burning. You might want to take a look at what's happening under that grill.'

Chapter Twenty-Four

The flash drive had been sitting right there on his desk the last time he looked. He searches the rest of the desktop, the floor, even the bin, but it seems to have vanished. Tom is scratching his head when a noisy altercation begins in the street outside. He peers through the window to discover that what sounded like a cat fight is a screaming and grunting tussle between two large dog foxes. A nearby first-floor light goes on illuminating the posturing opponents. Someone shouts out obscenities to scare them away to no effect. A second ferocious bout ends with one of the animals cowering in defeat before sloping off bloodied into the shadows.

As peace returns, the light goes out leaving Tom to stare into the darkness. He savours the renewed tranquillity.

On the subject of quarrels, he's relieved their unscheduled family brunch-up ended on a more harmonious note. Through teasing and fond recollections, they'd plastered over fault lines that never quite go away.

As soon as his parents left, Vega went off to a schoolfriend's birthday sleepover. (Knowing teenage girls, he doubts much sleeping will be involved.)

Once the two of them were alone, he'd apologised to Ollie. 'I've learnt my lesson,' he assured him – an uncomfortable role reversal moment.

Ollie spent the afternoon at some planning meeting connected to the town's Science Festival. He'd then rushed up to his room to work on a presentation, too preoccupied to welcome any interruptions.

With time to himself, Tom finally made the call he was dreading to Sarah Baynton – an awkward balancing act between declaring his sympathy while turning down the assignment. 'You'd only be wasting your money,' he told her, which then suggested there might be some wriggle-room.

'Isn't that something for me to worry about,' she said, forcing him to restate that his decision wasn't up for discussion.

'I see.' Her tone inferred he had let her down – which, in a way, is justified. Her simple, 'Goodbye then,' at the end of their conversation added to his sense of guilt. He's done what he assured his father he would do and that's the end of the matter.

His parents' visit must have been prompted by Matt's desire to deliver that warning. Was he acting as the mouthpiece for the "Organisation" – that unseen orchestra playing in the pits, their heads ready to pop up whenever the action on the stage fails to please them?

His son ought to have felt able to talk to him about what happened. Did he go to his grandfather asking for support or had the old man responded to an unintended mental distress signal from Ollie? He should have asked him what was in the package he delivered to Baynton.

Tom's gaze wanders from the blank screen in front of

him to the little Tex-Connex device still synced up to his IT system. The flash drive may have gone walkabout, but the coded information it contained remains available to view.

Hmm. He hates leaving any puzzle unsolved. What harm can it do to try to solve this one?

A single keystroke brings the whole thing back to the screen. Tom studies the complex table in front of him hoping inspiration will strike. It doesn't.

Relevant fact number one: David Baynton had been employed as a city trader – something he's failed to look into. The conversation he overheard sounded like it was about some dodgy dealings he was involved in. The way Baynton moved, his readiness to resort to physical violence, all adds up to him being, or seeing himself as, a bit of a tough guy – a player.

A quick search informs him there around sixteen subtly different types of city traders. Putting aside the precise nature of Baynton's job, what they all have in common is that they buy and sell stock.

Relevant fact number two: Given that Baynton was based in London, it's likely he was trading in equities.

Relevant point number three: How could a young man like that afford to buy a multi-million-pound luxury penthouse? It's a fair bet he had a source of income over and above his regular one – most likely from some highly irregular dealing. Not wishing to blacken a dead man's name, but it's not a giant leap to imagine the type of people who might employ the services of a complicit dealer to turn bad money into something shiny and new.

If the left-hand column identifies the stock being purchased, logically the corresponding numbers would be details of what had been bought and sold. Tom scrolls all the way down the very long document. At the end there's a small footnote – a series of letters he'd previously overlooked.

The door behind him opens. His back to the screen, Tom says, 'You're still awake then?' though the answer is self-evident. He notices Ollie's blue and white pyjamas are now too small for him – the trousers finish way above his ankles. Tom's surprised he hasn't asked for new ones.

Ollie yawns. In a sleep-thickened voice, he says, 'I knew you wouldn't be able to leave it alone.'

There's no point in denying anything when your son is telepathic. Tom shrugs. 'Caught red-handed – a fair cop. I just want to break this sodding code.'

'And then what?'

'Then nothing. As you must already know, I've told Sarah Baynton I don't intend to take the job.' He rubs at the stubble on his chin. 'All the same, curiosity got the better of me.'

'Yeah, I know what you mean.' To his surprise Ollie pulls up a chair alongside him. 'Like an itch you can't resist scratching.' The boy's sleepy eyes scan the screen for a matter of seconds before he points to the footnote's 36 random letters. Closing his eyes Ollie appears to be channelling spirits or possibly accessing another part of his brain.

He opens them abruptly. 'I think they've used a straightforward multiplicative cipher. If so, we just need to figure out what K is.'

'K?'

'K is the key – the number you start by multiplying by. Once you have that… Give me a minute.'

'D'you mean you're–'

'Shh, Dad. I'm running through the single digit possibilities, and I need to concentrate…'

'Okay.' It's both impressive and worrying that his fifteen-year-old son is managing to do these complex calculations in his head. Put in his place somewhat further down the evolutionary scale, Tom sits back and waits.

The silence is broken by Ollie's smug laugh. 'Bingo!'

'And?'

'Hold on a second, let me just double-check it first.' After a moment, he nods. 'Yep, I've cracked this one at least. It's Key 3 – simples! Those first three letters – HXO – give us T.H.E. The. Next ones are b, o, n, n, i. e.'

'So the bonnie something. Bonnie Prince Charlie?'

'Dad!'

'Sorry.'

'T,a,r,t,a,n. Tartan. D,i,s,t,i,l,l–'

'Distillery,' Tom guesses.

'Distillery Company,' Ollie corrects him.

He claps his hands. 'So, this information is about the dealings of an outfit calling itself The Bonnie Blue Tartan Distillery Company.'

Ollie shakes his head. 'I think we can safely assume this relates to certain dealings that company would rather not make public.'

After a search, Tom discovers there is indeed a Bonnie Blue Tartan Distillery Co. registered, not in Scotland as he expected, but the Channel Islands. The company names two directors – a Mr Guillaume Bastien Picot and a Dr John Hugo

Martin – most likely bona fide local citizens. From the scant information available in the public domain, nothing jumps out and says boo.

Ollie takes over, scrolling back up to the beginning of the document. After a moment's concentration, he says. 'Damn it, they didn't use the same cypher for the rest of the doc.'

'Which suggests the footnote might have been more of a spontaneous afterthought.'

'Quite possibly.' Ollie's face sobers. 'Like you, I love to solve this sort of stuff but…' He sits back in his chair. 'I reckon we might be better off not knowing about this so-called distillery and its shady dealings.'

'Yeah, you're right. Whatever this information relates to, I very much doubt it's legal and above board.'

'And I'm guessing the individuals involved are *very* protective of its secrets.' Ollie gives him a long look. 'To use a movie analogy – it's never a good idea to disinter a vampire.'

Tom chuckles. 'Point well made.' He turns off the screen then stands up, tousling Ollie's hair in the process. 'Talking of creatures of the night – I think it's time we both got some sleep.'

Later, it occurs to Tom the blue tartan throw that was draped across the bed in Baynton's otherwise rather anonymous apartment could have been the man's idea of a joke. A clue to his nefarious activities hidden in plain sight.

Chapter Twenty-Five

Vega

She feels bad about not telling her dad the truth – though it wasn't a total lie. After all, she is at Becky Owen's birthday party – or "dayger" as her friend insists on calling it. She'd omitted to mention that Beck's two besties are the only ones staying over tonight. By around 10:30, if not before, she plans to leave. (Having a dad known for his strict rules has its benefits at times.)

The occasion demanded a new outfit. After a bit of modifying, the purple and orange geometric print blouse she found in a charity shop fits perfectly. A couple of homemade, triangular pads sewn into the shoulder seams and voila! She's a bargain-basement superhero.

Miniskirts were a sixties thing, but a retro-fashion blog assured her they were commonly worn in the late eighties. She's cut a load of material off the bottom of a black skirt and hasn't done a bad job re-hemming it. Vega isn't comfortable about exposing so much thigh, so she's teamed it with three-quarter length, purple leggings.

Before she left home, Dad had frowned his disapproval of her new ensemble, but stopped short of sharing his opinion out loud. (As if that made any difference.) He'd cracked a joke about her looking like she was trying to smuggle jewellery through customs. Her many beads and chains jangle together creating a soundtrack to every action she makes.

She's not the only one who's overdone the makeup, which means no one pays much attention to her bright pink eyeshadow and top-heavy mascara. Though she'd made her entrance wearing the bomber jacket she wore before – this time slung across her shoulders – she quickly discards it.

Looking her up and down, Lachlan Gilbert says, 'Interesting out,' (meaning outfit) 'What have you come as?'

She ignores his mates' guffaws.

'You look nice,' Beck says after a fleeting glance. She returns the compliment, uncertain which one of them is lying the most.

Hours later, Becks is struggling to maintain her everything-is-perfect expression, trying not to show how bitter she is about the load of people who haven't turned up. Her mood is made worse by a shrewd suspicion they've opted to go to Darren Mangold's gathering instead. (She's not wrong.)

No one's had the nerve to tell Becks her party playlist is crap. The self-indulgent love song that's playing is further curdling the mood. A couple of sure-fire bangers might kick things off, but no such luck. A good percentage of her guests are wondering if – more like *when* – they can slink off to Darren's do. Bailing sooner than planned is an attractive option, except Becks is bound to notice her absence.

Vega sips the dubious, orange-coloured punch. (No one knows what's in it.) It's an effort to feign interest in the bitchy conversations going on around her. Harder to supress a groan when Wilf Hennessy saunters over to block her view. He runs a casual hand through his fauxhawk. 'Hi.' Wilf colours up in an odd way. (Fiery cheeks while the rest of his face stays deathly pale.) 'Can I get you a drink?' he asks, forgetting to disguise his posh-boy manners and acting like they're in some nightclub (if only) instead of standing around in the Owens' semi-trashed kitchen.

She raises her cup. 'Beat you to it.'

'Oh right.'

He picks up a bowl containing a couple of rejected olives and waves it under her nose. 'No thanks,' she says, before he can ask.

Legs splayed, Wilf sways a little as he struggles to decide what to say or do next. To save him from his own dilemma, Vega turns her back and walks away.

The abrupt change of temperature makes her catch her breath. This time nausea is only a passing sensation. She hunkers into the inadequate warmth of her jacket. As planned, she's arrived seventy-five minutes before the performance is due to begin. Caught between the fading day and the coming night, the twilight air has an eerie tension about it.

A dozen spotlights are trained on the ramparts of the former church. Vega steps out of the shadows and, scrunching a few fallen leaves underfoot, walks through the almost deserted car park. A black Golf GTI with red stripes is half-blocking the entrance – a proprietorial position. Glass doors have been fitted into the curvy contours of the ancient porch where a graffiti-style sign reminds visitors that, despite appearances to the contrary, they're about to enter an Arts Theatre.

The righthand door is unlocked as she knew it would be. She enters the stone-floored foyer with its residual air of reverence. Beyond it, high white walls host a dozen large, splashy canvases.

Vega shivers. 'Hello!' The word resounds like a cry for help. 'Is anyone here?'

No reply. The box office is closed, all the hatches pulled down. Overhead arrows point the way to the **Dress Circle** and undifferentiated **Upper Circles**.

Directly in front of her are a pair of doors with the words **Stalls, Main Entrance** etched into the glass. She peers through them into the auditorium. Its tiered seating rises amphitheatre-style towards the building's original, black rafters. She read somewhere that it's a theatrical tradition to leave what's called a ghost light on, so that the performance area is never in full darkness. Some actors believe it wards off mischievous thespian spirits. In any case, the central raised stage offers nowhere to hide either from the gods or mankind. How terrifying to stand up there with all those sets of eyes ready to judge your performance.

Vega backs away and, in the process, almost knocks over a display board advertising the current production. As she rights it, she spots the name Elizabeth Trevino at the head of the cast list. Her mum is pictured looking out to sea, her eyes haunted as if, in that moment, she's sensing the other life that's escaped her. Across the bottom of the poster someone's pasted a diagonal strip: **Final Two Weeks.**

Hearing footsteps, Vega swings round. A man in a black rollneck sweater and high-waisted denims is strolling towards her with a glowing cigarette in his hand. His early-George-Michael highlights contrast with his blunt, rubbery features. He takes a drag of his fag then asks, 'Lookin' for someone, sweetheart?' blowing smoke out through over-sized nostrils. Sounds like a line he might have used before. His dark sideburns look like two caterpillars that have just crawled out from under his loose curls. (Smoked out perhaps.)

'I saw in the local paper that you're looking for volunteer ushers,' she says.

''S'right, we are.' He reaches past her to stub his cigarette out in a sand-filled, fire bucket. There's nothing subtle about the way he looks her up and down to guess her age. He's not impressed by her outfit.

Vega remembers to smile. 'I'm eighteen, willing and, as you can see, able-bodied.' She makes a show of riffling through her shoulder bag. 'I've got my provisional driving licence in here somewhere if you need proof of my age.'

'No need.' He touches her hand to stop her searching. 'I believe you, darlin'.' He leaves his hand there a second longer than the gesture called for.

She steps back. Looking around, he says, 'There's not a lot to it – the job that is. You'll help check their tickets as they come in and then, if they look confused – which most of 'em are – you direct them to where they need to go.'

He rakes his floppy fringe to one side. She's taken aback by his next thought. 'If you don't mind me sayin', you look a lot like our current leadin' lady.'

'Yeah, I noticed that too when I saw her on the poster.' Jerking a thumb towards it, Vega gives a bold laugh. 'My cousin reckons that, back in his glory days, my dad was – how should I put it? Well, let's just say lots of women apparently found him attractive.' She shrugs. 'You never know…'

The man smirks. 'Bit of a lad then, your dad,' he says, with undisguised admiration. He scratches at one of his dark eyebrows. (Two more caterpillars.) 'Anyway, we supply you with a torch and a luminous sash. Oh, and a name badge of course. I'm Pete, by the way. And you are?'

'Vanessa,' she says, 'Vanessa Brookes.'

'Well Vanessa, why don't I start by showin' you where the fire exits are. You'll need to sit at the end of one of the back rows ready to intercept latecomers. And deal with any awkward customers. Not that we get a lot of them. I should warn you, it can get a bit much havin' to watch the same performance over and over.'

She giggles. 'A bit like Groundhog Day.'

He frowns. (Of course he doesn't get the reference – the film hasn't come out yet.) 'Oh, that won't be a problem,' she's quick to add. 'I'm really into acting, so it'll be an opportunity to study techniques – how performances evolve.'

'If you say so, darlin'. Jen's in charge of the rota, and the trainin' and all that. She should be here shortly. She usually gets new volunteers to shadow someone more experienced 'til they get the hang of it.'

'I can start straight away,' Vega tells him. 'Tonight, if you like. I'm more than happy to do a bit of shadowing.' She dials it back. 'See if I like it and that.'

'Jen's got a checklist she'll run through with you. What to do if the fire alarm goes off and all that sort of thing. We've had a few false alarms recently – which is a pain in the ruddy neck. (Ruddy wasn't his first choice.) The alarm system here can be a bit hair-trigger. A thunderstorm or a sudden electrical surge can set it off. Can't take any chances so we have to evacuate the whole buildin' in any event.'

In an effort to sound responsible, she says, 'I read somewhere that if people get used to nuisance alarms it makes them complacent, which means they're slower to accept it might be a genuine fire and so they stay seated for longer. In a rapidly spreading fire, any reticence can be fatal. An individual's response time can determine who survives and who dies.'

'Like the boy who cried wolf.' Pete shakes his head. 'Matter of fact, I was on the blower to the engineers earlier. I told them they need to come back and sort it out pronto.'

'Good to know,' she says. 'Fires can be a particular problem in theatres or cinemas because the audience is usually caught up in the performance. Their minds are engaged in the alternative reality being portrayed on the stage or screen, and so they're slower to accept a change in the real world.'

He narrows his eyes on her. 'I never thought of it like that.' A hint of suspicion has crept into his voice.

Chapter Twenty-Six

Tom

Ollie's already left the house to meet Cerys before school. His son seldom mentions Beth, whereas Vega is always keen to learn more about her. After gulping down her usual sludge-and-vomit coloured smoothie, she starts quizzing him about their mother's relatives.

Tom repeats the same bare facts – the wayward, hippie mother with a habit of hooking up with younger men and/or buggering off to "find herself". How Beth's Aunty Joan was left in loco parentis. 'Your Great Aunty Joan lived right here in Cheltenham,' he tells her. 'I'd take you to see her house, but it was demolished some time back to give access to a new car park.'

'Yeah,' she says, 'I remember you telling me that before.' She looks at him like he's some elderly man trotting out the same old stories. 'Joan's home was a special place for your mum. Her sanctuary. When we went back forty years on and she saw it was no longer standing, Beth was devastated.' A memory floats into his mind. 'Your mum used to sing this song about how paradise gets replaced by a parking lot.'

'Sounds highly appropriate.'

'It was – still is. The lyrics were all about not appreciating things until they've disappeared.' The words have left his mouth before he realises their significance. Tom clears his throat. 'Anyway, your gran would know the name of that song. I think – in fact I'm fairly certain, the singer was another Joan – which was a popular name back then.'

While Vega is getting ready for school, he hears music coming from her room. She's tracked down the parking lot song, is still humming it when she comes downstairs. These days she considers a hug unnecessary. 'Bye, Dad,' she shouts, rocking the door off its hinges with that slam.

His kids are used to him being a single parent. (Not unusual these days.) Before Vega started school, his mum was a godsend. Given the disparity in their ages, Vega must find her grandmother less relatable to as a role model. It's only natural for a growing girl to want to learn more about her mother. Maybe Ollie too, though he's never said so.

Tom heads out to his garage workshop. He recalls an expression about the cobbler's children going barefoot. As a detective, he habitually uncovers information about other people, but he's been remiss with his own family. Perhaps he ought to find out more about Beth's relatives. Although, if any of them are still alive, it's not like the kids can rock up and claim kinship.

He stands back to appraise the "lost kingdom" floating sculpture he's been working on – an overdue commission destined for the lake of the Hon. Artus Sandling-Cannard. ("Call me Artus – it's less of a mouthful.") As a visual pun on his last name, Artus wants it to function as a duck house for his soon-to-be-acquired Mandarin ducks. Since they're a species that prefer to perch and lay their eggs in trees, the house is likely to attract more commonplace squatters. Still, as agreed, he's adapted his design to suit the housing and nesting requirements of waterfowl – the rest is not his problem.

Absorbed in his work, the morning passes quickly. Tom is pleased enough with his progress to take a well-earned break. The café down the road serves decent coffee and an excellent lemon drizzle cake.

As he strolls towards his destination, a prickling sensation overwhelms him. He's being observed, though several glances over his shoulder produce no suspects and no supporting evidence. An absurd idea. Who would be interested in an ordinary bloke walking along an unremarkable, Cheltenham street?

On reaching the café, and after placing his order with Janice, he nonetheless chooses not to sit at his usual table but one next to the window where he can keep an eye on whoever might be lurking outside.

Through the glass he checks out the various passers-by. His eyes are drawn to an attractive woman who crosses the street and heads in his direction. When she gets closer, he recognises her as Gwen Roberts. Dressed down in jeans and a crisp white shirt, she comes into the café and strides over to the counter where he overhears her order a large black coffee. Head bent, her attention drifts to their tempting selection of cakes.

'In or out?' Janice demands in her usual forthright manner.

'Excuse me?'

'Takeaway or drink in?'

'Oh um, drink in.' Gwen wavers. 'And I'll have one of those little custard tarts as well.'

'A pasteis de nata,' Janice says, with homemade pride.

Once she's paid, Gwen glances around deciding where to sit. Their eyes meet across the uncrowded room. Tom raises his hand – not so much a wave, more like someone answering a question that's been posed. 'Hi there.' Why did he just sound American? He stands up, not sure what the appropriate form of greeting might be.

She comes over to his table. Her double air-kiss takes him by surprise. He inhales her perfume – woody base with a citrus edge. 'Care to join me?' he asks re-crossing the Atlantic but sounding like he's in First not Steerage where he belongs.

'Why not?' she says, like it's an act of self-indulgence.

'So, how's things with you?' He wishes his order would arrive, so he has somewhere else to look. And something to occupy his hands.

'Crazy busy, as usual.' She gives a heavy sigh. 'I've had back-to-backs all morning since 5:30. So I thought, damn it, I need a break; and a change of scene. W.F.H. definitely has its drawbacks.' (Why abbreviate the phrase to three letters when it takes the same time to say it?)

He asks, 'Does your husband work from home too?'

'Dom?' The idea makes her smile. 'Lord no. And thank goodness. We'd drive each other insane in record time. His work, well, it takes him away a lot.' Her guarded expression suggests she'd rather not elaborate on what her husband does. In a town where half the population works in what's referred to as "Government Communications", it's never a good idea to probe.

To fill an awkward silence, he says, 'So, do you come here often?'

She acknowledges his jest with a grin. 'My first time.' Gwen looks around. 'I like it. Unpretentious. So, is this one of your regular haunts?'

'I suppose you could describe it as that.' To signal a change of topic, he clears his throat. 'After your visit, I had a chat with Ollie like I said I would. As I'd assumed, he's only been tutoring your daughter and most definitely *not* doing her homework for her.'

She's nodding before he's finished speaking. 'Cerys said the exact same thing. In fact, she was pretty quick to turn the tables and accuse us of ignoring her needs by moving here so late in her final term. I'm afraid she has a point.' Gwen grasps the small silver-coloured locket she's wearing and holds on to it like a talisman. Looking him in the eye, she says, 'The other day – I apologise for jumping to the wrong conclusion.'

He shrugs. 'You were interceding in your daughter's interests. I reckon that's pretty much our job description as parents.'

'I'm grateful Ollie is willing to help her get up to speed with her maths. When I was a child I got used to moving from school to school. I was what they call an army brat. As a family, we've tended to do the same. Recently, we came back from Australia – my husband was seconded there for six months – and then we moved here. I sort of assumed Cerys would find it an easy transition. Turns out the syllabus is subtly different here. Especially maths.' Letting go of her locket, she shakes her head. 'Bottom line – Cerys has been finding it very hard to adjust. If she ends up with lousy marks in her exams, I doubt we'll hear the end of it.'

'Then let's hope Ollie does a good job.'

Janice arrives with a loaded tray. 'Okay, one Americano with cold milk for you Tom. And the lemon drizzle.' She's given him an extra-large slice. 'Black coffee's on the way.' She places a small tart in front of Gwen.

Tom rubs his hands together. 'Thanks a lot, Janice. Looks delicious, as usual. I've worked up quite an appetite,' he says, feeling the need to justify such a large calorie intake.

'Don't know where you put it all,' is Janice's parting remark.

He pours a slug of milk into his coffee and stirs. When he looks up, Gwen is giving him the onceover. 'Cerys seems to think you're some kind of pet detective.' She smirks. 'I loved the cartoon version of that movie when I was a kid.'

Tom's rattled though he tries not to let on. After a sip of coffee, he says, 'I'm a consulting detective. And, yes, I specialise in finding missing things. Mostly jewellery and other high value items. Sometimes, I try to locate missing animals – stolen pets predominately.'

'Fascinating.' He stares into her deep brown eyes trying to detect if she's taking the piss. 'How do you know where to start?' She sinks her teeth into the little tart's molten interior. Surprised by the way it disintegrates, she holds a screening hand in front of her face as she finishes it.

'It's hardly rocket science,' he says. 'As a general rule, I begin at the beginning – usually the missing thing's last known location.'

Swallowing the last segment of tart, she wipes her mouth with the paper napkin. 'And then what?'

He cuts off a corner from his cake and holds the fork in front of his mouth. 'I follow the clues and see where that takes me.'

'I'm sure you're being too modest. You must be good at picking up clues.'

He swallows the cake and then puts his fork down. 'I like to think so.'

They're sharing a smile when, in the corner of his eye he notices a young man sitting at the bus stop though the bus has only just pulled out. That stop serves only one route. The man's youngish. Grey baggy sweats and t-shirt. Heavy sunglasses and a beanie hat pulled down. Straightened out, he'd be tall and skinny. More of a runner than a bruiser.

'How interesting,' Gwen says. She picks up her cup, holds it with both hands. 'You must be very observant. I expect you notice everyone's weaknesses and foibles.'

'I notice details,' he admits. 'Although first impressions, as we know, can be misleading. I keep an open mind, at least to start with. A quick judgement can lead you astray.'

When he checks again, Beanie-hat has disappeared. Tom fails to spot him on either side of the road. It's possible someone stopped to give him a lift.

The clatter of crockery rouses him. 'I really should be going,' Gwen says. Her cup is empty, his half-full. Though they're right next to the window, Gwen's pupils are dilated. Could be down to drugs – over or under the counter. More intriguingly, it could be the result of elevated levels of oxytocin

– the hormone released when a person is sexually attracted to someone.

Chapter Twenty-Seven

Vega

Once the audience have filtered out of the auditorium, she's supposed to check for any forgotten possessions, before following them out and switching her attention to the bar area. She tries to follow Jen's instruction to, 'Keep a general eye on things.'

Pete is chatting to some people over at the bar, a lit cigarette in one hand, while the other constantly adjusts his hair. Vega stations herself on the periphery where she can observe the crowd through the haze of smoke. With last orders about to be called, punters are jostling to be served in time.

'Everything alright, Vanessa?' Jen says, sidling up to her. The Volunteers' Co-ordinator has a fondness for highly colourful scarves, worn mainly to distract attention from her sizable midriff. The roots of the woman's hair are aubergine, while the ends are a carroty orange.

Realising she hasn't answered her, Vega's quick to say, 'I'm fine. Loving it, in fact.'

'Good.' Jen smiles to disguise her suspicion that such

enthusiasm will wear off soon enough. Remembering her mission, Jen says, 'The gentleman over there has asked me to ensure Elizabeth – the lead actress – gets this note.' She nods in the direction of a tall, thin man in a pale grey suit. Drink in hand, he's one of the few not smoking. His oversized, black-rimmed specs are catching the light and obscuring his eyes. His note is a folded piece of paper. No envelope, no writing on the outside.

Jen hands her the note. 'Would you mind going backstage and giving this to her?' She checks her wristwatch. 'Better be quick about it.'

Vega has no choice. 'Yeah, okay.'

'Don't look so worried. He's no stage-door-Johnny. In fact, I'd guess he leans the other way – if you follow my meaning.' Jen nudges her with a knowing look that's just short of a wink. (For fuck's sake!) 'I've seen him in here before. He's one of those theatrical agents. Or possibly a scout. They're always on the lookout for fresh *thespian* talent.' The obvious joke in the woman's head doesn't make it to her lips.

Once backstage and alone, Vega is tempted to read the note, but the lighting is low, and she's been told to hurry.

The dressing room doors are distinguished by a male silhouette with top hat and cane and a female with a long skirt and feathered hat. The door to the women's room bursts open and two actors emerge giggling together about some man's toupee. Hard to recognise them in their everyday clothes. The one who played Harriet holds the door open for Vega. Another cast member (Landlady/Woman in Shop) brushes past on her way out.

Elizabeth is alone in front of a large mirror in a small alcove. Devoid of makeup, her face is pale against her dark hair. In her green, silky wrap, she's giving off a sort of ethereal, Pre-Raphaelite vibe.

Vega can sense how drained she is, how much the performance has taken from her. Her dulled expression shows the price of holding nothing back – delving into the depths of all those borrowed emotions. In the mirror that reflects them both, with Vega disguised by her own heavy makeup, the resemblance between them is hard to discern – a slight suggestion and nothing more.

Vega clears her throat. 'Um, sorry to disturb you…'

'What is it?' With an effort, Elizabeth turns, pulling her thoughts into the here and now. 'Sorry – I didn't catch what you said.'

'I apologised for disturbing your, um, reverie.' She holds out the note – her excuse for being there. 'It's just that Jen asked me to give you this.'

Elizabeth has forgotten their previous meeting. (It was dark, and she was knackered.) She doesn't take the note. Frowning, she asks, 'Who's Jen?'

'The Volunteers' Co-ordinator here. Woman with the strange aubergine and carrot hair? Has a penchant for flamboyant scarves.'

'Oh right. I think I know the one you mean.' Elizabeth narrows her eyes as if seeing her for the first time. 'You have quite a vocabulary.'

'Do I?'

'Reverie. Penchant. In fact, I would describe your own attire as rather flamboyant. Are you in the business? The theatrical business, I mean. Obviously not the other sort.' She shakes her head. 'Sorry, I appear to be talking gibberish – which tends to happen when I'm coming down after a performance. What was it you wanted again?'

'This note. It's apparently from some potential Mr Ten-per-cent.' Elizabeth is confused. 'It's from some, um, bloke who could possibly be a theatrical agent or their representative.' Met with silence, Vega adds, 'I think they use scouts – like they do in football – who go to watch smaller productions hoping to spot up-and-coming talent. The talent, in this case, being you. Because, well, you're an outstanding actress and why wouldn't they recognise that. Your performance tonight – it was extraordinary. Transformative.'

'Wow – that's quite an accolade.' She's studying Vega's face but doesn't register their resemblance. Elizabeth says, 'Something about you reminds me of someone I think I used to know.' She's conjuring up the shady outline of a young man, trying to remember how he might have looked. She can't make him any clearer because she keeps coming up against the fog in her brain that prevents her gaining access to a specific set of neurons – the ones that hold her memories of those missing four years.

'You'll have to excuse me,' Elizabeth says. 'I have problems concentrating sometimes and my memory – well, it isn't what it was.'

'That must be a nightmare with so many lines to learn.'

'Funnily enough I never have a problem learning scripts.' Looking away, Elizabeth tries once again to remember the man, but she can't push through that neural roadblock. She sighs at her failure. Rubbing her forehead, she says, 'I had some sort of accident a few years ago though I can't actually remember what happened.' A wan smile. 'That's the crazy thing. I'm not sure why I'm telling you this, but there's a period of my life that's a complete blank.'

Vega's heart is racing. 'Really? That must be disconcerting.'

'It certainly is. I used to picture it as a closed door that I might be able to prise open someday. These days I'm not so sure.'

This is her chance to fill that gap. There's no one else about – she could tell her in a single sentence: *You once had a husband and two young children.*

She jumps when Elizabeth reaches out – not to grasp her hand, but to take the note from her fingers. Flipping it open, she holds it to the light, scans it and then gasps. Her free hand flies to her mouth. 'Oh my God! He works for Hazel Mathews. I don't believe it. He wants us to *have a conversation*. They're a huge agency. They have an office in Park Lane... I walked past there once.'

She grabs Vega by both hands, her blue eyes shining, her cheeks no longer pale but flushed. 'Tell him I'd *love* to have a chat. Tell him... Wait, we can't talk in the bar it's far too busy. I only need a minute to finish getting dressed.' Her grip tightens. 'Whatever you do, don't let him leave.' She pushes her towards the door. 'Try to stall him for five minutes and then show him in here.'

Turning back to the mirror, she grabs a hairbrush then shoos her away with it. 'Off you go, girl,' she says, like she's nothing but a mere bit player.

Chapter Twenty-Eight

Ollie

Outside the circle of light from the lamp, he waits for her to return, taking care not to touch anything even though he's tempted to tidy up a bit.

She materialises near the bed, dressed in a confusion of orange and purple. Head down, she leans against the bedside chest for support before straightening up. On seeing him, she jumps. 'Shit – you gave me a fright, Oll.' Recovering a little, 'Lost your way? You seem to have forgotten, this is my private space.' A long inhale to steady herself. 'You've got no right to be in here.'

Keeping his voice low, he says, 'You're the one who seems to have lost their way.' *I know exactly where you've been, what you've been doing. Don't even try to deny it.*

Why should I? She's off balance in every way. Exhausted too. Out loud she admits, 'I'm knackered.' Her pupils stop drifting to centre on him. 'Can we have this little heart-to-heart, or whatever this is, another time?'

'A certain amount of curiosity is understandable,' he says.

'But this – this is becoming dangerously close to an obsession. You have to stop now before it gets out of control.' He walks over to her and places a steadying hand on her shoulder which she's quick to shake off.

'I don't *have* to do anything you tell me to.' *I don't need a big brother to protect me anymore.* Her eyes blaze with defiance. 'Why wouldn't I be curious about my mother – my personal heritage? Who wouldn't be?'

'You mean *our* mother.'

'Yeah well, *I've* chosen not to forget about her whole existence.'

He's finding it hard to stay calm and in control. *Do you imagine I can't see through such an obvious counterattack?*

She shakes her head. 'What harm can it do if I try to get to know her a little, from afar?'

'From afar?' He snorts. 'That's not how I'd describe getting a job in the same theatre she's performing in.'

'Yeah well – that was the plan.' The makeup can't disguise the look of loss he sees before she glances away. 'She didn't remember. Didn't even recognise me from the last time.' Her voice cracks. 'I was instantly forgettable.' She slumps down on the bed. 'You'll be pleased to hear that, as a lowly volunteer usher, I didn't begin to register on her radar.'

'And that's my point. She doesn't remember any of us. Believe me I know how much that hurts you.' Hand on his chest. *I feel it too, you know.*

She sniffs. 'Yeah well, our grandparents lived through actual world wars and awful shit like that. I guess by comparison, this is no biggie.'

'You're thirteen, Vega. All kinds of stuff is happening to the inside and outside of your body.'

'Eugh!' She pulls a face to demonstrate her disgust.

'I'm just reminding you of the facts. Puberty is like this hormonal minefield we're forced to navigate. It's stressful as fuck.' After a long look, he adds, 'And not everybody makes it out alive.'

Her face is set hard with determination not to hear. Throwing up his hands, he says, 'You've added a whole other level of complication to what is generally recognised as a volatile and stressful period in any parent-adolescent relationship. Pursuing a mother who can never recognise you as her daughter…' He shakes his head. 'Pretty much guaranteed to blow up in your face.'

'Except, I'm not some blundering, shit-just-happens-to-me human. In case you haven't noticed, you and me, even Dad to some extent, we're actual super-beings. We can control dimensions other people can't even imagine.'

'Listen to yourself, Vega. You seem to have forgotten we're also human.'

'But we're not, are we? Not really.'

'Okay, maybe not entirely, but enough to make us fallible. And psychologically vulnerable whether you choose to admit it or not.'

'I know exactly what I'm doing.' She hauls off one of her boots and hurls it across the room like she means it. 'Since you prefer to talk in metaphors, let's say I've taken a few knocks through the rapids but now I've got my balance again.' She holds out both hands to show they're steady. 'See, it's all under control. And, in case you were wondering, no I'm not naïve enough to go for the big reveal. Hey, guess what Beth, I'm your long-lost, time-travelling daughter.'

The other boot lands with a thud very close to his foot. 'Good,' he says, 'because if you were to–'

'Yeah, yeah – for starters, she'd assume I was mentally ill.' Pinching the bridge of her nose, she sighs. 'Look, Oll, I really need to get some sleep. If you wouldn't mind closing the door on your way out...'

He kneels down to her level. 'This has to stop, Vega. Please. I know you understand why it can't and mustn't go on.'

'And it will, *I* will stop,' she jabs a finger into her sternum, 'when *I* decide to. Not *you*.' Her stray spit hits his face. 'Now, if you'll excuse me, I need to undress.'

Shaking his head, he gets to his feet and walks out.

Cerys has football practice before school, so he and Vega leave home at the same time. Still angry with him, she's soon forging on ahead. He's surprised when rounding the next corner, she's sitting on someone's garden wall, legs swinging and apparently waiting. She jumps down in front of him. *Can you feel it?*

Ollie frowns. *Feel what?*

Vega rolls her eyes. *Get your mind off Cerys in her football kit and concentrate.*

She's right. *Shit – someone's following us.*

And not just us. He's left another one watching our house. Dad was right to be suspicious. Christ, Oll, don't look round!

It's hard not to. By unspoken agreement they carry on walking with what he hopes is an air of unconcern. He checks shopfront windows. Pretending to be interested in the merchandise, he catches glimpses of their stalker – a lanky, white man in a grey hoodie. Though it's a cloudy day, his eyes are covered by shades.

She laughs. *Might as well be wearing one of those trench coats with the collar turned up.*

Though he's not exactly a pro.

They're almost at the school when their stalker begins to dawdle, his interest tailing-off. By the time they've reached the gates, a quick glance confirms he's already turned round and is walking back the way they came. 'Dad must be their primary interest,' Ollie says. 'Did you get anything else?'

'No, not really. You?'

He shakes his head. 'Bit too far away.'

'So, what the hell do we do now?'

He hands her his schoolbag and pass. 'Could you put this in my locker for me?'

'Why?' She's reluctant to take it. 'What are you planning to do?'

'Not sure. I'll wing it.' Grinning, he forces his bag into her hands. 'Don't look so worried. I won't do anything daft. They'll assume we're both stuck in school and safely out of the way for the day, which gives me a big advantage.'

'Oliver Brookes, I can't believe you're actually planning to skive off school.' She narrows her eyes at him. 'What have you done with my brother?'

'I'm just prioritising.' The sixth form dress-code is loose enough for him to pass as a civilian. To add a casual note to his black trousers and white shirt, he rolls up his sleeves hoping he'll be mistaken for an employee taking a break.

But you've got no idea who they are or why they're watching Dad. It could be dangerous.

Strictly recognisance. I'm not planning anything heroic.

Good. She drops both bags on the pavement. 'All the same, I'm coming with you.'

'Bad idea. Two schoolkids bunking off is way more suspicious, more likely to attract attention than one. Plus, look at you – your uniform's a dead giveaway. I could be anybody. Besides, if we both skive off at the same time it'll be harder to wag it later. They'll be less likely to believe the excuse.'

'You mean you're actually planning to lie.'

'In this instance, telling the truth isn't a viable option.' Undoing the first two buttons of his shirt, he tries to adopt an I'm-on-my-break stance. A roll of his shoulder suggests he's stiff after his early shift. He rubs his hands together. 'Cometh the hour, cometh the man.'

'Fuck sake, you idiot.' She play-punches his shoulder. 'You're only fifteen remember.'

'Yeah, but I'm tall with it. People often think I'm older.'

Her face grows serious. 'You're not planning to do anything stupid, are you?'

'What, me act in a rash or irrational manner? You seem to forget I'm the boring, sensible member of our family. Cowardly too. Yep, first sign of trouble and I disappear. Literally.'

Smirking, she picks up their bags. 'I know we don't always agree on stuff, but you know–' He holds up his hand to stop her saying aloud anything that will embarrass them both.

Since their house is opposite the park, after entering by a different gate, he means to stroll past the lake before taking cover behind the overgrown beech hedge. He has no intention of confronting the two men – he only wants to get close enough to learn more.

It's peak dog walking time. Mutts of all different breeds are everywhere – sniffing out squirrels, rushing in or out of the water, relieving themselves against a variety of immobile objects or squatting on the scalped and bleached-out grass. To encourage responsible behaviour by owners, there's a poo-bag dispenser set back a short distance from each exit – including the one opposite their house.

As he gets closer to the gate, he glimpses the two men loitering with intent on the pavement. There could be others nearby.

Inspiration strikes. He abandons his off-duty-waiter persona and switches to frustrated-dog-owner. Leaning into this new role, he snaps off a poo-bag then bends down as if examining his laces while he fills it with soil and stones. (His fictitious dog is one of those cool lurchers.) For a further touch of authenticity, he calls out, 'Duke! Come here boy!' while carrying evidence of his dog's existence before him. A hostile observer ought to assume he's someone in search of a place to deposit this bounteous amount of dog shit.

To preserve his sanity, he's learnt to screen out the thoughts of strangers; now, deliberately homing in, there's nothing but the usual jumble of petty concerns and preoccupations.

Ollie dumps the poo-bag on the grass then takes a few steps closer to the high hedge that screens him from the men. He adopts the pose of someone engaged on a call.

The first thing he learns is that the two of them are bored to the point of irritation. Instructed via an anonymous message, neither of them has any idea who they're working for or why they've been sent to snoop on his dad. 'Yep, he's definitely still in there, I can see him through the window,' the one called Travis reports.

'I'm gonna need to take a piss soon.' The second speaker is a Jaxon Brady. He's twenty-nine and lives at…

'I want a word with you, young man.' Brandishing an accusing finger, an elderly woman is striding towards him on a mission, her voice raised by a combination of outrage and poor hearing.

'I was just about to–'

'Don't play the innocent with me. I saw you deliberately drop that bag on the ground.' She jabs her walking stick in the direction of the offending item and then sweeps it to the left. 'The right place for that is over there, in that bin.'

People have stopped to watch, all of them waiting to see how he's going to respond. A younger, fitter woman gets ready to intervene should he become aggressive.

Ollie retrieves the poo bag from the grass. A row of indignant stares follow his every step as he goes over to drop it into the relevant bin. With so many eyes still trained on him, he has no choice but to head back through the park calling for Duke – his fictious runaway dog.

Chapter Twenty-Nine

Tom

He glances skywards through the window as if assessing what the day's weather is likely to be. It would be hard not to spot the two young men hanging around near the park entrance. Casually dressed in jeans and muscle-fit t-shirts, both are hard-faced and serious.

Tom doubts the park authority is now employing bouncers. An innocent explanation is they're a couple of hardbodies waiting for their mate or mates to show up. The less innocent explanation – they're drug dealers touting their wares. (No visible evidence.) Or would-be burglars casing the houses.

Twenty minutes later, another peek confirms the two are still out there. He watches in the kitchen mirror as a stream of pedestrians pass them by without being waylaid or accosted. They don't appear to be soliciting. So what are they up to?

His gut tells him that he's under surveillance. The next question is why. When he's acting for a client, he asks them about gambling debts, jealous husbands or wives, someone who might be harbouring a grudge against them. Since none of the above applies to him, the most obvious explanation is that this troubling development is linked to his investigation into David Baynton's disappearance.

He's been ultra-careful to cover his tracks – or so he believes – and yet he must have left a breadcrumb trail that's led these two to station themselves directly opposite his house.

Did he ask questions of the wrong person? Away from their sightlines, Tom paces out his anger. Marshalling his inner Raymond Chandler, he lines up possible culprits for the snitch. He puts Baynton's work colleague, Simon Yardley, in the frame and can't rule him out. Hmm. Next he casts Katrina, the estate agent who showed him around Baynton's apartment, as the guilty party. That grumpy concierge is a more obvious candidate. Or possibly the chatty one who, come to think of it, might have been a tad too willing to spill the beans for such a modest monetary incentive.

Tom shakes his head, shakes his imagination out of the movie version of events and back to his current predicament. What happens next? He's damned if he's going to sit back and wait for the excrement to hit the aircon.

He could march over there and have it out with those two. If they "cut up nasty" he doesn't fancy his chances. He could call the police and report them for skulking about with a menacing air. Although, as far as he can tell, they don't have teardrop tattoos or suspicious bulges in their pockets.

At this point in the movie Marlow would slip his tail before making a house call on his prime suspect. Is Baynton holed up in that multi-million-pound penthouse? The only way to find out is to go over there and, if he is, confront him. And say what, exactly? His vision is a bit lacking in finer details – he can work those out on an ad hoc basis.

First off, there's the question of how to leave his house without being followed. Tom grins. That's not going to be a major issue.

Up in his study he asks for ariel footage from around the Grenewych Heights building then zooms in on a construction site about eighty metres away. Materials are stacked up some distance from the main working areas. It's now lunchtime and the chances are those construction workers will be having their break in or near the collection of staff huts. Perfect.

Tom's vision clears. 'Oh my sweet lord!' The girl is clutching her chest. 'Where did you just spring from?' American accent. He appears to be inside a fifties-style diner. Beneath his feet, its checkerboard floor is buckling like some Escher painting. Classic rock'n'roll is assaulting his eardrums. Elvis isn't the only one all shook up.

The startled young woman is standing behind a countertop and wearing a candy-stripe outfit complete with diminutive apron. Her blonde curls are restrained by a red scarf tied in a bow at the front.

He focuses on her name badge. 'Sorry if I made you jump then, um, Kirsty,' he says. 'I was just bending down to tie my laces.' Tom leans on an empty barstool for support. 'Guess I must have straightened up a bit too quickly.' He passes a hand across his eyes. 'I'm a little lightheaded.'

Calmer now, she says, 'Sounds like you might have a touch of orthostatic hypotension.' A Boston accent. Kirsty's pink lips slide into a smile. 'I'm a med student.'

'Really?'

'The dizziness you're experiencing could be down to dehydration.' She pours a glass of water and places it in front of him. 'Don't look so worried – it's not uncommon. Most likely due to low blood pressure. You might want to get yourself checked out sometime.'

Is this faux 1950s diner in London, or has he screwed up big time and ended up in the real thing in America?

She steps out from behind the counter to take an order to one of the tables. He notices the ankle socks, her red high heels. Seems like a lot of attention to detail. Her tiny apron has front pockets – the sort she might need if your customers pay with actual cash.

The diner's floor to ceiling windows are streaked by a heavy cloudburst that's now drumming on the roof and blurring his view into the world beyond. Through the fog of condensation, all he can see is a succession of headlights navigating a half-flooded roadway. Above the music, he hears a rumble of thunder.

Tom sits down on a barstool and sips the water hoping it will stave off his rising nausea. His grip on the glass is unsteady, the surface of the water ripples along with those restless black and white floor tiles.

Kirsty's back. 'You don't look so good, sir.'

'I'm feeling a bit nauseous.'

She frowns, her green eyes full of professional concern. 'Are you experiencing any chest pain?'

He shakes his head.

'Or maybe it's more of a burning sensation?'

He shakes it again.

'Do you have any other pain – like in your arms? Or your neck? What about in your back? Are you finding it hard to breathe at the moment, sir?'

'No – none of the above.' Tom swallows more water. 'I'm sure I'll feel better in a sec.'

He looks around for more clues. The shiny cash register sitting on the counter could easily be a prop. Against the back wall there's a curvy, fifties-style fridge. The coffee dispenser has one of those glass jugs – the sort they offer top-ups to the hero from.

Earlier, he'd been thinking about those black and white Humphrey Bogart films. (He's watched "In a Lonely Place" countless times with his mum.) Could thinking about those films have diverted him to the real thing? His accuracy has been a bit off before, but never by as much as eight decades.

'You seem a little anxious, sir. Do you mind if I…' Kirsty presses her cool hand to his forehead. 'Excuse my frankness, but are you feeling a little panicked right now?'

Other customers are watching. He needs to pull himself together. 'I'm absolutely fine, honestly. Thanks a lot for checking, but I'm definitely not having a heart attack. Or a cardiac arrest – which I imagine would be a lot easier to spot since I'd be clutching my chest and struggling for breath. As you can see, I'm not.'

He gives their audience a nothing-to-see here wave. 'For a moment I was a bit disorientated, that's all. Rest assured I don't have concussion – I haven't banged my head lately or anything like that.'

'Okay then.' She sighs, unconvinced. He's tempted to ask her what year it is, but she might imagine he's having a different kind of episode.

Part hidden by the highbacked bench, a man in a checked shirt is signalling to attract her attention. Kirsty puts on a professional smile before she makes her way over.

After a low growl of thunder, a young man comes in with a dripping umbrella which he proceeds to do battle with. Dark hair, generic mid-length haircut, denim jeans, soaked-through black t-shirt clinging to his muscle-bound chest. He could be an extra from "Grease" or equally "Fast XXL" – which means he's no fucking help at all.

Chapter Thirty

Vega

She dumps the schoolbags in their respective lockers. Freed of their weight on her shoulders, while everyone else heads off to registration, Vega goes against the tide and dodges into the toilet block and an empty cubicle that will allow her time to think.

The pre-lesson rush has left the air tainted by a repellent mix of natural odours and the various products intended to mask them. She's pissed off and indignant – no way is she going to remain an onlooker while the male members of her family take charge. It's the 2030s not the1950s.

To clear her mind, if not her nostrils, she stands up and begins to run through the various stretches they do before every tennis match. Both arms extended, she grips and then un-grips an imaginary pole.

With every event or development it's important to identify the causal root. One palm pulled down, arm still extended, she holds the pose for a count of five.

Ollie is trying to find out more about those two men,

though it's obvious their house is under surveillance because of what Dad's got himself mixed up in. Both palms up in the STOP position and hold…

It has to be connected to that missing man Baynton. (Even Dad should be able to join those particular dots.) Left foot forward, she moves on to the hip and calf stretches.

Dad visited his flat and would have been caught in the act if Ollie hadn't pulled that stunt with the package delivery. She sinks into the next stretch, steadying herself with one hand against the cubicle wall where someone's scrawled: lois jones = skank.

Yep, it all comes down to cause and effect. Actions and reactions. Next with her left foot forward.

What's to stop her rewinding that causal thread? With the two of them currently off on a mission, no one is likely to pay any attention to what she's up to. After holding the balance stance on the opposite side, she decides to cut short her warm-up and get on with it.

Vega unlocks the cubicle door. There's no one about. She washes her hands before scrutinising her appearance in the mirror. Her summer uniform is fairly generic with no identifying badges or logo. Vega smooths her hair into place then studies her appearance for any tell-tale signs that she's more than a hundred miles (and several months) off course.

Satisfied, she readies herself. She can hear approaching footsteps in the corridor. Time she was out of here.

Even in a bustling city there are unseen corners. Once her head's stopped reeling, she checks for aghast witnesses and is relieved there are none. This time the nausea is less severe and a lot quicker to pass, which is fortunate since the timing is crucial. She tests her balance with a few steps in one direction and then the other. Yep – she's good to go.

All glass and oversized artworks, the building's foyer aims for cool in every sense. Some sort of tropical-island aroma is being pumped out along with the chilled air. Clusters of exotic plants add to the pretence. (Estate agents must big up the oasis-of-calm-in-a-busy-metropolis angle.) It's 7.25 A.M. and the residents leaving are expensively tailored and coiffured. In this swanky, grown-ups building she's an object of curiosity in her school uniform. If their lives weren't so time-critical, the comers and goers might be tempted to stop and ask her what business she has in a place like this.

Vega tries to project entitlement – her perfect right to be where she is. It helps that she's much steadier on her feet than she was last time. She might be getting better at this. Maybe warm-up exercises even work with this stuff.

Her boots echo on the marble floor, the sound is then deadened by thick carpeting as she approaches the massive desk. The ancient concierge behind it engages full condescension mode. 'You seem a little lost, young lady.'

'Thank you for your concern, but I know precisely where I am,' she tells him in a fake posh accent. 'My aunt suggested I meet her here in the lobby.' (She doesn't indicate this absent aunt's whereabouts.)

'And this relative of yours would be...?' His mind runs through possible candidates of the right age and current location. (Despite claiming to be climate-aware, the residents here travel more than most.)

Time to choose. 'Ms Beauchamp-Huntley,' she says with full confidence. 'Florence Beauchamp-Huntley.'

'I'm afraid you've just missed her. She left the building a few minutes ago.'

'Oh, that's not a problem. Aunt Flo said she needed to pop out on a quick errand. She'll be back shortly. She was most insistent that I wait in here and not outside.' Lowering her voice, Vega adds, 'Between you and me, she has rather a vivid imagination; she worries about me wandering the streets unaccompanied in case I'm lured into a van by evil traffickers.'

'I see.' The concierge wafts an open hand. 'Then perhaps you'd care to take a seat while you're waiting.'

Dodging a man wheeling a large case, Vega positions herself in a vacant armchair exactly opposite the up lifts. Upholstered in scarlet velvet, for such an expensive chair it's remarkably uncomfortable. In her mind's eye she conjures up the various photos of Baynton in her dad's file. If her calculations are correct, he'll emerge from the far-left elevator within the next few minutes.

The lift doors part and he steps out into the foyer looking more attractive in the flesh. Delighted with her accuracy, she's ready to intercept him as he hurries towards the exit.

Their "meet cute" requires exact timing. The length of his strides forces her to rush and then slow down at the last minute. She remembers to turn her head like she has no idea he's in front of her.

The collision is more dramatic than she'd planned. Her head hits his chest with a force that bounces her backwards. He grabs her arm before she falls to the floor. 'Steady on,' he says, holding her until he's sure she's regained her balance. 'I'm so sorry,' he says. 'I didn't see you there.'

'I didn't see you either,' she tells him. 'So clumsy of me…'

He grins as he looks her up and down. 'No worries – the main thing is we both appear to be unscathed. Nothing broken.'

She holds her forehead like some damsel in distress needing smelling salts. 'I think I just need to sit down for a minute.'

Supporting her arm, he escorts her to a different chair. 'Are you sure you're alright?' Nice manners. 'Okay,' he says, raking his dark hair back into shape. 'I'd better be going. I'm sure you'll feel better in a minute or two.'

'Yes, I'm sure I will,' she tells him. 'In fact, I seem to be recovering already.'

He grins, amused by the quaintness of her phraseology. (She's channelling Jane Austen.) 'Bye then.' Watching him walk away, Vega tries to make sense of what she's just learnt.

So, it all began at a family wedding and the couple of dodgy near relatives who approached him when he was halfway hammered. They eased into it. 'Nice suit. Hear you're a big shot trader these days.' During the next round an idea was floated. David grinned at first, told them why it would never work, dismissed outright their over-simplistic, purely theoretical scheme. 'Everything's monitored these days. AI bots constantly search for any suspicious anomalies, routing out any inappropriate connections. Same tech they use in the big casinos.' Shaking his head, he declared, 'It's impossible to cheat the system.'

Ah, but then they knew of this genius kid with a brain like

a planet. A savant able to outsmart an army of bots. Patting his shoulder, the short one told him to sleep on it. Sharing a hangover hotel breakfast and the last to leave, he listened more attentively, already persuaded of the benefits if not the means. David couldn't stop thinking about those off-the-scale rewards. They would set up a shell company, start small. Suck it and see. Risk-free as long as he followed instructions.

A week later, in that rough-as-they-come pub, he met the planet-brained kid and was impressed. The men were only intermediaries, like spy cells, their masters able to deny any connection. It all added up, every last detail. Handshakes and another drink sealed the deal. The tall one assured him all angles were covered. 'As long as we all play our cards right, nothing can go wrong.'

Vega can still see Baynton through the glass wall, head up and carefree as he dodges a honking taxi with an apologetic wave. A man who believes in his gilded future, confident he knows what he's doing, cocky because he's in control. His newly acquired penthouse is tangible proof that he made the right decision. In this early morning moment he's still enjoying his freedom.

Chapter Thirty-One

Ollie

The lake sparkles in the sunlight, its smooth surface disturbed by the V-shaped trails from the many ducks and geese heading for the spot where a couple of children are lobbing enormous chunks of bread into the water, even though their parents are standing next to a sign asking people not to feed the water-fowl. Should he go over and explain that bread is not their natural food and so by artificially filling the birds up, it will stop them searching out the wide variety of things they should be eating and cause them to become malnourished. Judging their general demeanour, he doubts the parents will welcome his intercession. Better to choose his battles.

Ollie finds an empty bench, sits down, and shuts his eyes on everything around him. Some universal law appears to dictate that well-meaning acts often lead to unfortunate consequences.

Those two men are, albeit indirectly, connected to his dad poking around and asking questions about David Baynton.

By returning that flash drive to Baynton, he must have made things worse and not better.

He hates feeling culpable. Ollie rubs his hand across his chin searching out the various patches of stubble which seem as reluctant as ever to join up. What if he does what his dad had envisaged and goes back to the night Baynton disappeared. He knows enough about his movements to be able to pinpoint his entry time. All he'll need to do is follow Baynton and get close enough to read his thoughts without arousing his suspicion. He'll then know for sure what happened to him that night and why. And even if Baynton spots him, he'll assume he's some harmless kid.

Fired up for action, Ollie jumps to his feet. The park's toilet block would be ideal if it wasn't bristling with surveillance cameras. With the sun hot on his back, he recalls the gardener's composting area hidden behind a group of cedars.

The stench of fermentation hits his nostrils as he walks past the "No Public Access" sign. Underfoot, the ground is softened by layers of leaf mould with the occasional crunch when he steps on a hidden fir cone. As he'd hoped, the area is abandoned and screened from onlookers in every direction. He's all set.

His eyes take a moment to adjust to the low light. A series of shivers run through his body – not solely the result of the abrupt temperature change. After pausing to take in this new night-time reality, he strolls to the end of the alley whistling a nothing-to-see-here tune. (He stops once he realises it's the chorus of Zor Savage's "Drowning Man".)

Rounding the next corner, London is laid out before him – the city the Romans designated as their capital now grown out of all reasonable proportion. For the first time he senses the collective consciousness of so many lives; the myriad concerns occupying the city's population. The cacophony of voices in his head overwhelms him.

Shaken, Ollie shuts his eyes and focuses on the solid pavement beneath his feet, the wind tugging at his hair. He comes back into himself, unsure of what just happened. He puts it down to a delayed reaction to the change of time zone.

With no time for further reflection, Ollie strikes out along the pavement. The river is now in sight. Following it along, the paved area begins to funnel into the narrower Thames Path.

It's high tide. Ollie leans against the barrier to study the current running left to right, carrying the stench of brine and decomposition downstream; swift and silent except for the slap-slapping of the bow waves running ashore from the lit-up craft negotiating their passage upstream. At night the drab-by-day capital is transformed – glamourised by the thousands of lights patterning the dark waters of the river. A magnificent view to share on socials like the group of people ahead of him are doing.

He hangs well back as if taking in the sights. The metal barrier's cold touch seeps into his skin. The river is mesmerising for its sheer might – the unstoppable, primal force of water that can't be held back.

Baynton is about to appear on his left and then pass him by. If he's timed this right, he'll have the perfect opportunity to trespass on the man's thoughts.

In a disorderly fashion, the tourists up ahead abandon the path and turn into one of the side streets. Ollie is briefly alone before he hears approaching footsteps – a tread that's hurried and purposeful. There's a slight disturbance, an almost imperceptible ripple in the air as Baynton overtakes him without a second glance. Hands in his pockets, the man's topcoat is flying open, his confident stride almost a swagger.

A boat chugs past them – a river taxi slowing to deposit its passengers at the next stop upstream. Following its progress, Baynton checks out the people lining up ready to disembark. Apparently satisfied, he scans his immediate surroundings for cameras, is careful not to look at the one that's trained on the very spot where he's standing.

Ollie daren't get any closer. Fortunately, having come to a halt, Baynton is now resting his elbows on the metal guardrail, his scarf and coattails rising around him as if he might be about to take off. He watches the boats going about their business, then, satisfied none of them poses a threat, he drops his gaze to the restless waters below him.

With the smack of the boat's wake masking his footsteps, Ollie moves as close as he dares to that cam, close enough to know Baynton's mind is racing – assessing, then reassessing his predicament. He's thinking back on his evening, on the way Yardley kept insisting on another round. (He'd jettisoned his last drink into someone else's abandoned glass.) They spent the evening literally patting each other on the back. And he'd gone along with it all – played along more like, celebrating that bonus he's just received as if it wasn't a mere drop in the ocean to him these days.

David is alert, wary to the point of paranoia. He's reminding himself of the wealth he's amassed – enough to do just about anything that might take his fancy. If it wasn't for the curve of the river, his penthouse apartment would be visible from where he's standing. He pictures the view from his roof terrace, how it allows him to survey the city; a captain at his helm, the master of some great ship about to launch itself beyond the confines of the Thames into open water.

Baynton asks himself what he would do if he could go back to that wedding, to the moment when those two men approached him. With hindsight, would he walk away? Too late, he's thinking that none of it has come close to filling the hollowness he feels when he's alone. He looks down at his outrageously expensive shoes, the damp walkway stretching beyond him with no clear end in sight. He made his choice. He could have left his cousin's wedding a free and honest man. Instead he'd allowed those two nonentities to lure him into a scheme that promised to make all their fortunes. A better brain had already worked it all out, he only had to follow their instructions.

David shakes his head. He remembers the initial high at outwitting the system – sticking one to those ever-vigilant bots. Intoxicated by success at first, later he wasn't content to remain their facilitator. He turned the tables to prove to himself he was more than a minor linchpin in their scheming. They'd overlooked the fact that he's a fast learner, more than capable of thinking not just for himself but *of* himself. Once he understood how it all worked, he was able to cover his tracks without them knowing. And he pulled it off – they had no fucking idea what he was up to.

Who would have thought his nemesis would arrive in that small, anonymous package left for him at the concierge's desk. The flash drive that told him someone was shadowing his every move, knew all there was to know about what he was doing. The threat couldn't have been made more explicit.

What now? David's restless eyes spot an island of jetsam caught by the current. Against the moving background, a cormorant is silhouetted on top of it, seemingly unconcerned that the whole thing could break up at any moment. Not that it matters when your wings can launch you into the air and away. He snorts his bitter amusement. Comes to something that he's envying a sodding bird.

David may not know the identity of his partners in crime, but he's one hundred percent certain they won't be willing to bid him a fond farewell. Not while he's still living and breathing and knows far too much.

David walks on. Out of the cam's range, his scarf takes to the air and, though he makes a grab for it, the wind whips it away from his grasp. A gift from his mother now lost to the elements. He tries not to think about her as he keeps pace with the cormorant riding on an island of crap that's inexorably heading toward the estuary and from there the open sea.

How long before that bird bails? A plan is forming in Baynton's mind. Like the cormorant perched on its doomed raft, his own position is no longer tenable. He's a dead man walking. Nothing short of death can set him free.

Chapter Thirty-Two

Tom

The newcomer to the diner – wet t-shirt guy – sits down on one of the stools further along the counter. He orders in a voice so low Tom's surprised Kirsty understood that he wanted the coffee she pours him from the glass flask. The chalkboard behind her lists the variety of pies (unpriced) available but there's no coffee menu. The cliental in this place must like it plain and simple.

Tom sips his water while he looks for more signs that he's either in a modern-day, fifties-themed eatery or he's rocked up in the wrong era on the other side of the Atlantic – possibly, but not definitely, in Massachusetts of all places. He still can't see through the damn windows. If the rain would let up for a second, he might have a better idea.

A bluesy piano riff cuts through the general chatter – the unmistakable intro to that classic track – Blueberry Hill. While Fats Domino is finding his thrill, Kirsty does a little shimmy to the beat after serving Check-shirt guy. In his left ear he hears wet-t-shirt guy whistling along with Fats.

The source of the music is a glowing jukebox at the far end of the room. Squinting, Tom is able to make out its convex glass front and what must be a list of available records. Contrasting blue and red buttons allow customers to make their selections though he hasn't seen anyone doing so. If the jukebox is the real deal in working order, it must be worth thousands. If it's a modern fake – another prop – it's a damn good one.

Kirsty leans in to speak to him. (He does his best not to stare into her impressive cleavage.) With a slight backwards nod, she says, 'Gentleman over there was wondering if you might care to join him.'

'Really?' For the first time Tom notices his fellow customers are exclusively male. 'I'm flattered and, you know, cool about it and all, but, you know, I think I'll pass on his offer. I'm just not into other blokes.'

Giggling, she bats the air like he's made a great joke. 'I love the way you Brits say *blokes*. What's that other one? *Chaps* – that's it.' In an attempt at a British accent, she says, 'I met a *chap* down the pub...'

Less sure he's read the situation correctly, he puts a hand on her arm to stop her in her tracks. 'Out of interest, which particular gentleman wants me to join him?'

Her face sobers. 'Overdressed fella about halfway down. They reckon it'll hit 93 in the shade this afternoon and he's wearing a suit and vest.' By vest she means a waistcoat.

Shit!

A glance towards the exit tells him the rain has eased off. The steamed-up windows have cleared enough to allow glimpses of the cars splashing through puddles. He spots tailfins, loads of shiny chrome, bodywork mostly in pastel shades. It's unlikely to the point of improbable that this is some sort of massive fifties themed convention.

If this is the reckoning, there might still be time to escape. Tom pauses. He'd had a clear enough image in his mind of where he was heading, so how could he have made such a gigantic blunder?

Answer is – he didn't. Someone else is responsible for him being here. Someone who would wear a suit and waistcoat regardless of the heat. The person who's waiting for him a few tables down.

Submitting to his fate, Tom gets to his feet and strolls along the row of cherry leather benches until he's standing in front of him. 'Do take a seat, Mr Brookes,' Ford says, gesturing to the opposite bench. As always, a command disguised as an invitation. Tom notices his grey fedora lying on the table beside his untouched coffee.

Sliding in to face him, he's again struck by the man's resemblance to Liam Neeson back in his "Taken" era; so much so that he half expects him to begin reciting his particular skill set.

Deciding not to mince his words, he says, 'You diverted me.'

'Correct.' The bastard doesn't attempt to deny it.

'Why was that?'

Ford's smile is a learnt reflex totally lacking in humour. 'Please – we both know the answer to that question.'

'You wanted to stop me going to the place I was heading for.'

'Very good.' He snorts. 'The problem we keep coming up against, Mr Brookes, is that you have an annoying habit of blundering into situations without proper consideration of the possible consequences.' He repositions his cup in a way that suggests having the handle on his right is more aesthetically pleasing to him. 'You must understand, the intervention you had in mind would, first and foremost, have compromised the safety of others. In fact, your previous meddling has already resulted in what is rather vulgarly referred to as a bootstrap paradox. There's–'

He breaks off having sensed Kirsty's approach. 'Can I get you gentlemen anything else?' She takes a pad from her apron pocket and stands with her pencil poised. This is not an unreasonable request since an untouched cup of coffee and a complimentary glass of water aren't going to help pay her wages.

Tom is tempted to order a slice of pie just to piss Ford off, though he remembers he has no means of paying for it himself. 'I think we're both good for now,' he tells her with a wide smile.

'Okay, then I'll leave you two gentlemen to it.' She walks away – those frilly white ankle socks a weird sight on a grown woman.

Once she's out of earshot, Tom leans in. 'I really don't see what bootstraps have to do with any of this.'

'Feigning ignorance is an unattractive trait. However, for the sake of argument I will simplify the concept. You're familiar with the idiomatic expression "To pull yourself up by your own bootstraps".'

'Yeah – I mean it's a little archaic, but I understand it means people who have risen from poverty by their own hard work.'

'Now let us examine the metaphor itself and the apparent conundrum it contains. The generally accepted laws of causality should make it impossible for an individual to pull themselves clear of the mire they are stuck in by their own bootlaces. Would you agree?'

Tom chuckles at the man's pedantry. 'Yeah well, you still get the gist…'

Ford can't quite disguise his irritation. 'You appear to be deliberately missing my point, Mr Brookes. I am attempting to illustrate the problematic nature of what you and the average layman regard as the rules of causality. You see, I brought you here for this little chat to illustrate something you must already understand – id est, that what is variously termed the past, the present and the future are mere constructs since they are able to coexist at the same time. Thus questions regarding the origin of an object can be seen as an irrelevance.'

Tom throws up his hands. 'Genuinely, you've now lost me completely. I have absolutely no idea what you're on about.'

'I am, in fact, referring to that flash drive or memory stick – call it what you will.'

It takes him a moment to catch up. 'What flash drive?'

'Please spare me the tedium of your denial. As you know perfectly well, I'm referring to the object you found hidden in David Baynton's apartment.'

When Tom fails to contradict him, Ford continues. 'You took the object home and left it on your desk. Frustrated by your futile attempts to decode its contents, you injudiciously decided to return to Mr Baynton's apartment for a second time.'

Ford's ever-vigilant eyes range across their fellow diners. 'In error, you arrive before the man has moved out of his apartment and, thus, Mr Baynton is still in residence and, understandably, not too pleased to detect a possible intruder.'

He gives Tom an I-dare-you-to-contradict-me look. 'Realising you are in imminent danger of discovery and worse, and in order to create a distraction that will allow you to escape, your son Oliver takes said flash drive from your desk, wraps it up and leaves it at the front desk of Baynton's apartment block, asking the concierge to alert Baynton to the arrival of this urgent package. His intervention then gives you the opportunity to escape. As a consequence of your son's actions, the flash drive then passes into Mr Baynton's possession. Being already familiar with encryption methods, once he is able to decipher the contents – an impressive feat I think we can agree – Mr Baynton concludes he is in grave danger. Ultimately this will lead him to stage his own disappearance. However, before he makes this life-changing decision, on impulse and possibly as a clue should his envisaged escape scheme fail, he hides the flash drive in his apartment's underfloor storage space – the very place in which you subsequently discover it. And so we neatly close the loop of our aforesaid bootstrap paradox.'

Ford sits back looking rather pleased with himself. Tom stares at the man's cooling coffee while trying to unscramble his brain. 'Be my guest,' Ford says.

'Excuse me?'

'The coffee – you are welcome to consume it since, as you've guessed, I am not planning to do so.'

209

'Thanks.' Nonplussed, Tom gulps it down hoping the caffeine will help to sharpen his dulled wits. He says, 'Believe me, I had no idea about all this. When the concierge interrupted Baynton, I thought… Well, I just you know…'

'Unfortunately, I am all too aware of the nature, and indeed frequency, of your erroneous conclusions.'

Put in his place, Tom stares into the empty cup. 'When I was a kid there was this silly joke doing the rounds…' Ford couldn't look less interested. 'Anyway, the joke goes: what do you call a bus that goes from Bristol to London via Newcastle?' He waits. 'This is where you're meant to say, "I don't know, what do you call a bus that goes from Bristol to London via Newcastle?".'

Ford gives a weary sigh. 'Why don't we take that as read.'

'Yes well, anyway, the answer is – drumroll…' He taps the side of the table. 'A blunderbuss. Get it?'

Stern faced, Ford says, 'I assume you're referring to the type of short-barrelled musket use until the mid-eighteenth century.'

'That too. It's a pun – a play on the words *blunder* and *bus*.' Tom clears his throat. 'Anyway, the word is also used to describe someone who's clumsy or keeps blundering into things.' He rubs his eyes. 'That's me, isn't it? To your lot, I'm the human – or not quite human – equivalent of a bus that keeps heading off in the wrong direction.'

Ford doesn't deny it. 'I'm afraid this brings us to your latest impulse to go off to the Grenewych Heights in order to confront Mr Baynton thus, potentially, expose him to those who are convinced the man is still alive.'

'Now hang on a minute. Do you honestly believe that by showing up there I could, or would, blow his cover? I mean it's not like I was planning to catch a train or hail a cab with those two blokes staking out my house.'

Ford shrugs. 'With substantial funds at their disposal, you might be surprised at how resourceful his former associates can be.'

Tom shakes his head. 'You're serious?'

'You should know we have no intention of allowing that particular loop to be closed.' After giving him a long look, Ford reaches for his hat. 'Take my word for it, Mr Brookes, things are afoot. A sequence of events has been set in motion. Not for the first time, and for everyone's benefit, I insist you stay out of matters you *do not* understand.' The *do not* part of his warning resounds in Tom's head.

'What, so that's it, is it?' Whether justified or not, he's indignant. 'Just like that, we're all done here?'

'Indeed we are.' Reaching into an inner pocket, Ford extracts a dollar bill and slides it under the saucer of the empty cup.

'Wait!' Tom does his best to block Ford's exit. 'I'm still a bit puzzled about that flash drive business.' No response. 'Besides that, how am I supposed to get home?'

'That won't be problematic this time.'

'Oh right – well I suppose that's, you know, good to know. All the same, I still don't get why you didn't intervene before now.' When he doesn't answer, Tom demands, 'So – why didn't you?'

Ford seems more concerned with positioning the brim of

211

his hat to his precise satisfaction. A gesture that reminds him of Matt – well, the Matt of the past. When Tom goes to touch the man's sleeve, his hand ends up hovering a half centimetre from its target. He withdraws it. 'So the whole Baynton thing – was that just a way of teaching me a lesson?'

'You may find this hard to believe, Mr Brookes…' Ford's approximation of a grin drops like a stone. 'Our primary focus has never been on you.'

'What the hell does that mean?' Tom demands. 'What is it you're not telling me?'

Somehow Ford has gotten past him and is striding along the aisle towards the exit. Tom tries to catch up with him. A broad couple are standing by the entrance effectively barring the Guardian's way.

He's about to take advantage of this when the space Ford had occupied becomes air. There are no gasps from startled onlookers; no one appears to have noticed his instantaneous disappearance. People carry on as if nothing has happened.

Chapter Thirty-Three

'Dad!' Tom stares at the photograph on the wall. 'Earth to Dad!' There were four of them once upon a time. 'You look really terrible, are you alright?' Someone else asked him that recently. Not Beth. No. He grips the edge of the breakfast bar. It's unyielding, cold to the touch. 'Dad, are you stoned or something?'

He chuckles. That's it – stone. Granite. Grey like a headstone. Rest in Peace – that's the real joke. Or riddle. What's not alive but isn't dead? It should be who's. She's a person, after all. Or was.

'Dad, you need to sit down before you fall. There's a stool right here, almost under your bum.' A scraping sound. Gripping his arm. 'Careful.' He's sitting now. 'Okay, that's better.' Freckles across her nose the same. A different constellation. 'You're not having some sort of stroke, are you?'

Tom sniggers. 'You sound just like her. Kirsty.' The world is morphing into solid, identifiable objects. 'Ha – this isn't a diner. Good tune that Be Bop A Lula…' The floor's not black and white either but wooden. He might have laid it himself.

'Dad, listen to me, you're in the kitchen, okay? *Our* kitchen.

You know, at home where your family lives. Does 15 Park Close ring any bells? Bigger picture – we're in Cheltenham. Which is in England and, sort of, in Europe. On planet Earth – at least some of us are.' She comes into focus. Vega – of course it is. How could he forget?

'Your skin's gone a sort of living-dead grey,' she says. 'Maybe sitting you on a stool wasn't such a good idea.'

He shakes his head. Now *that* was a bad Idea. When things stop spinning, he says, 'I'm fine, um, Vega. For a second…'

'Let me look in your eyes.' She swoops like an owl. 'Have you been on the shrooms or something? Is this what you get up to when you haven't got much work on?'

'Ah, but there'll always be magic kingdoms.'

'What's wrong with you?'

Good question. 'If you must know…' He exhales. 'I've just got back from the States. Fairly sure it was some place in Massachusetts.'

'You're talking crap. You were right here this morning when we left for school, remember? Besides the idea being ridiculous, there's no way you could get over to America and back unless…'

Her eyes grow hard. 'Unless you didn't go by plane. Please don't tell me you nipped over there on a whim. Christ Dad, you've already pissed off those-who-shall-not-be-named. They'll be way madder if you zipped over to the States and back for the hell of it.'

'I'm not a prisoner on remand. There's such a thing as free will.'

'Ha! You realise you're preaching to the converted? Or, in

214

your case, the soon to be convicted. I doubt the Guardians operate an assumption of innocence principle.'

'Talking of Guardians – our friend Ford was the one who sent me there in the first place.'

'Sent you where?'

'Over to the States, like I said.'

She throws up her hands. 'Why would he do that? Are you seriously trying to tell me that he thought you needed a mini-break or something? All of us are banned from doing anything that frivolous. God forbid we might use our abilities to have fun.' She grabs his chin so he can't avoid her accusing eyes. 'Why would Ford do something like that?'

'It's complicated...'

'Yeah, most things are in this family.' She averts her gaze. He might not be telepathic, but he sensed something just then – something she's wishing he hadn't.

He says. 'Perhaps I'm not the only one who's ventured off piste.' That hit a chord alright and not the harmonious kind. 'You know that family discussion we mentioned before,' he says. 'I think it might be long overdue.'

He slides off the stool then, gripping the edges of the furniture like an old man, works his way over to the door. No comebacks from her this time. Leaning against the door jamb, he says, 'I believe my circadian rhythms are a little out of sync. I'm going to take a nap. Wake me when your brother gets back. Time this family was more open and honest with each other.'

Behind him, she mutters something he doesn't quite catch.

Ollie shakes him awake. Smirking, he says, 'I hear you've been on quite a trip – of one sort or another.'

Tom sits up to find he's still fully dressed except for his shoes – no wonder he's so hot. His mind is sharper for the rest. 'Yeah well, it's no laughing matter. One minute I was heading for present day central London, the next I arrived in 1950s America.'

'And you weren't tempted to stick around there for a bit? That was quite an amazing era. I fancy cruising around in those spaceship cars, listening to really great music, wearing sick clothes, the post war economic recovery in full swing…'

'Under the circumstances, sightseeing was hardly an appropriate response. Besides, a great soundtrack can't outweigh stuff like The Red Scare and McCarthyism, nuclear fallout shelters, regular drills in segregated schools…'

Ollie shrugs. 'Every era has its pluses and negatives. Like I was saying to Vega, the eighties might seem alluring in some ways, but there's always a downside.' He blushes. A dead giveaway. He's far too quick to add, 'Same as any other era you care to name.'

'We definitely need that talk,' Tom says getting up. After a few stretches, he rakes his hair into place and then makes his way downstairs. He can hear Ollie's tread behind him.

Vega is at the kitchen table, her hands cupping a mug as if it's winter. 'There's tea in the pot,' she says, not looking up.

Tom pours himself a mug. The tea is treacle coloured and tepid, all the same he sips it as he sits down. Ollie hesitates in the doorway, no doubt communicating to his sister that he might have spilt a few beans. There is no food on the table but he's not about to cater the event. Once Ollie's taken his usual seat, Tom spreads both hands on the tabletop in front of him. He takes a deep breath while deciding to start with the more straightforward items on the agenda.

'I've been running my recovery business for some years now and, before you say it, I'm sure you think it's a ridiculous occupation. However, since all adolescents are pre-programmed to find their parents embarrassing, I've always assumed it wouldn't do any harm if you disapprove of, or even sneer at, what I do for a living.'

'We would never sneer,' Vega says, a look of something close to condescension on her face.

Ollie squares his shoulders. 'Though, t. b. h. Dad, I guess we might prefer it if you had a regular sort of job like other people's parents.'

'What – in this town?' Tom chuckles. 'So, let's get this straight, you're referring to an occupation such as working for the government's main intelligence gathering agency? Seriously – that's your idea of a more socially acceptable job?'

'It wasn't so bad until they remade the film,' Ollie says. 'Now they make all these stupid Ace Ventura jokes...'

'By *they*, I assume you mean your fellow pupils?'

The two of them nod in unison. 'They call you a pet dic,' Vega adds. 'Which is meant to be a pun–'

'Yeah okay, I get it.' He studies their faces. 'And that genuinely bothers you?'

'You must remember how school works,' Ollie says. 'Kids look for weak spots and then keep jabbing away at them hoping to get a reaction.'

'And you react?'

'No, course not,' Ollie says. 'That would play right into their hands.'

'Okay so, having established I'm a source of embarrassment to you both, let's move on. My understanding is that, until recently, neither of you has felt the need to intervene in any of my cases. You've let me get on with what I do. Is that correct?'

More nodding. 'Okay so, while I appreciate you were only trying to help, Ollie, what possessed you to snaffle that flash drive from my desk and deliver it to Baynton's apartment?'

'I was only trying to save you from a beating, Dad.' He holds up his hands. 'And you have to admit it worked.'

Tom leans in. 'Maybe I actually deserved that beating? Perhaps getting beaten up would have taught me to stop poking my nose into things I shouldn't. Could that be a lesson we all need to learn in this family?'

'But hang on, you're my dad. There's no way I was going to stand back and let him beat you to a pulp.' Like he's laying down an ace, Ollie says, 'What would you have done if our positions were reversed?'

'That's totally different.' Tom jabs a finger at him. 'My job as a father is to protect you both. The principle doesn't hold the other way around.'

Vega clears her throat. 'Um, excuse me interrupting this machismo posturing, but shouldn't we be discussing the two men currently out there watching our house?'

He's taken aback. 'You know about that?'

'What – seriously? You thought we wouldn't have noticed?' She snorts. Leaning back from the table, she crosses her outstretched legs. He notices the heavy boots she shouldn't be wearing inside but lets it go.

She says, 'Since we're all showing our hands here, you might as well know that Ollie and me – possibly Grandad for all I know – are up to speed on the whole Baynton thing. We know he was frightened for his life before he disappeared, but he can't identify his "business partners".' After giving those words air quotes, she jerks a thumb towards the window. 'Oll discovered that those two out there have no idea who they're working for.'

'They must operate in a classic, cell structure,' Ollie says. 'It works even better now with modern tech. An individual's knowledge of any others involved is very limited so, if someone gets caught, they can't rat on the rest whatever pressure is applied.'

Vega says, 'They seem certain Baynton is alive. As yet, they haven't guessed he's holed up in a swanky penthouse apartment like a prince in a tower waiting for some knight to gallop up and rescue him.'

'Though I like your modern twist,' Tom says. 'Remember, none of us three are knights. It's not my job, and it certainly isn't yours, to rescue someone from the consequences of their own greed.'

'A high end prison is still a prison,' Ollie says. 'In the end, a person can only take so much isolation. Odds are, Baynton will make a break for it sooner or later.'

Tom rubs at the stubble on his chin. 'Well, from what I understand, he's unlikely to get very far. The people looking for him are what you might call highly resourceful.' He sighs. 'Still, his fate is no longer a matter for our concern. As you probably know already, I've been warned off in the strongest terms.' He opens his hands. 'Que sera, sera, as Doris Day put it earlier today. Whatever will be, will be without our involvement.'

He's interrupted by a loud buzzing. Someone is at the door. The next buzz is longer, more insistent. Whoever they are, they're not about to give up.

Chapter Thirty-Four

Ollie

After peering into the door cam, Dad says, 'Seems you have a visitor, Oliver.' Ignoring his sister's piqued interest along with his dad's smirk, Ollie hurries to the front door.

Opening up, Cerys, of all people, is standing there. He checks behind to make sure she's alone. She is. No sign of the two men, though he's sure they're watching. 'Hi,' he says. Then, as if it's no big deal, 'Come in.'

Instead, she takes a step backwards. 'You weren't in class today, so I thought you might be ill. Have to say, you look okay.'

'I'm absolutely fine.' He waves his hands and swivels his head to demonstrate they're in full working order. 'There was just a bit of a family situation earlier on today.' (Not a lie after all.) His shrug suggests it was of no consequence. 'Everything's, um, been fully resolved.'

'Oh right. Well, I don't want to intrude…' She's blushing in a really cute way. 'I'm glad whatever it is has been sorted,' she says. 'Maybe I'll see you tomorrow morning. In the library – at the usual time?'

She's about to walk away. 'Wait!' He dials it down, gives a casual nod towards her school backpack. 'Since I missed today's maths assignment, maybe we could take a look at it together now.'

Her brown eyes are uncertain. All the same she's wavering. 'I really don't want to intrude if this is an awkward time…'

'You wouldn't be.'

'It sounds like your family–'

'They're fine, honestly.' She's dithering, still unsure. 'Everything's totally tickety-boo,' he says. 'One hundred percent hunky dory. Definitely dope. Never better, in fact.'

He takes a breath. 'So, it's not like you'd be interrupting some high domestic drama or anything like that.' Ollie clears his throat as if to absolve the lie, opens the door as wide as it will go then stands aside.

'Well, if you're certain they won't mind.'

Yes! She's over the threshold. 'We've been given this stupid chessboard puzzle we're supposed to solve,' she tells him. 'It's meant to be about trying to escape from a prison.'

Musing on this coincidence, he closes the door behind her. In the confined space, the two of them are the closest they've ever been – physically at least. It's the end of the school day and she nonetheless smells of garden lilies. (Not those overgrown, pongy ones with the pollen that stains your hands.)

He needs to clear his head. Maths – concentrate on the maths they've been set. 'Doesn't sound like the classic Prisoners' Dilemma scenario so I'm guessing it's that puzzle where 64 coins are laid out on a chessboard in a random pattern of heads or tails.' He's on more solid ground now.

'Yeah – that's the one. Mr Godwin called it the Impossible Chessboard Puzzle – I mean the clue is in the name, right? We're supposed to work in pairs, so I thought of you.'

'I'm glad you did.'

'To make it sound *fun*, we're meant to imagine we're one of two prisoners stuck in jail and there's a secret key hidden by some maths-geek of a warden under one of the coins on the board.' She pulls a pained expression. 'The nut-job warden promises to set both of you free if you can figure out which coin the key is under. Oh, and I almost forgot – one of the prisoners knows where the warden put the key but can't tell the other. All he can do is flip just one coin. And that flip is supposed to help his mate guess the location.'

'It so happens…' He ushers her towards the stairs. 'I've got a chessboard up in my room.' Not the most enticing of lines. All the same he leads the way. Once he's checked that she's following, he says, 'If you think about the coins being either heads or tails, it's pretty easy to equate that to binary numbers – heads being one, tails being zero.' Ollie snorts. 'Though there's nothing to stop it being the other way around.'

She giggles. 'If you say so.'

They've reached the landing. 'I've got some old coins we can lay out on the board to help us visualise the problem.' He opens the door. 'Here we are.' With a mock courtier's bow, he says, 'Après vous.'

She walks inside. 'Shouldn't that be après *toi* – after all we're not strangers. And we're roughly the same age.' He's not about to correct her. Looking around she says, 'Wow – did your dad just make you clean up or something?'

Reading her expression, he says, 'Yeah,' like he's feeling resentful. 'Although it was quite a mess…'

She sniffs. 'Your room even smells good. I was expecting eau de old socks.' How many other boys' rooms has she been in? Does it matter? After all they could have been some friend's brother, or her cousin, or some other relative too close to contemplate ever having sex with. If he could read her mind, this would be so much easier.

She dumps her backpack on the floor with a thud they must have heard downstairs.

The chessboard is on his desk and set up with the game he's been playing remotely with Grandad. Though his mind is crowded, he tries to memorise their current positions before dumping the pieces in a heap on the bed.

He puts the board back on his desk, pulls out a chair and taps the seat for her to sit. (Christ, she's not a dog.) 'Please, take a seat,' he says. (Too formal. *Have a seat* would have done.)

Trying not to ogle her tanned legs, he reaches into the third drawer down where he keeps the bag of coins – mostly old pre-decimal pennies. He begins the process of placing one on each square in a random distribution of heads and tails. Randomness is a hard thing to achieve – he has to concentrate on not creating a pattern.

'Wow, where did you get these?' Cerys picks one up. '1862. And there's old Cruel Britannia sitting on a rock in her helmet and three pronged thingy, ready to re-conquer the world without a second thought.' Flipping the coin over, she tilts her head in judgement. 'Though I do like her hairstyle.' She lifts her own hair up at the back. 'What d'you think?'

Unable to think of an appropriate reply, he ignores the question. 'Victoria was young then,' he says. 'Those are called *bun pennies* because of that hairstyle.' He selects another. 'They call these *old head* for obvious reasons. This one's from 1885. It has Ind Imp – meaning Empress of India – on it. Apparently, they did that because the coins were also circulating in what was then the British colonies. She's in a widow's veil because her beloved Albert had died of typhoid in 1861.'

'Such a sad story,' Cerys says. 'She looks pretty miserable doesn't she? I read somewhere that after he died she wore black for the rest of her life.' Staring at the coin, she sighs, then says, 'Although black can be quite flattering.'

There's a sharp knock on the door. It opens. 'Oh, hi Cerys,' Dad says as if surprised to see her.

She gives him a wave. 'Hi, Mr Brookes.'

Dad's relief at finding them fully clothed couldn't be more obvious. 'We're just working on the Impossible Chessboard Puzzle,' Ollie says, pre-empting him.

'Ah yes, that old hidden key malarky.' Looking at Cerys, Dad says, 'It might seem like a waste of time, but this particular puzzle is quite useful in understanding how error correction codes operate.'

'Good to know,' she says. Her smile doesn't last.

Eyeing up the chessboard, Dad ventures further into the room. 'Would you like me to play the part of the warden?'

'No, we're actually fine as we are.' Ollie gives him a look even he ought to be able to read. 'We've only just started on the rules of the game.'

'Okay.' Taking the hint, Dad retreats. 'Well then, have fun

trying to solve it. Mindboggling stuff eh?' At the door, he says, 'Everything hinges on that one coin flip.'

'Dad, honestly I've totally got this.' If Dad could read his thoughts it would boil down to two words – *piss* and *off*.

'Right, well then I'll leave you to it.' His hand still holding the doorknob, Dad says, 'Oh, and would you mind keeping this open while you're in here alone. It's just, well, I'm sure you understand…'

They understand alright. The implication makes them both blush – in Ollie's case his embarrassment is mixed with anger so strong it robs him of speech. He hears his dad's footsteps retreating down the stairs. Hands shaking, his cheeks ablaze, Ollie carries on with the task of laying those damned coins in a random pattern on the chessboard.

'Think I'll just message Mum about picking me up,' Cerys says.

Chapter Thirty-Five

Tom

Back in the kitchen, Tom is less certain he did the right thing imposing that open-door rule. Then again, Ollie is only fifteen. At his age, his hormones rampaging, if he'd had an opportunity to be alone in his bedroom with a pretty girl and the door shut…

No, he was right about keeping it open. And, besides, he's in loco parentis here. Gwen would expect him to act responsibly. After all, if Vega was in some adolescent boy's bedroom… He shudders. Then again, Cerys is eighteen not thirteen.

Pacing, he rubs his forehead while imagining all the years still to come, all the judgement calls still to be made. Beth would have been so much better at this. Perhaps he should get some professional advice. Or join a local parents-of-teens group, if such a group exists. Kids should come with a downloadable handbook – and a really long one at that.

Looking up from her homework – "The Context of Dickinson's Poetry" – Vega is studying him in a critical manner.

She says, 'I think the relevant section of the manual would be called "Learning to Let Go".'

'Will you stop reading my thoughts, damn it.'

'No can do, I'm afraid.' She taps her temple. 'No off switch here. And believe me there are *so* many times I wish there was. It must be way easier and much less distracting being normal.' She laughs. 'Or relatively so, in your case.'

'Point taken.' He's chastened. 'I guess that was insensitive of me. And, by the way, I very much doubt there's such a thing as *a normal person*. You and Ollie, and me to a lesser extent, we're just a bit different.'

'A *bit*? That's quite an understatement even for you, Dad. Face it – we're total freaks.'

'That's a very unpleasant thing to say about us. Especially about yourself.' He's appalled she thinks like this. 'And entirely inappropriate,' he tells her. 'Look at you – you're amazing! What's wrong with being extraordinary? Since you can read my mind, you must know I couldn't be prouder of both my children.'

'Sorry to break it to you, Dad, but one day soon we'll be out in that big wide world where your opinion won't be the only one that matters.' The truth of it hits him. She's right – his time with them is finite. And these last few years have whizzed by.

Vega turns her attention back to her homework. He notices she hasn't made much progress with the Dickinson question. Hasn't even mentioned the civil war yet. She's keeping her head down, but he suspects she's not really concentrating.

She's seemed preoccupied quite often of late. Earlier, Ollie was embarrassed when he let slip something about him and

Vega discussing the pros and cons of the 1980s. Why would they?

Vega's head jerks up. 'You know, as a detached observer, Dad, there are times when your mind gets into a bit of a cat's cradle.' Before he can respond, she says, 'You might want to consider therapy. Could be time for a bit of mental house-keeping.' She's being provocative, winding him up and hoping he'll rise to the bait.

Swallowing his irritation, Tom says, 'Just remember this – while you're still young and living under my roof, I expect you to stick to my rules.'

How many times had his mum said the same thing to him? Echoing your parents – is that what everyone inevitably falls back on? His dad, uncle Matt as he'd known him then, tended to flit in and out of their lives before disappearing for years. Not an exemplary role model by any standards.

Time to change tack. 'So you're studying Dickinson,' he says peering at her screen. 'She was writing while the American Civil War was in full swing.'

Vega rolls her eyes. 'No kidding. So d'you think maybe I ought to mention that?'

'No need for sarcasm. I just noticed you seem to be a bit stuck, that's all.'

'I'm a bit stuck because you're standing right there doing all that *thinking*.'

'What – you expect me to actually stop thinking while I'm in the same room as you?'

'No, but you could stick to the stuff I can easily block out.'
'Like what?'

'Like what you're planning to do next to that ridiculous duck house you're making. Or the maths involved in that stupid Impossible Chessboard Puzzle Ollie's failing to explain to Cerys. Or what Walt Whitman and Emily Dickinson would have talked about if they'd ever met up. Oh, and then there's what you might have got up to at Ollie's age. And how Cerys looks quite like her mum. And by the way, that girl is only interested in Ollie because she's desperate to boost her maths grade.'

Shit – he's always known they could read his thoughts but not every single sodding thing. He's an open book – a movie version of his inner life they can never pause. Christ, it's a wonder his kids even speak to him.

Before he can work out how to respond (machinations she'll be fully aware of) the front door buzzer goes. 'That'll be Cerys's mum,' Vega says.

'What – you can see through walls now?'

'No, Dad. I recognised her when she walked past the window a few seconds ago.'

'Hiya,' Gwen says, when he opens the door. This time she's wearing shorts and a t-shirt bearing the ironic slogan: *Your Design Here.* Does she wear it on conference calls? 'I've come to pick up Cerys,' she declares.

'Come in,' he says. 'They're upstairs trying to solve a maths puzzle together.'

Seeing his face, her smile drops. 'Is this a bad time?'

'More like a bad lifetime.'

'That dire, eh?' She touches his arm, leaves it there a

moment before letting it drop. 'Don't I know that feeling.' Her smile is friendly, uncomplicated. A relief. She says, 'You know I reckon it must be wine o'clock.' When she glances behind her, he wonders if she's just spotted the surveillance team. Instead, she says, 'I reckon the sun is over the yardarm – or at least it must be somewhere in the world.'

'Sounds like a great idea.' He beckons her inside, then checks for the two men but there's no sign of them. Do they keep office hours?

'You know,' he says, closing the door, 'everyone assumes that expression about the yardarm refers to some vague time in the early evening.' He ushers her away from the kitchen into the sitting room, which is relatively tidy – well, by his standards. 'Actually, it refers to an old naval practice.'

Her laugh is unrestrained. 'A *navel* practise.' She pulls a face. 'Sounds a bit on the kinky side to me.'

He grins. 'A *navy custom*. No body parts involved. At least let's assume not. So anyway, where was I? Ah yes, apparently, when the sun had risen enough to appear over the upper spars on the main mast, which was usually around eleven o'clock in the morning, they'd call out, "Up spirits!" and have their first tot of rum of the day. A quick livener to keep them all going.'

'Is that right?' Her interest seems genuine enough. 'Bit of a rum do if you ask me,' she says, her eyes alight. 'No wonder so many ships got lost at sea in those days.'

His smile acknowledges her dreadful pun. 'So you see – following an established tradition, it's perfectly proper to partake of alcoholic refreshment any time after eleven in the morning.' He checks the time. 'Five thirty is, in fact, rather restrained on our part.'

'In that case I'll have a guilt-free glass of red if you've got it. Frankly, any colour is fine after the day I've just had.'

'Oh?'

She holds up a hand. 'Don't ask.'

He straightens the throw that's hiding a worn patch on the sofa and knocks a few cushions back into shape. 'If madam would care to take a seat, I'll be back in a sec.'

In the kitchen Vega watches him open a new bottle and take a couple of wine glasses out of the cupboard. Aware of his hunger, he finds a bag of Japanese rice crackers and pours them into a bowl. His daughter remains silent though her disapproval is written all over her face.

Sod it. He closes the door with his foot hoping that two doors plus the intervening space will be enough to shield his every damned thought from her.

In passing he looks up the staircase wondering if he should have shut Ollie's bedroom door after all.

Gwen is all smiles on his return. 'Tell me about *your* day,' she says.

'Let's just say it was unbelievable and leave it at that.' After a beat, he says, 'Are you sure you don't want to talk about yours?'

She bats away the suggestion. 'Hasn't been the best – at least so far.' She flicks her hair back before adjusting her position, leaning into the arm of the sofa. As she watches him pour the wine, she uncrosses her legs. Her silver sandals would look more at home on a beach.

Tom pours them both generous measures while reminding himself he could be misinterpreting her body language. Being telepathic might be a pain, but it must have its advantages.

When he hands her the glass, she doesn't sip it but holds it up ready for a toast.

He puts the rice crackers on the table and then sits down next to her. The extra weight makes the springs sag forcing them further together, their thighs touching. It's a big enough sofa but neither of them chooses to adjust their position.

Their glasses clink together. 'Up spirits!' His have definitely just risen.

Chapter Thirty-Six

Ollie

Cerys bites the side of her lip while he outlines the various strategies they might consider using to solve the puzzle. He notices how plump and soft her lips are. At first she appears to follow the various steps he suggests and his preliminary calculations, then her attention begins to wane, her eyes wandering along his shelves instead. After a while he can sense she's stopped listening.

He sits back, tries not to sound petulant when he asks, 'So – any thoughts?'

'You've officially blown my mind.' She mimes an explosion using both hands above her head. Is she referring to his summary or him? Ollie's sigh is more audible than he'd intended. She's not the only one out of her depth. How do regular people cope with so much uncertainty?

'Care to elaborate?' he asks, aiming for jaunty.

'Okay,' she says. 'Well, first off, if you think about that prison warden – even accepting this one's a maths geek – why would they set their prisoners a puzzle like that? The warden will get into serious shit if he lets two prisoners escape just because they're good at working stuff out. And those two prisoners could be... I don't know – axe murderers. Or paedophiles. Or axe-murdering paedophiles. Or a couple of terrorists about to blow up the entire world. Arrgh!' Her golden hair appears to float as she shakes her head. 'Seriously, the whole thing makes no fucking sense.'

'Okay, I accept the scenario is highly unlikely,' he says. 'But remember it's simply a premise to make the puzzle more immediate. And fun.'

'Fun?' Head on one side, she narrows her eyes at him. 'Seriously? I can think of much better ways to have fun.'

While he's pondering that last remark, she says, 'If I was banged-up I would rather try to dig a tunnel with my bare hands than attempt to get my head round all this stuff.' She snatches up the paper he's written some of his initial examples on. 'Guess what? I actually can't visualise a 64-dimensional cube – shocker eh? There might be 64 times 64 to the power of two possible strategies but I have no idea what that even means. I'd actually rather die of boredom in solitary confinement in some rat-infested cell than fill my brain with crap like this.'

He tries not to mind. 'Then another way you might want to think about it is in terms of yes or no answers–'

'You're not listening to me, Oll.' She makes a choking noise in the back of her throat. 'I don't want to think about it. Period. End of. Okay?'

'Right,' he says. 'Got it.' Crestfallen, he casts his eyes over the board in front of him, the coins he'd laid out with enthusiasm. He thought if he could help her catch up… For the first time it occurs to him that the two of them are very different. Almost diametrically opposed. Could the reason she's struggling in maths be because, for her, figuring out stuff like this is the very opposite of fascinating?

'This question might seem to be a bit insensitive,' he says, 'but if you don't mind me asking, why did you choose to carry on studying maths?'

Her shoulders droop. 'Crazy idea, huh?' Defeat lowers her voice. 'I suppose it was because of my dad. Like you, he loves all this type of shit. No offence intended.' Ollie's not so sure that's true.

Picking at the hem of her skirt, she says, 'I guess I wanted to impress him. You know, to make him sort of proud of me. Which turns out to be super dumb since I totally suck at maths.'

Her sad smile really gets to him.

'Anyway, c'est la vie.' She picks up a coin, flips it high into the air before catching it and slapping it onto the back of her hand. 'Heads or tails?'

Though he's still smarting from her implied criticism, he says, 'Heads.'

She uncovers a worn-thin George IV. 'Lucky guess.'

'Not really,' he confesses. 'I noticed the number of times it flipped over in the air.'

'Wow! You're like Invincible Ollie. Always one step ahead of the rest of us average mortals.'

'I'm just your normal, detail-obsessed, lanky nerd.'

A genuine smile at last. She says, 'You're not that lanky…'

They both chuckle. In the silence that follows he hears raised voices from downstairs. A high-pitched laugh followed by an echoing lower one. 'Ugh – that must be my mum,' Cerys says. Then after a while, 'Yep, that's her alright. Always the life and soul of the sodding party.'

Ollie lies awake, his head a maelstrom of competing thoughts. Cerys features in most of them. The two of them had listened to his dad and her mum enjoying themselves down there. Neither of them were surprised when Gwen messaged Cerys to say she was staying for another drink and there was no rush. It was mortifying to hear their parents chatting and laughing, while their own conversation was stilted and awkward.

Cerys had dawdled a finger along the shelf holding his model car collection. To salvage some credibility, he'd talked about their present value as if that was what mattered. The conversation downstairs had such an easy rhythm to it, while theirs was a struggle. If only he hadn't tried to help her with that stupid puzzle... He'd exposed a weakness she was hoping to overcome. She was embarrassed to admit she was only studying maths to please her father. He said something bland about how trying to live up to a parent's expectations is tough on anyone. Hadn't admitted that their dad just wants them to keep their heads down and blend in.

Cerys was right about the puzzle's laughable set-up. A maths-geek warden and his compliant prisoners – of course it's a ludicrous scenario.

Thoughts of prisoners send him back to thinking about David Baynton in his luxury eyrie looking out on the bustling capital. All the money a person could wish for, and he can't even venture outside.

Dad should never have got involved in the first place, wouldn't have done if he wasn't useless at turning down a damsel in distress. Though it was years ago – back when he was only a little kid – he remembers Meredith Schreiber. On the flimsiest of reasoning, instinct had led her to ask for his dad's help. Turned out her husband, Lange, had fallen through one of the Guardian's open portals. After declaring himself a time traveller from the future, Lange had ended up in the hellhole of a 1920s lunatic asylum. In spite of the many warnings he was given, Dad still felt compelled to try to rescue him.

Lange was being kept in solitary confinement in the grimmest conditions, but at least he had regular contact with the prison doctors and staff. How is complete isolation affecting Baynton? Ollie knows for a fact the 2020s Covid lockdowns caused a massive spike in mental health problems across the entire globe. When it comes down to it, humans need to interact with other humans. Right now Baynton could be deciding he'd sooner make a break for it than go quietly bonkers up there cut off from everything and everyone.

Following the same knight-in-shining-armour instincts, Dad had been on his way to Baynton's apartment when Ford intervened and sent him back to 1950s America. Granted, Dad has form when it comes to blundering into situations he doesn't understand, but there has to be more to it. Why did Ford stop him? Have the Guardians decreed Baynton should be left to his fate. Or his destiny – which is subtly different in terms of causality.

Quantum mechanics suggests traditional thinking about causality is outdated – that a causal relationship can be cyclical not linear; an effect can actually be causing the cause.

Whatever. How does "The Organisation" come to policy decisions? He pictures a sort of board meeting in the sky with individual Guardians casting their votes by raising their hands. Or choosing a black or a white ball. Or maybe floating through celestial archways labelled "yes" or "no" – a bit like they do in the division lobbies of the House of Commons.

Which brings him back to binary code. Ollie yawns and turns over, though he can't get comfortable. He can't shake his feeling of culpability. If only he hadn't sent him that damned flash drive…

He pictures Baynton stepping out of his building and walking straight into a fine tripwire. Boom! It's all over. Parts of his scorched body come to rest on that Phoenix sculpture like some gross additional embellishment. He shivers. Somebody really ought to warn him.

Chapter Thirty-Seven

Vega

She watches from the kitchen as Dad and Gwen say their goodbyes. Half scuttered, they go in for double kisses that only fractionally miss becoming a full-on snog. Several times they mention some parents' fundraiser night they might see each other at. Then there are lingering smiles accompanied by over-enthusiastic waves before they're finally done.

Urgh! She shudders at the nauseating performance.

Following her mother out, Cerys turns at the threshold and says, 'Bye, Oll,' like it's an afterthought.

'Bye,' he echoes, his voice redolent with defeat. Seems the mentoring sessions in the library are officially on hold. Possibly for good.

Oblivious to his son's misery, Dad comes into the kitchen whistling some old K-pop number. He puts their two wine glasses into the dishwasher, jettisons the empty bottle into the recycle bin and then spins around to execute a classic dad-dance end pose. (Emphasis on execute.)

Vega says, 'So, Gwen now wants you to make her a dovecot.' It sounds like a euphemism.

At least that stops him whistling. 'We discussed it.' He does his best to sound off-hand. 'But only as a possibility. Besides, I still haven't finished that duck house piece for The Honourable Artus.'

'Given our current financial situation, you might consider speeding up your output,' she says. He's shocked that she's aware of how little they have in the bank. 'Maybe you should try to avoid *unproductive distractions*,' she adds. Even Dad doesn't miss her implied disapproval of his growing "friend-ship" with Gwen.

He says, 'And maybe *you* should get on with your homework young lady and leave *me* to worry about our finances. After all, I haven't done so badly up to now. I've always managed to put food on the table.'

'Isn't that whole food-on-the-table thing a bit of a low bar?'

His buzz killed, he's now niggled. He says, 'Correct me if I'm wrong, but I'd say this is a perfectly decent house, in a perfectly decent street.' He spreads his arms as if to encompass the magical world he's created for them. 'As far as I'm aware, you and Ollie have all the material things you need. Or at least, you seem to want for nothing important. All in all, I don't think I'd describe that as a "low bar".' (He gives that air-quotes against his better judgement.)

'Yeah well, there's more to life than having lots of stuff.'

'Says the girl who's always had those things.' He shakes his head. 'So, is this where you accuse me of being an inadequate parent? Only I'd sooner we skipped that conversation right now.'

'No. I mean, I wasn't trying to suggest that. Overall, I'd say you've done an okay job.'

'Ouch. Talk about damned by faint praise.' He stops loading the dirty dishes. 'I don't need to be a mind-reader to sense your disapproval.' Waving his hands in the air again, he says, 'I may not be a perfect parent, but I've done my best to make up for the fact that there's only one of me.'

His hands drop to slap his thighs. 'I suppose you think it's my fault that your mother... That she left us.'

'No, I would never blame you for that.'

He stops right there because he's now thinking about Mum and the last time he saw her alive. He swallows hard as he tries to banish the scene in that dark lane, the escaping steam rising from their smashed up car... The terrible last image they all share when they think of her.

He says, 'What's this really about, Vega? What is it you're trying to tell me, only you need to put it into actual spoken words since I don't share your telepathic abilities?'

'It's nothing. Touch of P.M.T. I expect. Forget I said anything.' She shuts down the screen in front of her.

'How am I supposed to forget it when there's clearly something you're unhappy about?'

She stands up. 'Even if there is, it's nothing you can fix, Dad.'

'But at least I *can* listen.' He smiles at her in that goofy way intended to make her laugh. 'Though I say it myself, I'm a pretty good listener. And, just maybe, I can offer you a tiny sliver of advice based on my extensive experience as a semi-successful, mostly human adult.'

'I'm fine, really.' She squeezes his arm. 'Though you might want to go and have a word with Ollie. He's up there mooning over Cerys and what might have been.'

'Right.' Dad rubs at his chin. 'I see,' he says; but of course he doesn't – that's his whole problem. It must be like being partially sighted.

She says, 'F.Y. I. Cerys has at last recognised that she's utterly useless at maths. No point in asking why she chose that option in the first place since it's a long and complex story involving the heavy burden of unrealistic parental expectations. What you need to know is she's thinking of dropping the subject. Which means she'll no longer have any use for Ollie.'

'Wow – that must be quite a bummer.' He pinches the bridge of his nose. 'How come Ollie didn't know all that before today?'

'He can't read her. As far as he's concerned she's a complete enigma – which only adds to her allure.' She sighs. 'I guess he's blind-sided by love.'

'Aren't we all?' He pulls a pained face. 'Sounds like he might have had a narrow escape.'

'Exactly. Though possibly it's too soon to suggest that to him. Oh, and you might want to try to clear your mind of that idea, so he can't tell that's what you're thinking.'

'Christ, talk about a tall order...'

Vega's tempted to suggest he might want to apply the same "narrow escape" scenario to his own situation, but since he's already pondering what he might say to Ollie when he's sober, she leaves it there. For now anyway.

The school day drags on, only made bearable by her plans for later. Though they've extended the run of her mum's play, tonight is destined to be the last performance of it in that particular theatre. The production is about to move to a venue forty miles away. What then? She can't keep showing up without her mum becoming suspicious.

Straight after their evening meal, Ollie retreats to his bedroom muttering something about a presentation he wants to work on. Even Dad can tell from his body language that he wants to be left alone to brood. (Dad makes the convenient decision to put off having that awkward talk with his son.) She can't read Ollie since he's managing to block her out.

If only her dad could shield his thoughts. As it is, he'd spent way too much of their mealtime mooning over Gwen. As a displacement activity, he goes off to his workshop to apply several layers of wildlife-friendly waterproofing to his duck house so it doesn't rot. No doubt he'll carry on thinking about the bloody woman as he's doing it.

Getting away with her nightly visits has become almost too easy. After her first visit, Jen had tactfully suggested that, as a volunteer usher, she might want to dial it back a bit and wear clothes more appropriate for her semi-official position.

Up in her room, she cranks up the next track – Alice Cooper's "Poison". Over her white school blouse, she pulls on a black jumper then pins her official badge to it. She'll leave her bomber jacket in the staff locker room along with her usual shoulder bag. Achieving big-hair is easy-peasy thanks to her new hairspray and a subtle bit of back-combing. (Another technique discovered online.) Her makeup routine has become second nature, her smoky eyes, her self-made face a reflection of the new persona she's now comfortable with.

One final check in the mirror and she's ready. Except... What was that noise? She kills the music. 'Vega, I was...' Dad is frozen in the doorway.

'Oh, hi, Dad.' She opts for an off-hand, nothing-to-see-here tone. 'Just experimenting with an alternative look – as we adolescent girls tend to do when alone in our *private* spaces.'

'Alternative is, I suppose, one word to describe it.' The one he stops himself saying is slutty. 'I did knock but you clearly couldn't hear above the music.' He ventures further into the room, hands planted on his hips like a goalie getting ready to defend a pen. He's suspicious alright. 'Looks to me like you were planning to sneak out.'

'I can explain...'

His eyes have homed in on the badge pinned to her sweater. 'Volunteer Usher?' he reads aloud. 'What in God's name... Don't try to tell me that badge is part of your adolescent experimentation.'

She doesn't. He's not totally stupid after all. Time to drop the act. Like a bull about to charge, he's standing there glaring and mad as hell, breathing heavily as he waits for her to come up with a credible explanation.

'It's hard to explain,' she tells him.

'I suggest you try.'

She hesitates. There's a moment when they're eye to eye. She looks at his worn jeans and stained grey overshirt. Not ideal but it will do. Her mind made up, she says, 'Why don't I show you. Don't look at me like that, Dad. I promise what you're about to see will amaze you.'

Frowning, he's opening his mouth to speak when she grabs his arm. The world around them darkens as they make the leap together, just as he'd done all those years ago when he bumped into her mother.

Chapter Thirty-Eight

Ollie

Waking is like surfacing through treacle. Ollie drags his eyes open. He can sense he's alone in the house. Sitting up, he's certain of it. Something's wrong, though he's not sure what. He'd lain awake most of the night and now all his devices confirm it's nearly lunchtime. Today's a school day, but they hadn't woken him.

Sunlight is blazing through the gaps in his bedroom curtains. When he pulls them back, the glare makes him squint. He checks the area around the park gates and beyond for any sign of the two men. Nothing.

He can usually tell where Dad and Vega are, but today he can't – which is odd. Are the two things connected? Those two men might have snuck in while he was sleeping – though if his dad or sister had been kidnapped, he would know. And besides, both could instantly escape.

A more rational explanation is that Dad's gone off on some errand and Vega's at school. Dad's not known for his leniency. Maybe he'd assumed he was ill – though his forehead feels cool to the touch. If he goes into school now, he'll have to think up an excuse for missing the morning. Might as well write off the rest of the day and start afresh tomorrow.

Ollie turns from the window. His first priority is to take a piss. Washing his hands afterwards, he examines his chest in the mirror. The patch of hair running down his sternum is no wider or thicker than the last time he checked. Height-wise, he's grown a lot over the last year, but his torso hasn't expanded by the same proportions.

Striking a classic he-man pose, his biceps and triceps barely rise. Muscle development is the one way he lags behind all the other boys in his class. He's a lot younger than them, so it's reasonable to expect his chest and neck will broaden in time. What if they don't? Maybe he should pump iron or try the protein shakes Paul and Aaron are always swigging. They put a lot of effort into maintaining their so-called guns. Girls – specifically Cerys – might find him more attractive if he was a more manly shape.

Like an unseen audience, he hears excited, laughing voices. As the noise grows louder he can tell it's kids. He cracks the bathroom blind to watch a crocodile of children head into the park chaperoned by teachers carrying various items of sporting equipment. He likes swimming because that's for the practical purpose of preventing you from drowning. Exercise for its own sake is an urge that's so far passed him by.

Still no sign of those men. He knows they were watching Dad so why have they gone? Has it got something to do with Baynton? Ollie shrugs. They'd all agreed that man is not their problem.

He could go for a run around the park and try to enjoy it. (Although runners tend to be more wiry than muscly.) What if he bumps into someone from school?

On balance, it's not worth the risk.

Ollie goes back to his bedroom. Its usual orderliness is disturbed by the jumbled heap of chess pieces on his desk. He clears the board of those wretched pennies and tips them back into the bag which he returns to the drawer. He then places each chess piece in the square it occupied the day before. Ollie sits back satisfied that they are all precisely where they should be. What now? It's Grandad's move and he can't call him without explaining why he's not in school.

He's got the afternoon off and it's great weather out there, but he doesn't dare venture out. It occurs to him that Baynton is probably having the exact same thoughts at this very moment. For him, confinement is a temporary imposition, for Baynton it's a potential life sentence.

So why aren't those men watching their house? They could be following Dad – in which case they'd better enjoy a spot of grocery shopping or whatever boring chore he's gone off to do. Ollie smiles at the thought of them pretending to inspect vegetables or weigh up competing special offers.

There could be a more sinister explanation. Shit, what if whoever sent them to watch the house no longer needs to worry about Baynton because they've found out where he is and they're planning to deal with him. To "take him out" as they say in the movies.

It was his blunder with that stupid, fucking flash drive that kicked everything off. Ford may have warned Dad not to interfere, but Ollie still has a choice. If he's going to do something to save Baynton, he needs to do it now before it's too late.

Fuck it. Ignoring the inner voice cautioning him not to act on impulse, he pulls on jeans, socks and trainers. For luck he extracts the St Christopher from his drawer and fastens it around his neck. Downstairs he examines a pile of Dad's lame and obviously non-threatening t-shirts from the clean washing pile. He picks the one with the duck on the front and a speech bubble saying, "Trust me, I'm a quack". (A tortuous pun that's always made him wince.) He's careful to hide his medallion underneath it.

Ollie then checks the spare change tin and removes enough cash to cover what he needs. Fortunately, sunglasses won't look out of place given the weather. He pulls on the khaki baseball cap with a neck flap his gran nags him to wear on hot days. Not a brilliant disguise but it should do the job.

On leaving the house, he tries to stroll and not run. He kicks at a stone in case someone's watching. (Though he's pretty sure they're not.) Fortunately, the takeaway place at the end of the next but one street is one of those dodgy establishments that only accepts cash.

The man behind the counter stares at him as he enters. The food they're selling is congealing in heated trays in front of him and has clearly not been prepared by professionals who care about basic culinary standards. (Though it's mandatory, their hygiene rating isn't even displayed.) It's not his business to speculate about the actual business that goes on out the back.

He's careful to ask for extra sauce as the man scoops it into a non-environmentally friendly container – the continued use of which ought to be reported to food standards inspectors. Biting back the urge to point this out, Ollie exits with his polystyrene coated purchase and heads for the graveyard.

On a fine day like today the dead are predictably forgotten. All the same he checks that no one is occupying the shady benches or laying flowers next to the compost heap and its surrounding laurel hedge.

His nose is still full of the sweet corruption of decaying flowers. Though it's the same day and the same timeframe, he waits until his head is clear after such a rapid change of location.

Once he's ready, he leaves the toilet and weaves his way out through the busy restaurant. Outside, people are picnicking or sprawled out on the grass. The Thames sparkles by, busy with boats of all shapes and sizes. Up ahead the phoenix sculpture dazzles in the sunlight.

With what he hopes is an air of nonchalance, he walks through the open glass doors of the Grenewych Tower's building. In the echoing atrium the bored concierge gives him a friendly enough nod. If he takes his sunglasses off, she'll clock his age and wonder why he's not in school. She's dark-haired and very pretty. Her badge identifies her only as Kaylee. Approaching the desk, he takes off his hat though he then finds it hard to juggle it and the food container. 'Lovely day out there,' he says, hoping to sound matter of fact.

She looks wistfully through the surrounding glass walls. 'It sure is.' She's from New Jersey. This is a stopgap job – or so she keeps telling herself. A fine art degree (a high first) and a master's in Visual Communication haven't yet got her where she'd like to be at this point in her career.

'Lunch order for the penthouse,' he says, knowing this must be a frequent occurrence.

'I don't think I've seen you before,' she says. 'For Mr Logan, I presume?'

'Yep.' She must be able to smell those icky, sticky ribs. 'The regular guy's off sick today. I'm standing in,' he adds with a sniff. (No real reason.)

'Right.' Her smile reveals advertisement-ready teeth. 'Could be your colleague's pulling what you Brits call *a sicky*? (Upward inflection at the end.) Not that I'd blame him.'

'Well, it *is* a very fine day...'

'Tell me about it.' She sighs as she points. 'Service elevator's over there.' She doesn't add that it's apartment B because he would know that if he was bona fide. Muttering his thanks, Ollie heads for the lift.

It takes a matter of seconds to reach the 63rd floor. Before the doors open, he sabotages the container and even remembers to hang his sunglasses over the neck of his t-shirt. (It pays to look people in the eye when you're lying.) He steps out into the lobby shared by the two penthouse suites sensing the lenses of the half dozen cameras picking him up. When he presses the buzzer marked B, a man answers. 'Yes?' The visual feed is turned off at the other end.

Ollie musters his best, non-threatening smile. 'Lunch delivery for penthouse apartment B.'

'Just leave it on the table in front of you.' (No word of thanks.)

'I'd be happy to, only the damned sauce is leaking out all over the place.' He raises one stained hand to the camera. (It looks quite a lot like bloodstains.) 'I can barely hold the thing together. Before it all ends up on the floor, could I come in and just put it on a plate or something?'

The occupant hesitates. Ollie hopes he's hungry. 'Okay,' the man finally says. 'Kitchen's immediately on your left. Large plates on the shelf to your right. Leave the food there and go.' His voice has a slight Scottish lilt.

Ollie nods several times. 'Kitchen door's on my left, plates are on the right. Got it.' The door lock clicks to admit him.

The apartment's hallway would be too bright if the sunlight wasn't being filtered through numerous opaque blinds. A vibrant Turkish rug runs almost its full length. Fine artworks of the classical kind adorn the inner wall. Should he take his shoes off? No – inappropriate. Better to keep to the blond polished wooden floor. (Who does his cleaning?)

He enters the first door on his left. The kitchen he steps into is all stainless steel and high tech appliances, designed not as the heart of the home, but for a professional chef used to working in high end restaurants. Like the hallway, it's spotlessly clean suggesting no one has ever used it to rustle up a meal.

Following instructions, he slops the leaky contents of the container onto a large and pristine white plate. It looks like something a dog might have swallowed whole and then vomited up. As far as he can tell there are no cameras in the room to witness the arrival of such an abomination. He stops to rinse the red stains from his hand though not all of it comes off.

Back in the hallway, Ollie follows his intuition to the second door on the left. He takes a deep breath then opens it.

At the far end of the room, the back of a man's head is just visible above an egg-shaped, orange chair that's facing the glass wall and its spectacular view across the city.

'Thought I told you to leave.' The man doesn't turn round to face him but carries on sitting there looking out. Christ, what if he's got this all wrong? What if he's intruded on some other reclusive weirdo and is about to pay the price?

He swallows hard. 'Oh, I'll go, Mr Baynton, once I've said what I came here to say.'

The chair swivels to face him. Behind Baynton's calm expression, he's as mad as a bear in a snare. Dressed in pale chinos and a blue shirt, he'd be handsome if it wasn't for those stary, scary eyes.

After looking him up and down, he decides Ollie isn't much of a threat. (An insult on many levels.)

'You've successfully gained my attention…' Staring at the stupid talking duck on his t-shirt, Baynton steeples his hands like some movie villain bearded in his lair. (The man's a film buff. With not a lot else to do, he's rehearsed this scene many times in his daydreams – or nightmares. At this moment he's a bit disappointed not to be facing a more formidable adversary.)

Playing himself as the hero, Baynton says, 'What is it you wish to say to me?'

'That it's um… That it's quite likely, no, more like highly probable, that your life is at this moment in great danger. If you–'

He's interrupted by a buzz. Baynton swivels to one side.

Without getting up, he presses a button on the adjacent wall. 'What is it?'

'Mr Logan, this is Kaylee, your concierge. Please excuse the interruption, sir, but, weirdly, the regular delivery guy has also just arrived with your lunch order. Seems they've doubled up today. Should I send this one up too?'

'I think not,' Baynton rubs at his lower lip. 'Please pass on my apologies and ask him to leave.' She's still talking when he releases the pressure on the buzzer, cutting her off. 'Well, young man, where were we?'

Ollie could be standing before a pissed-off teacher. (In retrospect, it's possible "Trust me, I'm a quack" wasn't the best choice of slogans to plead his case.) Looking him full in the face, Baynton sighs as if saddened by this unacceptable behaviour. He leans forward in that Bond-villain chair of his, playing for time while he figures out his next move. Out loud, he says, 'I suppose I should congratulate you for being a most unlikely would-be assassin.'

Chapter Thirty-Nine

Tom

Tom opens his eyes to darkness. For a moment he wonders if he's dead. No, he can hear voices – lots of them. All talking at once. Music too.

A grey light takes over though he can't yet make sense of his new surroundings. He can pick out low lights – enough to see he's standing in the side-aisle in a blacked out auditorium.

'You okay, Dad?' The question is Vega's. His daughter. With some difficulty, he turns his head to find her beside him, holding on to his arm to keep him upright. She looks like a different person with all that makeup obscuring her natural features. Older. More like…

'Excuse me.' A man pushes past.

'What the hell…?' They're definitely in a theatre, near the back of the stalls. His suspicions gather. 'Why have you brought me here?'

'You'll see.' Her voice is light, hints at amusement as if this is a regular family outing. 'The performance is about to begin,' she tells him. 'Why don't we take our seats?'

The music – he recognises Tracy Chapman's "Fast Car". Given a choice, he'd get the hell out of here too. Most of the audience is seated, chatting, settling themselves ready to watch whatever show this is. Sweets and snacks are being unwrapped and shared. He can smell smoke. It's rising from a number of people who are actively smoking cigarettes regardless of the effect on those sitting near them. Outrageous. He's minded to protest, but sitting down appeals more given that he's struggling to maintain his balance.

To any onlookers his dutiful daughter could be leading her infirm father to his seat. She guides him to the end of one of the less populated back rows. A flip-down seat is a complexity beyond him. She holds it down until his knees and then his full weight can prevent the wretched thing from springing back up again.

The music is switched off before Tracy can escape. Everything begins to solidify as the house lights dim. An unthinkable suspicion is adding to his lingering nausea. 'What the hell have you brought me to?' he demands. Vega doesn't reply. Good or bad, the show is about to start.

A perky folk tune sets the scene, the distinctive sound of a bouzouki or possibly a Cretan lyra. The curtain trembles like it's uncertain. It finally rises on a theatrical set containing two steamer-style loungers against a painted backdrop of a view out to sea with the distant suggestion of an island. A low, faux-stone wall runs behind the loungers. The small table placed between them holds a jug and two cocktail-style glasses. Warm yellow lighting indicates this should be taken as a sunny day. To one side of the stage artificial flowers have been twisted around a section of pergola to add to the illusion of a garden.

This must be Greece, he guesses. Or one of its islands. The music fades to silence as a fair-haired man in a blue and white striped one-piece swimming costume strolls onto the stage smoking in an effete manner. A towel is draped over one shoulder. His hair appears to be wet. A buzzing sound comes and goes. The man swipes the air in front of him with his towel as if swotting at an annoying insect. The buzzing fades as he turns to admire the view out to sea.

After a loud sigh, he stubs out his cigarette, places the towel on the back of one of the chairs and pours himself a peachy-red drink. He raises his glass as if celebrating the view, takes a sip and then turns to face the audience. In a clipped English accent, he says, 'It seems we are to endure another day in paradise.'

The audience chuckles. This must be a comedy – at least Tom hopes that's the intention. Could be one of Noel Coward's more obscure works.

Off stage a woman calls out, 'Bertie, darling?' Something in her voice sends shivers through him. Christ, it couldn't...

After a quick conspiratorial look to the audience, the Bertie character downs his drink and exits stage left seconds before a woman enters from the opposite wing. 'Bertie, is that you?' Her dark hair is pinned at the nape of her neck 1920s style. Dressed in a yellow halter-neck beach suit, she strides with confidence to the centre of the stage where she turns to the audience to deliver her first line. 'That man is infinitely more slippery when wet.'

While those around him are laughing and enjoying the show, he grips the sides of his chair. Framed by the many heads of those in front of him, the woman on the stage is stunningly beautiful with her flapper-style, smoky eyelids. He's too far away to be sure of the colour of her eyes and he doubts the band of freckles across her nose would be visible beneath all her theatrical makeup, but she is recognisably and most definitely Beth.

Tom groans, overwhelmed by too many competing emotions. He tries to look away from the temptation in front of him. He might turn to stone if their eyes were to meet. 'Just look at her, Dad,' Vega whispers. 'Isn't she amazing.'

'She is,' he croaks. He would leave now if his ability to do so wasn't in serious doubt. Christ, he swore he would never do this – never give in to this ultimate temptation. It's too much; his body and soul can't take it. Heart thumping, he has to turn his head away. If he walks out he'll look like a dissatisfied customer. And the last thing he wants, or needs, is to draw attention to himself. Or worse still, to risk drawing *her* attention to him.

Safely flanked by others, he allows himself another peek. The audience is lapping up her performance, responding to her tiniest gesture, every perfectly timed pause.

Even from such a distance it's obvious she possesses the most extraordinary stage presence. Between lines, her lip-stick-defined mouth forms a perfect cupid's bow. When she turns her head away to stare out to sea, he imagines planting kisses down her neck like he used to...

Watching from afar, he's entered another realm. Physically,

she's almost unchanged and yet she's no longer the same person, the same young girl he'd so fatefully bumped into on that train to Cheltenham. They'd been soulmates – as close as any two people could or can be. Or so he thought. She'd had his children, loved and nurtured both of them in those first few vital years. During their time together he'd assumed he knew everything there was to know about her, and yet all along this other Beth had been lying dormant, ready to blossom given the right conditions.

After she disappeared from their lives, he'd searched out the bare facts of her successful acting career; they'd even watched her on film a few times, but nothing could convey the experience of seeing her up there in her element, of witnessing her remarkable, mesmerising talent first hand.

She strides across the stage, the skirt of her playsuit dividing into shorts. How many times has he run his hands over those long, bare legs...

He shuts his eyes to bask in the sound of her voice. Losing Beth has been the defining tragedy of his life. Nothing and no one has ever come close to what they had together. For her, those few missing years are a mystery no doubt dismissed by a medical diagnosis of amnesia. With no recollection of her time in the twenty-first century, she hasn't had to deal with the regrets that have plagued him for so many years. Freedom from knowing about the other life she'd stumbled into, has allowed her to discover where she truly belongs. Erasing her memory of their time together was a mercy – a final gift Ford had bestowed on her.

At this moment in time, for Beth, only a few years have

passed. While his hair is beginning to grey, hers is as dark as ever. Her face and body haven't aged a bit while he's now middle-aged. For the past twelve years he's been the sole custodian of their time together. In his reality, she's been dead and buried all that time.

Tom's vision blurs and yet he continues to watch as Beth walks toward the wings. Looking out into the audience she declares, 'When I married the man, I had no idea he was a more impressive escapologist than Houdini.'

The irony isn't lost on Tom. While the audience chuckles, he cranes his neck to catch a last glimpse before she makes her exit. In this unplanned, stolen moment he's happy for her, proud of the woman she's become. The bouzouki music fades in to round off the first scene and introduce the next.

'Dad.' Vega nudges him. He's not sure if he should be angry or grateful for this moment of revelation. Either way, he wants her to leave him alone with his thoughts and memories.

'Dad.' A sharper dig this time. 'We need to go,' she whispers.

Beth is striding back onto the stage. He hisses, 'Now that you've brought me here, I want to watch her for a bit longer.'

'Dad, it's Ollie...'

'What about him?'

It's an effort to turn his attention to Vega. Her expression is serious. She's genuinely worried. 'I think he might be in trouble,' she says.

The spell is broken. 'What kind of trouble?'

A nearby woman turns to shush them. Into his ear, Vega says, 'Can't be sure. He's too far away right now.' Her hand is pressed to her chest. 'I just have this really awful feeling. Something's wrong. I think he's in danger and needs my help.'

Tom ignores the shushing woman's hostile stares. 'You're certain?'

'No; but I think. Look, I'm pretty sure, Ollie's life is in danger.'

'Jesus!'

Leaning in she whispers, 'It could be nothing. Why don't I go while you stay here for a bit…'

'No chance.' His son's in trouble hundreds of miles and more than four decades away. His stomach in freefall, Tom hauls himself to his feet.

Heads turn to watch their abrupt departure. On his way out, he glances up at Beth one last time before following her daughter into the auditorium's shadowy passageway.

Chapter Forty

Ollie

They continue to stare at one another hombre-a-hombre style. (Or face it, hombre-a-adolescente.) Baynton is a lot bigger and stronger – in a fair fight there's no question who would win.

'Since you know who I am,' Baynton says. 'Perhaps you'd care to introduce yourself.' A ploy to distract him while he considers the best way to get his hands on the gun hidden in the top drawer of one of the console tables. He's also wondering if he's capable of shooting someone in cold blood. (Jury's out on that.)

Standing in front of that particular console table and so, in effect, blocking his path, Ollie musters his most disarming smile. 'My identity is irrelevant,' he says. 'However, I'm afraid you've just made a very big mistake.'

'Oh really?' Baynton grins, confident he's holding all the cards. 'And what might that be?'

'You really should have accepted that other takeaway. I guarantee it would have been better than the disgusting plate of sludge I just left in your kitchen.'

Mildly amused in spite of the situation, Baynton snorts, 'You're a cool one, I'll give you that much.'

He's about to lunge for the gun when Ollie raises a blocking hand. 'Hold it there for just a second, take a minute to think before you do anything rash.' He stands firm though his legs have gone very wobbly.

Amazingly, it works. Maintaining eye contact while lowering his hand, Ollie says, 'I promise it's in your interest to hear me out.' He points to the relevant drawer. 'For a start I know about the handgun you keep in there. You might think you can get to it faster, but since you're further away and sitting down, I'm fairly sure I can grab it first.'

That's thrown him. Baynton holds up his hands in a classic you-got-me pose to disguise the fact that he's now thinking of rugby tackling Ollie to the ground before he goes for the gun.

'As you can see, I represent no real threat to you.' Ollie takes a step backwards to illustrate his point. 'I came here to warn you.'

'Warn me of what, exactly?'

'Well, the thing is…' (Now might not be the best time to confess he was the one who sent the flash drive that made him so paranoid he staged his own suicide.) 'You're up against some pretty determined people who are convinced you're still alive. Which, let's face it, they're 100% right about.'

Shaken by this revelation, Baynton tries to keep his expression neutral, though a nerve has started to twitch just below his right eye. Ollie continues, 'The individuals looking for you have a substantial vested interest in locating you. I'm guessing it's a multi-million pound incentive. It's therefore not unreasonable to assume they're what you might call *highly motivated.*'

'Go on.'

'Let's imagine, for argument's sake, that your former associates have acquired friends in high places. They may not know precisely where you are right now, but thanks to these newly acquired *friends*' (big air quotes) 'the next time you step outside they'll be on to you almost straight away.'

Baynton scoffs. 'I'm prepared to take my chances.' A reasonable assumption as he's been able to come and go a few times in disguise.

'You're probably thinking that if you wear a pair of sunnies and stick something over your head, you'll get away with it again. I'm sorry to tell you that's not going to work anymore.'

Less sure of his ground now, Baynton has at least stopped thinking about that gun. 'Oh really, and why's that?'

'Because your previous associates have managed to gain illegal access to the Security Forces' top secret, state-of-the-art surveillance system. They're calling it Panoptes by the way – after the all-seeing giant in the Greek myth. The salient point here is that this new system is capable of identifying individuals by their unique stance even when the subject is standing still. As soon as they take a step, it measures their stride length and other vectors that, taken together, can distinguish the subject from those around them. It can do this even in really crowded places like airports.'

Ollie waits for that to sink in before he continues. 'Okay, so if someone tries to get around that by, let's say, pretending to be disabled and acquiring a wheelchair, Panoptes still has many more tricks up its metaphorical sleeve. Its facial analysis tech is something else. So if, for example, you paid some dodgy doctor to perform facial surgery on you in here – which, no offence, would be a less than ideal environment in which to carry out major surgery – after all that pain and suffering, you'd have wasted your time and money. Panoptes sees through a subject's surface features to digitally reconstruct their skull. It looks for tiny anomalies. It can identify any modifications made to the subject's original bone structure – intentionally or following an accident. It's capable of reconstructing the skull's original shape before layering over the person's original features. Which means that this new tech can, quite literally, see through any and every disguise it encounters.'

'Fucking nonsense!' Baynton is shaking his head, his thoughts running all over the place and getting nowhere. Swallowing down outrage and growing panic, he says, 'Putting aside whether I believe you or not, how in God's name would a puny little kid like you know something like that?'

It's a good question. Come to think of it, Ollie's not sure how he knows all this stuff. He just does. The information is there in his mind like his brain's received some data download – an unsourced and unasked for update. How's it happening? Should he see this as a positive or a negative addition to his personal development?

To cover his confusion, he shrugs like the answer to Baynton's question is no big deal. 'Same way I knew you hadn't drowned and were hiding up here,' he says. 'The same way I was aware of the loaded gun you keep in this drawer here.'

'Which is…'

'I'm not prepared to say. And, just so we're clear, I wouldn't tell you even if you were holding that Glock to my head.'

Baynton's frown gets even frownier. 'How in God's name do you know it's a Glock?'

Ollie grins. 'I think we're in a bit of a loop now.'

Like salt sprinkled on snow, the man before him is visibly shrinking into himself. Where a moment ago he'd been cocky and self-assured, he's more rattled than he's letting on. And thoroughly spooked that some kid has not only breached his defences, but also claims to know about a nightmare new surveillance system, one he's never even heard of, that would rule out any possibility of him ever escaping his apartment.

His plans in tatters, Baynton is rubbing his forehead repeatedly while running through possible alternative scenarios. If this new surveillance system exists, he'll never make it out of London alive. If he transfers all the money he's taken back to the investors, it's not going to end there. Cross those sort of guys once and there's no coming back. After stealing their money and faking his own suicide, when they track him down, they're not exactly going to forgive or forget.

Right now he wants to shoot the messenger. 'Who sent you?' he demands. 'More importantly, what the fuck do they want?'

'No one sent me. I came here on my own initiative.'

Baynton scoffs. 'You expect me to believe that?' His brain's in overload. He's trying to conjure up images of the anonymous individuals bent on destroying him. Ollie would feel greater sympathy for the man if he was more likeable. And if he hadn't just called him a puny kid to his face. Then again, being amiable ought not to be a criteria, or even a prerequisite, when deciding whether to help someone or not. After all, doctors don't give their patients a personality quiz before deciding whether to try to save their life.

Hang on – he's getting carried away. He's no doctor – he's not an actual anything. He needs to get a grip and remember he's a lanky, fifteen-year-old schoolkid in danger of getting above his station.

'If what you're telling me is true, it seems I'm royally fucked.' Baynton's staring at the floor, the fight gone out of him for the moment at least. His faceless opponents are all formidable if rather shadowy figures. At the same time he's outraged that a boy with a terrible duck pun on his t-shirt has ostensibly outwitted him. The aspect of his situation he's focusing on is that his sanctuary has been breached. He's not thinking ahead. Instead, he's fixating on how it's possible he could have been outsmarted by such an underwhelming person. And he's becoming more convinced every second that someone of greater significance must be pulling the strings.

Baynton slumps back in his designer chair appearing to acquiesce. 'Since you seem to have all the answers, young man...' He's trying to spot the earpiece or device through which instructions are being relayed by an unseen yet formidable puppet master. 'What happens now?'

Though Ollie's tempted to demonstrate he's nobody's stooge, he needs to put his own ego aside if he's going to figure out how they're both going to get out of this alive.

Chapter Forty-One

Vega

Her dizziness doesn't last this time. Back in their hallway, she wants to let go of Dad, but his eyes are still half shut, and he looks like he might be about to fall.

'Beth's not here,' he mutters. 'Left her behind again. Can't be right.'

Perhaps the sitting room with its softer surfaces would have been better. She shakes him. 'Dad! Dad we're back home.'

That rouses him a bit. 'What's it… look like?' His pupils are making those involuntary movements you're told to look out for in stroke victims. His free hand searches and finds the wall. 'My fucking head's spinning like… some sort of spinning thing.'

Now they're in the same timeframe, she's more certain of Ollie's predicament, where she needs to be right now. But she can't let go of Dad or he'll faceplant on the hard floor. He mutters, 'Like I've just aged by several decades…'

Vega does her best to prop him against the wall. When that doesn't work, she manoeuvres him towards the staircase, holds him while he lowers his arse onto one of the bottom steps. 'Better,' he says. Head in hands, he's remembering now. He looks up. 'Where's Ollie? You said he's in trouble?'

'He is.'

'Ah yes, the old psychic connection.' He rubs his eyes. 'Then we'd better get going.'

'Not you,' she says, 'Just me.'

Dad shakes his head. 'There's no way I'm letting you do this – this whatever it is – alone.'

'You're in no fit state.'

'I'll be fine in a few minutes.'

'We don't have a few minutes. Dad, look I'm sorry but I can't wait. Besides, they won't let you go there, remember? They're watching us, monitoring what we do.'

'What, those two men out there?'

She scoffs. 'No – not them. They're just a couple of non-entities. In any case, they've buggered off.' She touches his shoulder. 'I'm going now.'

'No!' He grabs her hand. 'If Ollie's in danger like you said, *I* should be the one to handle the situation, not you. You stay here where it's safe. I'll go.' By hanging onto the banister, he hauls himself to his feet. 'Although, you'll have to tell me where he is and explain what I need to do.'

Even if she tells him, there's no way he'll be able to get past them. Under her breath she mutters, 'I haven't got time for this.'

To him, raising her voice, 'Listen, Dad, the situation… how can I put it? Look, everything's on a knife edge. Look at the state of you. If you go blundering in there, you'll only make things worse. I can do stuff you've never been capable of.'

He recoils like she's hit him in the face. 'I'm your father. I should be the one protecting you and your brother. Don't imagine for one second I'm prepared to sit idly by while you put yourself in danger...' He shakes his head. 'Not gonna happen. If you think you can stop me, think again.'

'Erggh!' She grabs her head in frustration. 'Look, it's not like I'm dissing you or anything, but you have limitations I don't have. That's a fact and not any kind of judgement.'

'All the same...' He grabs her arm. 'I'm going – not you.'

Exasperated, she concentrates on making him let go of her. Once he has, she forces him back down onto the step. It upsets them both to witness his body bending to her will, but he's left her no choice.

'Jesus, Vega! I can't... I can't move my fucking arms or legs. I don't... Did you just...?'

'Dad, I'm sorry.' She's close to tears. 'I can't allow you to interfere.'

'Allow me? How in God's name are you...'

Already overheating, she pulls off her jumper and loosens the collar of her blouse. 'I'll be right back,' she says. 'Don't go anywhere. Not that you'll be able to, um, go anywhere.'

Her attempt at levity misfires. She turns away from the horrified expression on his face. 'Won't be long,' she says, like she's just popping out to the shops or something. Immobilising your parent is undeniably a big deal – the sort of thing that's bound to have hideous repercussions afterwards.

If there is an afterwards.

Ollie's standing directly in front of Baynton, the two of them staring at each other in classic stand-off style.

'Holy fuck!' Baynton says. 'Where did you just come from?' The charming and helpful man she'd met in that foyer has left the building. This one is a mess of paranoia and aggression.

She's struggling to master her balance, the spectacular view over the city below is disorientating. Ollie's furious as she knew he would be. Not even looking at her, he says, 'You shouldn't be here.'

'Neither should you.'

Not allowing his eyes to leave Baynton, he says, 'I can handle this. Honestly, I've got this, okay. So bugger off.'

'I've got a better idea,' Baynton says. 'Both of you kids fuck off and tell whoever sent you they can fuck off too.' Men! Always masking their fears with bravado – like that alone is going to get him out of the shitstorm heading his way. *Their* way, in actual fact.

'You know that's not a bad suggestion, Mr Baynton,' she says, 'Not a bad suggestion since, thanks to my brother here, ATM we're all royally fucked.'

Without speaking, she tells Ollie, *The people looking for him sent those two men to watch our house. They've taken loads of photos of us. You know all about Panoptes, and yet you completely failed to factor it in.*

She can sense him joining the dots. He risks a glance at her. 'Shit!' he says out loud.

'Make that shit squared,' she says. *The cams will have picked you up outside this building. If it hasn't already, it's only a matter of time before Panoptes picks you out as a match. By coming here, you've led them straight to this building, you moron. They'll piggy-back on this building's CC cams.* She nods at the terrified man in the orange egg-chair. *Which will show you heading straight up here to meet him.*

Ollie takes his eye off Baynton to stare at her. *If they find us here too, we'll just be collateral damage.*

Exactly.

Before she can process what's happening, Ollie is falling. Baynton lunges to pull out a drawer and grab the handgun in it. In charge now – or so he imagines – he points the barrel at Ollie and then at her. Then he swings it back to Ollie again perceiving him as the greater threat.

The hand with the gun is shaking so much Baynton's forced to steady it with his other hand, gripping it two-handed com-mando style. 'Don't fucking move,' he says. 'Both of you need to stay exactly where you are.'

He takes a backwards step, though that just backs him into the surrounding glass walls. At this height, he has nowhere to go.

She says, 'I hate to point this out, but your instructions seem a bit contradictory. How are the two of us meant to fuck off and at the same time not move?'

As she'd hoped, Baynton turns his attention and his gun in her direction. 'Who sent you here?' he demands. Then, 'Wait a minute – Don't I know you?'

He can't quite make the connection to their brief meeting in the atrium of his old apartment – back when he was a better man. He doesn't recognise her as the same person since she was dressed as a schoolgirl at the time and not an overly made-up, late eighties, theatre usher.

'I doubt it,' she tells him. Then wordlessly to Ollie: *He might be a prat, but I don't think he's a killer. Although people can do rash and stupid things when they panic.*

Yeah okay – guilty as charged. That still leaves the two of us stuck in a room with a terrified man currently pointing a shaking gun at us.

Good point.

Baynton's trying to work out what his next move should be. He runs a hand over his mouth several times as if the answer might be about to spring from his lips before tightly gripping the gun again. 'I might...' His gun barrel twitches. 'I'll let you both go if you tell me who sent you.'

'No one sent us,' Ollie tells him. 'Like I said before, I only came here to warn you.'

'And I only came here to warn him,' she says, drawing the gun's aim away from where Ollie is still sprawled out on the floor.

While trying to connect the pieces of the puzzle he's facing, Baynton's better nature is telling him to calm down and not do anything in haste he'll later regret. Great advice he should listen to. Logic and decency are gaining the upper hand. Everything's heading in the right direction...

They all hear the thud of a controlled explosion.

Terrified and cornered, Baynton loses his shit big time. Given that flight from here would require a parachute he doesn't have, fight wins the battle.

Like spinning the bottle, his vacillating gun barrel ends up pointing at her. She glances down at Ollie. *This might be the bit where I die.*

Chapter Forty-Two

Ollie

Disadvantaged by his prone position, Ollie can do nothing to physically stop the man. 'Try to stay calm,' he says. 'Don't do anything you'll regret.' Baynton's brain is in a tailspin, even his two-handed grip can't keep that gun steady. Already there are voices in the hall, heavy footsteps heading their way. The gun's magazine holds twenty-two rounds, but Baynton's worried it won't be enough, for God's sake. His instincts are urging him to act – to kill or be killed. And Vega is directly in his line of fire.

He can't let this happen. Shutting his eyes, Ollie touches his St Christopher and prays.

The silence that follows is absolute. When he dares to open his eyes, he sees an ejected bullet casing hanging in the air, the unmoving whiff of smoke expelled from the gun's chamber. More smoke has escaped the barrel to form a static cloud. The glinting bullet itself is suspended mid-flight, its lethal, pointy end halted millimetres short of Vega's chest. His sister is open-mouthed, her emerging scream petrified. He'll never hear the end of this.

Facing her, Baynton is a poised action-figure, both arms extended as he finally holds the Glock in an immobile grip.

Shaking, Ollie looks around the room to find the door is half open. Behind it, several impressively armed, balaclava clad individuals are caught in the act of bursting into the room.

He scrabbles to his feet while staring at the bullet – a miniature rocket on its horizontal trajectory, its surface scarred with tiny grooves from the barrel it's just left. He wants to pluck it from the air but hesitates in case it might still burn his fingers. Worse still, such an act could break the spell that's stopped the world in its tracks. Ollie holds his hand up ready to block the bullet's path should the laws of physics decide to reassert themselves.

Things can't stay like this forever. For starters, he needs to find a way to free Vega without reactivating all the rest.

An intermittent sound penetrates the stillness – a regular pattern he recognises as someone clapping. The applauding hands are attached to a tall man in a dark grey suit. He's over by the window as if he's just materialised through the glass. Since the top half of his face is hidden by the brim of his hat, he could be any age. 'Bravo!' The man drops his hands to his sides. 'Congratulations on a most impressive demonstration, young man.' His accent is hard to pin down.

Ollie swallows. Trying not to show how intimidated he is, he says, 'I'm guessing you're a Guardian.'

The mouth beneath the hat's shadow falls into a lopsided grin. 'Guilty as charged.' The man's skin has a pale tinge to it. He looks like someone who's just stepped from a black and white photo.

Faking nonchalance, Ollie says, 'Yeah well, as you can see, I've got the situation wrapped up. Job's a good un, as we say where I'm from.' The muscles in his extended hand and arm are beginning to ache. Looking around he admits, 'Well, I'm not quite finished but, you know, since no one is going anywhere in a hurry, I'm sure I can figure out the next bit by myself.'

'Oh, it's not my intention to interfere. Perish the thought.' (Posh British accent) In mock innocence, the Guardian spreads his arms wide. 'This type of stasis tends to become unstable, though this one is as solid as it gets. I'm here to acknowledge an important milestone in your career.'

'You're joking right.' Ollie shakes his head. 'What career? I haven't even taken my A-levels yet.'

'As you might guess, in our line of work we tend not to worry too much about formal qualifications.' (Bostonian American that time.) Grey-guy turns his attention to Vega. 'Your sister here has shown herself to be, by any standards, equally impressive. One to watch – no pun intended. Though, I'm sure you'll agree, she can be rather impetuous.' He tuts. 'Heart before head. Without wishing to be unsympathetic, her recent actions suggest a certain lack of self-restraint.'

Trying to read the man's thoughts is like coming up against steel. Ollie says, 'I'm not going to allow you to – well, to treat this like it's some kind of audition for a job that, I assure you, I don't even want.'

'You should have realised by now that we're *allowed* to do whatever we see fit.' Grey-guy spins on his heels. 'And I have to say this is quite some tableau you've got going on here. Quite a situation to be untangled.' He sighs. 'The young so often want to handle things by themselves but is that wise in this instance? Given your relative inexperience in these matters, perhaps you might like to consider accepting a little assistance from…' He looks down at his nails as if assessing them for a manicure. 'A vastly more experienced colleague.' (Antipodean rise at the end that time.)

'You're not my colleague.'

Grey-guy snorts. 'Why argue about semantics when you have more immediate matters to deal with?'

He's right. First off Ollie needs to figure out how to release Vega without setting everything else in motion again. The Guardian clears his throat. 'With your permission, of course, I'm more than happy to send your sister home where she'll be safe.' His mouth approximates a benign smile. 'I'll even throw in a touch of amnesia as I'm sure you'd prefer not to deal with her adolescent outrage.'

Ollie hesitates. He's tempted to tell the smug bastard to go to hell but the locked muscles in his arm are burning to be released. Can he trust him? Then again, what choice does he have? 'Okay,' he says.

'I do think you might show a little more grace when accepting assistance.'

Ollie remembers their gran insisting on the "magic word" when they asked for something. '*Please* could you send her home,' he says. 'But make sure you don't do any of that weird shit to her memory, okay.'

Grey-guy shrugs his indifference. 'Condition accepted.'

Though he was expecting it, Ollie's taken aback when Vega disappears. 'Christ – that was fast. Is she going to be okay?'

'I'm not an amateur.' The Guardian meets his eye. 'I assure you she's quite well.'

Ollie drops his outstretched hand. What now? He starts by massaging the ache in his shoulder. The puzzle in front of him is the same as it was, but minus one crucial element. After what almost happened to Vega, should he retreat and let them shoot it out? It's tempting.

He turns to the man with all the answers. 'I'm curious. You lot seem to have gone out of your way to protect Baynton. There are people getting shivved or shot every day in this city. He's only holed up here because he stole a vast amount of money from some shady businessmen.' He points to the accused. 'If I hadn't intervened, that fucking man there would have killed my sister. So why the hell are you lot helping him?'

With an edge to his voice, the Guardian says, 'Why indeed. You've heard that tired cliché – every day's a school day. As a fledgling tutor yourself, you'll appreciate the value of allowing an individual to reach their own conclusion. Hmm. I think on balance...' Grey-guy rubs at his chin. 'Yes, I think I'll leave you to work it out for yourself.'

'Now hold on a sec...'

Too late – he's already melted into the glass wall behind him.

Shit! What the hell is he supposed to do now?

Chapter Forty-Three

Tom

He's livid – mad as a homicidal hornet. If there was any justice, the sheer strength of his fury would break the hex Vega's put on him. He's never felt, or in fact been, so utterly powerless. His kids could be anywhere. Anything could be happening to them, and he can't do a fucking thing about it.

One minute Vega had, without any prior discussion, whisked him off to watch Beth give the most amazing performance up on that stage, the next she left him immobile in his own hallway like some bag of groceries she'd dropped off. He's in limbo. No, more like fucking purgatory.

Damn it, he's half Guardian – and biologically that's a greater proportion than they are. He should be able to break her hex.

Tom concentrates on moving his fingers. He stares at the hand he can see more of hoping it'll twitch, but it remains locked and immobile.

He's within range to make a voice-activated call but who to? Not the emergency services – he can't imagine what they'd make of his predicament. (Yaay – he might make the evening news!) It surprises him that his first and only choice is Matt.

Tom can't believe it when his father doesn't pick up. Damn him.

His arse aches from sitting too long on the hard step. (How come he can feel that?) He's still mad at Vega for rejecting his help and leaving him stuck on the bloody naughty step. For her to pull a stunt like this – well, it's unforgiveable. When she gets back…

What if she doesn't come back? She's just walked into the lion's den. He doesn't even know who the lions are or why they're threatening Ollie.

Yes but, with their extraordinary abilities, nothing bad is going to happen to his kids. They're both way more powerful than he ever was. Together their combined abilities are off the scale. They were little more than babies when they managed to reverse time for heaven's sake. Through their collective will, their mother was able to cheat death. Well, for a while at least. Between the two of them, they're bound to triumph, so of course they'll come home.

Maybe Ollie wasn't in that much danger and now Vega's too shamefaced to come home. That's a joke in itself. Being forcibly confined to a step by your youngest child is a stark illustration of how far his authority over his family has waned. Never mind head of the household, his position as their father and guardian – with a small g – is becoming a joke. And not the ha ha kind.

But what if they don't come back? He banishes that thought. They'll be back soon – after all, they've got school tomorrow.

If they were never to reappear – then he'd be past caring about anything. He can't even wipe the tears he sniffs away. If he didn't have his kids… If they don't come back, it's game over for him. Stuck on this step, eventually the stench of his putrefying flesh will alert one of the neighbours. Or some unfortunate delivery person. When they break down that door, he'll be nothing more than a pool of liquefied nutrients on the floor – not so much ashes to ashes, more goo to goo.

When he raises his head, Vega is in front of him – so pale she could be a ghost he's conjured up. She's standing there like a statue with her eyes shut though her chest is rising and falling in time with her breathing. Thank God she's alive and back home – nothing else matters.

Relief floods through him. When he says her name, her eyelids open to stare at him unseeing. Past him, in fact. He turns his head to check and, as far as he can tell, no person or object has materialised behind him.

Recriminations can wait. 'Christ, I'm so glad you're back in one piece.' If only he could jump up and hug her. 'Are you okay?'

She appears to consider the question. Her 'Yes' is barely audible.

'Are you in pain?' He's not sure what to do if she is.

'No.' She blinks several times then touches the centre of her chest. Is it really her or is this a monosyllabic doppelganger sent here in her place?

'What about Ollie – is he alright?'

Her answer is a slow to form frown.

'You told me he was in danger.'

'Yes. I forgot that.'

Tom swallows down his exasperation. 'So Ollie – is he okay?'

'I'm not...' She looks around her as if assessing her surroundings for the first time. 'I think so.'

He clears his throat. 'Listen, that thing you did before you left – so I couldn't move my arms and legs – do you think you could possibly cancel that now? Only I've been sitting here for quite a long time, and I would like to be able to move again.'

She says, 'I'm sensing some hostility towards me.'

He does his best to soften his face. 'Okay, I have to admit I'm still a bit annoyed at you for forcing me to stay here against my will.' If he could shrug he would. 'But, you know, bigger picture, right now, I'm not mad at you. No, I'm more *concerned* than anything else.'

'Oh,' she says, her voice rising like she's curious.

'You seem a bit... How should I put this? Well, a bit out of it at the moment. Ollie isn't with you, and you don't appear to be sure if he's alright or not.' He takes a deep breath. 'If you release me, maybe there's a chance I'll be able to help him. Or your grandad might be able to do something.'

There's more colour in her cheeks now. 'I don't think they'll allow either of you to interfere. They've decided... They're waiting to see how Ollie handles things.'

'How he handles what?'

'Men. Guns. That sort of stuff.'

'So, hang on a minute, you're telling me your brother is facing men, *plural*, with guns, *plural*, and he's meant to handle the situation by himself.'

She nods. 'Yes.'

'So these people who are waiting to see how he handles things – are you talking about the people who sent in these gunmen?'

'No.'

'Then were you referring to our old friends the Guardians?'

The question elicits a wan smile. 'Guess.'

He can guess alright.

'You got there in the end,' she says, like it's a game.

'But why would they do something like that instead of helping him?'

'They're testing his reactions. You could call it an audition.'

'Shit a brick!' Tom stares at her. 'And what exactly is Ollie auditioning for?'

'Don't you get it yet?' She snorts. 'It's the role of a fucking lifetime.'

Chapter Forty-Four

Ollie

He needs to unravel the scene in front of him. Christ, where to start.

Ollie dodges under the expelled bullet still stationary in mid-flight. Judging by the angle of its trajectory, now Vega's no longer in its path, it's on course to hit the woman in the renaissance-style painting on the wall behind. Immortalised by the artist, whoever the sitter is, or was, he doubts she deserves a bullet hole between the eyes.

The bullet glints in the sunlight. He's tempted to grab the bloody thing before it can do any damage but stays his hand. What if by removing it, he sets everything else in motion again?

Hmm. If he re-imagines this as a chess game, which piece should he prioritise?

The bunch of armed figures frozen in the act of bursting through the door are anonymised by their balaclavas. Hired guns, they might be warm and cuddly human beings at home, but in this game it's easy to see them as pawns to be ignored. Or sacrificed.

Which leaves Baynton – the man who by now would have killed his sister. For starters, he's tempted to punch him in the face a few times, though, like Snow White's kiss, that might be enough to rouse him. And he is still holding a gun with twenty-one shiny bullets left in its magazine.

Whatever he's going to do, if it's done fast enough, the element of surprise will be on his side. First off, he needs to take Baynton out of the equation because nothing much is going to happen up here without him.

What's his exit route? Earlier, he'd arrived in a restaurant toilet cubicle hardly big enough for two. Although stuffing Baynton's head down the toilet and flushing it does hold a certain appeal. He peers into the man's eyes and sees beyond. Interesting. A more effective option presents itself. Okay, so all he has to do now is grab Baynton's gun to disarm him while, in more or less the same movement, he leaps with him to a new location where no civilians, or surveillance equipment, will register their sudden arrival.

Once the two of them have left, will the men at the door spring back to life? If they rush into the empty room, they'll only find one stray bullet and a still-warm Glock lying on the floor.

But what if they stay frozen? As Baynton never allowed anyone into the apartment, it could be a while before anyone finds them standing there like a posse of poised-for-action G I Joes. Someone must have heard them use that explosive charge to get through the outer door. Won't they have called the cops already?

Wait. Whoever sent them is bound to realise they haven't

emerged from the building and come to investigate. Ollie tries to shrug away any responsibility. Under his breath he mutters, 'C'est le guerre – or, as we say in English, tough shit.'

He rubs his hands together. Right, he has a plan so he might as well go for it.

When Ollie looks down, the world below them is receding. They're still loading people in. Each time the wheel shudders and stops, their cradle rocks back and forth. Beside him Baynton is groaning. 'What the hell–' He leans over the side before he throws up. It's an ugly sight. After a final spit, he slumps back in the seat, eyes shut as he prays this is only a bad dream.

With each small turn they climb higher, their seat swinging freely in the air. All that movement induces the next bout of nausea. Good job he didn't eat that takeaway.

When he opens his eyes, the horror on Baynton's face makes it all worthwhile. 'How the fuck did I get up here?' More retching – this time the dry kind. (The crowd below must be thankful.)

'I gather you're not happy,' Ollie says. 'And there I was imagining we might enjoy this fun experience together.'

Clutching his stomach, Baynton moans. 'I've always fucking hated Ferris wheels.'

'Oops. How was I meant to know that?'

Baynton's not daring to look down. 'I need to get off this fucking thing – and I mean right now.'

'Shame you're not the one calling the shots.'

His response is a deep, prolonged groan.

'You know, as a special bonus we're getting a free ride today,'

Ollie says. 'Do take a look down there – we're almost at the top now. Look how tiny everyone else seems from up here. The view's almost as good as the view from your apartment. Or I should say your *former* apartment since I doubt you'll ever go back there again.' Ollie leans forward making the whole cradle tip with him. 'Yep, the rest of the seats are full. Any minute now this ride is about to start.'

Baynton shakes his head. 'Kill me now.'

'Tempting, but I think, on balance, I'd better not.' Ollie waits a beat. 'Talking of killing, do you happen to recall firing that gun at my little sister?'

As the memory of it floods his mind, Baynton buries his head in his hands and groans. 'Oh God!' His very next thought is to shift the blame. 'Out of the blue you two appeared in my apartment. They were coming for me – what did you expect me to do? You must have tipped them off. I was shitting myself. Lord help me I...' Hair is streaming into his eyes, he grabs the front of Ollie's t-shirt with both hands. 'Tell me I didn't kill her.'

'If you fire a gun at someone from near point blank range, what do you expect?'

'Christ almighty!' Baynton lets go of him to stare at his own hands like he's checking for signs of his guilt. 'What sort of person does a thing like that?' Then, shaking his head over and over, 'I should have drowned myself while I had the fucking chance.'

The wheel is beginning to rotate, building up speed, and the man beside him is feeling suicidal. They're nearing the top, it's a hell of a long way down and Baynton is seriously contemplating ending it all. And he's given him the perfect opportunity to do that right here, right now. Fortunately, his hands are shaking so much he's struggling to unbuckle the strap that's holding him in. They're going faster. As they plunge back down Ollie's stomach flips and people scream out through fear and delight.

Shit – this wasn't the plan. 'No, no, no!' Ollie grabs Baynton's seatbelt. 'My sister's fine, honestly. You missed her. She's back at home and unharmed, I promise you.'

'Who the fuck are you anyway?' Baynton shouts above the din. 'And how did you get me up here on this damned thing? Was I drugged or something?' He narrows his eyes. 'You're lying, you little shit. There's no fucking way I could have missed from that distance.'

Leaning in, Ollie shouts. 'Your gun – the Glock – it misfired. This may come as a shock, but the man who sold it to you was a criminal, and they tend not to be overly concerned about the quality of the goods they supply. I mean, I doubt many of their customers have the nerve to ask for a refund.'

Baynton wants to believe him. 'She's okay?'

'Listen, she's my sister and I love her – if she wasn't I'd throw you off here right now and then claim you slipped.'

They're climbing again. Hating every second, Baynton can't decide whether to hang on or let go. 'So that lets me off on a technicality.' He snorts. 'We both know I would have killed her if that gun hadn't been an expensive piece of crap.' He pushes Ollie's hand aside. 'I was backed into a corner, but that's no excuse. That girl would be dead right now and that would make me a fucking murderer. I'm worse than pond scum. I should do the world a fucking favour and jump.' They're reaching the top – roughly 120 metres above the ground with nothing to break his fall.

'Wait!' Hand to the man's chest, Ollie holds him steady and waits for the stomach lurching drop to come. Down and down they plunge like the wheel is never going to stop. He shouts above the noise. 'Suppose you get another shot. No – I didn't mean to put it like that. What if we could make all the crap you've got yourself into go away?'

They're climbing again. Baynton shouts back, 'Like this fucking awful ride, there's no getting out of it unless you've got a magic wand. Believe me, I've thought about it long and hard.' He lets go to throw up his hands. 'I'm well and truly fucked.'

They're nearly at the top again. Ollie shouts, 'What if I could offer you redemption? Instead of giving in and topping yourself, which would, by the way, make one hell of a mess down there and ruin a lot of people's day out. What if this is your chance to reinvent yourself? You could try to achieve something that really would do the world a favour.'

The air is whistling around their ears as they plunge down defying gravity. Reaching the bottom, Baynton shouts, 'Is this the part where you lure me into some kind of cult?' An unamused smile. 'Or recruit me as a secret agent?'

Ollie's relieved to see he's now holding on to the edge of the seat. Hair battering his face, Baynton yells, 'No offence, but you seem a very unlikely spymaster. Or divine saviour.'

'Yeah well, as you might have guessed, I'm neither.'

Instead of leaving it there, Baynton feels the need to add, 'I mean you're not even shaving properly yet.'

Running a protective hand over his chin, Ollie wants to tell him to fuck right off. That last remark takes some swallowing, but he drags his mind back to the task in hand. How's he supposed to come up with a believable explanation for any of this? If only that sodding Guardian hadn't buggered off...

They're already halfway up again. Since all other options won't cut it, Ollie decides to come clean. 'How do you think I tracked you down in the first place?' he yells. 'Or got you out of your apartment and up here with both of us still breathing?'

'Mate, I have no idea.' Baynton shuts his eyes, ready for the coming free-fall.

Though he bristles at the "mate", Ollie lets it go. To be taken seriously, he needs to convince Baynton he's not talking about a plan he's just thought up, but one with some kind of official authorisation. He yells, 'As you might have guessed, I belong to a secret organisation. We're the sort of outfit that makes a point of knowing everything and everyone.'

'Wait a minute–'

They've reached the bottom of the curve. Ollie says, 'In case you're wondering, I don't represent a foreign government, or our own useless lot, for that matter. The organisation I'm a part of is both apolitical and non-religious. And, before you ask, we're not some criminal cartel either.' Baynton's gripping the seat but listening. 'As I've amply demonstrated, we're able to do things and go places you can't begin to imagine.'

'I'll give you that much.'

The ride is slowing down. Ollie's glad not to have to yell when he says, 'Look, David, consider this a one-time deal. We'd like to offer you a fresh start. In fact, we're prepared to whisk you away to a different location – somewhere you can begin to build a better life.'

Baynton shakes his head. 'Not in some witness protection program.'

'Oh I think we can be a lot more ambitious than springing for a bedsit in Swindon.'

Baynton's unconvinced. 'What's the catch – the downside of this deal? An offer like that always comes with a catch. If you expect me to testify, you can think again. In fact, if that's the condition, I might as well throw myself off this thing right now.' A threat that couldn't be hollower since they're now near the bottom heading for the part where they turf you off.

Ollie sighs, wishing he liked this man more. 'The catch, David, is that you'd better not turn out to be a self-serving, unprincipled, avaricious arsehole this time around.'

Chapter Forty-Five

The two of them walk away from the funfair into the main body of the park. Baynton is visibly shaken up, a shadow of his former, cock-sure self. He stumbles along, dawdling behind Ollie like some sulking kid. His hair is messed up, he smells of vomit and his smart shirt is now crumpled with enormous sweat stains down the back and under both arms. In a weak voice, he says, 'I'm all in, mate.' Then, looking around. 'Why the fuck are you leading me in circles?'

'We're dodging around the cams, so you need to keep up and stay close to me.' Exasperated, Ollie adds, 'No, don't look up. We don't want to make it obvious we're aware of them. Act natural if that's possible. We're just two guys taking a stroll in a park on a sunny day.'

Baynton nods and begins to walk alongside him. 'No offense, kid, but we're an unlikely looking duo. And if this new surveillance system – this Panettone or whatever you called it...'

'Don't say its name out loud. Not ever.'

Baynton clears his throat. 'Yeah well, if this unnameable, all-seeing system is as good as you say it is, then there's literally nowhere to hide from it.' He stops dead, plants his hands on his hips, his forehead beaded with sweat. 'I might as well give myself up.'

Ollie is forced to retreat to where he's standing. 'I'm taking you somewhere safe. Somewhere that's way off the beaten track, okay?'

'A safe house is just another prison, so what's the point?' Baynton glances down at Ollie's t-shirt. 'Out in the open like this, we've got to be sitting ducks. In fact, I might as well go for one last swim in that lake over there.'

Ollie shakes his head. 'Given the water quality, I wouldn't recommend it.' He's not going to physically coerce the man. 'You know, even sitting ducks can fly and that's what we're going to do as soon as I find the right spot.' He sniffs. 'And I reckon it's around here somewhere.'

'What's with all the sniffing? What are you hoping to smell?'

'Decomposition, if you must know.' Ollie scoffs at his reaction. 'No, not rotting corpses, only rotting vegetation. Every park needs composting areas. This one has several, and unless I'm mistaken, one of them is just over there behind those bushes.'

It's easy enough to locate the entrance and move aside the no-public admittance barriers. Baynton says, 'Okay, so now we're out of sight and surrounded by heaps of shit, what next?'

'Not shit, just compost.'

'Well, it smells like shit. Anyway, that's beside the point. What happens now, Sherlock? Are you going to snog me or something?'

'Ha – not a chance, *mate.*' Ollie checks there's no one in sight, no gardeners pushing wheelbarrows heading their way. 'Right, well as they say in the movies, we're about to go dark.' Before Baynton can object, he grabs the man's arm.

It's been a while since Ollie was in this house. Same low ceilings, same indefinable, comfortingly familiar smells. Nothing's changed here – it never has. They're in the kitchen, Baynton's head grazing one of the oak beams. Though Ollie's holding him up, he starts to sag at the knees, about to fall.

He steers Baynton into the nearest chair and the man's head flops forward hitting the table with a force that would have hurt if he wasn't more or less unconscious.

Blocking the light, a dark shape fills the doorway. 'I imagined you'd seek my assistance at some stage,' Grandad says. He comes forward to squeeze Ollie's shoulder in a perfunctory greeting, then examines Baynton with a disdainful look. 'So this is the wretched man who fired a gun at my granddaughter. A would-be murderer whom you've nonetheless decided to rescue.' Seeing his surprise, Grandad lifts one eyebrow. 'I may be past my prime these days, but I know enough.'

His dark eyes examine Baynton like he's seeing right through him. 'Not much of a specimen, is he?'

'Not right now, no. I mean, to be honest with you, back there I was tempted to let them gun him down. I'd still love to kick him in the ribs a few times while he can't fight back.'

'I'm not surprised.'

'But I've brought him here because–'

'You don't know exactly what to do with him, but you think he might turn out to be worth saving.'

'I assume there's a reason the Guardians have been protecting him. So I thought, you know, it has to be worth a try.'

'People have fought duels over much less.' Grandad looks at the ceiling like he might be thinking of going to fetch a pair of antique flintlocks. 'Fortunately, Lana's gone to see a play in Stratford,' he says. 'On a regular coach of her own free will so no, young man, I haven't just transported her there against her will. Give me some credit.'

'I give you loads of credit, Grandad, or I wouldn't be here.'

'Hmm. I see you're wearing that talisman your mother gave you.' When Ollie checks, the St Christopher is still hidden under his t-shirt. It seems his Grandad's powers of perception are as sharp as ever.

The old man pulls out a chair and sits down opposite Baynton. 'You might like to know that those gunmen you so successfully deactivated have now been arrested and charged.'

'Christ, they're not still frozen?'

Shaking his head, Grandad chuckles. 'Now that really would have caused a stir.' His face becomes serious again. 'As things stand, this man here remains filthy rich – with an emphasis on *filthy*. Despite its dubious source, with that sort of money under a person's control, it's easy to make things happen. Whether those things are desirable or ethical – well, that's another question.'

Grandad runs a hand through his iron grey hair. 'As the wronged party, it seems to me Vega should be involved in deciding this man's fate.'

'In that case we might as well sling a rope over one of these beams and string him up right now.'

Seeing the look on the old man's face, Ollie laughs. 'I was joking. Well, half joking. I suppose you're right about involving Vega. Victims should always be heard.'

'Good, then let's—'

'Although I think perhaps we should hold off a bit,' Ollie says. 'Give her time to calm down. If someone had just tried to shoot me, I wouldn't be feeling especially well-disposed towards them. And I can sense she's mad at me too for immobilising her along with everybody else.'

'Since she knows you're here now, I don't imagine we'll be able to stop her.'

Ollie nods. 'Fair point.'

'She ought to be grateful to you for saving her life. How you managed to do that is irrelevant in the greater scheme of things. You did a fine job of neutralising a difficult and complex situation. I'm proud of you.'

'Thanks Grandad.'

'With a bit more practice you'll refine the technique.'

'Perhaps there's a Guardian Proficiency course I could sign up for during the summer break?'

'No need for sarcasm, young man.'

Ollie sits down. 'Since we're going to do this by committee, what about Dad? Vega's his daughter, shouldn't he be given a say in what happens next?'

Grandad wrinkles his nose. 'If this man wakes up to find you, me, Vega *and* Tom sitting here ready to interrogate him, he'll assume he's facing a kangaroo court.'

Ollie shrugs. 'Is that such a bad thing?'

'Then why stop there? Why don't I whisk Lana back?'

With a straight face, he adds, 'Better still, let's rouse the whole of Stoatsfield. If you ask me it's about time we re-established the old ducking stool method. Yes, we'll tie him to that chair, parade him through the village and lower him into the river to see if he floats. If he drowns, he's innocent; if he survives, he's guilty.'

'Now who's being sarcastic? Seriously though Grandad, why not scare the shit out of him for a bit. As a deterrent.'

'Didn't you already try that?' Head on one side, those old brown eyes see right through him. 'That Ferris wheel stunt you pulled. Don't pretend you were ignorant of Baynton's long-standing phobia of being stuck on one of those contraptions.'

Ollie grins. 'Although it sort of backfired on me.'

Stern-faced, Grandad says, 'To quote Hesiod one of my favourite Greek poets: "He fashions evil for himself who fashions evil for another, and an evil plan does mischief to the planner".'

'Yeah okay, busted,' Ollie says.

Chapter Forty-Six

Vega

She's there before either of them can stop her. It's strange to be back in this familiar kitchen for something other than a social visit. Standing up to greet her, Grandad is tearful as he throws his arms around her and hugs her tight. 'Vega sweetheart, I'm so glad you're alright.'

She pulls away, too angry to be placated. 'Hi, sis,' Ollie says, on his feet now. Seeing her face, he decides not to hug her after all. 'Glad to see you're, um, feeling a lot better now. How's Dad? Is he still mad at you?'

She ignores his questions. 'You both know exactly how I feel.' Nodding over at Baynton, she says, 'If Oll hadn't intervened, I'd now have a big hole right here.' She thumps her breastbone. 'So how do you expect me to react?'

'Exactly as you are.' Grandad clears his throat. 'That said and acknowledged, going forward as we need to do—'

'Hang on, I'm not finished. There's way more I want to say so don't try to shut me up.' She holds up a hand to block any objections. 'He – that moral vacuum there – he needs to take responsibility for what he's done. Or would have done.' She turns to her brother. 'Thanks for stopping him, by the way. I owe you big time.'

'You're welcome,' Ollie says. *Maybe you should try to calm down a bit.*

No fucking chance. She walks over to where Baynton is slumped across the table. Her hands itch to throttle him. 'I'm thinking that, before he comes round, I should lie out on the floor here with a fake bullet hole just about there.' She taps the spot on her blouse above the place where she can still feel a slight ache. 'Have you got a black magic marker somewhere, Grandad? I'm sure one of you could draw a convincing entry wound. We can put a load of tomato ketchup coming from the hole and make it look like blood that's oozed out. And maybe some more ketchup can spread out over the floorboards here, so it looks like I've bled to death. He'll have the fright of his life.' She chuckles. 'He might even think I'm haunting him.'

'Although he knows you're not dead,' Ollie says. *What? I just felt he should know the truth, okay.* 'If it's any comfort, he was suicidal with guilt immediately afterwards.'

Grandad chips in. 'You're understandably angry…'

'I'm not angry, Grandad, I'm… Aaargh! I'm beyond livid. Right now I'm out of my mind crazy. As fucking furious as it's possible to be.' Her vocabulary runs out.

Grandad does that patting motion in the air he always did when they were little if he thought they should calm down. 'Emotions are running high at the moment…'

'*Running high?*' She gives a hard laugh. 'Oh they're *high* alright.' She stabs a finger towards the culprit. 'But let's not forget that he – that man right there – actually shot at me. By rights I should be dead. My life cut short, finished off at thirteen by him and his stupid gun.'

'No one is denying any of that,' Ollie says. 'But let's all try to be rational about what happens next. Leaving aside his fraudulent dealings, I think we can all agree that the main charge against David Baynton is attempted murder. Plus an additional charge of possessing and firing an illegally obtained and unregistered firearm.'

'Too right,' she says. Grandad nods.

'Okay so what should we do now?' Ollie looks at her. 'It's not like we can report him to the police. So, once we've all had a chance to calm down a bit more, the three of us are going to have to decide what happens to him next.'

'Yeah well, I'm not fucking planning to calm down any time soon.'

'Anger is a highly destructive force,' Grandad tells her. 'It's–'

'Is this the part where you quote some ancient Greek poet at me?' She's spitting nails. 'Because the ancient Greeks weren't exactly renowned for their leniency. Didn't Artemis turn some poor hunter into a stag so his own dogs would then rip him apart just because the man had accidentally seen his wife and her mates skinny-dipping?'

'Acteon's punishment was rather disproportionate,' Ollie says. 'Though, to be fair, that story is a myth.'

'Yeah, well those myths didn't just spring up fully formed out of nowhere. I hate to break it to you, Oll, but humans made them up in the first place.'

'I think we may have digressed somewhat,' Grandad says.

'Can I suggest we stop talking about people being torn limb from limb.' He sits down next to Baynton. 'Let us suppose for a moment that this man was duly charged and sent to trial. In his defence, he would probably claim he was under extreme duress at the time. That these were mitigating circumstances.' Before she can speak, he says, 'Just hear me out, Vega.'

'Go on,' she says.

'The jury would, I imagine, nonetheless find him guilty. He'd then be sent to prison for an unknown length of time. Assuming he wasn't murdered in prison – which, I think we can agree is a highly likely scenario – the prison system would attempt to reform him so that, when he finally emerged from his captivity, he wouldn't reoffend.'

Ollie sits down on the other side of Baynton. 'That's quite a rosy view of how the prison system works, but I guess the principles hold.'

'So you two are suggesting we try to reform him.' Vega folds her arms. No way is she going to sit down with them. 'Exactly how do you propose to do that?'

Grandad looks at Ollie. 'The floor is yours.'

Oll clears his throat. 'I might want to ring his neck for what he almost did, but I'm trying to master my emotions. Baynton was horrified when he thought he'd killed you, Vega. Genuinely, he was suicidal.'

'Pity he didn't see it through,' she mutters.

Grandad says, 'I think we can all agree he's made a few grave errors of judgement.'

Vega scoffs. 'Oh, they were grave alright.'

'He wasn't always an arsehole,' Ollie says. 'When he was at

302

uni, Baynton spent the summer in the Fiji Islands volunteering on a project that helps to conserve and restore the coral reef there. It's one of his happiest memories – a place he's in the habit of mentally retreating to when he's in stressful situations. I happened to have read about the project – how they've made enormous strides over the last decade, and they've been able to share their knowledge and techniques worldwide.'

She shrugs. 'So?'

'So imagine what they could achieve with a massive injection of funds – donated anonymously, of course.' He spreads his hands wide. 'If we send him back there, Baynton can live off-grid under a new ID–'

She snorts. 'And where's he going to get that from?'

'The man's been paranoid for some time,' Ollie says. 'He's acquired quite a selection of false passports. We just need a volunteer to go and get them from a safe deposit box he's been renting.'

Grandad raises a finger. 'Happy to oblige.'

Ollie's getting carried away. 'Think about it – his ill-gotten gains won't benefit him or the sleaze-merchants he's been associating with. Instead, that money will potentially benefit the entire planet.'

Vega's incredulous. 'You're seriously suggesting that his punishment for almost murdering me is being sent to live in paradise? No way.' She shakes her head. 'He would have killed me and now he gets to swan about on holiday for the rest of his life. What sort of fucking punishment is that?'

'Haven't finished, okay.' Ollie gives her a look. 'What if a certain "Organisation" (air quotes) keeps a close eye on him. They make sure he gets stuck into the work and doesn't just spend his time pissing about on the beach. He'll need to demonstrate he's serious. And, like I said, he'll lose all of the dodgy money he's accrued by giving it to the project. The Panoptes System will soon be spreading like a pandemic. If he tries to take off, as soon as he shows up at an airport, or a port, it will spot him. I doubt he'll ever be able to leave.'

Grandad says, 'Well, the man is obviously ambitious. Perhaps he'll keep his head down and even retrain as a marine biologist or something similar.'

'What you're advocating is the Norwegian prison model on steroids.' She looks at Grandad. 'I always imagined the Guardians were more on a par with the Old Testament God. That they were okay with all that wrath and smiting. Are *they* going to be happy with this rather enlightened solution?'

Grandad smiles. 'I imagine we'll soon find out.'

'And the Norwegians have one of the lowest reoffending rates in the world,' Ollie feels the need to tell her.

'Then the least you can do is let me play dead for a bit. I just want to scare the shit out of him, okay.'

Baynton groans like he's coming round. It strikes her that Grandad might have been controlling his consciousness levels ever since she arrived. Ollie squeezes her arm. 'What if we let you slosh some ketchup over your shirt, will that do?'

'And a fake bullet hole,' she says. 'Or the whole deal's off.'

Chapter Forty-Seven

Tom

Tom doesn't see them arrive. One minute the house is unnaturally quiet, the next he can hear music, the upstairs shower running. It seems they're back without a "Hi, Dad" – never mind an explanation about what they've been up to.

Still smarting from the indignity of being immobilised by his own daughter, he's determined to go up there and demand to know what happened. Halfway up the stairs it occurs to him that Matt will know already. His father might be less all-seeing these days, but no one keeps *him* in the dark for long.

Reaching the landing, he can't decide which door to bang on first. The music – Soul ii Soul's classic "Back to Life" – is coming from Vega's room. He can hear her singing along like she's celebrating, which suggests everything must be fine. Would it kill her to say so?

When did they decide to keep him out of the loop? Undeniably, he's the amateur in the family, the person Vega so forcibly prevented from becoming involved.

Ollie emerges from the bathroom with a towel around his waist. Thank God there are no injuries on him – at least as far as he can tell. 'You survived then,' Tom says.

'Yep.' He jerks his thumb in the direction of the bathroom. 'Things got a bit messy towards the end – so I thought I'd clean up before putting in an appearance.'

'Good to know.'

The boy's face becomes serious. 'You're right, you deserve a proper explanation, Dad.' He scratches his neck like he does when he's thinking. 'And I'm sorry you feel, you know, sort of excluded. The situation – well it got a bit more complicated than any of us anticipated. Vega really needed to change – her clothes that is. Her school shirt took a bit of a hammering. Not literally, you'll be pleased to hear. Oh and I've also managed to get ketchup on that duck t-shirt of yours. Sorry about that.'

Ollie grins like this is one big joke. Above his sister's off-tune wailing, he says, 'It's all my fault really. I was the one who screwed up in the first place. It was me who set certain wheels in motion. Although, that's maybe not a particularly original or apt metaphor what with causality being way more complicated than that implies.' He takes a breath. 'Anyway Dad, what I'm trying to say is, you're not the only one who can screw up in this family so you shouldn't feel bad or in any way inadequate. Not that I'm suggesting anything of the sort.'

Tom recognises something close to pity in the boy's eyes. 'I'm relieved you're both back safely,' he tells him. 'Thanks for the pep-talk. I feel a whole lot better already.'

'Don't be like that, Dad.' Ollie grabs his arm and then drops it to rescue his towel before it slips. 'Let's have a chat once I've thrown a few clothes on and Vega's sorted herself out.'

'Yeah well, I'd love to stay and *chat* with the two of you but, as it happens, I've got a duck house to deliver. An absurd object, no doubt, but one that nonetheless will help keep the wolf from the door.'

'Or the fox from gobbling up the Honourable Artus's precious Mandarin ducks.'

'Let's hope so.' Tom retreats down the stairs.

'We'll fill you in on everything that happened when you get back,' Ollie yells after him.

'Don't wait up,' he shouts back.

Tom stares into the remains of his pint, the many columns of tiny bubbles forever making their way to the top. Good for them. It's so-called Happy Hour in The Red Lion – better known locally as the Dead Lion. Heads bowed, his fellow drinkers are concentrating on their devices, or worse still, staring open-mouthed at the floor. The music comes into the category of "easy listening" with banal, saccharine lyrics that make him want to smash the old-school speakers pumping it out.

Jermain Jenkins – Aaron's dad – strolls up to the bar and orders a drink. After a sideways glance, he says, 'Evening Tom.' Then, 'You look to be a man drowning his sorrows.'

'Not *just* my sorrows. I can think of several people – if you can call them that – I'd personally like to drown. Or at least waterboard for a while.'

Jermain's booming laugh turns a few heads. He claps him on the back so hard it hurts.

Tom says, 'Hope you're not going to tell me to cheer up.'

'Not in this place.' Jermain takes a sip of his drink. 'Good drop of beer that. I sometimes pop in here for a quick one just to take the edge off the working day – know what I mean. Shame it's such a dump.'

'Hi, Tom. Hi, Jermain.' The voice belongs to Gwen. She looks great in tight jeans and a surprisingly low cut top. A sight for sore eyes.

He sits up. 'You're the last person I'd expect to see in this place.'

'Just popped in to buy a bottle of wine for this evening.' Ah yes, he's heard about the landlord's mysteriously sourced and heavily discounted off sales. After ordering and paying for a decent-looking Malbec, Gwen says, 'Either of you planning on coming to the barbecue at the school tonight? Should be fun.'

'That's a definite no from me,' Tom tells her.

Jermain raises a hand. 'I'm off there shortly. Three-line whip seeing's my missus is on the organising committee. They've really pushed the boat out this time according to my Lizzie. Suckling lamb, whole keg of beer, live reggae band... And all the money's going to the music department.' He chuckles. 'Beats me why they want our kids to make even more noise.'

After grabbing the wine bottle by its neck, Gwen shrugs. 'Guess it keeps them off the streets.'

Jermain snorts into his beer. 'Ask me, it would do most of them kids good to mooch around by the burger van like we used to, 'stead of spending all evening on their socials in their bedrooms.'

'I should probably go home,' Tom tells them before he downs the rest of his pint.

This elicits another hearty slap on the back from Jermain. 'Why not tag along with us, instead? Not that you'd know it in this place, but it's a mighty fine evening out there.' He nudges Tom. 'Single, good-looking bloke like you ought to be putting himself out there – know what I'm sayin'?'

'I'd be poor company,' he says.

Gwen raises an eyebrow. 'Why don't you let us be the judge of that, Mr Brookes?'

It's been such a relief to be with ordinary people who can't tell what he's thinking every damned minute of the day. Tom's just finished his pork and apple sauce bap when Gwen dances up to him. He's drunk enough to ask, 'So your Dom didn't fancy coming along tonight?'

'He's away again.' She's nursing an almost empty bottle. 'Sometimes I envy women with ordinary husbands – the sort who come home every night. Men who are happy to discuss their work over dinner, even if it's boring as hell.'

He taps his beer against her bottle. 'Here's to all the ordinary, boring folks out there.'

She laughs in that unbridled way she has. 'I think you might be a little drunk, Mr Brookes.'

'Only a touch inebriated, Mrs Roberts.'

He looks into the embers of the dying fire then surveys the scant crowd still gathered around it. 'Looks like the party's over,' she says. 'Don't know about you, but I'd rather not get cajoled into the clean-up operation. I've just ordered a cab. Would you like me to drop you off?'

'Yeah, why not?' Realising that sounded a bit ungracious, he adds, 'It's good of you to ask.'

'My pleasure.'

Ten minutes later they're stumbling into the car together. It's been a while since he shared a backseat with an attractive woman. 'You seem a lot happier,' she says.

'I expect it's the calibre of the company,' he tells her – which is the truth after all.

As they're nearing his street, she leans in closer, her fingers trailing down his thigh. 'Fancy coming back to mine for a nightcap? Cerys is staying over with a friend, so we'll have the place to ourselves.'

He can see his own house now, the downstairs lights still blazing. They must be waiting up for him. Gwen is a married woman and yet she's offering him no-strings sex in such a casual manner. Does she do this all the time? Unbidden, a picture of Beth comes to him – this time not a static, faded image in a frame, but the living, breathing, beautiful woman he watched on that stage.

'Maybe another time,' he says. Raising his voice, he tells the driver, 'Could you stop right here, please. This is me.'

Chapter Forty-Eight

Vega

He comes in smelling of booze and unsteady on his feet. 'Hi, Dad,' they say almost in unison. He nods but doesn't utter a word while he takes a glass off the shelf, goes over to the sink, glugs down a glass full of water and then tops it up again. When he spills some of it on the floor, she stops short of grabbing his arm to steady him as he wipes it up.

Ollie shoots her a look. *He's beered up, we should do this another time.*

He's not totally hammered. And he's in a much better mood now. If we put this off, it'll fester like – like some thorn in your finger that you ignore and then it turns into sepsis.

Raising his water glass at them, Dad says, 'Nighty-night you two,' a phrase she remembers from when they were little. 'I'm off to bed.' In the hallway, he mumbles, 'To sleep, perchance to dream...'

'Yeah, I'm totally knackered too.' Following him out, Ollie's pleased to be getting his way after all.

'But we need to talk,' she pleads from the kitchen doorway.

'We should sit down and discuss things as a family, like we always do.' They take no notice. 'And there won't be enough time in the morning,' she says to their backs.

One hand on the newel post, Dad pauses. 'Ah, but then time isn't an issue for you two, is it? I expect you could probably put the whole of Cheltenham on hold just like that.' Having failed to click his fingers, he looks down at his feet. 'Oh look – there's that step, the one I've grown so familiar with. Unless you plan to imprison me on it again, I'm going to catch some z's.'

Ollie smirks, damn him. *So, not such a good mood after all.*

What's she supposed to do? She can't stop her father from going to bed. Well, she could, but that's not exactly going to help the situation.

Vega gets up early to set the breakfast things out ready and grind the coffee that helps to determine Dad's mood in the morning. He comes in yawning, hair like an abandoned bird nest. 'Sit down,' she says. 'I've got everything ready.' She's quick to set the hot coffee in front of him.

Ollie comes in, hair wet from the shower. He sits down in his usual place, tipping out cereal and milk like this is any other day. Dad sort of chuckles. 'That boy is infinitely more slippery when wet.' He looks at her and they share a smile, both of them remembering.

'Ollie is now going to tell you exactly what happened.' She glares at her brother. 'Aren't you, Oll?'

Dad makes a point of finishing his coffee before he says, 'I'm listening.'

'Okay.' Ollie clears his throat. 'Well, as you guessed, Dad,

Baynton was holed up in his penthouse, had been ever since he went missing.' He waves his spoon like a conductor. 'His original plan was to lie low until the heat died down.'

She snorts. '"The heat died down" – this isn't a gangster movie.'

'You wanted me to tell Dad what happened, so shut up and let me tell it my way.'

Not taking the bait, she narrows her eyes at him. *Now who's in a bad mood?*

'You shouldn't tell your sister to shut up,' Dad says.

Ollie's about to answer back then changes his mind. 'It was me who made him so paranoid he faked his own death. I couldn't stop feeling guilty about that, so I went there, to the Grenewych Heights building–'

'And no one tried to stop you?' Dad asks.

'No. I think the, um, Organisation wanted to test me to see what I would do. I only went there to warn Baynton he wasn't safe. Not sure how, but I knew the people who are after him had access to this state-of-the-art surveillance system, which is only supposed to be used to track terrorists and really serious stuff like that. It's called Panoptes–'

Dad's geek-mode kicks in. 'After Argus Panoptes – the Greek giant with a hundred eyes.'

She interrupts. 'The people looking for him knew you'd been sniffing around his old apartment, Dad. They got suspicious and that's why they had men watching our house. So, when this genius over here surfaces in London, Panoptes soon picks him out as a match. And then he goes and leads them straight to Baynton's apartment block – the dolt. That's why I needed to go there to warn him.'

'Those men he swindled really mean business,' Oll says. 'They accessed the building's own CC cams before sending in these commando-style armed men. Leastways, I think they were men. I mean I didn't look that closely.'

Get on with it, she tells him silently.

'Anyway, those faux commandos have to set a charge to get inside his door. Baynton hears them coming and gets so spooked he's ready to fire at anyone and anything that comes through the door. They're about to burst into the room when he fires his gun. Unfortunately, the first person in his line of fire is Vega.'

'Unfortunately!' Dad's fists are balled like he wants to hit out. 'Christ almighty!'

Ollie touches his shoulder. 'Yeah, but the good news is I manage to freeze everything and stop Vega getting shot by about this much.' His thumb and finger are almost touching. 'I mean that close.'

Don't remind me. Pain stabs her chest like a knife plunged, though in the next breath it's gone.

'I don't know what to say,' Dad still manages to say.

'You've not heard half of it,' Oll tells him. 'I'm standing there wondering what to do next when this weird Guardian shows up and, after we have a bit of a conflab, he agrees to whisk Vega back here. So now she's out of the firing line, I'm still left there in this room that's like some stage set with a load of human puppets all holding guns. And I have to work out what to do next. So anyway, I figure if I can take Baynton out of the equation—'

'That was your first thought?' Dad's looking daggers. 'You

chose to protect him even though the man almost shot your sister?'

'Yes well, there was that to consider. But, you know, I felt a bit bad about my flash drive cock-up and then making it worse by blowing Baynton's cover. And I worked out that once he's out of that room no one else is going to get shot – unless they turn on each other. So I move him to this fairground. He's genuinely suicidal once he realises how close he came to murdering Vega. Anyway, I'm thinking – what do I do with him now? I didn't trust my own judgement so, long story short, I move Baynton to Grandad's house.'

'You sought your grandfather's help but not mine.'

She looks at her brother. *You could have skipped that particular detail.*

I think he needs to hear it all. Out loud, Ollie says, 'After two major screw-ups, I wanted to be sure to do the right thing. And I had this idea, which seemed to me like a good one, but I needed to confer with someone, and since Grandad has loads of experience…' He shrugs. 'Seemed like the best option at the time.'

'I see.' Dad stares into his empty cup. 'And what was your agreed solution?'

'Okay, you need to hear me out.' Ollie puts his spoon down and spreads his hands along the edge of the table. He takes a breath. 'I took Baynton to the Fiji Islands.'

'You did what?'

'When he was a student he'd worked on this really brilliant conservation project over there.'

'Let me get this straight,' Dad says, in that calm voice he

puts on when he's about to lose it big time. '*You* went to the Fiji Islands with the man without even telling me?'

'It was just a flying visit. Who else was going to take him? I was in and out in no time. I know it's a long way away – but then so is Massachusetts for that matter.'

Dad thumps the table. 'Yes but I didn't exactly choose to go there.'

'Well I wasn't exactly taking a vacation either. I mean, I would – it's a beautiful place and all that.' Catching Dad's expression, he sobers his face. 'The project he's working on is no doss. And the research going on over there is helping in the regeneration of coral reefs all over the world.'

'So the scientists running this project just accept this stranger who shows up out of the blue with open arms?' Dad's shaking his head.

Ollie smiles. 'Once Baynton happened to mention the massive donation he was about to make to the project, they were more inclined to view his application in a positive light. By the way, he'd already laundered that money more thoroughly than a hotel's sheets after a stag do. And remember, he'd worked there before and was genuinely enthusiastic about what he might do to help them. He even offered to muck in with the other volunteers to begin with. If I'm honest, it felt good to give him a second chance. I really believe he cares about what they're doing over there and wants to contribute to their work.'

'If you say so.' Dad is a long way from convinced.

Ollie leans back in his chair. 'Moving on, I'm sure we've all been wondering why the Guardians got mixed up in all this in the first place.'

'And?' she says.

'Seems to me,' Ollie says, 'the only logical explanation is that Baynton goes on to do something of real significance. Something he needed to survive the mess he'd got himself into in order to go on and achieve.'

Dad scoffs. 'Or does he get the false credit for what the project achieves thanks to his sizable donation? Seriously, what's to stop the man absconding or living the life of Riley over there?'

'For a start he's being watched,' Ollie says. 'Though he thinks it's by members of the Secret Service. I may have led him to believe that if he puts a foot wrong they'll haul his arse into jail.'

'So this was actually a joint venture between you and our overlords.'

Dad's sigh is more resigned than anything else. 'The first of many perhaps.'

Ollie frowns. 'I wouldn't put it quite like that.'

'And then there's your grandfather – let's not forget his part in this.' She hates to hear that bitter edge in Dad's voice when he talks about his dad.

'Remember *I* went to him,' Ollie says. 'He wouldn't have been involved if I hadn't rocked up with Baynton on his doorstep – well in his kitchen actually.'

'And your grandmother?' Dad asks. 'Was she party to these discussions?'

'No, of course not,' Vega says. 'She was on a theatre trip with her friend Sylvie.'

Dad rubs his chin. 'How very convenient.' He looks at her.

'So I gather you were there too.' She can only nod. 'It was the three of you who decided Baynton's fate, not the Guardians.'

'Pretty much,' Ollie says. 'Although, if we're being pedantic, I guess the three of us *are* actually Guardians.'

No one says anything for a bit.

To lighten the mood, she says, 'If it's any consolation, I gave Baynton one hell of a fright. Seriously, he nearly pissed himself when he came round and saw me lying on the floor all covered in what looked like blood. We used up a hell of a lot of Gran's tommy sauce, but it was worth it. I mean, you should have seen his face, Dad...'

'If only I'd had the opportunity.' He's not amused. After a bit, Dad says, 'That's why your school blouse is soaking in the sink.'

'Maybe we should have asked Baynton to launder that too.' Her joke falls flat.

Looking at her, Ollie says, 'I believe, on balance, we did the right thing.' He takes a mouthful of muesli and chews on it for a while. Eventually, he adds, 'I guess time will tell.'

Chapter Forty-Nine

Ollie

His visit might have been fleeting, but all the same the Fiji Islands were a revelation. He'd needed those sunglasses to block the glare from the white sandy beaches and that clear sparkling sea. He's never been anywhere so perfect. He must have looked a dweeb rocking up in a place like that wearing one of his grandad's ridiculously formal shirts. (The tomato-stained duck t-shirt would have raised many more eyebrows.) Ollie had thought about taking the shirt off. He would have done if he hadn't been surrounded by so many tanned, buff bodies.

That was then, this is now – just another same-as-always school day. Another morning of negotiating packed corridors; the smell of cleaning fluid mixed with sweat and cheap perfume; irrelevant notices about lame events; hollow banter and joshing by the lockers – all of it so small-scale and irrelevant when, on a whim, he could be out of there and on the other side of the world.

Vega would tell him to get over himself.

During registration, he occupies his usual place on the

margins of other people's friendship groups. He homes in on one conversation when he hears them discussing Cerys. In his absence she'd announced to the whole maths class that she'd had enough and wouldn't be showing up for any more lessons and then she walked out.

'She said they were all small-minded, fucking morons,' Minnie Blackman tells them. 'I couldn't believe Mr Godwin didn't even say anything about her language. All he did was tell her to calm down. Cerys apparently then swings by the office and tells them, like, "Oh and by the way I'm not planning to sit my exams". On her way out, she waves at us through the window and says, "You won't be seeing me again". And no one's seen her since.'

Paul's enormous hand clamps his shoulder. 'Eh Ollie, weren't you meant to be getting Cerys up to speed?' Behind Mrs Fulmer's back he makes an obscene gesture then repeats it several times.

Ignoring him, Ryan Elliot says, 'I heard the head told her she should go home and think about her future. If that was me, once I'd calmed down, I'd grovel so I could sit the exams, at least.'

'Makes no sense not to even take the exams.' Aaron shrugs. 'Okay, you might get crap marks, but you might get lucky if the right questions come up. What's the worst that can happen?'

Minnie leans in, 'You could tell something wasn't right when Cerys burst into the class with a face like thunder. Jazz tried to ask her what was up, didn't you Jazz, and she totally ghosted her. I don't mean to slag Cerys off or anything, but she must be a fucking idiot to jack it in with only a few more weeks to go.'

Ollie's heard enough. 'I'm sure Cerys will be delighted to learn she has such loyal friends,' he says, walking away and ignoring all the comebacks.

He's never set foot in the Roberts' house. Built of honey-coloured Georgian stone and situated in one of the posh parts of Cheltenham, number 15 Regency Close is at the end of a cul-de-sac. Due to its high hedges, he can't see the ground floor of the house from the street. All the upper windows have blinds drawn. As he walks up the path, he worries some territory-defending dog might come hurtling out of the bushes to see him off. (Though Cerys has never mentioned any pets.) On the doorstep, he presses the old-fashioned bell. It buzzes. Her mum answers. 'Yes.'

'Hi, it's Ollie,' (Stupid when the woman can see him.) 'Is Cerys in?'

Gwen Roberts says, 'Yes she is.' Nothing more.

'Right, so could I possibly come in and have a chat with her, please?'

She appears to think this over. In the end she sighs and says, 'Wait there while I go and have a word with her.' In the background he hears a male voice mutter something unclear.

A robin hops out of a bush and, head on one side, stares at him as if confirming he shouldn't by rights be standing there.

The intercom crackles. 'You'd better come in,' Mrs Roberts says. Not much of an invitation. He pushes on the open door and walks into their hallway. The floor's patterned Victorian tiles give way to a pristine grey rug. No furniture, no coats or shoes littering the place. Should he take his off? There's no time to before Mrs Roberts emerges from one of several closed doors. She seems cautious, wary. Dressed in a smart silk blouse over formal trousers, her mid-brown hair is pulled into quite a severe bun. Apart from her face, she could be a different woman to the friendly one he's met several times. More like her embittered twin. He has no idea what this version might be thinking.

'Cerys is in her room,' she says. 'You'd better follow me up.' She must be worried that, left to his own devices, he'll snoop around or open the wrong door.

Her heels ring out as she leads him up the cantilevered stone staircase to the first floor. She stops outside the second door on the right and knocks. 'Come in,' Cerys says from within. Her mother opens the door and then stands aside to let him through.

Cerys is lying on her bed fully clothed in denim jeans and a plain blue t-shirt. Her feet are naked, her golden hair spread across the pillow behind her like some artist's muse posing. The blind at the window is filtering out most of the sunlight. To say the room lacks personality is an understatement. The floor is carpeted a sort of greige colour. A bookshelf covers most of one wall. On its shelves there are matching rows of expensive leather books that look like they were bought as a job lot. No fluffy toys on her bed. No action heroes either, just a cleared desk with an uncomfortable looking wooden chair that looks like it could do with a cushion. No posters or pictures on the pale grey walls. Cerys is lying on a pristine, white duvet – the sort you might see in a fancy hotel.

He offloads his backpack and waits. After marking her

page, she puts her book aside. (Proust in the original French, of all things.) 'Thanks, Mum,' she says looking past him. Mrs Roberts huffs as if disapproving. Taking the hint she shuts the door leaving the two of them alone.

Attempting to read Cerys's thoughts, he comes up blank as usual. Still standing by the door, he says, 'I heard about what happened at school and I, um, thought you might want to talk things over with someone.' Blushing he adds, 'With a friend.'

'I've left that place,' she says, uncrossing her ankles. 'It's as simple as that.'

'Look, if something I said has upset you, then–'

'It didn't. You haven't.' She sits up. 'If you've come here due to a guilty conscience, you're mistaken. I left because it was time. It's as simple as that.'

He shakes his head. 'Cerys, I don't understand... Something must have happened to make you want to leave before the exams.'

'Ah, my exams – so that's your big concern.' She pushes herself up from the bed and comes forward to look him in the eye. Her scent makes him think of windswept beaches. Like her mother, this Cerys could be a whole other person. Smirking now, she says, 'All this fuss about insignificant examinations. I would have thought you'd be the first to see that type of assessment is crude at best. But then, of course, there's the hidden curriculum – the assumptions and expectations one imbibes without being fully conscious of the process.'

'I guess that's inevitable,' he says. Nothing's right here – a very large piece of this puzzle is missing. Less sure now, he asks, 'What do your parents think? Aren't they worried about you throwing away your future?'

She snorts. 'I'm not throwing away my future.' Up close, her deep brown eyes are lit by amusement. 'The thing you should remember about any assessment is that it can be a two-way process.' Her smile is more than self-assured – she's the one in charge here. 'Tell me, Oll, why did you really decide to come and see me?'

'Like I said…' He's shocked when she reaches up to slide her hand around the back of his neck and into his hair. 'I came…'

She pulls his head forward until his mouth is close to hers, her warm breath playing on his lips. Looking into his eyes, she says, 'I think it might have been for something like this.' When she kisses him it's a dream come true. The pressure intensifies until it begins to hurt his lips. She opens her mouth wider and her tongue slips into his. He responds, wanting more, physically aroused like he's never been before. The hand on his neck is exerting more and more pressure, her tongue half blocking his airway. Against his will, he begins to imagine her tongue growing and growing until she's ramming it down his throat and he can't breathe.

Shaken, Ollie pulls away. He wipes his mouth half expecting his hand to come away bloodied.

'I can see that wasn't quite what you were hoping for,' she says letting go of him. 'As you might have guessed, I'm a long way past my first rodeo, though I believe it might be yours.' There's no warmth in her expression.

'I think I should go,' he says, picking up his school bag.

'Good decision.' Her face softens a little. 'Sorry to be harsh, Ollie. You're a really great kid with amazing potential and all that. You just need to learn not to rush into things you don't fully understand.'

She picks up her book. 'You should know that we're leaving here soon. Not just this town, but the country. Since I won't have another chance to say goodbye, I'll wish you bonne chance and all that. You're cute and smart – the next girl is going to fall head over heels for you. But I was never going to be that girl.'

Ollie wishes with all his heart that he'd stayed away. He can't get out of there fast enough. 'Bye then,' he says, not looking back as he closes the door.

Out on the landing he takes a deep breath, shuts his eyes, and gives himself a moment to get his act together before venturing downstairs. It might be bad manners, but he's tempted to make a bolt for the front door before Mrs Roberts can come out from wherever she's lurking.

Too late, he hears footsteps on the staircase leading up to the second floor. Before he can move, a pair of trouser-clad legs come into sight. The other half of the man emerges. Matching grey jacket, white shirt, pale face, dark hair combed back from his face, sharp as hell ice blue eyes. 'Hello there, young man.' He lingers on the bottom step taking stock of him.

Feeling the need to explain his presence under such scrutiny, Ollie jerks a thumb at the door behind him. 'I'm a friend of Cerys's – from school. We've just been having a chat and, um, we've said our goodbyes, and now I'm about to leave.'

The man – surely the elusive Mr Roberts – frowns. 'That was quite a summary, young fella.' (More American that time.) His mouth slides into a sideways grin. 'Are you feeling alright? You seem a touch pale around the gills, if you don't mind me saying so.'

'I'm absolutely fine.' Ollie waves away the suggestion. 'Anyway, got to run. Goodbye and, um thanks for your hospitality. Hope the move goes alright.'

'It will. We're old hands at it.'

Ollie rushes down the stairs and out of their front door, only catching his breath once he's through the gate and safely back on neutral territory. Further down the street he's reassured by the presence of a bickering couple hauling heavy shopping bags up their path.

A black and white cat strolls past him. In no hurry, it brushes up against his legs leaving hairs on his school trousers. He bends to stroke it's arching back, to feel the living warmth of its little body. It starts to purr under the attention. Looking past him, the cat could be checking out the Roberts' front garden. 'I wouldn't go up there,' he tells it out loud. 'The people in there are...'

Are what? He thinks back to the man on the stairs. That wide, grinning mouth. And his voice – the way his accent ranged freely between several continents. Ollie grasps the bigger picture – this time in colour. He looks the cat in the eye. 'Be careful, little kitty, those people aren't what they seem.' In case they're listening, he's careful not to utter the word Guardians.

Chapter Fifty

Tom

Outside the day's heat is intensifying. Tom shuts the windows and makes sure all the outside doors are locked. Alone in his stifling house, he runs through his preparations. The kids won't be back for ages – tick. In the bathroom he sticks a line of motion-sickness patches to his stomach – another tick. Nothing untoward strikes him when he checks his appearance in the mirror, apart from the fact that his grey hairs are multiplying at a rate of knots. Unlike Matt, his Guardian genes haven't stopped him looking exactly what he is – a man in his mid-forties. Statistically classed as middle-aged. He rubs over his newly shaved chin.

Should he be doing this? Staring himself in the face, he admits that a small part of his motivation is to demonstrate that he's still capable of pulling off something pretty bloody amazing without anyone else helping him. His previous visit had been cruelly cut short and, after all, it's only for this one last time.

Discarding his habitual shorts and t-shirt, he pulls on jeans and a padded jacket over a plain navy sweatshirt – an outfit that's never been era-defining. He's already boiling – if this doesn't work, he might melt like chocolate.

It wasn't easy to discover which venue the production moved on to next. Now converted into a nightclub, various contemporary images reveal that the Elysian Playhouse was purpose-built and had a jutting, half-polygon stage surrounded on three sides by tiered seating. He's already studied the surrounding streets and earmarked a suitable entry point – a nearby, dead-end alleyway. If he gets the timing right (an optimistic assumption) it should be early evening. Surprising a rough sleeper or illicit lovers can't be fully ruled out.

His checklist complete, Tom crosses his fingers hoping no one will intervene to screw things up this time.

A variety of disgusting smells fill his nostrils while the darkness thins. It looks like he's arrived precisely where he had planned. Already nauseous, he staggers out from behind the heaps of carboard next to a row of overflowing wheelie bins. He sits down on the hard kerb. Head in his hands, he waits for his internal roundabout to stop spinning. Not exactly first-class travel.

An unfathomable amount of time passes before he's roused by a scratching sound. A large rat is scurrying towards him, its whiskers twitching. When Tom shoos it away, it retreats to a safer distance but continues to study him. Rodent aside, he's feeling better. Once he's confident he's not about to fall, he stands up. So far everything's going to plan. And look – no hands.

The sudden drop in temperature is making him shiver, although some of that is down to his growing excitement. He buttons up his jacket before raising a fist to celebrate his triumph. Still got it.

For better or worse, he walks out into the open. Though it's after dark, the streets are still busy. Distancing himself from the squalor of the alleyway, he checks his clothes for besmirchment but can't spot any blemishes. His jacket seems to smell okay. He's reassured when passing pedestrians pay no attention to him. Most of the shops have closed up for the day – the low prices in their lit windows hard to get his head around.

Reaching the end of the street, he emerges into the town's main thoroughfare. Despite the blinding effect of so many headlights, he spots a Ford Escort Estate on a D registration plate. Right behind it, a silver E reg Peugeot 205 GTI catches his eye. Nice car. The next vehicle he picks out is a red B reg Polo with aspirational black stripes. Unless they're all heading for a classic car convention, this has to be the late 1980s. A boxy, blue and white bus splashes past. A cyclist gets in the way before Tom can read the plate. The only living being to regard him with any curiosity is a passing cocker spaniel. As the dog gets closer, it emits a low growl then strains to sniff him out before the elderly owner pulls it to heel.

The theatre is exactly where he expects it to be, its name picked out in lights above the main entrance. The poster on the A-frame sign outside confirms everything he had hoped it would. Smiling to himself, Tom hunches into his upturned collar, the drizzle curling his hair as he waits in the growing queue. His fellow punters are mostly middle-aged, umbrellas up, all chatting and smoking in groups or couples while he stands alone, one hand clutching the currency in his pocket.

Once inside, he picks up a souvenir leaflet from the box office counter and folds it with care before zipping it into an inner pocket. Without a hitch, he pays the admittance fee in cash and manually selects his seat – four rows back in the central tier. 'No interlude,' he's told.

Tom swallows his impatience as he follows the stream of theatre fans making their way into the auditorium. He takes his seat with time to spare, then stands up again to remove his jacket which he stuffs under the seat in front. He keeps expecting some po-faced individual to emerge from the crowd to spoil everything. To calm his jangling nerves, he focuses on the exposed set. It must travel with them because everything is identical, although on closer inspection the flower-clad trellis is further back, and the two steamer chairs have been placed more to the fore.

He yelps when a heavy woman steps on his foot. Heads are turning. The woman's apology is fulsome. 'I'll live,' he tells her. Then, because that sounded ungracious, 'It's absolutely fine, honestly. I hardly felt it.' He's relieved when she locates her seat further along the row.

The atmosphere is literally changing due to the thin veil of cigarette smoke hanging like a mist over the audience. Much of the seating around him has filled up though not yet to capacity. Whoever chose the upbeat background music is doing nothing to induct the audience into 1920s Greece. A Billy Ocean banger morphs into Kylie who's feeling lucky alright.

Him too. Bill Withers is having a lovely day, but the lights are dimming, and he's faded out in favour of the same Greek folk music. By the time the male lead comes on, Tom's heart is pumping so hard he worries he's about to suffer a coronary arrest with no handy defibrillator to revive him.

The Bertie character's first line about enduring another day in paradise couldn't be more apt. Tom takes a series of deep breaths – slow inhale, slow exhale. It helps a bit. When Beth finally strolls out onto the stage, almost within touching distance, it feels like he's having an out of body experience. Everything about her dazzles him. Without his mind-reading daughter at his side, he's free to remember their many intimate moments. Watching her, he can't believe his younger self was capable of securing the affections of such an extraordinary woman.

For one scene she shimmies on in a flapper-style midnight blue dress complete with a peacock feather in her hair. It's an astounding transformation. Later in the play, the besotted chief of police gets down on one knee to kiss Beth's hand and for one mad moment Tom imagines running onto the stage to throw himself at her feet and declare his undying love.

The performance is exquisite torture. He can't concentrate, can't take it all in. And then, far too soon, the final curtain is falling.

There's a moment's silence before rapturous applause begins. The actors reappear. They form a swaying, hand-in-hand line for a series of bows that acknowledge the standing ovation they're receiving. A roar of approval greets Beth when she steps forward for her solo bow. After one more curtain call, a collective understanding runs through the audience that the players have given their all and should be allowed to leave the stage.

It's over.

The bustle around him gradually dies away while Tom sits on in the dimly lit theatre trying to savour something of the last hour and a half. He wants to drink in the glamour and excitement of Beth's make-believe life. It ought to be enough that he's stolen this opportunity to see her in her prime, living the life she always dreamed of. He wonders where she is right now, picturing the company backstage taking off their makeup while they relish the high that must follow such an enthusiastic reception.

Cleaners have come in with bin bags and noisy vacuum cleaners giving him no choice but to retrieve his jacket and leave. He walks out into the throng in the bar then weaves his way past people drinking and discussing the play in raised, insistent voices. A couple of individuals are peering at him as if they recognise that, by rights, he has no business being amongst them. When a man in a smart suit turns around, it turns out not to be Ford after all. In any case he's past caring.

He's made it this far, what's to stop him making the most of this last opportunity? He takes the pamphlet from his pocket and there she is again smiling up at him. Abandoning caution, he heads away from the marked exits into a passageway that appears to lead deeper into the building. If he can find Beth's dressing room, there's a chance he'll be able to tell her to her face just how brilliant she is. If he doesn't even try, he might always regret it.

Up ahead he hears and then sees a raucous gaggle of young men and women heading his way. Tom stands still, his nerve failing him. Amongst them various cast members are almost unrecognisable reduced to their civilian clothes. Instead of continuing in his direction, the actors pour out through an open fire door into a back street. When he moves closer, he can see they're congregating in an animated mob, their collective breath misting the night air as they laugh and loudly disagree about where to head off to next.

With so few streetlights it's hard to be sure, but he thinks one of the girls in the thick of it with her back to him is Beth. When she moves he's less certain. The girl squeals at something, her dark hair bouncing around her shoulders. How spirited they all are, buoyed up by tonight's success and the many possibilities that lie ahead.

Discussion apparently resolved, they set off along the street in a noisy gang. It is her – he can see that now. If he were to follow, wheedle his way into their midst until he's alongside her, what then? Beth would be polite, while inwardly disdainful that a dodgy and obsessive older man could be so persistent. As the father of a teenage girl, he's all too aware of the nuisance, and worse, posed by delusional older men.

Tom shudders. He doesn't belong with them. Or with her. He watches the last of the raucous posse turn the next corner and disappear from sight.

Time he went home to his family.

Chapter Fifty-One

Vega

When she walks into the kitchen, Dad is sitting at the table staring into a half-drunk mug of tea. He looks up, his smile a strain. 'Hi, sweetheart. How was your day?'

'Averagely boring. School was hot as hell.' She dumps her school bag on the floor. After grabbing a lemonade from the fridge, she takes the chair opposite him and gulps down half the bottle. She says, 'So, your day was quite eventful.'

He looks sheepish, is uncertain how much she knows. To put him out of his misery, she says, 'You went to see Mum in that play again. I'm not surprised. She's amazing, isn't she?'

'She certainly is.' He shakes his head. 'Anything else you care to comment on while we're having this little heart to heart?'

'Well done for turning down Gwen Roberts.'

'Jesus, can't a man have any secrets?'

Matching his gesture, she throws up her hands. 'Not in this family.' Before he can go off on one, she says, 'You had a lucky escape with that Gwen woman – if that's even her real name.

If you knew… Anyway, I'm delighted to inform you that the Roberts family are leaving town right away.'

He frowns. 'You're serious? Surely not before the term ends.'

'Oh yes.' She gives a sage-style nod.

'But that's crazy. Cerys must at least be coming back to sit her exams.'

'Nope.' (She makes the P pop.) 'She told the head she wasn't going to be darkening their doors again – or more derogatory words to that effect.' After another long swig, she says, 'Curious, is it not?'

'Or foolish.' Dad rubs at his chin. 'Poor Ollie – he must be devastated.'

'He probably would have been, if he hadn't gone around to theirs after his last lesson to try to talk Cerys out of it. Seems he discovered a whole other side to her and her family.'

'And he told you this himself?'

She gives him a look. 'It's not like he can keep stuff like that from me for long.' She finishes her drink. 'I was right all along about Cerys being a bitch. I knew she was a total fraud, though I couldn't tell what she was really up to.'

'Which was?'

'Let's just say she had an ulterior motive for befriending Oll.'

'But you're not going to tell me what that is.'

'Think I'll leave that up to Oll. I expect he'll say something to you when he's ready.' She gets up to put the empty bottle in the correct bin. Dad doesn't comment because he's gone back to staring into his cold tea. Perhaps now might be the right time to say it. While the iron, or whatever, is hot.

She sits back down to face him, rubs his arm as if their roles are reversed and she's the comforting parent. 'You know, Dad I've been thinking about us as a family and the fact that one very important person is missing.'

He sighs. 'Your mother.'

'Let's not forget we have options other families don't have. I reckon there could be a solution if we use our imaginations.'

'Sweetheart I understand–'

'Hear me out, please, before you say anything else.'

'Okay.'

'This might sound a bit ambitious, but what's to stop us all moving back to the late eighties? Or maybe the early nineties? It was a really cool era – in lots of ways things then were tons better than they are now. And if you were to arrange to bump into Mum, and she got to know you again, who knows... What's to stop her falling for you just like she did the first time you met?'

He's already shaking his head. 'I'm sorry Vega, but it won't work. The Beth I saw up there on that stage is a very different person to the woman I was married to. And it's not just that. I've changed too.' He pulls at a strand of his hair. 'And in more ways than this.'

'So what? Lots of women marry older men. A silver fox is still a fox.'

His smile is all sadness. 'Sweetheart, I honestly don't know where to start,' he says using that patronising tone he reserves for telling her she's done something stupid. He draws a slow hand over his face. 'It pains me to say this, but your mother is a lot happier being free to pursue her career unencumbered.'

'Unencumbered – is that how you think of us?'

'I used the wrong word, but the truth is she successfully moved on in her life. Don't ever doubt that she loved you and Ollie with all her heart when you were little, but that was her other life.'

'And she loved you too, Dad. If we all lived in her era, and frankly, you made more of an effort, it could work out like it did before. Just think – the four of us could be a proper family again.'

Covering her hand with his, he says, 'I'm sorry to say Elizabeth Travino has no room in her heady new life for a middle-aged man and a couple of teenagers. That's the harsh reality. I wish it had been and could be different, but today helped me come to terms with that fact.'

She pulls her hand away, but he hasn't finished. 'It's okay to miss her, Vega. And remember a part of her will always be in you and your brother. Today I realised that as long as I have you two, then in a way I still have her.'

'That's just sentimental bullshit!' She stands up. 'You know, Dad, you could grow a pair and not always sit back and let stuff happen to you.'

She's lit a fuse. His chair almost topples as he stands up. 'Now just you hold it right there, young lady. This is not a question of how big my cojones are and the implied, and frankly ridiculous, concept of masculinity that metaphor suggests; it's about coming to terms with what's possible and what isn't. Your scenario is a beguiling fantasy that can't ever become reality.'

'What if we choose another time, when she's nearer your age now?'

'It would make no difference in the end. We need to let her go,

sweetheart.'

He might be tearful, but she's not going to feel sorry for him. 'Yeah well, that may be your decision, but it's not mine.'

'You're only thirteen so, right now, the two happen to be inextricably linked.'

Vega narrows her eyes. 'You forget, I can do whatever I like, and you can't stop me.' She doesn't mention imprisoning him on that step, doesn't need to. 'The fact is, Dad, me or Oll can decide to live in a different era, and you won't be able to stop us. It's our choice to make, not yours.'

'Speak for yourself,' Oll says from the doorway where she realises he's been standing for the last few minutes. 'Dad's right. Face it, Mum has no fucking idea who we are anymore. You know all about her stellar career. You remember that one time we met her on the village green when we were tiny, and she was an old woman. She gave us those St Christophers not because she remembered we were her kids, but because you kept popping off to see her at night like some baby ghost. You even pointed to Marshy Bottom on a map, for Christ's sake. All she did was follow her instincts. Nothing more than that. And then she just got back on that coach and went off to live the rest of her life.'

His face softens as he comes over to her. 'Our mother died more than twelve years ago. Fact. You need to stop giving Dad a hard time about something none of us can change.'

'You can't tell me what to do.'

'I can when you're behaving like a...'

'Like a what?'

'Like someone who's immature.'

'Sod off.'

'Sod off yourself.'

'Stop it both of you!' Dad slams his fist on the tabletop and the cold tea leaps out of his mug. 'I don't need this,' he says, not even bothered by the mess. 'I've had more than enough to deal with for one day.'

'Me too,' Oll says.

'Everyone needs to calm down,' Dad says. 'And that includes me.' He brushes past Ollie on his way to the door. 'I need some fresh air.' No mention of when he's coming back or what they're supposed to eat this evening. He even slams the front door.

Oll gives her a sideways smile. 'Not sure about fresh air,' he says. 'It's close to forty degrees out there.'

'That's another thing about the eighties,' she says, 'Back then it was way cooler.'

Chapter Fifty-Two

Ollie

The atmosphere at home is better than it was because the three of them can't stay mad at each other for long. Well, Vega can – she tends to revel in perceived injustice like it's a warm bath. When her friend Rani invites her to join their family on a fancy villa holiday in Portugal, she starts being super nice to Dad because she needs his permission. (It doesn't suit her.) Dad might not be able to read her mind, but he sees through her sucking-up.

Once the exams begin, the mood at school is one of suppressed panic. As they line up to file into the hall for the first history exam, Aaron looks like he might be about to throw up. 'Good luck,' Ollie tells him, even though chance is not a major determining factor in the examination process.

'Cheers.' Aaron grins. 'This must be a walk in the park for you, Brooksie.' Ollie decides not to explain that he finds the exams a strain because it's hard to condense everything he knows into the simple and concise answers they require.

He doesn't go to any of the end of exams parties – now

they consider themselves free agents, his former classmates won't welcome some fifteen-year-old tagging along. At Dad's insistence, he attends the Leavers Prom all dressed up but without a partner. (Gran insists on him posing for photos.) Minnie and her friends make him their pity project for the evening and force him into a few stumbling dances. Playing along, he pretends it's amusing to watch people throwing up down their hired suits or expensive dresses. Thank God he's excluded from Greg and Aaron's drunken plan to break into the caretaker's shed so they can use his white-line machine to draw a giant cock and balls on the front playground.

And then school is over and the summer stretches before him – a succession of hot and airless days with no specific purpose. To impose some kind of routine, he takes himself off on runs in the morning while it's still relatively cool. During these circuits of the park, his brain keeps picking up information about the people he jogs past like he's tuned into them and not the music in his ears. More frequently now, his mind feels like it's in overload. He reads voraciously in an attempt to wrest control of the images and information in his head.

A week after the end of school, he spots the head of physics, Miss Harrison, in Cullimore's bookshop. The novel she's perusing seems an unnatural choice for someone of her intellect. 'Well now, Oliver,' she says, 'I'm intrigued to know what your plans are now you've finished your A-levels. Are you planning a break before university?'

He shrugs in a noncommittal way as if the same question hadn't been rattling around in his brain for months. 'Still considering my options,' he tells her.

'I see.' She's disappointed, had expected him to have everything worked out in advance. Before going up to the counter with her *True Love in Tuscany* novel, she says, 'Better not take too long about it, young man, or you might find certain opportunities have passed you by.'

Approximately six aimless and yet thought-crowded days after this conversation (Who's counting?) a smartly dressed woman sidles up to him when he's queuing for an ice cream in the park. 'I'm a friend of Winifred Harrison's – the head of physics at your school,' she says by way of introduction, while failing to explain how she could possibly know the two of them share that specific connection.

'That must be nice for you.' She's irritated by his reply, more so when he turns away to ask for a ninety-nine with an extra flake.

'I should introduce myself – my name is Jennifer Briggs. By all accounts, you are a remarkably gifted young man.' The two flakes could be flicking her the V, but she doesn't take the hint. Jennifer – if that's her real name – is fiftyish, short grey hair, determined jawline. She waits for him to pay and move out of the queue. 'Winifred thought you might be interested in discussing your future with someone.'

He takes his time before replying, licking up the many escaping drips around the cone. Having cast the bait, so-called Jennifer is annoyed he hasn't bitten. 'I have a rather interesting suggestion you might want to consider,' she says. 'That's if you can spare the time.'

'Are you a careers advisor?'

'I suppose I am.' She tries a smile. 'In a way.'

'In a way,' he repeats. 'Interesting answer. Let me get this straight – we haven't met before, but you approach me in a public park claiming to be a friend of my ex-teacher and hinting that you are about to offer me some sort of opportunity. Have I got that right?'

'Put like that, it sounds a little–'

'Creepy? Sinister? Illicit?'

'I was going to say irregular.'

'I imagine making this type of approach is in fact highly *irregular* since I'm only fifteen and a minor according to the law. Shouldn't you be advising me in an office, possibly in front of a responsible adult like a parent or a *guardian*?' He tries to read the effect of that last word but can't.

'If you'd prefer it that way.' She opens her crocodile handbag (Got to be faux, surely) takes out a regular looking business card and hands it to him. She snaps the bag shut. 'If you'd like to know more, call that number. If not, then have a nice life.'

He looks at the card. No logo or name, just a number on a plain white background. Could she be a spook? It seems unlikely but, then again, this is Cheltenham. (Though they must have a lower age limit.) Why couldn't he read her? He watches her stride along the path until she rounds the corner and is out of sight.

When he wakes the next day the info-dumps in his head arrive with a vengeance. He sits up in bed in a state of confusion. Something is happening to his brain. Could he have a tumour? It's possible. Christ, this is serious. He needs an urgent appointment with the doctor so he can get a brain scan.

He jumps when Grandad materialises by his bedroom

door. 'What the fuck! Can't you pay regular visits instead of popping up like some Dickensian advising spirit.'

'I apologise for this unscheduled arrival.' Grandad sits down on the edge of the bed next to him. 'I thought I should intervene before the situation got out of hand.'

'What situation?'

'You are beginning to experience what, for want of a better term, I'd characterise as a form of collective consciousness.' Ollie's hands automatically cover his head like he might do in a fight he wasn't winning.

'You need to relax,' Grandad says. 'I promise you this development is nothing to be afraid of. Your brain is – how can I put this? Your brain is in the process of, as it were, rewiring itself. It's creating an enormous number of new neural connections within certain parts of itself – areas that in the mass of the human population lie dormant. Before you ask why, I should explain that this is happening in preparation for your future role as a Guardian.'

Ollie bridles at this assumption. 'Hang on a second – you're telling me my brain is re-wiring itself, but that's no biggie?'

'It's a natural process that occurs in people like us around your age. It didn't happen to your father, but I suspect Vega will experience the same process in a year or two.'

While he's freaking out, Grandad's just sitting there in his smart shirt and perfectly ironed trousers like this is an everyday intergenerational conversation. Ollie says, 'I want a regular brain like everybody else's.'

'Ah, but then you wouldn't be you.'

'Is there a way to stop it happening?'

'It's been happening all your life. This is merely a more noticeable period of acceleration. You're more aware of it because your brain is what you might call idling at the moment. It pays to keep busy during the transition. You'll learn to block most of it out – a bit like people living with tinnitus learn to block out all that ringing in their ears.'

Ollie pulls a face. 'That's not exactly encouraging.'

Grandad shrugs.

'So this collective consciousness thing – are we talking hive-mind like bees or something? Jesus Christ – is it like the Borg?'

'Not at all. You're still you and will remain so. You'll still have free will – although that is rather a flawed concept.' Grandad clears his throat. 'Perhaps a better analogy might be that you're becoming part of a network – a bit like mycorrhizae.'

'Fungi?'

'As you know, mycorrhizae refers to a symbiotic underground network that enables trees to communicate with each other. By the way, that word comes from combining the Greek word *mycos* for fungus, and their word *rhiza* for root.'

'Don't try to distract me with the etymology at a time like this.' *And besides, I already knew that.*

When Grandad smiles he looks like a stereotypical, elderly gent. 'When I was your age and it was happening to me, I have to confess I was somewhat alarmed. A more senior Guardian advised me to think of all that extra knowledge and understanding as an extraordinary resource available instantaneously when needed.

'Like the internet.'

'You may prefer to think of it that way.' Grandad twists his mouth to one side in preparation for what he's about to say next. 'You've been monitored over the last few months.'

'Spied on, more like.'

'Try to consider it as a positive development – a reward for amply demonstrating that you're a level-headed young man, able to blend in to the general population, calm in the face of provocation and capable of making sound judgements in a crisis.'

'Sounds like the sort of bullshit I might put on my CV.' Grandad refuses to be amused. 'So,' Ollie says, 'You're saying I've passed some sneaky assessment and, as a result, the Guardians have given the go ahead for my brain to be fried by a download of all sorts of stuff, including lots of crap I'm not interested in and some things I would rather not know.'

'Oliver, listen to me, your father has always harboured a negative attitude towards the, um, Organisation. We're fully aware that this has tainted your own views. We wanted to be certain of your character, and I'm pleased to say you've shown you're naturally compassionate and not given to using your re-markable abilities unless you judge it necessary. Those are key pre-requisites – a sound foundation that can be built on.' The old man's eyes are twinkling. 'Oliver, you should be delighted to have an opportunity to become a powerful force for good in a highly troubled and chaotic world.'

The hard sell, eh? Ollie smiles. 'When you put it like that, it does sound pretty epic.'

Grandad pats his shoulder. 'You have a lot to assimilate. Any time you would like to talk things over with me, send up a bat signal.'

'Did you just slip in a contemporary cultural reference?'

'You can blame your grandmother for that one.' The old man stands up with a lot more effort than he used to need. 'Now if you'll excuse me, I'm going to disappear and then knock on your front door and pay a regular visit as instructed. In the course of my conversation with your father, I plan to suggest that, before deciding on your future, you might like to do a bit of travelling.'

'Hmm – I'm not sure he'll be keen on the idea. Although he certainly did plenty of travelling when he was young.'

'I think I might suggest a trip to the Fiji Islands and a certain conservation project that should help you keep out of mischief for a while.' He winks before he disappears.

Chapter Fifty-Three

Tom

On the day she leaves, Vega gives him a tight hug and then climbs into the back of the Dhariwals' car. She's so preoccupied with her friend Rani, she barely looks up when he waves.

Back in his echoing house Tom tries to think of the positives. He can eat when he wants, whatever he wants. He can play the music he likes at a volume that suits him. He's been handsomely paid for the duck house and so, for the next two weeks, there's nothing to stop him going anywhere he fancies on the merest whim.

He's in his study deleting some old files when a photo of Sarah Baynton pops up on his screen. Tom takes a moment to study her face. Her pale blue eyes seem to implore him to put an end to her protracted misery. How bereft must she feel not knowing whether her only child is dead or alive? Tom tries not to imagine. When he does he feels guilty. No way can he tell her where her son is, but perhaps he can give her some hope he might still be alive. Worth a try.

The next day he catches the 7:40 train to Edinburgh. He

won't reach the city before lunchtime – enough thinking time, he hopes, to work out what he's going to say to her. Several hours later, Tom emerges from the stifling depths of Waverley Station with no clearer idea but trusting it will come to him in the moment.

It's some time since he visited Scotland's capital city and he's captivated anew by the grandeur and scale of the towering granite buildings and cobbled streets. If this was a regular visit, he might hike up to Arthur's seat or take a tour of the castle, but today he's a man on a mission.

On foot, his route takes him past Blackfriars Kirk and he allows himself a brief detour into the kirkyard with its memorial to Bobby – the touchingly loyal Skye Terrier who guarded his former owner's grave for fourteen years. The inscription tells him Bobby died in 1872 aged 16 – which means the dog spent 87.5% of its short life in mourning instead of running around chasing rabbits or whatever. A moving monument to outstanding loyalty, it also commemorates how grief can waste a life.

Since, like Rome, the city is built on seven hills, there are plenty of steps to navigate. He's sweating in his shirtsleeves, envious of the bare-chested men in shorts he passes. A further twenty-five minutes at a brisk pace and he's reached the street where she lives – a crescent of stone-built, two-storey houses with small front gardens enclosed by neat hedges. Away from the bustle of the city centre, he can hear birdsong, someone mowing their back lawn.

Various trees provide welcome patches of shade as he counts down the numbers until he's standing thirty metres or so from number 11 – a well-maintained house with flowering pink roses trained around its wide front door. He lingers on the pavement in the shade and anonymity offered by a hazel tree. During his walk from the station his confidence has been gradually evaporating. He pinches the bridge of his nose. Christ, what was he thinking coming here like this? Unless he tells her the truth, nothing he can say will offer Sarah any comfort.

Tom is about to turn around and walk away when the front door of number 11 opens and a dark-haired woman in a green dress emerges. As she strides towards him, he notices she's around his age or possibly a bit older. He steps out of her path, and they exchange a brief smile of acknowledgement. Further along the road, the woman stops to speak to an elderly man who puts his shopping down on the pavement while they chat. Tom's curious. Could Sarah Baynton have moved? Has he got the right number? She hasn't got a sister – in fact she has no immediate family. The woman could easily be a friend who's staying, but his instinct tells him something's not right here.

Their conversation over, the dark-haired woman goes on her way. Once she's around the corner and out of sight, he rushes up to the old man before he can shut his front door. 'Hello there.' Tom takes a step back, holds his hands up hoping to demonstrate he's no threat. 'Sorry to bother you when I can see you're busy, sir, but I'm looking for Sarah Baynton. I know she lives somewhere around here, but I'm not sure I've got the right number.'

The old man puts his bag down on his hall floor then straightens up to study Tom with some suspicion. 'And who might you be, laddie?'

'A friend – well, more of an acquaintance.' Seeing those rheumy, blue eyes unconvinced, he's forced to add, 'It's about her son.'

'David?' The man points a gnarly finger. 'Are you the polis?'

'No, I'm absolutely not.' Noticing an overgrown hedge further along, Tom takes a punt. 'I thought she lived at number seven, but the bloke there said he didn't know her.'

'Aye, well he wouldn't know his arse from his elbow that one.' Head on one side, he adds. 'Even on the rare occasions he's sober.'

Tom chuckles. 'So, I gather you know Sarah. If it's not too much trouble, sir, could you point out her house?'

The old man shakes his head. 'If you're not the polis, then I've a mind to think you're one of them wretched hacks from the papers.'

'I promise you I'm neither.' Tom tries another smile. 'Like I said before, I'm an acquaintance of Sarah's.'

'An acquaintance is it?' A sly smiles creeps across the man's face. 'Then how come the lass herself walked right past you just a wee moment ago and you failed to recognise her?'

Before he can think of an answer, the man steps inside his house and shuts the door.

On his way back to the station, Tom speculates about the identity of the woman who came to his house. She'd certainly put on a convincing act. It worries him that he hadn't seen through her. Damn it, he allowed a plausible imposter to drag him, and then both his kids, into a dangerous situation. In future, he should probably stick to finding stray dogs.

Chapter Fifty-Four

Vega

When the door opens, she's taken aback because her mother is right there in the living, breathing flesh. The morning light seems to illuminate her silky, blue dressing gown – the same colour as her eyes. Before she can stop herself, Vega blurts out, 'Hello. I've come here because…' She takes an enormous breath. 'You may find it hard to believe, but I thought you needed to know that I'm your daughter. The long-lost variety.'

Elizabeth's face has already hardened. 'Don't be absurd.'

'Believe me, I'm aware that it sounds totally preposterous, but think back to that period when you had amnesia – though I suppose you can't think back as that's the definition of amnesia.'

She's in danger of losing it. 'Anyway, Elizabeth, what actually happened during that time is that you bumped into my dad, Tom, on a train and, long story short, you got pregnant with my brother – who's called Ollie by the way – and then you had me.' She holds out both arms ta-daa style.

Elizabeth is angry. 'Is this some kind of sick joke?'

'No, of course not, I'm completely serious. My name's Vega by the way. Which is actually my second name. Celia is my first name – the name you preferred – which is after my dad's dead gran. Anyway, I should also explain that the reason you have no memory of those missing years, is that this interfering Guardian erased all that.'

Though her mother hasn't responded, she keeps going. 'I probably need to explain to you what a Guardian is. Well, they're a bit like supercharged hypnotists. They can alter your brain and that sort of thing, just like that.' She snaps her fingers. 'I expect you're wondering how I can possibly be your daughter when you're far too young to have a kid of my age. Or Ollie's. He's fifteen, by the way. Look, I can see this is a hell of a lot to take in at once, so maybe we could discuss it over a cup of tea or something stronger.'

'Bugger off.' The door is slammed in her face.

Vega stoops to holler through the letterbox. 'Please, if you just let me

explain…'

There's a waft of air as the door opens again. Instead of her mother, a man is standing there. An angry one. Mid-twenties and stern looking, his handsome face contorts. 'Like she said, piss off,' he says. 'No one wants you here.' Before she can protest or plead her case, the man's face turns from angry to sad. He opens his mouth and starts to sing, 'It's time to let the curtain fall, and say goodbye to one and all…'

Vega wakes with a start. As her breathing slows, she lies back and sighs with relief to find it's daylight and she's in her bedroom at home. The familiar chaos of her room greets her. On the floor her open suitcase lies amongst her scattered clothes. A heap of dirty washing is by the door. On her chest of drawers there's an eclectic pile of souvenirs – some waiting to be added to the montage of photos and memorabilia covering most of one wall. The room might be a bit of a mess, but it's all her mess.

She can hear voices – someone talking to Dad down in the kitchen. Sounds like Gran.

Vega leaps out of bed and stumbles downstairs in her pyjamas. 'Hello there, sweetheart.' Gran comes forward to give her a big, gran-style hug enveloping her in the perfume of old roses. Vega has to fight back tears. As they separate, Gran says, 'I hear you had a lovely time in Portugal.'

'Yeah, it was nice hanging out with Rani and her sister. And Mr Dhariwal's a ledge.' She looks over at Dad who's hunting through the fridge. 'Still, it's good to be home.'

'I thought, to celebrate your return, I might rustle up some Portuguese baked eggs for us.' Dad shakes his head. 'Though I'm not sure we've got enough eggs, or the right type of cheese for that matter.'

Gran pats her stomach. 'I had breakfast before I left home.'

'And I'm happy with cereal,' Vega tells him. 'Have we got any fruit to go with it? In Portugal, we had this weird, knobbly fruit called Anona da Madeira which tasted a bit like…'

Dad's nodding. 'A sort of combination of pineapple and banana.'

'And sort of like strawberries too,' she says.

'We're a bit short on fruit,' he says, 'And we're almost out of milk. Think I'll just nip out and get some. Won't be long.'

Once the front door bangs shut, Gran gives her a meaningful look and sits down at the breakfast bar. This has got to be a set-up. Taking the stool next to her, Vega says, 'You're about to say something about Mum and how I should learn to accept the situation and move on.'

'I certainly wouldn't have put it as starkly as that.' Gran sighs. 'You know, it would be nice if you could pretend not to know what I'm going to say before I say it. Especially since, these days, I'm not even sure myself.'

'Just thought I'd save you the trouble.'

'It's only natural for you to be curious about your mother.' Gran squeezes her hand. 'I got to know Beth very well when you and Ollie were little. Living in that tiny village miles from anywhere, the poor girl didn't have any friends her own age she could confide in. Being a full-time mother of young children is exhausting in more ways than one. And, of course, she wasn't much more than a child herself at the time.' She smiles at the memory. 'I suppose I thought of her as the daughter I never had.'

Her eyes lose focus for a moment. 'Although we all missed her terribly after she... well, after she went; later, when I learned about her successful acting career, it was good to know she was leading the life she always dreamt of. If you were religious – not that I am – I suppose you might say she found her true path in the end. I came to realise that her time with us was a sort of unintended anomaly – if I can put it like that without making light of what she meant to those she left behind.'

Gran's watery eyes look into hers like she's seeing right through to her soul. 'Tom tells me you're thinking of leaving us.' She sniffs. 'Losing Beth was the hardest thing for him. None of us could bear it if you–'

'Don't say it.' Vega looks down at the crinkled skin on Gran's hands, the network of blue veins running close to the bones. 'You'll be pleased to know I'm not about to leave home. If I'm being honest, I was starting to feel homesick by the end of my second week in Portugal. So you can tell Dad he's got nothing to worry about – I'm staying put.' She smiles. 'Well, at least for a few more years.'

Chapter Fifty-Five

Ollie

Scuba diving for the first time opens up the underwater world to him. Ollie's astounded by the colours, all the teeming, interconnected life going on just below the surface.

He grows used to the different rhythm of life on the islands. Locals and blow-ins alike have a languid, profound connection to the earth and the ocean. On the smaller inhabited islands there are no shops or bars. Surrounded by the natural world in its abundance, the young people living in these remote communities get along fine without being in constant electronic connection with others. Islanders by birth have a reverence for the natural world, and protecting the islands' fragile biodiversity fits easily with their traditional beliefs about guardian spirits in the form of such things as mountains or trees.

As for Baynton, his memory has been adjusted to exclude Ollie's part in his flight to the islands. He now believes he engineered his own escape before the ruthless people he double-crossed put a bullet in his head. (Ironic that now he's literally swimming with the fishes.) Observed from a distance,

Baynton is enthusiastically engaged in what he's working on and in no hurry to leave.

Back home, Ollie finds it hard to adjust to not waking up to the sound of the ocean, or walking barefoot on white sand in the warm evening air while the dying sun bathes the water in glorious colour. Most of all it's that colour he misses.

Assessing him from head to foot, Dad decides he's grown. 'And put on a bit of muscle,' he says, play-punching his arm. (Which actually hurts a bit.)

'Nice tan,' Vega comments in passing. *You look like a beach bum with those bracelets and that ratty hair.*

After their reunion breakfast, she goes off to hang out with friends in the park. *You might want to consider getting a haircut,* is her parting thought.

Dad claps him on the back. 'You'll adjust,' he says, guessing his feelings not from reading his mind, but from recalling how he felt returning from his own travels. 'It won't last long,' he adds like it's an illness Ollie needs to recover from.

They clear up in the kitchen and then Dad leaves the house – a man most definitely with a plan. (Though not an especially honourable one.)

Left alone, Ollie looks around, seeing everything through a sharper, more critical lens. Needing fresher air, he strolls out into the back garden. For a town plot it's not a bad size. Lost in thought, he stares up at the developing cumulus clouds for a while. With Gran's encouragement (read insistence) Dad has planted up the skinny borders enclosing the parched lawn, but all the flowers look like they'd rather be someplace else. This same garden seemed so much bigger when he was a kid.

'Perceptions change,' a voice behind him says. 'Especially when viewed from a different perspective.' Without looking around, he knows his uninvited visitor is Ford.

'To what do I owe this honour?'

'Consider this a social visit. I thought I should touch base – as I believe it's termed in modern parlance.' Turning round, Ollie shakes his head as he looks into the Guardian's smug, know-it-all face. 'I thought we might have a conversation about your future.' Ford's blue eyes look like they're in danger of icing over. 'I assume you have no objections.'

Ollie snorts. 'Would it make any difference if I did? You're not renowned for respecting people's boundaries.'

He hears the front door slam. The resulting gust runs through the house, stirring the curtains. Dad's back. Ollie can't actually hear him humming the Kings of Leon track that's going around in his head. He'll hide that betting slip somewhere obscure like it's his drug stash. (Which in a way it is.) This time it's the horses – an accumulator that will yield a relatively modest five grand and, Dad hopes, not cause too much suspicion.

To distract Ford (as if) who is now sitting down, he joins him on their rickety garden bench. Avoiding the bird shit, he's careful to keep some distance between them. Ford says, 'Adjusting to the new consciousness can have its difficulties.'

'Yeah well, I seem to be handling it okay. The filtering bit can be quite a challenge at times, but I'm getting there.'

Dad's shocked when he spots their visitor through the window. From his perspective, the two of them must make unlikely bench-mates – him barefoot in shorts and a crumpled

"Dive Fiji" t-shirt, Ford immaculate in a dark blue suit, the brim of his fedora at an almost jaunty angle.

'You might care to remind your father that the tax authorities may begin to query his consistent run of good luck.' Ford laughs like a drain – a blocked one.

'I'll pass on your advice.' When Ollie dares to look him straight in the eye, all he sees is his own reflection. 'It was nice of you to make time out of your busy schedule to ask after my mental health,' he says. 'Rest assured, I'm taking things in my stride.' He clears his throat. 'In fact, now I'm more used to it, I find this omniscience thing is actually pretty cool.'

Ford bristles at his vocabulary. 'It never pays to let these things go to one's head,' he says, giving him a long, meaningful look.

Ollie says, 'Thanks for stopping by and all that.' About to stand up, Ford beats him to it.

'You will have further need of my guidance,' he says, which sounds more like a threat than an offer of help.

Ollie doesn't deny it. 'Just before you go,' he says, 'can I ask you about that flash drive business?'

Ford doesn't respond though something shifts in his eyes.

'Okay, so my dad finds that flash drive *after* Baynton disappears. He takes it home where I eventually grab it from his desk and deliver it to Baynton's apartment *before* he's moved out. What it contains makes Baynton lose his shit. He hides the flash drive in his old apartment before faking his own death. And it's there that Dad finds it.'

'As I took pains to explain to your father, you are merely describing the apparent contradictions within a classic Bootstrap paradox.'

'Oh, I totally get that non-linear causality part. But you see, that still leaves the fact that someone must have put the information about the dirty dealings of The Bonnie Blue Tartan Distillery Company onto that flash drive in the first place. Can't have been Baynton or he wouldn't have gone ape when he discovered what was on it. It wasn't me and I'm pretty sure it wasn't my dad, so who else knew about what he and his associates were up to and then decided to download all that incriminating information onto that drive? My further question is – exactly how did that pivotal object get inserted into an otherwise closed loop?'

'Something for you to ponder perhaps.' Ford stands up. 'Suffice to say, it always pays to be concerned about the ongoing accumulation of an excessive amount of wealth and whose controlling hands it is likely to end up in.'

'You know, Ford, I'm reminded of that magician's trick with the three cups and the ball hidden underneath one of them. Like most sleight-of-hand tricks, it relies on the viewer's distraction. If I had to guess, I'd say the Organisation's intervention was never primarily about saving Baynton from himself. Or even testing my particular responses to a difficult situation. No, I imagine it was more about stopping certain parties from getting their hands on all that money and so preventing whatever the consequences of that would have been.'

Stonewalled.

Ollie says, 'I thought Guardians were only interested in putting right time anomalies, not rectifying social ills.'

'On occasions the two are linked.'

'I see.' What wouldn't he give to be able to read Ford's thoughts? Then again, maybe it's just as well he can't.

Ford adjusts his hat though the difference is imperceptible. 'And now I will take my leave.' With an edge, he adds, 'Please pass on my felicitations to your father.'

The space he'd occupied becomes a ripple in the air and then nothing.

Framed in the doorway, Dad says, 'Shame he buggered off before I had a chance to tell him to sling his hook.'

Ollie chuckles. 'Don't worry, I think he got the message.'

Dad comes out to inspect the bench where Ford had been sitting as if, like the birds, he might have left some tell-tale trace behind. 'So, are you going to tell me what he wanted?'

'I expect you can guess.'

'They're keen for you to join their merry band.' Dad's sigh is a long one. 'You know, part of being a halfway decent parent is realising when to let go and allow your kids to make their own decisions. What I'm trying to say is, whatever you decide to do next I won't stand in your way. You might be young in years, but I'm the first to admit that, as a way of assessing maturity, that measurement alone is deeply flawed.'

He squeezes Dad's shoulder. 'Thanks for the vote of confidence, but you won't get rid of me that easily.'

'Glad to hear it.' Dad pulls him into a hug.

Over his shoulder, Ollie says, 'By the way, Ford knows about you nipping back to place bets and he's not too happy about it.'

Dad holds him at arm's length. 'Trouble is, it's just too damned easy. I mean, who wouldn't be tempted to bet on a certainty?'

'You know,' Ollie says, 'whether it's the past or the future, no outcome can ever be considered certain. If things were immutable, there'd be no need for Guardians.' After a moment's pause, he says, 'But since there is…' He shrugs. 'I'm thinking, you know, why not give it a go?'

'So you're planning to join them?'

'I thought I might try it for a bit. I mean, what's the worst that can happen?'

Dad pulls a face. 'Fate might be a flawed concept, but perhaps it's better not to tempt it all the same.'

They both touch the back of the bench, just in case.

About the Author

Before becoming a writer, Jan Turk Petrie taught English in inner city London schools. She now lives in the Cotswolds area of southern England. She holds an M.A. in Creative Writing from the University of Gloucestershire. As well as her published novels, Jan has written numerous, prize-winning short stories. She is a big fan of Margaret Atwood, Kate Atkinson, Kurt Vonnegut, and Jennifer Egan – authors who like to take risks in their writing.

As a writer, Jan is always keen to challenge herself. Her first published novels – the three volumes that make up **The Eldísvík Trilogy** – are Nordic noir thrillers set fifty years in the future in a Scandinavian city where the rule of law comes under threat from criminal cartels controlling the forbidden zones surrounding it.

By contrast, **'Too Many Heroes'** – is a period romantic thriller set in the early 1950s. A story of an illicit love affair that angers the mobsters controlling London's East End at that time.

Jan's fifth novel: **'Towards the Vanishing Point'** is set primarily in the 1950s and depicts an enduring friendship between two women that is put to the test when one of them falls under the spell of a sinister charmer.

'The Truth in a Lie' was her first novel with a contemporary setting. It is the story of a successful writer who has a complex and often difficult relationship with her mother and her own daughter as well as with the men in her life.

'Still Life with a Vengeance' also has a contemporary setting. Married to a famous rock guitarist and apparently living a picture-perfect life, a young woman's life begins to unravel when her husband is accused of rape.

'Running Behind Time' (Cotswold time-slip series Book 1) Jan's first time-slip novel. Written during the unprecedented events of 2020 and the new social norms arising from the pandemic, she was inspired to imagine a wrinkle in time which accidentally brings her main characters, Tom and Beth, together.

'Play For Time' (Cotswold time-slip series Book 2) continues the story of Tom and Beth with the birth of their extraordinary son Ollie and an existential threat to the family.

'Turn Back Time (Cotswold time-slip series Book 3) After welcoming daughter Vega, the Brookes family settle down to life in a tiny Cotswold hamlet before an act of compassion by Tom leads to unforeseen consequences.

Dear reader,

I really hope you've enjoyed reading 'Time to Choose. Thank you so much for buying or borrowing a copy, this book means a great deal to me. If you would like to help other readers discover it, please consider leaving a review anywhere readers are likely to visit. It doesn't need to be a long review – a sentence or two would be just fine. Many thanks in advance to anyone who takes the time to do so.

If you would like to find out more about this book, or are interested in discovering more about my other published novels, please visit my website: https://janturkpetrie.com

If you'd like to follow me on X (formerly Twitter) my handle is: @TurkPetrie.

My Facebook author page: https://www.facebook.com/jan-turkpetrie

Contact Pintail Press via the website: https://pintailpress.com

Acknowledgements

Once again I genuinely hadn't planned to write another volume of these time-slip novels and I certainly wouldn't have done so if an interesting new angle to the story of the Brookes family hadn't occurred to me.

I can hardly believe this is my eleventh published novel. This one took longer than most to write and presented me with numerous challenges. My lovely husband, John, always encouraged me during moments of self-doubt. I'm enormously indebted to him for reading and commenting in detail on the first and subsequent drafts of *Time to Choose*. His feedback kept me going during the long and sometimes arduous process of writing and then rewriting this book.

Thanks go once again to my daughters Laila and Natalie for their love and support. And to our toddler grandson, Leon, for being a source of constant delight. I'm relieved his teenage years are unlikely to be as complicated as Ollie's or Vega's.

Grateful thanks also go to my wider family including my daughters' partners Ed and Sam, my sister Jenny and brother-in-law Geoff and especially my mum, Pearl Elizabeth Turk, for those highly prized 'Pearls of Wisdom'.

Writing is a solitary occupation and so considered and insightful feedback from other writers is always invaluable. I'm very grateful for the comments and suggestions made by the highly talented members of *Catchword* writing group in Cirencester and my fellow *Wild Women Writers*. Your feedback most definitely helped to make this a better book.

I'm indebted to my enthusiastic and talented editor and proof-reader Johnny Hudspith for all his comments and corrections.

Final thanks go to Jane Dixon-Smith, my very talented cover designer, for her outstanding work on yet another brilliant cover.